Andrew Bramwell was born in Walsall. He was educated at Bluecoat School and St. Martin's College, Lancaster.

Since 1982 Andrew has worked as a teacher in a number of schools in the Midlands. A life long fascination and attachment to the history, literature and people of Finland is reflected in much of his work.

Karelia is his first full length novel and follows the production of numerous articles, stories, poetry, and most recently the children's book 'The Adventures of Theodore Snowflake' and the radio play 'The Last Deckchair'.

Andrew is married with three children and lives in the Midlands.

KARELIA

Also by the same author

The Adventures of Theodore Snowflake (2005) Published
by Nightingale
ISBN 1903491347

Andrew Bramwell

KARELIA

Vanguard Press

VANGUARD PAPERBACK

© Copyright 2010
Andrew Bramwell

A CIP catalogue record for this title is
available from the British Library.

ISBN 978 1 84386 574 2

Vanguard Press is an imprint of
Pegasus Elliot MacKenzie Publishers Ltd.
www.pegasuspublishers.com

First Published in 2010

Vanguard Press
Sheraton House Castle Park
Cambridge England

Printed & Bound in Great Britain

To

Janet

Thomas, Peter and Rees.

Introduction

In December 1939 the Soviet Union launched a massive assault across the Finnish border.

Throughout the winter of 1939–40, despite being heavily outnumbered, the Finnish army held their positions, causing massive casualties to the Soviets in the process.

In spring the defences were overcome and the Eastern lands of Karelia were ceded. The peace lasted little more than a year before Finland joined with Germany and counter attacked. While lands were initially re-taken, final defeat came in 1944 and once again Karelia was evacuated, never to be re-gained.

This is the story of Hannu the carpenter in those extraordinary times. This is more a work of poetry than history. While the contexts and settings are based on fact, the military historians amongst you will spot inaccuracies and discrepancies. I hope you can forgive this licence in the pursuit of a human story.

There have been many books and articles of invaluable assistance to the production of this work. They are listed in the appendix.

MAP OF FINLAND

PART ONE
1939–40

Chapter 1

Karelia

'You will soon die', the angel said. 'You will leave the battlefield with me and enter heaven...I am permitted to carry one memory for you, but no more. What shall it be?'

So hear my tale as the quiet milk-white sky drifts to a merging of conifer green, as soft autumn lays the hay dry and a single Finnish sun splinters my hair. Listen if you have ears to this story of enchantment as it threads through my fingers like a snake writhing.

It is a new salmon morn.

Corn licks the lakeside. A morning mist whispers its way across the water to those vague and distant hills. And beyond those hills pours melting black the universe and in its wake the day rises across the pastel-layered horizon.

It is the beginning, like the very first when the world was brought into being by song and the great white swan burst from her nest spreading wings for the sky; when the vapour of her breath licked our ancestors into life to tame this land with axe and fire. When we crouched in fear of spirits and hid our faces from the moon.

So it has come to this.

This feeling furnacing my veins, that the end of these things, all that we know, is coming and soon; with the first flurries of snow, with the first cry of the wolf, the storm will strike. We are not well prepared. Few listen to the portents. They nod or smile, or murmur he's a strange one, full of those thoughts, such thoughts. He should keep them to himself. So I have learned to be circumspect.

But those dreams. I am cursed by them. They are not so easily dispelled.

Last night in my sleep the hunters swept through landscapes barren, devoid of habitation, landscapes full of wrath. Clothed in fur they tracked the bear as a tribe. Guttural calls snapped the air, animal grunts and then shrieks as they drove spears deep into the body. While still alive they peeled the flesh away with flint knives. The screams of the bear woke me. My eyes shot to the ceiling and in the still of night between the shingles of the roof a hay cart lumbered its way down the lane laden with raspberries, so many they tumbled as the cart rolled and left a trail for children to follow. Excitedly they picked them up and swallowed, the juice running down their faces. One boy turned to look at me but he had no eyes and the children and the hay cart vanished. All that was left were crushed red berries in the dust, like spots of blood.

What does it all mean?

It is autumn now but this tale took root that last summer. I will unpack it for you. It is a story harnessed with memory, sinewy and clad in steel. When the midsummer bonfires were lit the whole village threw logs and kindling onto the flames. The heat was terrific and the noise like bombs exploding. We thought for awhile it was out of control and would spread to the forest but old man Hannu puckered his lips around his pipe and said it would be alright. So it was.

Then one of the Kuisma girls edged too close and singed her new dress. She got a scolding for that from her mother, but her father laughed and swigged his vodka.

'It might have been worse,' he said. 'No harm done,' and his wife gave such a look that could have wrung a chicken's neck but he took no notice and drank and smoked and laughed with his friends until he fell over, curled into a ball and went to sleep. This would be his last midsummer celebration. It would be a last midsummer for them all, for the family did not leave in time and the little girls were covered with the earth not far from here, frozen unforgiving earth.

As the daylight ebbed and the yellow husk of night descended I found myself sitting on the edge of the fire nursing my thoughts. The flames flickered and curls of smoke spiralled into the thin air. Warmth wrapped around me and though people say it is impossible to think of nothing, well I was, and happy with it. The men's snoring made me smile and the gentle cracking of pine cones spat bars of wild staccato music.

I was shaken out of this reverie when Maarit came and sat beside me. For awhile she said nothing, just staring at the embers. The smoke made her eyes smart and the firelight tigered her cheeks. My hands clutched my knees and she must have noticed.

'Your hands are filthy, they are covered in grime. Where have they been?'

'They have been with me always,' I said.

At this she raised an eyebrow and flicked sand into the ashes with the heel of her foot.

'So you haven't been drinking?'

'No...vodka makes my head burst, you know that.'

'I've been looking for you all day. Where have you been?'

I paused to think.

'Collecting wood mostly. I had to repair the roof of the cow sheds, and then build up the fires. The wood was dry as a crisp. It was too brittle. It took an age,' I said.

'That family harnesses you to work like an ox.'

'I don't mind.'

She frowned. I smiled and sidled my foot towards hers.

'If it would make you happy,' I said, 'I will wash my hands in the stream.' So I rose and walked along the now deserted track to where a small stream sliced an arc through pasture. It was an ancient parish marker but now, in the orange sunlight, shone like a band of copper. When I dipped my fingers into the water I half expected it to be solid. I splashed water onto my face and turned around to where Maarit stood watching. She started to laugh.

'That's better. In the darkness you are almost handsome.'

You are beautiful I almost said but did not have the courage, for she was beautiful in all ways heaven could provide. In this stillness waves of light moulded her features and every twitch of her nose or flick of the hair sent my nerves jangling. Her smile was torrent or cataract and swept me off my feet.

In the animal light of this midsummer she moved in silence, like a gazelle, like a ghost uncaught. Then she took my hand and we followed the stream, upwards to the summit of a swinging hill where the birch curled in tentacles and we were hidden from the village by a canopy of branches that might have been taken for a cathedral roof. In the sand there were elk prints and I saw the distant field where I had learned to handle a plough until becoming a carpenter. I was proud of my trade, for Joseph was a worker in wood. Moses too washed ashore near here, so legend states. In the bulrushes of Ladoga lapped the basket, captured in reeds before the Tsar's daughter saw him and claimed him. I would have made his crib, I thought. If they had asked.

'I will miss you when you go,' I said.

'I will miss you,' she replied and after a pause, 'You know why I have to leave?'

'Yes,' I said.

We walked until we reached the summit and resting our backs against a pine tree gazed over a landscape young and fresh and finally free of winter's hammer. She tore a stalk of grass and put it in her mouth.

'I need this job in the Technical Institute. I will make a good secretary and I can send money home.'

'Helsinki is a long way,' I answered. 'You will soon forget about me.'

'I will not.' There was a touch of hurt in her face. But we had raced this conversation into the same circle many times. Our words were locked into pattern.

'I will not forget you,' she repeated. 'I will write...and you will reply.'

'I will,' I stated firmly and it suddenly sounded like a vow. 'I will even wash my hands.'

'No, let me see the trace of your fingers on the paper and I will touch them and know that it is you.'

Now I knew she was slipping into sadness. Helsinki seemed so far away and her thoughts foamed with the turmoil of it all. We stayed the night, a northern night which never really slipped into darkness. We talked, she said there were trams in Helsinki, but I had never seen a tram or the sea, or an orchestra, or those things you read about in the great cities. I said there would be a lot of students and she replied that obviously there would. She hoped they wouldn't laugh at her accent and her primitive country ways. I secretly hoped they would and leave her alone.

Then morning came, yellow beams cleavered a path between our shoulders so when I looked to the east there was a hint of butchery surrounding us. Layers of green rose, dark shells, yawning, and I caught the whispers first in my pocket and then in my mind while the day tingled and prismed.

And the sun rose glowing to a red core, flaying the horizon with razor sharp edges, amber tipped, slicing black earth. Birch leaves twisted on the branch and a flight of swallows splintered the sky.

Maarit shivered. 'Someone just walked across my grave,' she said and wiped sleep out of her eyes. 'We should be going.'

We re-traced our steps, she holding onto my sleeve. We parted by the church. I watched her walk away until she slipped into her cabin. I crept through the window of my room and fell upon my bed. When I slept I did not dream and was thankful for it.

Looking back I saw now that there was something strange about that day. There was a wildness. Wilder than usual I mean. There was more dancing and drinking and falling out. It didn't strike me at the time but looking back I saw it was so. It was odd because there was a wedding in the morning. A half-brother of mine, I had so many, was getting married. Everyone hoped that it would calm him down. Not much chance of that. But it was a happy affair even though the village was hung over and the pastor warned about the evils of excess but probably realised that everyone felt too ill to care. He shut up after that. He was a pragmatic man that pastor. I liked him, even if no one else did.

There wasn't another wedding for a long time so I record the details for posterity. There was a farewell party at the bride's home. My half-brother, much the worse for wear, set out for her home with the rest of the family in tow. I followed dutifully, grateful not to have been made a peacemaker. Those two had already gone ahead to begin the negotiations in homage to an ancient ritual. Once it was a necessity, a business transaction, but now a sop to form. This had been completed with more drinking before the groom's party arrived. We all knocked on the door and he was supposed to seek out his bride but he was too hung over to notice until he tripped over her foot. There was a great deal of laughter. I laughed because it was expected.

The ceremony began in the living room with my brother and the bride standing at the writing table. The bride wore a long white dress and a circlet of flowers in her hair which glistened like barley. She was very happy. The groom looked uncomfortable in his black suit. I thought he was going to be sick but he stared intently at the candles on the table... it was soon over. The pastor, who had few friends, mumbled a prayer. Everyone repeated Amen and the cat on the window sill scraped her claws across the glass. The congratulations began with the wedding feast. It was a good spread: potatoes, rice, carrots, liver and ham, pies, gooseberries, almonds and cream, coffee and speeches, tears.

My half-brother came across to shake my hand.

'Congratulations,' I said.

'It's been a fine day... your turn next.'

'Not for while,' I replied.

'Marriage is good for a man.' I smiled and slapped his shoulder in a brotherly way. His arms were like tree trunks and at that moment he seemed to genuinely believe it.

'I'm sure you're right,' I said and caught sight of Maarit in the corner of the room. She was making obscene gestures which no one else could see. Maarit was no great fan of the groom. I winked and slapped his arm again. He slapped me back good-naturedly and I thought I would leave it at that. Old and young departed, the day ended.

Summer progressed through July and August. There was a heatwave. Streams dried to a trickle. Swarms of mosquitoes made walking uncomfortable; they bit like the devil. So I took to my workshop to escape and hammered and nailed, felt the soothing motion of the plane under my arms, studied grain and weave until the call for outside work arrived. Then I was a wheelwright, fixing carts, repairing roofs, forever keeping out the rain or snow. Some complained, but as I said, if you pay a proper price you get a proper job. Still they grumbled and above them the storm clouds gathered.

On occasion old man Hannu paused to pass the time. He sucked a pipe through gaps in tombstone teeth, turning his tobacco-stained hands to the sky, feeling the air.

'Morning, Hannu,' I would say.

'Hello to the one who brings the greeting and another to the one who sent it.'

There he would sit on the workshop step saying nothing for awhile, then making his thoughts public would utter some comment.

'There are more crosses in the forest,' he pronounced.

'I've noticed.'

'We must be careful they don't go too far.'

'Yes,' I said.

Although the heat was stifling he wore still his jacket and muffler. Even in the summer he slept in the kitchen, and in winter on the stove itself. So thin and brown was his frame he could be taken for a tree, were it not for his movements. His large peasant hands flapped if there was nothing to do, every year his eyes sank deeper into the skull until they looked like pools in caverns where light has never penetrated. Yet he did his rounds and baked his bread and sprinkled flour on the floor with a 'God Bless' prayer. When he was young, so legend tells, he pulled the village schoolmaster out of the ice and was rewarded with a meal a day for a month. A meagre reward if you ask me. Now I picture him sucking yeast out of bread through lips that for many years had only been kissed by frost or flame; scouring the forest for cloudberry and juniper and mushrooms with that ever present trail of tobacco smoke behind him and a wattle basket over his arm.

'Hello Hannu,' I would always say.

'Hello to the one who brings the greeting and another to the one who sent it,' he would reply.

There were times, in those days, when I would lock myself in the workshop, bolt the door and the shutters, especially when I was repairing my tools. My chisels were sharp as diamonds and I fancied myself as a carver of wood. Eyes I would gouge out of offcuts, all lines and furrow, but never the whole head; hands sometimes but never the fingernails. When I rubbed linseed into the handles of the bow saw I followed the grain. I paused only when I heard footsteps outside. I hated being disturbed, it broke the spell and if my half-brothers ever came for conversation I could not work again that day for they were wastrels and their chatter caused me no end of irritation.

And I remember one evening, working by the light of a lantern, when I thought I heard a cry: some old crone from the forest's edge, a shriek, a witch. I had a particular fear of them. I had seen them lay the cattle low and whip away the still born. It made my flesh creep. I took up my shotgun which I stored always beneath the bench, and gripping the trigger, I glared at the door so when the wind raced through the walls scattering nails and shavings and wood dust I was ready. But the wind settled and she did not enter. I took it as another warning, like my dreams, but still could make no sense of it. After that I took to working only in daylight. I was uneasy.

*

When the church bells sounded I was in the house. Merja, my only sister, was eight years old and learning to serve coffee and lay the table. She was quiet. She was alright. Sometimes a travelling teacher came to take a few lessons but mostly she stayed in the house, due to her shyness.

I heard my mother utter a cry of 'Lord Preserve Us' and rushed to the church porch where many others were gathered.

'What's happened?' someone asked.

'Risto the woodsman, there has been an accident.'

We followed him and saw that Risto was no longer a middle-aged man full of worry and concern but was dead. The axe he had been wielding embedded in his skull where it had ricocheted from the trunk. His hands grasped the handle as if he had, for a moment, attempted to pull it out. There was a red jelly everywhere. His blood ran into the land as would our own with time. One of the villagers closed his eyelids for respectability... another exclaimed that it was a new axe.

Between us we carried his body on a board to the drying barn before his widow saw him. It was the women who washed away the blood, trying to stem the flow of brain tissue. They dressed him in his best shirt and waistcoat. We mumbled a few prayers and sealed him into a coffin. After the funeral and the burial his family crossed the river and scratched crosses on the bark of trees so that his soul could find its way back to the parish boundary but no further. They did not want him haunting the paths of the village. Nor did we.

It shook us, that accident to Risto. It was a bad omen. Some of his friends remarked that he was plagued with ill luck. He had lost his cattle to disease. Others were sure that had he put them out of their stalls on May Day like everybody else, they would not have died. The men nodded their heads in assent and departed with the thought that Risto's widow would not be lonely for she had the only radio for miles around. They nodded their heads in assent to this too.

So it is that this allegory returns to the beginning, in September, when the forest floor was thick with berries and the fungi sprouted, poking the earth, when the world was russet and amber, cherry red, coffin brown, weary green.

Maarit left for the station in the back of a cart. She had a new suitcase and a scarf around her head. She was as smart as she had ever been and waved her arm through the cooling air. I watched her go and could not imagine what would befall us before we would meet again, in another age, another country. There were no tears, it was an adventure and the people left behind were split between admiration and fear for her in that place.

It was Michaelmas and the cattle had to be rounded up and returned to the winter stalls. We were all on hand to push these obstinate creatures bellowing into quarters, which would save them from the raw. Their bodies oozed steam and we boys too were red faced with effort and impatience. I knew all the village boys, their straw hair and risqué language, families and alliances; we were all related one way or another. We whipped the cattle home with willow switches and searched endlessly for those who were missing. To be honest they were brutes and caused me unparalleled trouble even though I had the way of handling them. In the old days the pastor would have come to make sure we did not work on Sunday. They were hell and brimstone preachers then, fiery characters, their Bibles reinforced with steel. Woe betide the boy caught playing on the Sabbath; he would be flogged and made to listen to those 'warning stories'. Our pastor was too gentle for the harshness of this parish, too fond of order and cleanliness, and the church bell, which was almost like a wife to him. After hours of crashing through the undergrowth we had driven all but one through the fields and apple orchards. One was lost, trapped and bewitched in the mire, long since returned to worm, with the maggot still picking off the remnants of flesh. The eye had gone, I noticed, and the bone was already beginning to sink. All that crawled was there. So we left and turned for home, damp, cold, ready for rest as the night cloaked ever earlier around our shoulders and spirits sank.

When we met at the widow's house later that evening the news was not so good. The radio churned out a language we barely understood. But even the most innocent among us could appreciate the gravity of tone. It was often our only connection to the outside world. We had become accustomed to it, relied upon it for information. Our homeland was losing its isolation and likely to soon be in the centre of things. It was a thrill in some ways to be noticed, like a public execution I imagine, where you cannot tear yourself away; so many faces. One or two looked in my direction for I had many times talked about my strange dreams and feelings of unease, but I could not articulate them.

So we are a threat to Russia the announcer seemed to say. We a poor strip of land with no mineral wealth and a soil so barren only blood will cause the seedlings to stir. He explained the strategic position, an hour from Leningrad, a threat from the sea, from ships we did not have. Had it been less serious I would have laughed, but my laughter would be out of place in that room, intense and concentrated as it was.

We were many of us in the Civic Guard and drilled with ancient rifles, and that not so successfully. We had no parade ground and would only have planted it with potatoes if we had.

When the demands were repeated that October day we knew that war was coming with its entrails smearing the snow behind it. We could not give up our Suursaari, Tytarsaari. Lavansaari, Koivisto, Hanko, or our arctic lands. We could not destroy our fortifications. What foolishness was this? There was anger in the room, I could pick it up with a spoon.

We separated in silence. I lay on my bed for awhile and re-read Maarit's letter where she talked about a meal of crayfish, about the markets loaded with cucumbers, runner beans and tomatoes. There was a rock near the harbour, she said, which cried, and a railway station with an echo louder than a cannon and a glass-domed roof higher than any church she had visited. And at the end she told me not to worry, that we Finns smile without smiling and God was with us.

In the distance the river surged. It clawed and wore away the bank, spitting it out like teeth. Stones and gravel tumbled along the bed and fish scurried to their holes and hiding places. I heard it in my room as I pulled a blanket to my chin and again in the morning; in the quiet of a workshop the rumbling grew.

I resolved to tidy and sweep till not a speck of dust was found. First I sharpened the chisels, wrapped them in rag and carefully placed them in a storage chest. I repeated the process with my hammers and saws and planes and mallets. Soon they were gone. In the empty room I saw the eyes of Joseph looking at me, and in the iris I could see that he knew, he knew; there was no longer any point in caring for things, he seemed to intimate. His son, he said, was beyond manual labour and would not be coming home. Why do you take such care? The dust of Nazareth swept through boarding; his sandals lay by the door where they had been left. So when I looked ever deeper into his tough brown face I beheld the visions he once had shared contorted by tears.

Still I dreamed. Two dark-skinned strangers emerging from the trees, growling, with stones in their hands. I shouted a warning but they took no heed and cast a stone through the window; glass shattered and I swept it up. They returned and the window broke again, once more. But was this window ice or glass? Why did these strangers persecute me? I knew not but I woke with a start, parched.

With a final glance I turned the key and placed it in my pocket. Across the fields mist settled, and a haze gathered around the whole frontier. At the edges naked birch trees webbed and laced. The lichen on its bark already curled for winter. A wagtail scurried, bobbing across my path. There was usually a pair but I hadn't seen the other for some time now. Cobwebs silvered the branches and water dribbled to the ground one atom at a time, and in each atom I could see the blue and green of earth and sky.

When old man Hannu appeared it took me by surprise. I greeted him but he did not reply. He did not even notice my presence.

'Ah the village boys,' he whispered, and disappeared. In the forests wooden crosses grew and the scratches in the bark on the opposite bank were still clear enough to offer protection from ghosts.

Already my feet were wet and I fancied I heard a peel of thunder, though the sky was clear. Then I heard it again and wended my way home. In the living room Merja poured the coffee but said nothing. We were all subdued. I asked if father had been in touch...but she said not, and that she didn't care. Nor did I. The clock ticked. A cow bellowed. Somewhere an owl took flight. The clock ticked. A cow bellowed, the rafters groaned. There was nothing to do but wait.

Outside, Hannu completed his round. In his hand he held a club and wore his best boots. He sniffed, packing more tobacco into his pipe.

The clock ticked. Merja lay across the table with her head in her hands.

'Let me read you a story,' I suggested. She waved her head and closed her eyes.

The clock ticked. Mother took the scrubbing brush out, splashing water on the floor. I moved my feet helpfully. We were all waiting.

The clock ticked.

When the floor was clean, she moved into the kitchen and started on the pots and pans, scouring, clattering with a curious harmonic. I could not help but smile. When the door opened our hearth neighbour entered, enquiring if we had heard the news.

'Yes,' I said.

She looked worn out. Three sons of military age already packing their bags. Before long there would be only old men in the village, and women and children. She was right.

'We will all be walking in the great giant's tread,' she whispered brushing the hair from her forehead; so little here, so much nothing and all and sundry trying to grasp it...the monsters.

My workshop key rattled in my pocket. Merja stirred. The clock ticked and then fell off the wall. We gasped and watched it as it rolled away. In a quarter of a century that clock had never moved and now, now in the corner of the room, it had stopped.

I walked our neighbour home and on the way retrieved the shotgun. It was loaded. It was a gesture, no more.

A hill fox barked a solitary whine. There was nothing we could do.

Later, when we had become accustomed to this tension, the church bell rang. No one rushed. There were a few parishioners sitting straight-backed upon the pews, eyes fixed on the communion table.

'It has begun,' said the pastor, in a voice trembling and close to tears. 'Shots have been fired across the frontier at Mainila.'

The congregation shuffled but did not speak. I looked across at my friend Harri. He had his Civic Guard rifle with him.

'Lot of good that we do you,' said one of the men.

Harri just smirked. 'I'll come with you in the morning,' he said.

I smiled back and began to laugh at the absurdity of it all. The air inside was still, still as glass, cold as marble.

The pastor paused. He was expecting some sort of response, but there was none.

'May the Lord have mercy on us all.'

Chapter 2

Man says in his wisdom that the earth is a sphere, which spins in space, which is infinite, which like man's imagination knows no limit or boundary. So it was on the final day of November when the first snow had fallen and ice laced the pools and watering places. When the ground was heavy with frost he unleashed his fury upon his enemies to make carrion of us all. From the mountains of Ethiopia or so it seemed they sliced the atmosphere baring teeth and uttering war cries. No mercy did they show; no pity, no thought for our mortality.

And through the cloud banks of the Baltic Sea they screamed, screamed with an intensity that turned the blood cold and would ever be remembered. Nine, ten, more levelled and wheeled in the sunlight, aeroplanes hawking their prey.

First the harbour where their cargo fell uselessly, where sailors clutched the deck with their fingers and bit into the steel shells of their ships. Then with all-seeing eyes they scooped out the railway station and from there proud jealously caused their bombs to land upon the streets and squares of the city, scattering confusion. Where men raised their fists in blunt anger, pouring curses from gutters where blood ran and bicycle wheels turned upended, in dust and masonry and fractured water mains, in the crazed galloping of dogs they showed no awareness or concern.

Further they ranged to the airport, releasing their incendiaries, strafing pavements where workmen once toiled and in the morning had closed their doors one final time. Nominating widows and orphans, the fitters and teachers and flute players.

High explosives fell upon the roof of the Technical Institute.

The first Maarit noticed was a fluttering of something white against the window of her third-floor office. Arms draped around the keyboard of a typewriter, she watched another fall, and then another. Thinking it to be a dove she moved across and saw the sky full of paper, like tiny pillowcases tumbling earthwards. In the streets below curious passers-by were examining the contents.

'What is it Maarit?' said her friend at the opposite end of the desk.

'I don't know.'

In the corner of her eye she caught a vapour trail heading south but other than that it was quiet, ordinary. The shoe-shine boy on the corner still plied his trade; students sauntered through the main entrance unaware of anything unusual.

'I'm going to have a look,' she said.

'You can't...we'll get into trouble.'

'I'll be a few moments. I want to find out what's going on. Come with me...'

Her friend joined her at the window and tried to make sense of the scene. A few people raced after the leaflets, some screwed them up and flung them away. A policeman spat.

'I think an aeroplane dropped them. Come on, join me.'

'I daren't,' the friend pleaded. She fiddled with a ring on her finger, unsure. 'The professor doesn't like me, if he finds me out of the office there will be more trouble and I'll burst into tears again. I know I will.'

'Don't give him the satisfaction.'

'I can't help it,' she said.

'Keep a look out then...if he comes...say I've gone to retrieve a file or something. I'll pick one up from the second floor just in case.'

Maarit opened the door and looked along the corridor.

'Be quick.'

'I will.'

Maarit raced down the stairs to the hurried tread of her own footsteps. There was no one else around.

When she pushed through the glass doors of the entrance she was momentarily blinded by sunlight. Blue specks danced across the retina until she adjusted and found her way to the street. There were few leaflets left. Most had already been pocketed or blown away. Eventually she found one, in a small square some distance from the Institute.

Before she had chance to read it her senses were assaulted by noise. The roar of engines danced upon her ear drums. It was then she saw the squadron of aeroplanes circling above. Ugly they were, blasphemous, working against all the laws of nature but they held her gaze. When thin metal tubes fell from the undercarriage her fascination merely increased and she could not tear her eyes away. She followed the trajectory until they were lost to view. Even when the explosions blasted scabs of metal against her coat and the pressure wave quaked her hair she did not move, thinking only that she had left her gloves and handbag in the office, that she would be cold. More aeroplanes cut across the sky, slowly as if in freeze-frame animation and delivered more of those strange sparkling tubes.

When a young man with spectacles awry started screaming at her to move she was most indignant. He was too close; his face was almost in her own. Was he spitting at her?

'Excuse me,' she said.

The man seemed stunned.

'Move,' he shouted. 'Get under cover...can't you see we are being attacked?'

When Maarit looked, she could see.

'Attacked?'

The man, a young man, more frightened than she but more aware grabbed her by the arm and dragged her to an alcove beneath some basement steps.

'In there!'

She was thrown against the wall and he dived after her, squeezing as close as the bricks allowed...she did not notice the cut on her forehead for a long time, only when a tiny red dew drop trickled onto her hand did she realise, only then did the trembling begin and the amazement as shock waves bowed the building which encased her body. Zing, zing, zing the pattering of shrapnel like a demented xylophone and the young man buried his head in her shoulder so he would not weep, and removed his glasses so he would not see, and the statues on the portico of the old apartment fell to the ground.

They were enveloped in noise and dust, wasps stung them, needles poked at their eyes and veins burst pumping liquid into cell, which, in their turn, burst. When they could see nothing the air raid siren set off its whine and the pale thud of anti-aircraft fire pounded.

There was smoke, so much that visibility was obscured and it was only when it lifted that the two were able to picture the results of this very first raid. They parted in shock and the young man in the spectacles hurried home, his name and origins and outcome unknown. A minor character in this tale gone.

Smoke cleared and the ruin fell around Maarit. There were no birds, here and there a cat cowered and spat. There was glass, fragments of wood, pockets of flame and for awhile it took Maarit's total concentration to decipher events. There had been a raid, several planes, out of the blue. There was a trickle of blood running down her face but it was not much; she wiped it away with the sleeve of her coat. She must write to Hannu about it; he had left the village but there would be a forwarding address. He would be very angry. It was nothing personal she pondered, the Russians were not after her specifically, merely operating in a general sense…then she thought again that Hannu would be incandescent with rage. She began to cry and cursed herself, wiping the tears and blood into a mess on the only coat she owned. Get a grip she thought. You are not badly hurt, there must be others worse. But she was hot and thirsty. It was then she decided to head back to the Institute. There she could get cleaned up, get some water; maybe a hot drink…talk to her friends. She took the leaflet out of her pocket and glanced at it briefly. The clumsily phrased writing urged her to overthrow the government. It seemed pointless and she used it to wipe away the stains on her sleeve.

Sirens wailed. She staggered across the park, kicking away branches striping the snow. There were no people and she thought it strange, only sounds in a blurry slow motion shrilling, bells, phut, phut, phut of anti-aircraft fire and her head ached. She was not seriously hurt. My hair is a mess, she thought.

It was not real. The two dead swans in the middle of the path were merely props for some cheap movie. Yellow flowers arching through a broken window as if trying to escape. Well, they were part of the set too. It was then she saw the first body, a woman slammed against railings, razored by shrapnel and gnarled like the bark of an old tree. There was no privacy now, only the pornographic. This was the picture in her frame. A personal icosahedron.

She paused for a second before moving on quickly, still wiping the sleeve of her coat with the paper until it disintegrated. When the Institute came into view it caused her to stop in her tracks. It was no more. A shell eaten by moths, a piece of wedding cake crumbled. No entrance, no door or windows, no front or back or beginning or end. No water or ice but girder, steel, brick, tile, guttering, snow thawing where fire burned, stairs on a mushed-up lawn, desks like tombstones and the arm of her friend poking out of the ruins. There were lines of people, all in black, shovelling the masonry backwards in a heap. There was order of a sort. A policeman directed proceedings, a fire engine arrived. An old man pushed past with an empty violin case and the wind whistled through the openings of a flute.

'Are you hurt?' asked a bystander.

'No,' said Maarit, 'it's a scratch.'

'You need to get it seen to,' he said with a gentle voice. 'They are setting up a first aid post over there.'

'I will,' she replied. 'What's happened?'

'Direct hit,' he said with the Institute filling his field of vision. 'There are some casualties, students; faculty staff.'

'My friend is over there...I left her minutes ago. She should have come with me but she was afraid of the professor.'

The man shook his head.

'There is nothing you can do now. Go and get yourself cleaned up.' And he pushed her away. More and more people arrived as she watched from the edge. Sometimes she heard a call for silence or a stretcher. The cold returned and the blood on her face froze as a web freezes in the forest. So she stood in line and waited for a nurse to wipe away her blood in a matter of fact way.

'That will do,' she stated.

So the brushes of the workmen bristled and the snails crept across ruins still hot, and the serpents cast their eyes to the sky for surely they would return to sow more seeds, there was nothing to stop them. So slabs angled the pavements into rickety decks, and the honey oozed from jars where the nails had shot, and Maarit brooded the journey to the outskirts of Helsinki where her lodgings were located. Her thoughts she parked within her. The cold chilled. Her flesh caught the embers of fire. Hannu will be so angry she thought. And the story watches her lonely tread for a time, on the road, shrinking, where the worms gyrate and a hundred beds are emptied. Here men carried their dreams like anvils and the women waited and the phut phut phut dimmed with winter. Here the story tripped into tunnels without light.

In Helsinki many lay in rows upon the bare earth. Hosepipes strangled the squares. Tiredness and shock spread. Newspapers clattered out their headlines as ammunition rushed up to the batteries but the guns were slow and ineffective and wrought no more holes in aluminium than had curses.

*

So it was war.

In that beginning was the eye. The all-seeing, all-scanning pupil, worming the retina and infiltrating all that was visible. All forest and lake and cloud banks came within its compass and the holes within which men were settled pitted its rods and cones and the roads cascading twisted the cornea into wild contortions and the movement of animals coloured the iris all. Where once crops grew now only the crow prouded its call. Fences fell, the metal beaters clattered their music.

So when at last the bear shrieked its sharp call, sharpening tungsten claws, there answered a multitude from the Arctic to the Crimea, the Uzbeks and Cossacks, Tartars, camel drovers, the hordes of Mongolia, the driven and the free, the weavers of the great silk road, steppe dwellers converging as the red voice from Moscow beckoned. The black bear called and its voice resonated with the armies trekking northward as did men in the census of old. All humanity crossed this spot. Ox carts, wagons piled with bread, endless, endless, exhausts, stubble-faced soldiers, trucks and tank tracks churning the snow into tempest.

At first the defenders waited, counting, noting, making their preparations with lips that smiled in on themselves, knowing that the key to Finland was the Isthmus, barring their windows and bolting their doors. Fourteen divisions closed upon them and a thousand tanks. Tens of thousands more in Ladoga, rifle divisions, butchers sharpening their cleavers and rubbing hands on aprons heavy with sweat. And in the north, the far north, more men still like ants scenting home, readying the strike as mourners approach the slab. The skies buzzed. The sea lanes opened and ships without sails scraped across shingle beds where the steersman had planted the prow.

In the Finnish lines, waiting, always waiting, as the steam curled from coffee pots. As the marten poked curious whiskers from the pine tree, as the fir cones heaped. Homes they made and gun sights adjusted, and cards played. Still the bear shrieked demented cries as the wastes became populated and the men in their holes practised a saintly patience, carving masks and putting on the strange white garb of ghosts, the apparel of their ancestors. The brethren huddled until the whisper came to climb out of the den and stalk, patrol, in a slinking company. No wolf howled, no owl flew. Reindeer gloves they put on their hands and prayers they uttered with curses and incantations. Like beasts selecting prey they slid through the ice, utterly at home. No movement did they miss, no smoking camp fire escaped their attention, no shout, no whimper. The same souls many times drenched in blood unrolled a carpet for the next performance. But no boots sullied its texture only the smooth slide of skies or prick of ski poles touched the surface.

So reader pick up again this tale of young Hannu, slender in the telling and short of flight. When I with my friend Harri joined this company on the Isthmus, entrenched within the Mannerheim line, hostilities were still many days away. Viipuri lay at our backs and the citadel flew the Finnish flag as it had done for many years. We were both of us knotted with homesickness and longed for the village with a quiet aggression but we helped to clear the vicinity of civilians as duty required.

We packed sledges and carts with bedsteads and chairs and blankets until the final cabin door swung shut. Our lads torched them in a wave of slash and burn, a primeval act, a new cutting of the cord. It made our young hearts heavy when we saw them looking to the eastern skies with a fresh intensity. But marvel did we at their toughness, faces set like granite, tearing out rivets that had held them to this spot for generations. While their bloodline snapped its connection to this earth we tempered it with youthful exuberance, reassuring them, putting on a brave front, cocky even, heaven knows what they must have thought.

'Leave them nothing but bones,' one old man said. He burned the cabin down himself, didn't trust anybody else to do the job.

'I was born in this spot, in the days of the old Tsar. There were real witches then, shrieking and carrying their broomsticks. Bandits lay waste to it many times over, and all my kin born, married, died within the parish boundaries. But I will leave them nothing but ashes.' He poked the still flaming embers of his home, wrapped his memories and put them in his pocket. The smoke made my eyes smart. I coughed a little, pulled my cap over my forehead. We do not shed tears, not we, not we with dialects thick as potato soup. We smile without smiling. Maarit said that in a letter from Helsinki several weeks ago.

It was gruelling, unsettling work, hard on the soul. In those days I was not so sandpapered, there were chinks in my armour.

We watched the drays stomping the ground, foaming at the bit, almost lost in spirals of steam from the flanks. Occasionally a plane flew high overhead, the red star just visible and in those moments we knew that Karelia would be forever maimed. We were losing a limb. The old man waved and I recall him teasing his neighbour good-naturedly because she had whitewashed the walls before burning it down. She looked a fragile, slender creature, even in her winter scarf, but she swore like a trooper, shocking it was for us to hear a woman swear so.

So the sleds zithered away. He was a real old Job that one, a proper Biblical Job with his gossip and the grey ash sprinkling his beard in spots between brown tobacco stains. But our labours were not complete. When the last civilians had gone we prepared our welcome. Manure was poured down the wells. We left booby traps at every door and window that remained. That's why they were spared. There wasn't a chicken run or outhouse that would not explode at the triggering of a wire. Pipe bombs we left in snowdrifts that would blow a man in half and mines so deviously hidden that only angels would escape their menace. We were proud of our work, even though it made us sweat and fumble. Even the ice had mines suspended beneath it. There was no safe passage brothers, might as well go home. Only a watery grave or a journey to oblivion awaited you in this place.

In the end Harri and I were glad to return to the line and rest our backs against the trench wall, pouring coffee down our throats. We heard the sergeant shout maliciously to pipe down in a voice that could have carried to Leningrad, to keep our eyes and ears open. I checked the catch of my Lahti machine gun and glanced across to Harri. There was nothing to read in his face, no more than when the teacher had asked him questions he could not answer. Usually he charmed his way out of trouble. Nothing was ever serious, even this was a game, even this a carnival. He saw me looking and whispered across.

'What's the matter?'

'Nothing.'

'Trying to read my mind again?'

'Maybe.'

'Reading a man's mind in broad daylight,' countered Harri laughing. 'I won't attempt to discover what goes on in that brain of yours.'

'I was thinking of Maarit.'

'She's fine.'

'She is like porcelain.'

'She scares me to death…far too clever.'

Last night (but I didn't share this thought) I dreamed Maarit was shaking me, trying to rouse me. I was in my room at home and the door was ajar from where she entered. She was feverish and her blue eyes turned to black. No matter how violently she tugged my hair or slapped my face I did not stir. It was only when she turned and slammed the door that I woke. It was my guard duty and as I scanned the barrenness of no man's land, picking out specks in the moonlight, trembling with cold and boredom I wondered why she had taken the trouble to enter my head and communicate.

'Come to think of it,' continued Harri oblivious, 'all women scare me to death. They are all abstraction.'

'Don't you mean distraction?'

'I know what I mean,' and he threw a piece of hard tack at my head. 'Anyway I was thinking what an ugly lot of soldiers we are.'

'You've been talking to Simo.'

Harri ignored me and continued with his train of thought. 'Our army must be the ugliest in history. How can you expect to win a war looking as we do? I'm sure our corporal is a troll.'

As darkness fell, an early black descended for midwinter approached. We sank ever deeper into our great coats, trying to rest, but it was so cold. The occasional flurry of snow flirted with our faces, a criminal mechanics pin pointing gaps in our clothing. I cast my eyes down to my boots, already clogged with mud and layered with frost. The trouble with times such as these was time itself, time to think and ponder, neurons connected in my brain almost as if I had been drinking. They flashed on and off. So the state of my boots caused me to worry what my mother would have said about my uniform. She would have had me carry an iron into battle! She was always so smart, smart as a meagre income would allow anyway. Every Sunday, without fail, marching to church in her work shoes, sitting on a rock within sight of the porch to change into best, despite the fact they pinched and bit; always the same stone. As if God cared what you wore on your feet. I envisaged her loading the sled with that stone when the call to evacuate came, just in case she had to change her shoes on the journey. The thought roused me and I called across to Harri.

'Are you awake?'

'Yes.'

Then I said nothing. Harri pulled a letter from his pocket as if our thoughts had fused.

'Did I tell you my family had left for Hämeenlinna? Half the kitchen's been buried in the garden. They'll be digging up pots and pans for a year.'

'My mother is still in the village...and Merja.'

'I suppose your brother...half-brother (wisely corrected) will help them pack if the time comes.'

'He's a fat head,' I said addressing Harri with some scorn.

'I agree... but still.'

Then I started to snigger at the thought of my mother telling him to fold everything carefully and mind the bird cage, make sure the stone isn't creased; serves him right. I'd sooner face the Russians than my mother in one of her moods.'

'He has a skull like a pig's head,' I remarked.

'No wonder I'm your only friend. You should have joined the diplomatic service.'

'I know...I know they all talk about me. But I don't care. I tell it as it is.'

He stamped his feet on the frozen ground. The sky was ink black: black as infinity and cold to the core.

'You don't hold conversations, you daub them on walls.'

'But friend,' I said, 'would you rather be anywhere else, with anyone else?'

Harri just grinned and stamped his feet even harder.

'Yes,' he replied, 'anywhere else…and with anyone else.'

Then suddenly there was a shout.

'Stand to…stand to,' roared the Sergeant.

A flare exploded into the night sky illuminating the landscape. It was bright. It was a miracle. It was a miracle freeze framed.

We stood there shoulder to shoulder, as if in a shield wall. I felt so calm and Harri perched on the fire step with the muzzle of his rifle wedged into his body smiled insanely.

'Can you see anything?'

'Nothing.'

Even though my eyes strained for movement, there was none, just the vapour from my breath rolling across the gun sight.

A false alarm maybe. A patrol returning spooked.

Another flare illuminated, bounced beneath the clouds, parachuted down and fragmented. Then it was we saw them in the distance, specks, flocks of snipe issuing strange cries, advancing with a slow parody of soldiers. It seemed so unnecessary. Did they have nothing else to do? But still we hugged the lahti and maxim. A troglodyte army faced up to them. A fuss of an army playing games and in all honesty I felt nothing but curiosity. What were they doing?

'Steady,' called the sergeant although he didn't need to for they were far away, miniature creatures shelled in unreality and as far away from human as the huge granite anti-tank blocks teething the plain. They wore black or grey or green with coats swaggering at the ankles and no attempt to camouflage. It was difficult not to feel a sense of pity. Looking along the line of my section there was no tension, just a quiet resolve. We were workers and this experience was an impediment to our labours. We too had better things to do.

More flares, and onwards they crouched in a vast herd, knee deep through snow and bog and weeds. No features wore they, we viewed them with awe, amazed that they did not feel our presence. Yet I felt they did for I could sense despair in their tread.

'Steady,' he called again.

We wired our thoughts and flexed our fingers, increasing the circulation of blood. We village boys steadied our nerves. We one hundred holding this section of the line held our breath so the fog of condensation would not envelop the view. Harri brushed his hair back out of his eyes and I could feel his excitement.

'Ready.'

So we were and willing to get on with it.

'Mark your target.'

So we did, as best we could, we were pointing at clouds.

And when the order to fire was given, we did, quite naturally. There was a blast of noise, the air vibrated, we recoiled and heard the bullets zing across snow like magnetic mosquitoes and when they found their mark there was a thud of expelled air, or a shout, or a clump...as cattle are pole axed so they fell, so they drown slipping through ice, eating snow and being trampled in a ceremony that could have been from another age.

'Poor sods,' said Harri as he fired away and reloaded.

So fell the hunchbacks in their heaps and we the seducers, the inmates of a zoo grotesque, flashing teeth or biting lips participated in the dance. Fire, reload, call for ammunition. Yet nothing came our way. No reply, no casualties on our part. No hint of flames to worry our heads.

From a support trench the thud of mortar. An artillery shell looped overhead. Still they assembled and reassembled, charged on, fell, vomited, the unencumbered sleepers rolled as our children's scythes cut them down.

I thought again that it was all so unnecessary. What were they doing? Which mad man ordained that it should be so? Only the radio operator's voice bore any resemblance to humanity as he gave a running commentary in the fire breaks.

'Cease fire.'

So we did.

Smoke cleared and canyons of the dead rippled from the front. Black mounds smouldering. Someone attempted to climb out of the trench but a stern bark called him back.

'Stay where you are,' he cried, 'we are not finished yet.'

We watched and waited. There was a scratch on Harri's forehead where a spent casing had grazed. No one else was touched. It was quiet and warm now in our den but hellish cold beyond the perimeter of our guns.

Some minutes later Corporal Murto crawled across to where the bodies lay. A sparrow flopped out of the sky. There was an abundance of these dead: a physical presence already turning stiff with cold. He called for others to join him but I stayed where I was. Weapons were collected and sent down the line. Pockets turned out for scraps of intelligence which might prove useful. Some did not even have gloves. They were all races under the sun, slumped in mounds beneath the sky. Red ran in tides from them, rivulets scarlet slashed the battlefield. A runner was sent to report on the action and the rest of us felt proud for we had not run. War did not come any easier than this.

These sluggish, ponderous enemies lay where they fell, frozen arms protruding as the wind whistled through their fingers. Rumours from returning patrols of many tanks began to circulate. Officers quickly quashed them, ordering the men back to their trenches. We prepared ourselves as the short arctic daylight penetrated the ground. We heard the trucks of more Russian battalions trundling up the road, fumes from many exhausts hazing the air. They were in no hurry to continue the fight. It was this lack of urgency that so impressed me. Nothing more happened that day. There were no more attacks. We said our prayers, warmed ourselves on campfires and poured hot potato soup into our stomachs in the manner of soldiers. We were subdued. We felt uneasy living so close to corpses. I prayed that their spirits should not haunt us. Already I saw their ghosts milling around, some bewildered, some crying and then walking away.

When evening settled we in the Taipale district took our turn to scan the promontory where the frozen Vuoksi and Ladoga waterways funnelled together. It was a bleak posting. We cleaned our rifles, combed our hair, searched the seams of our uniform for lice, chatted, peered beyond the edges of no man's land into the murk.

Chapter 3

This much I know.

When the mighty wail died, Maarit, in her shock, stumbled through rubble, the streets now even more unfamiliar. Cobblestones marked the walls of civic buildings. Already defence workers were digging through remnants of the city. Long lines stretched around new born craters, elements of the moon dropped on earth. This much she recalled with clarity, others like the cries of the injured, or the calls for silence tempered into dereliction and her memory shelved them.

Lines of volunteers reefed the places of worst impact until a whistle blew and all went quiet, listening for that tell-tale signal, a scratch, a cry, a whimper. When there was none they continued.

In Senate Square she paused. She felt weak, blood still dribbled across her face, not seriously, but enough to be noticed. Several passers-by asked if she was alright as she lent against the steps of the great cathedral, still dominating the square. The cupola was lost in layers of smoke now embellishing the city in the manner of enamel.

When an old woman wrapped heavily against the cold stopped and asked if she could help, Maarit barked back that she was fine. The old woman nodded, tapping her on the shoulder. Maarit relented, calmed a little by the woman and reported, this time in a more conciliatory tone that yes, she was fine; it was a scratch looking much worse than it really was. She was returning to her lodgings to get cleaned up and then she would return to the city to see if she could help.

'Pray to God,' the old woman said, 'only He can help us now.'

'I will.'

Maarit could tell the woman was not satisfied. She still betrayed her anxiety and did not take her eyes from Maarit's face, now marbled in red and white.

In the distance there was another thud, the petrol tank of a car exploding, and then another of unknown source. Or was it a new pounding in her head? So dream like this state, so difficult to distinguish the inside from the outside.

'Get yourself home Miss…quickly. There is no safer place than home.'

'I will.'

'God be with you.'

'And with you.'

She shuffled off through the smoke and flotsam with a shopping bag over her arm, muttering.

From these steps, which in autumn's yellow glow she had first surveyed the city, she now watched water from fire hoses trickle, saw the city telescoped to the ground, stone cold. Catching her breath in nets she occasionally coughed, wiping her face with a handkerchief. She must not give the appearance of distress when so many people rushed with their ant legs to and fro. This vantage point gave the panorama of the day. Great coated fire wardens, anti-aircraft fire grazing upwards although the bombers had long gone. Mere pea shooters.

But yet.

Yet she felt easier now, had gathered her thoughts and pulled a robe around her body.

It had been rough, this last hour, but now she gathered her thoughts and determined to return to her lodgings. As he had told the old woman she would clean herself up and then see if she could help. It was a duty. These people, who she did not know, were now her neighbours. So she thought.

Northwards the road led, from Senate Square to the railway station, still the all-pervading stench of smoke and a haziness. Thousands it seemed swarmed that beautiful building; it was a place of complete confusion. The desire to reach the countryside overwhelmed and the station entrance echoed to the beat of many dialects, of mostly women and children caught in the storm.

Then it was the siren moaned once more, a bitter conversation as Maarit passed beyond the city museum, a place she intended to visit one day. She crouched in the doorway and could hear the soft groan of bombs near the harbour and airport as they were targeted again. The sing-song patter of machine gun bullets caught her attention. The bombers strafed streets on their return. So soon it was over, mercifully far away.

Her journey continued, a coppersmith heart beating and oxygen difficult to catch. How her head ached, how it caused unpleasant feelings of nausea. But she did not want to be sick, not here on the pavement, in public, it would be so undignified.

Across bridges now, spanning the many threaded lakes of the suburbs. Into districts where the poor dwelt, where the labourers and servants nestled, she stepped, where the wooden houses rooted. It was quiet. Empty.

Pushing the front door with her shoulder the creak was the same, the same handle she had pushed that morning on the way to work, on the same doorstep. It was eerily unchanged.

Halfway up the stairs she bumped into her landlady. Then it was she fell into her arms, exhausted and white, then it was she wept when Mrs Rajala laid her on the bed in the little bedroom. The womb she had carved as a home from home. Returning with a bowl and water she bathed her face, wringing out the blood-soaked towel, wrapping a fresh bandage around the wound. Then it was she sleepways sank.

In weariness too deep to number she washed in and out with the tide and her memories poked or probed, electrical impulses sparking thoughts as a battery sparks into life but without logic or meaning.

She saw a mirror but could not tell if the refection was the room or some corner of a mind confused. Her face was alabaster and her eyes the colour of green tea. What a mess, she thought. I must comb my hair, no…it must be washed and scented but only when my strength returns, till then I drift where the current leads me, even to death. Is that overstepping the mark?

The pillow was a bank of snow. Warm snow lined with eider feathers from the far north.

Then it was, she later stated, she saw me for that first time, even though we had been to school together, not that I had much schooling, book work was not my forte. Hannu fishing with a line from a boat. May I presume to enter her head now?

Hannu, it was the boat I noticed first, the bow splitting the water as a knife slides through butter. Waxed and polished and I know you would not speak but watch. I wrapped my shawl around my shoulders.

'Hannu,' I called. You looked up expressionless and jerked the line.

'Hannu,' I called again as the dragonflies skimmed the water's edge and the whirligigs performed their maddening dances.

But then you knew why I called for your attention and rowed to the shore. I couldn't tell if you were pleased or irritated.

'You have lost her again.'

I must have blushed.

'I know…I know. The stupid creature.'

'Where have you looked?'

'Everywhere…beyond the birch hills, almost to the railway track. She hates me that stupid, stupid creature. She taunts me with her hide and seek.'

'Do you want me to help you?'

'Yes,' I said.

You know these forests, I thought, if anyone can find her it is you.

'I will then, maybe she has walked homewards.'

'Do you think so?'

'Maybe.'

Hannu pulled the boat onto the shingle beach and stowed his fishing gear away.

'I saw the miller earlier but all he would say was that some crone had bewitched her, that she was a rock or tree stump now.'

'Then you will be in need of a sorcerer.'

'Some say you have those powers,' I stated with some courage. It was difficult to know how Hannu took to conversations, he blew hot and cold.

'Who?'

'Some people.'

At that moment a crow flew across my path and startled me. Hannu laughed.

'What was the miller doing out here?'

'Picking berries and mushrooms as you would expect.'

'Are you sure?'

'What else would he be doing?'

'Some say he has the mark of evil upon him, the one-eyed miller.'

'Who?'

'Some people.'

Mrs Rajala's eyes peered into her own.

'Poor child.'

She changed the pillow for it was wet and unclean.

And she was in the 'dwelled in' place. Roads quartered the village. It was all very familiar. She belonged to a house in that village. It did not belong to her; it was another dwelled in place heavy with the scent of golden rod and watercress.

She heard the train whistle to Viipuri beyond the hill and the timber mill loomed large. Splinters shot into the air, as the owner often remarked, you cannot cut wood without splinters. There was Hannu again, following the heifer home as it turned her doe eyes upon him and spoke.

Maarit regained consciousness in the early hours of the morning. A candle flame flickered on the bedside table. It bore a lion's face with amber mane and blue sword shimmering in the centre. There was a fierce heat to it.

Mrs Rajala was asleep in a chair. She still wore a work apron, her aged frame wore gullies and frowns. Her lips moved softly.

It was dark outside.

Mrs Rajala must have sensed her wakefulness for she lumbered from her chair and sat on the bed.

'How do you feel?'

'Fine,' uttered Maarit. 'Have I slept for long?'

'Some time...you were exhausted and in shock I shouldn't wonder.'

'There was an air raid. The Institute was hit.'

'Yes...yes I know.'

'Were you there?'

'No, I slipped out to see what was happening.' She paused. 'I should have been at my desk.'

'You have someone watching over you child,' whispered Mrs Rajala. 'Lie still and in an hour or so I will bring you a plate of soup.'

'I should get up.'

'Ah such foolishness. You are in no state, rest a while, that wound of yours is not serious but if infection should set in.'

With that she departed, closing the door behind her.

It seemed like seconds when Mrs Rajala returned with a plate of soup and hunk of black bread.

'Build your strength,' she advised. 'There was a tear in your overcoat, it's repaired now, and the rest of your clothes will be ready soon.'

'You are too kind Mrs Rajala.'

'Eat that soup before it goes cold.'

Maarit mechanically forced three or four spoonfuls of soup into her mouth, but the bread was too much, like cobblestones.

'When we heard about the Institute we were very worried. The neighbours have been in and out ever since you got back, though you had all the appearance of a ghost when first I saw you on the stairs.'

'Was it only yesterday?'

Mrs Rajala pulled the curtains aside and a quartz like light flooded the room. Another day.

'We should be safe enough here, there is nothing to interest the Russians in this district.'

'I had such dreams.'

'You were feverish Maarit, delayed shock and a temperature from that injury. Goodness how hot you became. Who is Hannu?'

'Did I speak of him?'

'In and out of sleep.'

'He is a boy I know, a friend. He will be making his way to the border now.'

'A great many will.'

Later, in the morning the air raid siren sounded another alert. It was distant, far, far away but the roll of engines carried even to this place and Mrs Rajala muttered under her breath.

'You know,' she said. 'I was born when the Czar – whites and Bolsheviks' daggers drawn and a good many injustices on both sides. I saw the cruelties of the civil war but never thought it would come to this.'

'No,' agreed Maarit.

After a few more moments Mrs Rajala left the room, obviously tired after an all night vigil. Emotion had seeped into her thoughts too and the strain that was to become commonplace surfaced for the first time.

Maarit dressed and stood by the window, gazing out into a landscape dripping with snow. Beyond the road was an orchard of fruit trees, each one a tower with star-flecked branches defying the north wind. Geese roamed beneath them challenging, bellowing in strange catches of song but nervy at

54

the same time for even the animals of the earth knew something was afoot. A cart horse lumbered towards the city and somewhere a trumpet played. She felt like Noah's wife.

Where would it end? From where would help come? Divine intervention? As for herself, she had no work, no income, a home on the edge of a battlefield. She surely was a passenger on her own ark. Like this she observed the world outside her own mind, only partly understanding until the urge to activity overcame and she helped Mrs Rajala with the housework, cleaning pans, checking the stores of food.

'You are of course welcome to stay Maarit,' said her landlady. 'There will be much to be done. Things will become organised in a short time, you'll see. Likely as not we will have to prepare for a siege.'

*

In the froth and frill of this winter war, at the start of it, in the bleak, grey days we did not have the luxury of hindsight. We travelled, our people gnawed pathways through forest and lake. From the Isthmus moved this human wave, children west to Haem or other such places, while the farmers and grooms and factory workers, and the glass blowers donned their forage caps and buckled their belts. Such bleak days in December when roads became clogged with refugees winding away from the centre. Russian planes strafed the columns, biting and stinging as does the scorpion all under the vast, empty sky. In the snow banks they lay, the child bearers, the old or weary, pushed aside so we citizen soldiers, we brave, happy souls would reach the front. So whirled the bicycle wheels and the hot breath of horses souping the air, mixing our channels of communication with animal spirits. Sleds curdled the ice like melting honey. The sight of this first evacuation made my throat burst. Even Harri, happy heart, could not cast his eyes from his boots.

There was a pulse to the movement, it was a directed madness. All these people leaving their homes, carrying as much as their shoulders could bear. I watched it without comment. Saliva would not wet my tongue sufficiently for me to speak.

The cold tore at their faces and the raw blade of it liquefied the fingers. Children sucked blood into their hands and no one spoke. Our village was safe for the time being, it was not yet in the killing zone, but this was no real comfort. It was in the line of advance.

But we of the infantry witnessed all this with our own eyes. It saddened our hearts, and for some it roused anger and defiance. When they had passed by we left our trenches, torching everything, laying traps. Every opportunity to lay a snare was taken. Open a barn door and the entrant would be atomised by explosives; pick up a rain cape, prod the pig left dead in the sty and enter a Soviet heaven.

Already the first attacks, strangely half-hearted, were repulsed by our advanced positions. Now the field was clear for action. It was a dangerous place. Mines littered the ground as seeds litter a poppy field. Only the maggots harvested the carcasses of animals slaughtered in the yards and meadow. They would not feed the enemy, instead they froze and thawed and rotted and froze.

But on the other side where the roads from Leningrad radiated towards the Isthmus, what of those men? So it seemed even greater collisions were on hand.

From the time of the first whistles, before that shrill cry had died upon the wind, columns of green machinery, all manner of motorised transport, slewed across the roads, trucks, lorries, mechanised infantry, ambulances, workshops on wheels, clogging every avenue, moving ever closer to our own positions. These were gnawed in their turn by snow storms making communication even more difficult. Every tentacle of their army writhed independently, blinded by storms to the others. The red army floundered before it really began, unable to see or speak with each other in an alien land the name of which the common soldiers did not even know. A jigsaw before even the initial advance units had blundered into the Finnish trenches. So we had a chance.

In time it soon became apparent to the enemy that this war would not be so simple. Engines halted frozen as early December temperatures fell to 40 degrees below. Some did not wear gloves so the bite of bare metal on skin tore skin and fingers away. Blood froze inside the veins. Bread became as bricks to be thrown.

Their olive-coloured uniforms held neither cold or snow or rain at bay, merely draping the body in readiness for burial. Yet still this menagerie struggled to advance, cumbersome, uncertain, but not lacking in courage.

There was one thing more than any other that Mannerheim the great Finnish commander feared. That Harri and me and others of our kind sheltering in dugouts miles to the east would cast away our rifles and flee when the squadrons of tanks appeared on our front. It was his greatest nightmare that we would run in terror at its first appearance. It was this panzer army rumbling onwards painfully slowly, chain by chain, at five miles an hour through snowdrifts and entanglement s of barbed wire. This was the test, the great unknown. Would we stand?

With the motion of mammoths the war was beginning...no longer a game for soldier/civilians. Within these steel boxes bullets could be repelled and trenches cleared. From the air they gave the appearance of roaming skulls, alloy boned and spitting, prehistoric clanking through the white silence. The Finn men processed none, nor had they seen their like before. The steady thump of their engines a recital to the winter air. Rolling onwards, infantry in their wake, as a factory lathe burnished and spoiled. This was the Russian strength and Finnish dread. How would defenders who had weeks before been farm hands or butchers or boat builders react when these dinosaurs descended on the village of Taipale, a small place, once innocent.

*

Waiting, always waiting. The stench of damp earth in my nostrils. The man next to me sniffing, coughing, eyes misting over, freezing. In this trench we had the perspective of snails on a wall. We felt vulnerable.

'Can you stop that God forsaken spluttering?' I snarled to my comrade.

'I have a cold,' he replied, 'what do you want me to do?'

I just looked at him. Harri sniggered to my left. Then I started coughing in sympathy.

'Can't you stop that God forsaken spluttering?' he mimicked and I threw a clod of earth at him.

'Pipe down,' bawled the corporal in a hail of expletives. 'At least try to behave like soldiers.' Corporal Murto had many times stated his view that we should be in a kindergarten. His aggression dampened the spirits. We did not like him, he was not over fond of us.

It's a rum thing this war business, all hurry, hurry, hurry, wait. I suppose we were buoyed because we had repelled the first attack, though it was an uneven affair and later we realised that it was merely a clash of patrols rather than a real attempt to break through the lines, something of a turkey shoot and we took no losses. Maybe if they had closed upon us, baring their teeth, growling or pale we would have felt anger. I wanted to feel the rage of earlier when we saw the civilians on the road but once they had gone I could not. But in those early days, in the initial brief engagements, the Russians were olive-greens, not men, stiff as animal carcases when we rolled them away into a ditch. It was dark then and they were tubes of humanity cold to the touch. Some unfeeling crimes we committed.

So we molluscs waited. Subterranean creatures clutching our mugs of black coffee, stamping feet, wriggling fingers in frost repelling gloves, and occasionally, when there was sufficient light crumbling, our retinas against the horizon to catch glimpses of movement or a sound. But for two days there was nothing, just the whistling of the wind through fishing boat sheets, a hoary, timeless sound jumping out of the black.

By the third day we were embedded in the soil, growing roots.

'Taipale, Taipale, Taipale.' I kept singing until all words seeped into the liver and heart and pancreas. If only something would happen. But out there beyond the cover of our fox holes the bleak unravelled towards the horizon. So this land became known simply as the bleak, the hungry land, the mouth swallowing; we simpletons passed the time in whatever way we could.

The wind reaped our faces, the atoms of space ruffling the hair and smarting the eyes. Time was our deceiver, our daydream. There, exploring the gaze of the parapet in a line I saw my fellow travellers. There was of course Harri, jack the lad, never one to despair or take anything seriously, even this situation. That grin, that all-the-world-must-love-me grin lightened the atmosphere. Next to him a different generation. Simo the sniper. How that man loved his stomach! He had a scar like a crow's claw on the side of his face but would never explain how it got there. Poor Simo was always hungry, a ravenous cove with dark humour. The first night we arrived, nestling into what was then just drainage ditches intended to clear the farm land of swamp water, he started a little pot of stew bubbling on a campfire. He claimed to be not afraid, his mother-in-law was more ferocious than any Russian, so he said, and as long as she wasn't in the lines opposite he would be alright. When we laughed he stroked his beard and stirred the pot which bubbled a language of its own. For a while we thought he had fallen asleep, but no, merely musing he opened a conversation.

'You know lads,' he said with that slow, lazy voice, 'my own son is not much younger than you, but more intelligent.'

No one was ever sure when he was serious.

'Better looking too. Ugly brutes in this trench and thick as two short planks.'

'Salt of the earth,' replied Harri.

'Aye,' he conceded, 'I'm not saying I don't think a lot of you lads, but there's not likely to be too many sweethearts worrying about you.'

' You speak for yourself,' shouted Pekka Salakka.

'No...let's be honest, there are not many sweethearts around here, no actual women.'

'What?' I said. 'In this trench?'

'Exactly.'

It was a diverting conversation, if pointless.

'Do you mean,' shouted Pekka, suddenly becoming worked up, 'that the ugliness of the men in this sector – which incidentally I dispute – is the reason for the absence of women?'

'Obviously.'

'And,' he continued, still riled, 'that it has nothing to do with the fact that we are living in a ditch in the middle of winter, likely to be attacked at any moment.'

'You must draw your own conclusions,' replied Simo, stirring his stew again.

'What has this got to do with your mother-in-law?' said Harri.

'Nothing...she's not here is she!' There was a hint of panic in his voice.

'Have you ever considered joining the Russian army?' grunted Pekka.

'No lad...not seriously...and smoking is bad for your health.'

I attempted to stifle a laugh.

'So how did you meet your mother-in-law?' I asked.

'It was through the wife,' said Simo, quite seriously.

Harri was in hysterics.

'My wife', he continued, 'is a big woman.'

'How big?'

'Like so,' he indicated, 'and when I first saw her, it was a picture. Her face in profile on the cow shed wall holding a pole axe to the skull of this cow. That's when I saw the mother-in-law, with the sledgehammer, waiting to swing.'

'What was she like?'

'It was a black and white heifer if I remember correctly.'

'I meant your mother-in-law.'

'A big woman.'

'How big.'

'Like so.'

'I saved that cow's life. My Liisa was smitten that day, dropped the pole axe and came with me there and then, carried my pack all the way back to Lappeenranta. The mother-in-law,

God Bless her if she still lives never forgave me, even when I bought her a new sledgehammer.'

Then silence.

'Anything else?' asked Harri.

'No...just keep your nose out of my stew.'

All Pekka could do was growl and mutter under his breath. 'He's mad he is...mad.'

I suppose we didn't have much choice in being there but I was strangely content at that time, we were all a little unhinged. I didn't stand out and the sense of order which prevailed, the routine, made me easier in my mind. We were a temporary band bound by a blizzard that would soon disperse us all.

More and more men of the 10th Division arrived, more youngsters like ourselves. If they only knew how green we were, how lacking in battle hardness. They did not know that our experience amounted to one skirmish. But we understood that God in His wisdom governs the deeds of all men, as He did in times gone by, as He does now. It was a period of patching up, mending, cleaning weapons endlessly, guard duty and at night, ski patrols, a slithering, zinging nightmare where even our breath wore the acoustics of a cannon roar and our hearts thundered the night air.

Our corporal led these patrols with a demonic intensity. He lived for them and in a darkness of the unimagined poked out his red, bloodshot eyes, scouring the unseen as a wolf. If he had chanced upon a Russian my conviction is that he would have torn him limb from limb and brought the pieces back for Simo's stew pot. But this no man's land was lair to him, ice and sludge and marsh bore his skis and his teeth bit the air unnervingly. He was a terror to us and I was not alone in fearing his temper. Once I caught his face in my line of sight and sucked my breath.

A real demon. I crossed myself once his back was turned. In those short daylight hours we witnessed lone reconnaissance planes flying overhead, low and stately, bubbling eastwards, banking, turning back to forest airstrips once they had seen what they wanted to see. Things were building up. More men and supplies coming through the trenches, more patrols, more guard duties. The officers whispered in their dugouts. Simo ate and ate with real determination, we were so proud of him. Harri combed his hair and Pekka sulked, rooted to the fire step in a mood. It was a matter of time we knew and sensed new movement across the Taipale river and the waterway known as Suvanto.

Then it was this theatre of ours, this drama into which myself and others equally unaccustomed to the stage were drawn.

Towards the end of the first week of December we were called together. The captain stood on sandbags near the entrance to a dugout and began to speak. He said what we thought, new attacks were expected, that intelligence reports had drawn conclusions about armour and artillery and infantry and Stalin himself for all we knew would be rolling towards us.

The corporal was standing alert, blazing a gaze at the officer as a sniper would. That corporal, that corporal had nothing in common with himself let alone anyone else.

Anyway, the officer knew we would do our duty, would defend the motherland. It was a good speech I suppose for an officer and brewery manager from the district of Joensu. It did not have enough blood in it for the corporal's liking and his scowl became even more canine.

Throughout it all Simo chewed on a husk of bread. What a man.

'I hope you shoot better than you march,' the corporal spat across at Simo. I felt there was no need for such language but it caused him no disturbance. Even when he pulled his finger across his throat Simo made no indication of taking any notice. For it was true that Simo could not march, or stand to attention in a straight line, or at ease for that matter. It was true that his salutes caused fits of hysterics in the officers' mess, that they mimicked him, that he was an unusual soldier. But I knew that he could drill a bullet into an eyeball from a thousand metres, that he never missed. That much was clear to him. Besides, you did not kill Russians by saluting them, what a thought!

And as the last caramel drops of daylight flooded the promontory we knew the battle for Taipale would soon begin. Smoke from every campfire grew closer and more numerous. Simo polished his spoon in readiness for the assault, ammunition was distributed and a thought occurred to me, 'Do not be afraid for I have redeemed you. I have called you by name. You are mine.'

Chapter 4

Thoughts clustered on the inside of Maarit's head, she could neither select nor dismiss them. They had cut a groove inside her mind and spun around and around even when to the outside world she was occupied. Still their presence hung heavy.

She sat in the corner of Mrs Rajala's kitchen on an ancient chair that squared not to the floor but rocked this way and that in a humorous way. The flames of the fire licked against the grate, warmth oozed into her toes as the logs spat and crackled. Smoke breathed clouds into the room swirling and dispersing. She had written but as yet had received no reply from the village. This was no surprise for the countryside was in turmoil. Her immediate fears were not for the family. They were as yet some distance from the front line and if they had to leave there were good roads and a railway. No, her anxieties followed Hannu. There had been no word from him either and she knew he would be near the border with countless others. She did not know how he would take to life in the field with its lack of privacy, had she but known the life suited him maybe her worries would have been appeased. But as her mother always stated, 'we must endure, it is the way'.

Frost coated the kitchen window, distorting the image of any movement outside, giving the world a pale intricacy. Water beads traversed the inside pane where heat from the fire had caused a melt. Like sap it streaked the glass adding even more pattern to the world.

It was Mrs Rajala's return that broke the spell. She had checked the storehouses and was grateful to report an abundance of potatoes, sausage, salt hams, enough for winter whatever shortages may come about. She settled herself on the bench opposite Maarit and rubbed her hands.

'It's getting colder,' she said, 'the path is like an ice rink.'

'Good skiing weather.'

'Yes...I suppose it is.'

After a pause Mrs Rajala opened the conversation again.

'Have you resolved to go then Maarit?'

Maarit felt slightly uncomfortable but nevertheless answered.

'Mostly. I shall go into the city today. I have to make enquiries about people at the Institute. I want to make sure they are safe. Then...well there must be things I can do. Sometimes I feel I should go home and be with my mother, but I'm not so sure it will be easy to return. The roads are clogged and the weather worsening. Maybe I am needed in Helsinki. I can cook, I can nurse, I have my wits about me, every pair of hands will be needed I'm certain of that.'

'True enough, but you are welcome to stay here.'

'Thank you. You have been more than kind and I have no plans to leave immediately. To be honest I'm not sure what I should be doing, just something. I want someone to tell me to do this, go there.'

'Well...when you go be careful, the roads are dangerous, there are unexploded bombs and craters, not to mention more air raids. Keep to the centre of the street and in that way, if a building collapses, at least you will have some warning.'

'I will,' conceded Maarit 'and God Bless.'

In winter coat she opened the door and began the long walk back to the city, bare headed with hair trailing vaporous and youth saturated in both optimism and vulnerability she counted steps in fresh air between blasted trees. The Baltic wind raised perfume into her throat and mocking she twined her fingers into Hannu's and saw his nervous smile. She had survived the first ordeal, the first examination, bruised but unbroken, no veins split, no flesh turned over to maggot. The same sun now dusting snow from roof tops shone down on Hannu wherever he lay, the same fluid flowing through her body flowed in his lean frame. The gruffness which in some caused offence caused only smiles in her, and his old, old ways of thinking was a comfort. We will have a serious talk when next we meet, she thought, and bounced through streets now dense with shuttered windows.

Helsinki was mute. Strangely quiet the walkabouts swathed in cold weather garments seemed lost within themselves. At the corner stores queues developed, uneasiness seeping into people who spoke not except in whispers as if the ankle grasping stones were threatening to pull them down. She noted the faces, bespectacled or triangled in head scarves. Was this a mood swing, she pondered, a peak to be followed by a trough? Was this a reaction to events? She knew not but found herself outside the railway station. Curiosity bore her to the precincts. The crowds carried mostly women and children, populations of them moving through swing doors as the announcer broadcast destinations in hieroglyphics. Still hunched in corners, as they always had been were the vagabonds and alcoholics, the leavers of society, tormented mortals spitting and snarling and staring uncomprehending...wounded souls, sad, jittery, even they sensed something unusual was happening; the watchers and the watched, aimless as grey-suited soldiers strode purposely through the concourse to ripples of applause and sailors returning to their ships traversed the platform like skaters on a pond.

Maarit stayed and watched, transfixed by the ebb and flow. Children boarding trains for safety in the countryside, mothers waving them off, blinking the light from eyelids heavy with time. Straining to discern faces, jogging the brain like dreams. Dust settled on the floor or floated in prisms of glass. Waves, weary waves of travellers chasing through tunnels with the knowledge that this place was a prime target should the bombers return. And the sun's rays melted across her hands, her fingers moving like the inner workings of a heart. And the train standing at platform six began the long haul to Oulu province where the

Baltic shield hammers on the doors of the earth and scars appear as the watchers watch and the rail to rail melody grinds.

The sense of strain was palpable and emotions of relief, sadness and anxiety melded when the trains cut their moorings and began the journey north and west.

Smoke particles still clung in the air, a scent she would forever associate with Helsinki and it walked with her until she reached the burned out ruins of the Technical Institute. Many mental rehearsals had prepared her for this scene but it still hurt to see the mangled remains of her work place, though in truth she had been employed there only a few months. It was half-shell, half-ruin like a cake crumbling on a plate. Students milled around and gangs of workmen were busy clearing rubble, others picked through the remnants looking for salvageable equipment or materials. Paper rolled across the ground, pages from text books or periodicals, memos, administration sheets, that was the abiding memory, all of these words tumbling, meaningless now they had lost their anchors and connections. What was it about monkeys and the works of Shakespeare Maarit had once heard? Something about probabilities and the randomness of words. But it escaped her. There were a few faces she recognised, faces passed in corridors or in the canteen but she did not know their names. By the main entrance, or what was once the main entrance, there was a hand written list of casualties, the dead and the injured and the missing. A small knot of people scanned the information, a few attachments asked for news. 'Have you seen the whereabouts of?' Appeals from mothers, sisters, sweethearts. Her friend's name, she who shared a desk and typewriter was listed as dead, as she had known it would be. Other names had no association or some she recognised only as names on lists or invoices rather than faces.

For some time she watched as some departed and some arrived, all spoke in whispers. Professors, bearded many and with spectacles across the bridges of their noses looked as if their whole world had collapsed, it was a wondrous scene of descent and dislocation.

Then her name was called.

'Maarit,' she heard, and then 'Maarit' once more. On turning she saw a face dimly known, the voice gave it away.

'You are the girl on the switchboard.'

'Yes.'

'We have spoken a few times.'

'You have very distinctive vowel sounds,' said the girl, 'there is no mistaking you are from Karelia.'

'Is it that obvious?'

'Afraid so...but no matter. My name is Liisa. I've seen you a few times, coming and going. A mess isn't it?' She stood scanning the debris field. She was very confident this creature, this small well set inhabitant. Sparks flew from her and it was what Maarit needed, some one to take command, a purpose.

'How did you know my name?'

'The professor pointed you out. Said you might be in need of some company after all this...I'm sorry to hear about your friend.'

'She was a child really...always nervous about something. How are her family?'

'In pain I imagine, like so many others. How are you?'

'Fine.'

'Really?'

'Yes...pulling myself together now, after the shock.'

'Do you have any plans?'

'No...none other than to go home. See if there is anything I can do.'

Maarit's tone dropped and she looked beyond Liisa to the hive of activity, where it seemed even the ground quivered. Liisa suggested a walk to the harbour, unconsciously Maarit followed.

As the narrow, wall-encrusted lanes led down to the water's edge her eyes began to sting, the smoke perhaps or the whip of wind channelled through mute corridors. She did not want to give the impression of crying, it was not her way. Nor was she unduly troubled, more curious, seeking space, quietly she wiped away a tear with the sleeve of her coat and they walked as if funnelled to the water's edge and sat upon a bench there.

The harbour was almost empty of ships. Strange and bloated baggage bobbed in the waves, an oil slick grasped the surface coating. The cup of the quays resounded with workers and sailors and stevedores strengthening defences and strong points with sand bags. There were sentries too with bayonets fixed and barbed wire scything through exits. Here were men ramshackled in their chains and oblivious to all but the whirr of seagulls overhead who sensed their dangers with a shrieking expectancy.

'Will they return?' asked Maarit connecting the ways of the birds with those of aeroplanes. 'Will there be more bombs?'

'Maybe…but I expect there is more call in the east. I'm lucky, my parents are in America. I have no one to fear for but myself. And you Maarit, where do you call home?' Maarit paused, momentarily picturing the fields and forest and the little railway station.

'It is a village to the east of Lapeenranta, a small place, of no consequence. It is quartered by roads and streams and a mill and a church. A typical village…quiet.' Then as if anticipating Liisa's next question, 'As far as I know there is no danger, we are some distance from the border. The Mannerheim line and most of the Isthmus is before us, but who knows? I expect it is a fearful time there too, empty of men. My Hannu is somewhere near the border but I know not where. He will write when the opportunity presents.'

'Are you going back?'

'Probably,' replied Maarit wiping her sleeve across her face again. 'I can stay with my landlady Mrs Rajala for the time being. She is of the old school, but so kind. She sort of adopted me.'

Liisa coughed, smoke catching her throat, but after a moment of silence she started the conversation in a rather blunt way and her tone made Maarit sit up.

'My friends in the union are organising a group to go to the front…north or east I'm not sure yet. Would you be interested?'

'I'm not in the union.'

'I know but no matter. We never thought to ask you to the meetings, we never thought you would be interested.'

'What will you do?'

'We will be volunteers…nursing, cooking, washing, anything that might be useful. What can you do?'

'I can cook and clean, heaven knows I have experience of that. I've nursed my cousins through fevers and injuries.'

'Sure…this is nothing official you understand. It will be no picnic. I'm not even sure our presence will even be welcomed but it's better than sitting here waiting for something to happen.'

Maarit sank thoughtfully into the bench where frost had recently melted. Vapour clouds betrayed her breathing as her eyes jumped from scene to scene and memory to memory.

'It would be good…to do something. But what would I need, what are the arrangements?'

'Bring whatever you have, winter clothing obviously, blankets, food, bandages, salt if you have any. Don't forget your identity papers.'

'I will need to let my mother know.'

Liisa looked so certain, so confident as she placed a cigarette to her lips and lit it. The aroma of tobacco permeated the air with a fragile reassurance. The scene grew into celluloid, two young girls on the bench, a trail of smoke and burning Helsinki rising as a back drop, an imaginary camera panning away, soft focus, feet crossing, staring, whispering eyes scanning the herring barrels, dockside workers repairing hoists with the seriousness of gallow makers. They called out, the outspoken one breathing hard and listening for the preliminary notes of the aid raid siren. Seagulls circled, bilge pumps gushed molten from a lone freighter hugging the quay side. Hoses clamped like huge determined leeches to the side, ships all and sundry prepared to leave this dangerous place.

'We are meeting at daybreak on Wednesday, outside the university. Bring only a rucksack, pack it as tightly as you can…we will know by then our destination.'

Maarit forced a smile, blood flowed to her cheeks, an axe landed on a tree and a spring old nest fell.

'You will not be alone, there will be others from the Institute, you will recognise them by sight at least.'

Maarit nodded but said nothing.

'The world is unravelling Maarit, soon this war will spread into every corner and we have to participate one way or another. Action for sake of action, save us all going mad.'

'I know my landlady Mrs Rajala will think it a bad idea. I wonder how she will cope on her own.' But Maarit knew she would endure, she was made of steel that woman, a body in an armoured shawl.

And the wordy mouth continued to vibrate but Maarit...well she was no longer listening. Her path was clear now, that's all she wanted. That was the reason for the trek, to unearth a reason and a road.

*

In the village snow fell from the branches in great clods, with a thud it drummed the gardens and farm yards. A blunt instrument in this marginal land was winter, carrying away the weak and infirm year on year. A solitary mister plodded humpbacked through the drifts to where the pastor stood blowing on his hands and stamping his feet at the entrance to his church. The bell was silent now, swathed in blankets even its appearance was muffled as it lay on the porch floor, crated and ready for departure.

'Are you sure you want it to go Pastor?' asked the mister through his scarf.

'Certainly...that Godless race of heathens will not carry it away for their war materials.'

'As you say Pastor...but some will see it as a mite defeatist, the Russians not yet being at our door so to speak.'

'The bell is my responsibility. I will take no chances with it.' He looked harassed and impatient, aged even.

'Many a fellow's been eased from this world with that fine sound.'

'So will many more if we can but move it to safer territory.'

''Tis the heart beat of the village that bell.'

'And I'm ensuring it does not undergo surgery…now where is the cart, are we to freeze to death before anyone does anything?'

'It will be here soon, don't you fret Pastor, we'll have it on the station platform before nightfall. Are you sure it is crated securely?'

'Of course.'

'Can't say I've ever transported a bell before sir, most other items and bodies a plenty of course. People always have a habit of dying in inconvenient places and always me has to rectify it…must be a Karelian tradition dying away from your bed, well your own anyway,' smirked the mister. 'I recall once…'

'I really don't want to know. Now have you my instructions? Nothing is to go wrong, do you understand?'

'Yes sir.'

'Good. If I'm needed I'll be at the mill with the rest of my parishioners. The police sergeant will be there to guide us.'

'So he will.'

'You will do well to take heed.' The pastor was irritated, his patience with the waggoner and the world in general wearing thin. 'And look to the care of your soul at times like these.'

'Don't you worry sir, my soul is always tucked safe in my pocket.'

'Glad to hear it.'

'Well goodbye Pastor I spy the horses coming, take care now.'

The mill was empty of all timber. Hessian sacks flapped in the wind outside and a white dust settled on plank and shingle. The great saw bands were cold and still. All had assembled in this place, the largest building available now the church had been commandeered for a lookout post.

The police sergeant stood on a crate and checked the villagers off on a list as they entered. He looked nervous, set his teeth to the crowd. His voice was unconvincing.

'This is the situation as far as I have been informed. The government expect the Isthmus to be attacked in strength. We know that, it has been a feature of our history so many times before. The Mannerheim Line is now occupied, defences are in place. This much you have suspected. The region of the line has been evacuated of all civilians.'

There was a murmur of disquiet. More dust settled on hair and clothing. The sergeant continued in a weary voice, trying to keep the tone official.

'What about we?' piped up old Hannu. 'Do we have orders to move?'

'No…not at the moment, but there are precautions. The government has stated that this district should be prepared to evacuate at short notice if necessary. Be ready with essential items, blankets, food, tools, but the essentials mind, no luxuries.'

'What might they be?' uttered a voice from the back. There was strained laughter. The sergeant took no notice and continued.

'Be ready, make sure the horses and sleds are prepared, you are to go west towards Mikkeli. Keep together but only move if the order comes. The roads are dangerous, they are constantly attacked. We need to keep them clear for reinforcements and supplies for the front. Those of you who have no transport, well now might be a good time to leave though it will be a long and uncomfortable journey. Obviously the railways are targets. If you have relatives in the west, go to them, if not there are other arrangements which may be made. Officials at the station can issue passes. Make sure you have your papers, you will be asked for them. There is intelligence concerning spies and fifth columnists. We have to be on our guard.'

A wave of unease saturated the villagers. The police sergeant attempted a smile.

'It may not come to this, this is a precaution. I have every faith in our boys at the front and this winter will make life difficult for the Russians. I'm sure if the worst comes to the worst we will have warning.'

'In the meantime what do we do?' asked old Hannu again. He did not seem the slightest perturbed.

'Carry on, do what you can to help others who will pass this way. Viipurri is almost empty now, our people are on the move, give what aid you can. Hide and camouflage the buildings that stand out, don't advertise your presence. Stay away from the main roads. Those amongst you who have strength dig trenches, construct dugouts at key points, they may need to be occupied quickly. I can advise as to the best locations.'

'Is it true that the land in the east has already been scorched?'

'I have heard,' he stumbled 'that is the case, anything which may offer comfort or protection should be obliterated...and here too, if it so comes, be prepared for that, store gasoline and matches.'

'So be it,' said old Hannu and you could sense the tears inside the others as he said it, the withering, the skin shivers.

'There is one more thing,' he said. You could tell he felt uneasy, more than uncomfortable.

'Spit it out man!' shouted the mill owner.

'We are having reports of deserters in the forest, not many, a few young lads but I have orders to inform you that anyone helping them will be in serious trouble. There are orders on the police station wall stating clearly that any soldier found deserting his post could be shot. The orders are signed by Mannerheim himself. Offer no aid or succour to these men should you be aware of them. Inform the authorities if there are suspicions, it is in everyone's interests to do so. The farmers and foresters among you, keep your eyes open, report anything unusual, however small or insignificant.'

Gradually the idea of soldiers in the wilderness combed both men and women. Light filtered through the boarding and the sergeant departed. The villagers drifted away, preoccupied, evaporating. Hannu's mother was amongst them, she walked back to the cabin where Merja sat gazing out of the window, a doll on her lap.

'Are you alright my child?'

'Yes,' she answered, puzzled. 'Where was everyone?'

'Nothing to worry you...'

'Do we have to leave?'

'No...not yet. Maybe not at all, we just have to be prepared.' She busied herself immediately. There was no rush but somehow it was a comfort to arrange things. First she hung the outdoor hats and coats and gloves on hooks by the door. She placed identity cards, legal documents, marriage certificates in a leather bag, anything the family might need. The old tin trunk was dragged to the door too and loaded with blankets, spare clothes, family photographs, a cooking pot, cutlery, pieces of soap...it was so difficult. And in the canvas laundry bag she placed coffee, flour, bacon, dried fruit. Whatever they had. Merja helped without understanding but watched with curious eyes.

'I shall take my doll.'

'Of course you shall my dear.'

'There...I feel better. We have the trunk and the laundry bag, we can get by.'

She went outside and wheeled the hand cart to the front of the cabin, oiling the axle and looping rope around the frame, all ready, all prepared. Her brain grappled with unfamiliar chemistry. When she was moving, when she was doing things, it was fine, but on resting, on thinking, the tears came and her face she hid from the child's sight. Others too were busy, checking on horses, repairing wagons, collecting, looking to the forest. The cattle were in their stalls...but if need be they could be driven out.

She looked at Hannu's workshop, marched across and unlocked the door. Tools were displayed immaculately, razor sharp, stowed and stored with precision. It was so quiet and she thought for a long time before taking a small axe, it might be of use. Finally, with a heart remote she put the padlock back on the door before adding the axe, a sewing kit and the sewing machine to the pile.

'If we have to leave Merja we will be ready, less than an hour to load this and away...if you help.'

'I will. But where will we go?'

'God will be our guide.'

It was obvious Merja was uncertain about something, unsettled.

'What if Hannu returns and we are gone?'

'Hannu will find us, never fear.'

*

Well my friends, all this I discovered once the war was over and we were at peace of a kind. These discoveries and more were passed up to me as ingredients in a meal, one at a time with a good deal of cooking in-between! Of course I had thoughts about home but drew comfort from the fact that they were some distance from the front line and that the villagers would stay together. They would move as one, more a transference than an evacuation.

As for the actions of my half-brother, the newly wed, that sly beast, well rumour reached even the trenches of his doings, though it was difficult to believe. As I understood his tale unravelled as string. There was a knock on the cabin door, late at night and mother was startled. Her blood ran cold for such disturbance was uncommon. On rousing herself she realised it could not be the order to leave for there would be tumult outside and there was none, just the cloistered silence of the forest, a forest deadened of noise by snow, thick and unleavened. With some trepidation she put her ear to the door and called out.

'Who's there?'

'Tuija, your daughter-in-law,' came the response.

When the door was opened she fell through.

'Whatever is it at this time?'

'Paavo...Paavo has gone.'

'Gone where...to his unit you mean?'

'No, disappeared...taken his clothes and left.'

She slumped in a chair, cheeks streaked and hair stranded, wild. After fumbling in her coat she withdrew an empty cash box and a letter scrawled in pencil.

'I found this, the money has gone of course but this...' She held the letter to the light.

When you read this I will be gone, no one will be surprised.
I am aware of local opinion. I do this for us dear. This war is
senseless. We cannot hope to win. No one will come to our aid.
We are a speck, of no interest to other powers. They have more
pressing issues. There is no time to explain but I hope to join
Kusninen's men. Soon all this madness will be over and we, you
and I my dear will come up smelling of roses. Do not worry I
will send for you as soon as possible.

> *Your Loving Husband,*
> *Paavo*

My sister-in-law was a ghost, so I discovered, she could
hardly speak between tears of bewilderment but my mother was
of sterner material and cursed in the old dialect. She took her
into the home and made a bed for her and promised that no one
would hear of this. Men were leaving every day, no one would
detect his running, not from her lips and so the family was three.
Though of course such things cannot be kept secret and word
spread like wild fire. It soon became common knowledge that he
had gone over to Stalin. The women were on their own now,
come what may, there would be no help. But Paavo, though we
shared a father (wherever he was) was no friend of mine, his
poor wife...so short a time of marriage deserved some
sympathy... a n'er do well, a shifter, coaxing words from a belly
full of vodka. I was not finished with him, not I, though I did not
know it our paths would cross again. Kuusninen was welcome to
him and the rest of his 'government' in Terijoki, our lads did not
leave that place without a fight. But once I heard, once the war
had ended and we were picking up the pieces my anger re-
surfaced. I had sharpened my teeth for our next meeting. The
shame of it, the duplicity; deserting his homestead as in a
business transaction, weighing the odds, spreading risk. So you
see reader my story has many threads, some prowling with
deceit and accusations, dripping cloudward from where they one
day fell.

If I can steer your mind away from that place of waiting to
another of divine patience, from home to frozen swampland, to

we. For those parallel tales weave themselves together with time. We lived through anxious ignorance in those days.

*

Sparks soon flew from rocks. Bayonets we sharpened, brandishing our weaponry to the rising sun, the last sun for many, we metal smiths and carpenters closed ranks and locked shields in a wall around Taipale.

Chapter 5

When the storm broke it was with the stride of a giant, pebbles kicked from his boots flicked the lid of our trenches. The defenders, that is, we, found our brains being picked in a number of ways. Let me draw you the picture while it is still clear.

While this district was largely low lying, devoid of trees we were fortressed on slightly higher ground with views of the promontory before us. Much land had been given up as indefensible, because of the need to concentrate on strong points. The open tongue before us had no defenders but we knew that such artillery as we had and the coastal batteries ranged their guns upon it. With this information we were confident of the test.

It began in an unexpected way with our own troops racing towards us, sliding into the trench and then continuing into support and communication trenches. We heard them first, reconnaissance patrols emerging from no man's land. Such raging, such panic in their eyes caused us all to stare in horror. They did not pause or report but shrieked words we could not catch, shouts that turned the blood cold. I glanced along the line and saw my comrades were equally affected, nonplussed, we had not anticipated this development.

One young fellow, white as a sheet, jumped beyond me, weapons, long since gone, his voice dry, clogged, screaming, 'Tanks! Tanks!' and we heard the mocking of their tracks in the distance. Harri watched him burrowing into the parapet.

Then it was the corporal put a bullet through the young man's head, an expression of blunt shock on his face as he fell.

'I'll kill any man who moves,' he yelled pointing the pistol towards Simo who merely spat into the ground. When more came running through us he fired again and again spitting raw rage, but he missed his marks so we focused our attention on the armour as it approached.

The lieutenant poked a periscope towards them and tried his best to calm nerves.

'Don't worry men,' he said, clearly unnerved himself. 'They will soon be in the killing zone, our artillery have them in their sights...load your weapons. Signaller, tell the mortar platoon to fire on my command.'

Metre by metre, like sulking agricultural tractors they trundled across open land, twenty, no thirty long-barrelled thugs. Infantry pin pricked behind in their exhaust fumes. We had not seen their like before and it sorely tested our nerves. Some I could tell were ready to run as they edged nearer, others aimed rifle sights at the following infantry. When the mortars shot upwards it was with an ineffective pop pop pop. This would not do!

'What are they waiting for?' I heard the lieutenant mutter under his breath and saw our favourite corporal re-load his pistol and fire that too. When this act left his anger unappeased he picked up the body of the soldier, now stiff with cold and threw it into the communication trench, shrieking and growling like a beserker. If this was to be our final test it was ridiculous.

'Look to your front...look to your front or you'll get the same, first man to twitch...'

We could hear the signallers desperately calling for artillery support but here was no response.

'Tell them to fire will you!' yelled the lieutenant to the poor radio operator sinking ever deeper into his shirt. Through these dramas the iron clads advanced, ferrosed and welded, ever closer. Cannon blazed from them but the shots arched way above our heads, only the pressure of their passing rattled our helmets.

'You can tell them to fire Hannu, you have the way!' shouted Harri. 'Just give the order.'

There was fear in his voice so I screamed out loud. 'Fire...fire.'

At that moment, at the predetermined location poured mountains of explosives and shrapnel. A new genesis wrinkled the promontory. Men writhed like adders and the tanks became pyramids upended in the sap of flame. And the following infantry were as salt crumbling where they stood. Rifles they dropped and hands covered brows fending off sparks, skin scalped away and limbs imploding into the earth or ferris wheeling across the mush. For us it was a disturbing sight, the power of Joshua surveying the battlefield. Blood and fluid flowed from their bodies and the stench of burn stabbed my nostrils. Still more shells landed, socketing peat and soil. Pustules bursting from the surface made more impacts throwing up titanic debris. Planning for this barrage had been long and execution quick.

When the bombardment lifted and the smoke cleared we charged, uttering our battle cries and firing as if in some mediaeval war until they fled, hundreds running towards their own lines. All that remained was incineration. One dead Russian among many with his head half-buried and arms deep in the ground as if burrowing from danger as a cave man would. When we could run no more a whistle blew and the lieutenant called us back. I shouldered my rifle and tiptoed. The adrenalin and elation still pumped through me, the scene was cinematic and external.

Harri ran up and slapped my shoulder.

'You called it down Hannu. You called for the fire, murder it was, beautiful murder.' The whites of his eyes poked out and I had never seen him so excited. 'You called it down,' he repeated, no one else could.

I did not reply but I knew that night I would dream, dark dreams as I did at home. Once we had returned and answered roll I glanced across at the young patrol soldier with a volcanic hole in his skull. I saw Simo looking at the corporal's back and knew he was not happy, that he felt the act had been unnecessary. When the corporal turned in our direction I sensed the hatred between Simo and he. I knew there would be trouble between them.

'What are you looking at old man?' said the corporal. 'Never seen a body before?'

At first Simo did not reply. He was ruminating, as was his way.

'That was someone's son, no more than a school boy.'

'Not any more,' snapped the corporal. 'You have a problem?'

Simo said nothing.

As that day progressed we were busy in shoring up defences, cleaning and repairing weapons. Some men were detailed to recover weapons and ammunition from the dead, it was a gruesome task, many were mangled and mutilated and in the cold of that winter stiff as steel within minutes of hitting the ground. Such scraps of information as could be gleaned from the bodies: letters and regimental insignia had to be carved away with bayonets. It was cold store butchery of a particularly unpleasant kind, the scraping of the knives across frozen flesh a source of horror to this day even. There was little anyway. It was soon clear that many of the soldiers did not know where they were. Small numbers of wounded prisoners were sent back to the clearing stations, and a pitiable sight they were. Many had frozen to death before we could get to them for they wore summer clothing with no gloves and boots no thicker than paper. It was a wonder they got this far. Vast numbers of rifles and machine guns were collected, pistols, ammunition, grenades, binoculars, aluminium canteens. All useful for we were short of everything. As the war progressed we became more and more reliant on captured equipment. This was just the beginning. It was a puzzle, so much unpreparedness. Where was the thinking behind it all? As we surveyed the field we marvelled at the accuracy and timing of our own guns, at the flight at our charge. In the afternoon as the first needles of darkness began to fall we returned to the trenches. The Russians were probing our defences and we could hear the sudden pattering of small arms fire as they clashed with our own patrols. The young soldier's body had been removed. We settled down to sleep as we could between sentry duties.

My rest, my slumbers arrived with a hand bell, semi-crouched as an animal at bay from wolves. I fell into the tunnel of sleep, that rest where minds are skewered with spears and thoughts are disconnections. For awhile I fought against it but exhaustion both physical and mental caught me out and I could not resist. Sinking slowly into my dreams until I hit the hard, rocky ground, a slope of granite rolled upwards with crevices and moss and lichen growing. It was autumn for the leaves were just beginning to turn. I felt compelled to climb this slope but my footfalls were uncertain and I slipped many times, the gradient sharpened, sweat dripping from my brow. On the top of the hill was a mighty fir tree broad of girth and black-green, a sentinel and from its shade I viewed a landscape unknown to me. A lemon-gold sky with a stream running into a lake surrounded by silver birch. There was an encampment on the shore and a boat pulled up. As I gazed my senses were assaulted by foul odours, sulphur, phosphorus, and carbon and behind me was a creature more hideous than imaginations could grasp.

'What do you want?' lisped the creature, her tongue flicking to a nose curved and boned. 'What do you require of me?'

For a moment I was dumbfounded. I could not unscramble my reasoning and the location meant nothing. All was muddle. The look of this furry beast with claws and talons and horns and ears like drinking cups and wings of feather caused me great fear. Instant flight was my instinct but the smell of her caused my eyes to water and stomach to retch. I was in no fit state for my tunic was drenched with sweat and boots ill-fitting.

'You require?' rasped the beast, tapping a willow switch on a rock.

Looking beyond her, in the distance there were undulating fells, no sign of habitation other than the encampment. In my mind it occurred to me that this might be Lapland. Yellow spells writhed within the roots of trees. I noticed a cuckoo twitching his head from side to side obviously listening to every word. Juniper berries vibrated. The magic of this place was beyond my understanding.

'Speak!' screamed the hag and all the earth shook with violence. 'Thou hast summoned me, now state your requirements or shall we contest with riddles?'

'No...no,' I responded, finding my voice. I could not hope to defeat such a creature with riddles. So many wayfarers lost their lives by being tricked in this way.

'The land is hungry,' I said glancing at the lake. 'I desire that you bring me luck in my fishing.'

'And my payment will be?'

'I will pay you with a song,' I said. So I sang in the clearest tone with a voice majestic of loves lost and gained and gold and silver and the spinning of fine cloth into tales. The hag's blood red eyes closed and she slipped into mute revelry, soothed by my voice. I sang until twilight, when sure of my ground I crept away.

Down the berry strewn path where the vapour from the lake lulled me and bracken caught my ankles, looking back constantly, looking over my shoulder with a sense of the unclean. The hag's odour seeped into my very skin so on reaching the water's edge I dived in. The cold took my breath away like a thousand knives stabbing. Arctic waters splashed my hair until it dripped icicles and my uncontrolled shivering caused palpitations of the heart. Pincers of many crabs attached themselves to every part of my body. I was guillotined but such was my drive to wash away the encounter it did not cause me anxiety, serving only to sing out counter spells and incantations. At last, feeling shredded by razor blades, I left the water and dried myself by the flames of a campfire. My teeth chattered and the cuckoo still watched and the twilight fell like a net upon the lake and with it my hunger returned. I pushed out the boat and jumped aboard rowing with fresh strength. The lines were cast east and west and soon fish of every size and colour I pulled into the bows. And when the line was pulled and stowed more leapt aboard, salmon and trout with fixed grins until the boat was over burdened and began to sink. I bailed furiously with my hands but no sooner had I tossed the catch overboard than more jumped in. There was no end to it. What magic was this? Then it was, in the shadow of the sinking sun, where the surface of the water was gold a great malevolent pike steered towards me. He laughed and bared his teeth sucking air through gills, waiting.

'Desist,' it said, 'there is no hope for men on this lake, it is my kingdom and your coming is an intrusion. No man returns to the shore, the encampment once made is ever deserted.'

'I will not surrender,' I yelled, red in the face, heavy of brow but I tired for the fish grew heavier and more difficult to throw. Silvery scales covered my fingers, water lapped higher up my legs and the great malevolent pike swished its mighty tail broader than a tree and snapped its jaws mockingly. Then it was the boat capsized and I was thrown into the water coughing and spluttering and struggling with all my strength. Then it was the great malevolent pike surged towards me opening its huge cavern like mouth. I saw my own face reflected in an eye; saw the coiling tube of its body as my head and shoulders and trunk it swallowed.

I woke with a start, unsure of myself, disorientated and gasping for air. At first I thought I was in the body of the pike and tried to pull myself out of sleep but my lungs were crushed and my eyelids forced shut. Panic took hold of my mind and I scrabbled with my fingers but could not move them. It was hot and when once my lips were parted soil spilled into my mouth and worms wriggled there. What was happening? Still I could neither breathe nor move, glimpses of the village flashed through my thoughts and I heard Maarit calling to me. My lungs were balloons ready to burst and my ribs felt like cracking such was the pressure pushing against them. Then, a glimmer of light, mere photons greyed by the earth. Something clawed at my arms and I was out, sucking in air and choking and swallowing soil and vomiting and spitting and clasping at the boots of a man who shook my shoulders and brushed debris from my eyes and hair.

What hell was this? An almighty storm of thunder and lightning split my ear drums and like a child I curled still short of breath on the ground and moaned and tried to shut out the clamp and crump of explosions. In amongst the collisions of sound I could make out screams that soaked my thoughts like acid corroding the senses. The palm of my hand closed and it felt as if I was crushing the tender bellies of slugs which were for some reason slithering across skin exposed by my writhing. In the sky were vapour trails, smoke of every shade of darkness, flames of blue and red and yellow and magenta and the slush of what once was snow rolled in waves down the trench. Wonderful pyrotechnics that in origin could only have been celestial blazed across the sky, traces and puffs of white. I fancied I heard a horseman riding by and once my eyes were cleared and focused, chaos I saw, and all was unrecognisable. I had no idea what abyss this was and the battering on my skull drummed holes into the brain which pinned me to the floor unable to hide or run.

When it seemed the earth could withstand no more from this assault it stopped...as a bird ceases its singing so the barrage lifted and the trenches were becalmed. I staggered to my feet, helped by Harri, who pulled my arms, and even in my state of dizziness I could see the grey upon his face and blood trickling from his ears.

'To the fire steps,' the lieutenant ordered, calm now. He fancied himself to be a veteran after all this. I rose and slumped across the remains of the trench which in many places had slipped and shifted. Sandbags seeped sand and I pointed a rifle which was not my own towards the empty space of no man's land. My eyes strained, particles of soil still encrusted them and it was difficult to discern anything through smoke. Nothing moved but vapour, which might have been of spectre or ghost for all I could tell.

Everyone was there, the infantry and clerks and cooks and signallers. The dugouts were empty. The communication lines deserted. We all peered out into the murk from defences that were largely destroyed. I noticed there were gaps, my friends

...but in the chaos of bombardment they could have been anywhere. Still we looked. My finger played with the trigger nervously. I aimed the barrel iron sighted but still there was no movement. What were they waiting for? Even we of this small army knew that a bombardment of such ferocity was a precursor for attack. Any moment now the hordes of Russia would come screaming and snarling towards us, but as time ticked, with every second passing, their advantage lessened. We were ready. Runners had already departed to call for reinforcements. In small ways the trench was being repaired.

'Keep your eyes open,' the lieutenant whispered, clips of ammunition stacked by his hand.

It was tense. In the distance someone loosed off a round, but there was no response. We could see more clearly now and it began to dawn on us that maybe the attack wasn't coming. It was a puzzle. A real puzzle. What was the sense in it?

One by one the non-combatants shouldered their guns and slipped away to get on with their jobs. The lieutenant frowned but maintained a vigil. You could tell he thought it was all a trick to lure us into a sense of security before the strike. Maybe they were creeping like beetles across the ground, cunningly camouflaged. But the ground before us was devoid of cover. It had been chosen for that reason. Nothing moved but the wind.

Gradually the tension eased as it became obvious that no attack was coming. Harri sauntered up to me with a mug of black coffee.

'Here, get this down, it will help clear your throat.'

'What happened?' I asked.

'You were asleep...as usual, when out of nowhere the bombardment started. It wasn't very accurate at first but bit by bit they found our range. There's been a hellish amount of damage, some places in the line are worse than this, not that you think they could be. One of the first shells landed metres away from this section and the wall caved in. You were buried my friend. Simo and I dug you out with our hands. We thought you were done for until we carved you out of the soil spluttering and coughing. Some one is looking out for you, Hannu, that's clear.'

'I was in the middle of a dream, I didn't know what had happened.'

'You were lucky that's all I can say.'

The blood around Harri's ears had dried now, a river of baked brown down his neck.

There were scorch marks on the timber frames of the dug out. Pieces of kit smouldered, the smell of cordite and smoke hung in the air. Soon after the lieutenant came round, encouraging, slapping us on the shoulder, saying how well we had done. He ordered one in three to be on guard duty. You could tell he didn't know what to expect any more. Rocks and huge splinters of granite perforated the trench walls where shells had displaced them. Fire and heat melted another layer of soil which quickly turned to mud. Once darkness fell it would freeze again into ruts and tram lines. The lieutenant barked his orders with confidence now.

'Corporal Murto,' he called. The corporal was seething as usual. 'Detail three men for a search party. There are still three missing. I want them found if possible.'

He did not reply, but pointed at Harri.

'You'll do,' he said matter of factly. 'Take two others, work your way south to north, if you find anything make a note of it, bring it back if you can...and keep your weapons close at hand. There's no knowing what Ivan will do next.'

I went with Harri and so did Simo, just to escape the glaring eyes of Corporal Murto. He was a good man, Simo, nothing perturbed him. He was like a piece of granite himself.

Harri shouted, 'Do you know who's missing?'

'Ask the lieutenant,' was all the response he got. We didn't ask, just tidied ourselves up, shouldered our rifles and walked hunchbacked through the maze of channels in a roughly northward direction, towards the lake. All the daylight hours we toiled (of course there were not many at this time of year). When darkness fell we switched on our torches to poke into every hole and crater. There was so much debris scattered, helmets, discarded clothing, a shaving kit, it was difficult to make anything out. In one of the dugouts there was a youngster, the beams of our flashlights must have disturbed him, nerves frayed and babbling, incoherent, he could not answer our questions but curled back up and rocked. No one noticed him and for a second I thought he might have been one of the missing before realising he could not be for others were with him in the dark.

'This is useless,' Harri said. 'In this lot half the garrison could be hiding and we still wouldn't find them '

'Poor souls be buried more likely than not,' added Simo. 'Like Hannu here.'

'True...let's get back and try again at day break. It's too cold to be wandering about like this, dangerous too, some of these lads are jumpy. I don't fancy a Finnish bullet much.'

'Me neither,' I said feeling ready for sleep myself. I felt unclean, the taste of soil still lingered in my mouth. So we made our way back through the mildewed corridors of Taipale anxious for a hot drink and rest. We had found no one. It was close to our section that we saw the body. Slumped in a corner and covered by some old duck boards. My torch caught the mangling of his torso, arms and legs twisted like spaghetti and a face sliced clean off by shrapnel. The light focused in so closely I almost retched.

'What's the matter? Never seen dead meat before?' spat the corporal who must have been waiting for us. 'He's one of the lads you were supposed to be looking for.'

The light fastening to his remains seemed almost solid and my eyes, try as I might, would not be deflected from it.

'It's Pekka,' said Harri. 'I recognise his hunting knife, it can't be anyone else.'

'That's right...friend of yours, get it moved before the others see it, things like this are bad for morale. If you'd done your job better it would have been removed by now.' At that the corporal turned on his heels and marched away. I swear I saw a thin smile playing on his lips.

'Pekka,' repeated Harri.

'Why did he let us go blundering about all day if he knew he was here already?'

89

Simo said nothing, shuffled his feet and watched Corporal Murto's back as it disappeared into the gloom. I saw his lips move but no words came out.

'What are we going to do?'

'We have to take him into no man's land. We'll find a shell hole, that's the best we can do,' muttered Simo with all the wisdom of his years.

So, in that sad gloom, in that time that was not real we fetched hessian sacks and shovelled the remains of Pekka, friend and soldier into them. Sometimes we used our hands; his flesh was hard to the touch, frozen like alabaster. We dragged the sacks out in front of the lines, for some distance. Our thoughts were to find a place that would not be disturbed. Eventually we found a crater several metres deep and carefully placed the sacks into the pit of it. Simo stood and said a few words. We did not stand to attention or salute or any of that nonsense. It was not our way. Instead we piled whatever branches or moss we could find. We marked the spot with Pekka's hunting knife. He was proud of that knife, the handle was delicately carved and he was constantly sharpening it. Flares occasionally lit up the night sky, a distant rattle of small arms fire indicated a clash or a nervous sentry. In the morning, if we could, we would return and try to heap more branches and soil onto the grave, make it more respectable. It felt like we were casting Pekka away but looking back I knew we had done all we could.

On our return Simo uttered all manner of threats against the corporal. He'd better watch his back he said. We told him to keep his voice down but still he raged and raged. The next day, when the winter sun was at its highest and some at least of the earth had thawed, we crept out and finished the job. I was pleased we could at least do that. And Pekka lies there still, at peace I hope, clear of pain and distress. No one know his whereabouts, his grave was never marked and now of course it lies in another country and it is tended only in our hearts and memory.

*

There was a lull in the fighting at Taipale for two weeks. We had chance to repair our defences and replenish supplies, tidy ourselves up. We were aware that war could resume at any moment but we were largely preoccupied with keeping warm and eating and cleaning. Patrols sometimes ran into each other but withdrew without firing under some kind of gentlemen's agreement. It suited all of us. The shortest day came and went. Our thoughts turned to Christmas.

Mail arrived, a letter from Maarit full of the agonies of Helsinki and hints that she was moving on, though where I could not tell. No news from home; it did not cause me anxiety, no one there was a great writer and nor was I. In the lull we all had time to think and the sky larking lessened. I had no children to worry about like some of the older men, but my little sister's welfare did cause some concern, she would not like these changes, she would sense the tension and maybe, maybe, fall into herself even more. Still there was nothing I could do.

On Christmas Eve we were becalmed in melancholy and, brave as we tried to be, our spirits spawned unnatural quiet as if the curtains had been drawn down. Just a year ago I brought the bundle of straw into the family home and made the star of Bethlehem on the floor with Merja; we tied it up and pinned it to the wall. Cones of straw we made too to ask for a blessing for the harvest, perhaps the last harvest after all these thousands of years. We put a stick through the middle and rammed it into the wall. The rest of the straw we scattered on the floor and only swept away at Epiphany. Such delight Merja took in it all, so easily satisfied with a pair of mittens and some dried fruit. How was she now? Who was there to carry the straw, if there was any? We had pig's head soup and barley bread and in the morning barley cakes and meats roasted in fat. It could set you howling the anticipation. Then church once the light had come and raisins from the hand in the evening or a tune on the fiddle or accordion with hearth neighbours. It was a joyful time; we knew the days were lengthening bit by bit and the bruises of the old year would pass. I remember it now in my brooding as I watch Simo sucking on his pipe.

When Christmas Day came I was assigned the morning watch. Peering from a machine gun emplacement across the promontory idling time until relieved. There was a dense fog, nothing to see, just the mist swirling into castles and trees and horses, a mesmerising scene made more surreal by the heavy frost and ground vapours.

So silent.

Not a word was spoken, not a heart was broken as my mother would say. Even the air was creased. I did not know, I could not know, such was my lowly status of the movement of the Russians not far from this place.

Under cover of the fog and with a purpose the Soviet 49th Division crossed the frozen Suvanto waterway. More soldiers crossed further down, establishing beach heads. Reinforcements flowed and we saw nothing, suspected nothing. Still they came, many thousands. Then it was I fancied angels gliding through transparencies that were never still, swords in hand and wings a shimmer, smiling I thought upon us on this holy day. But where they flew a veil was lifted and the fog burned away and to my shock and horror Russians, many, many of them setting up their own mortars and machine guns almost within touching distance. When I sounded the alarm their faces betrayed the same shock for the fog had hidden our own presence and regiments of the enemy stood helpless in the glare of our guns. Pandemonium, we fired with everything we had, maxims, lahtis, rifles, pistols. Some ran towards us but were felled, others ran backwards or into each other. Hundreds ran into wire hidden in snow banks to guard the perimeter, writhing and dying suspended in the barbs, arms in the air and eyes blank. I could feel the heat from the maxim next to me, heard the frantic call for more ammunition. The ice bounced, tremors clawed my boots and the oscillation of bullets ripped everything in its path. When the artillery opened up the whole front was rendered with quake and noise. Sections of the ice split sending dead and wounded into the water. Yet still they came, crawling, and clambering over the corpses of their comrades to get to us...but none did, we cut them down as a scythe. So when the order came to cease firing and the last

Finnish shell landed, there were thousands of corpses strewn across the promontory. Some groaned pathetically but most lay still, already covered by flakes of snow from a new fall. It was all too much for me. I did not climb out of the trench as others did but watched, still shaking with the waves of projectiles passing our front. Only Corporal Murto paced the lines of fallen, flicking the bodies with his toe or searching the still warm pockets. From time to time he drew his pistol and put a bullet into the head of one of the unfortunates. It was a bleak portrait he gave before he too slumped to the ground. The bullet that ripped into his head was plain to see and hear. It was plain too that it had come from our own lines. I instinctively turned to look for Simo but he was nowhere to be found.

Chapter 6

Now reader remember please that this story is told in retrospect, with the addition of hindsight. How events would develop at the time I knew not, and with the passing of time sequences and conversations are placed on hooks. But when I talk of Maarit, as shortly I will, you will understand the nature of my bias. She was young in heart and in experience, younger than many in High Schools today. She was sensible and mature, but shared the bewilderment of us all. There was a touch of fire in her but no calculation, a confidence from being descended from the elders of the village, though now as poor as the rest of us. In most respects strong and considerate, of compassion full, of humour serious, courageous too, brimful with sense, which made her attachment to myself even more surprising. I was not easy to belong to!

If then we leave the horrors of Taipale briefly and following Maarit's tale we see her striding forcefully with winter coat and rucksack, snow drifting into her pale face towards the steps of the University. She ventured no further than the corner from where the site was clearly visible. There was a lorry waiting and equipment being loaded into the back. Maarit watched; she saw Liisa scanning the street with her eyes. A few muffled shouts and queries carried on the breeze but real words could not be deciphered. It was clear, once the lorry was about to depart, that Liisa, on the top step, was looking for her, pacing, checking, re-checking her watch. When it was clear that Maarit would not be coming she jumped into the back and was gone, out of the city, to the north, the far north.

Maarit did not go because she felt uneasy. A hunch, an instinct, warned her against throwing in her lot with this group. The organisation and purpose was too haphazard for her, so she held back.

There had been a final, fitful night's sleep and a tearful departure from Mrs Rajala. She too had reservations about the enterprise, a natural wariness caused her to ask many questions.

'This Liisa person, well, how well did you know her? She sounded impulsive, loose if you like.' Maarit knew she was talking sense so when morning came she left most of her belongings with her landlady, promising to return at some indeterminate time and decided to be sure of Liisa's (and her companions') departure from Helsinki before making her way to the Red Cross building where the Lotta Svard were registering in some numbers. Now Maarit was not in all honesty a member of the Lotta Svard organisation, though like everyone she agreed with their aims, patriotism, home and fatherland. She realised that in the current confusion such administrative details as previous membership could or would not be ascertained. Her objective was to present herself as an honest and trustworthy young woman, skilled in the art of nursing, morally sound and willing to serve in whatever capacity thought appropriate. There was an endless queue, frozen to the core, chattering and silent in turns.

When finally she reached the front, an elderly woman, all grey-starch, looked her over before opening her lips.

'What is your name?' she croaked, pen in hand.

'Maarit Harmala. I come from a village to the east of Lappeenranta, near the Saima canal. I am 18 years old, willing and able to serve my country.' It was a fine speech, thought Maarit, but the starch did not stir, no muscle moved.

'And you were a member of the Lotta Svard in your home village?'

'Yes Madam.'

'Then why are you in Helsinki now?'

'I moved earlier in the year, for work as a secretary. My district is poor and family of little means. My wages I sent back to my mother.'

'And you are pure of heart and body?'

Maarit cast a glance of steel at the woman and pursed her lips.

'Most certainly Madam, I can obtain testimonials from the pastor and others if required. I want simply to serve my fatherland.'

'As do we all,' she responded hard as nails.

'You can cook?'

'Yes Madam.'

'And tend wounds?'

'Yes Madam.'

'Are you prepared for hardship, for hunger and pain and heartbreak?'

'I can bare it. Karelia is rich in pain and heartbreak.'

She stopped writing and looked again at Maarit.

'Wait here.'

She walked away, shoes echoing on the wooden floor like a limpet-headed angel. Out of the corner of her eye Maarit could see her deep in discussion with a superior. From this distance her pock-marked face was more obviously cratered and transparent by turns. The tininess of her frame too and the hushness of her tone gave a melancholy feel to the proceedings.

Maarit waited nervously while the clock ticked. Surely they needed everyone, she thought.

When she returned the interview continued in the same terse fashion.

'We have no records of your village unit.'

Maarit began to protest.

'Let me continue,' interrupted the woman. 'We are unable to clarify your details. But we are operating under war time conditions, and whatever you may think we will make allowances for that fact. We are not stupid. When you joined who were your sponsors?'

Maarit was not a good liar, concealment did not come easily, but she embellished the truth with fingers crossed, mindful that these were mitigating circumstances.

'The pastor and the station master, both honourable men of impeccable character, both would vouch for me if they were in a position to do so.'

'I'm sure.' There was the faintest flicker of a smile creasing the water. 'And your political views?'

'I have no real understanding or interest in politics. I am a village girl, such things are not expected of us.'

'And your family?'

'My brothers are in arms defending the fatherland.' She lied again.

'But their views are sound? There is no family association with communists or socialists?'

'My family are upright citizens Madam.'

'Very well.' She drew papers from a box beneath the desk, produced another pen and passed it to Maarit.

'You have been accepted, fill in this form now, address, next of kin and so on. You are to join the nursing section as you appear to have some experience in that field. Do you have your luggage with you?'

'Yes. I have everything I need.'

'Once you have signed the papers follow the corridor to the right. You will be sworn in by an officer. From there you will be taken to an assembly point with others. You will receive some further training, a few days, make sure you attend well, it will be all the preparation you will get. From there you will be most likely taken to the front. Where I know not. Do you have any questions?'

'No Madam, thank you.'

For the first time the woman's weariness betrayed her and grey from within and without permeated the smile she attempted to form.

'God bless you child. Remember your moral responsibilities and duties at all times. Show compassion, show gentleness and strength. Do not give in to temptation, no matter how difficult.

At the assembly point you will be issued a new uniform, from then on Maarit you are a representative of the Lotta Svard.'

'I will remember.'

'On your way then,' said the woman before putting on her body armour once again and shouting. 'Next!'

Maarit followed the corridor to the right.

*

At that moment of time, as the dew drop drizzled down the stem and the background red suckled those beads with the colour of blood, at the time when the merest raising of the temperature caused the convoy of students from Helsinki to slide across the ice bound road, the now familiar aluminium hawks flew out of a low sun and shot their bullets into the snow. Some ripped, some spat, some hissed into radiators or canvas roofs offering no shelter. One vehicle soon burst into flames and men and women poured out like reptiles escaping. Some stumbled, some fell, one was ripped apart, one unpeeled, one frayed at the edges and groaning lay slumped and curled. Not one of that spawn escaped the net, not one lived, not one would-be engineer or doctor saw the sun set. They were defenceless, sitting ducks, target practice. They froze where they lay injured on a lonely lane so many miles distant from a destination that was only ever adventure. Too late they realised this war was no game, no jest, but the rim of savagery.

Where Liisa lay with eyes open, blinking, surprised, life seeped and she stared at the sky of glass with a curving smile more mock than merry and slipped away.

At that moment, in that time, Maarit shuddered and wrapped a shawl around the grey-shouldered uniform. Instinct channelled her fate as she warmed her hands around the stove of a church hall now doubling as a barracks, thinking of home.

*

Winter in the village quartered by roads, saw those who remained screwed tight to bonds of earth that succoured them. The widow's radio was a source of information and anxiety. It

98

was a querulous period. Neighbours communicated in whispers, performing mental acrobatics, especially at night when only the wind moaned its music through the rafters.

The swinging hill was empty of souls, boys and girls dispersed to their various corners and the apple trees bent under the weight of ice and frost.

Hannu's mother lay with her head on the pillow, eyes open and ears alert to the breathing of little Merja and her daughter-in-law. Vapour rose in clouds in the cold room, cold penetrated even the neurons of the brain, it needled the skin beneath the rugs and blankets of the bed.

She chuckled. Couldn't help herself. What with the pastors visit, so naïve that man, so easily shocked. She recalled his hurt tones as he recounted his visit to the aged widow in the log house by the oat field. So said he as she lay dying.

'How far have you travelled on this earth?'

'Not far Reverend. No further than the parish boundaries my whole life long.'

And, in tones deep. 'Where do you want to go now? Heaven or hell?'

She paused before answering. 'We old folk don't mind where we go as long as it is warm.'

Such a face, such hurt was almost as funny as the aged widow's responses.

It was good to smile, so infrequent these days. As she lay she reflected on the harshness of times and her own life where work had sapped her energy and spirits. She had a fairness of complexion once but now it was tired and her hair greyed day by day and her hands red raw from water and ice, beaten down by manual labour. She was becoming stout and bad tempered, that much she knew. While she fought against it...it was not easy.

Her eyes peered into the darkness of the room and breath sparkled as mineral, warming the air but briefly. The cabin creaked like a ship and she imagined it sawing through the waves, and the sailors trimming the sails in response to the wind. In the mist that was between sleeping and waking she reviewed her life, every nut and bolt, every clamp and lever, good and bad. Like currents the joys and anxieties swirled within the mind, concealing nothing, nor deflecting any savagery. The men in her life, useless for the most part, husband feckless, disappeared drunk somewhere now. His son, the one he called his own, she took him in out of goodness and pity, called him her own but he too gone now, blood will out. She cared not for either of them. But Merja, so young and awkward, so drawn into that world of silence only Hannu could really penetrate. So frightened of everything and barely educated. What was to become of her? She folded her shames and guilts into the blanket and pulled them tight around her body for at this darkest hour the air was bitter, painful.

Somewhere a mouse scuttled and the eagle from its eyrie circled overhead. The cabin now took on the persona of a cave, stone age at this hour where light could not penetrate. Only the natural world intruded and all movement was receptive to the ears. This was the world of the winter primitive, a mediaeval beacon, hiding from the hordes of orthodox from the east as many ancestors had done. The forest dwellers hammering on the roof, altar candles, an underworld of peasants speaking dialects of devilish complexity. She felt the closeness of her forefathers. They were in the room, soothing her mind and resting. She saw the crosses in the forest multiplying day by day. The crossroads and bridges protected by spells. The cabin and the land enfolded her.

Still the clock ticked.

Where was Hannu? Where was my son? How cruel the world that tore him away. She saw him smiling, sawing wood, cursing the neighbours for their laziness, or sulking in the forest after some imagined insult. He was too like Merja, she thought. They shared an understanding. Where are you Hannu? Are you well? Do you eat? Is your uniform clear of dirt and lice? Do you ever think of me and home? Do you know my son that we lay a place at table for you every night though it breaks my heart to see your empty chair. So frayed my nerves. I seem to be plucking responsibilities and cares. But what else can I do? We are fortunate and I reproach myself for my selfishness. We have shelter though cramped, food enough, and distance between the village and the battlefields. But my son I dream of charnel houses and cannot labour without brooding. God be thanked that the boys of the village are still safe. Not one gone so far and praise loud and long I do for that fact. But forgive me Hannu. I feel shrivelled when you are not here. So much did I rely upon your exertions, more than was acceptable.

So my son, where are you now? Are you safe? Do your friends engage you in wild talk and profanities? I have little news to relay. We close in on ourselves in this forgotten corner. The trains pass through from east to west, and on occasion planes attack them, though not here, not yet. I cannot gaze into the carriage windows for fear of what I might see. Maarit is in Helsinki, though her parents grow restless. No letter has arrived for awhile. Your half-brother is gone and his disgrace is another burden. Fortunately our neighbours show only pity and harbour, no animosity.

The wolves howl and the nightjar is departed.

*

The crag of dawn crushed the night down. Heavy it fell, unveiling a day short in daylight. After a rushed breakfast little Merja and Tuija sat on the floor unravelling bundles of wool. Nothing very much was said between them but threads of blue and red and white untangled between semi-numbed fingers. Merja was more than usually subdued and coughed intermittently. Her face looked flushed as if an infection was in the making. More worries, more concerns.

So when the knock came it was part relief, part fear that caused the activity to cease. My mother glanced out of the window and relaxed when she realised it was not a telegram boy, only the timber mill owner who was beginning to take on the role of an elder now so few men were left.

'Greetings,' he said in that deep laconic voice of his while stamping the snow from his boots.

'Hello master…this is a surprise. Please, take a seat, warm yourself. Tuija put some coffee on the stove. You look half frozen.'

'True. Bitter it is outside and all morning trudging through ice and sleet delivering bad news to every hearth.'

'Bad news you say.'

'Unfortunately yes.' He paused and accepted a cup of coffee. 'Many thanks. Well there's no use beating about the bush. We have to leave. We must evacuate the village.'

'Tonight. There is a train west. All must be on board, without exception.'

'But whatever for. There is no fighting, not here, not yet.'

'It must be tonight. Those are my orders from district. Who knows how the war is going ? We are mere mortals, we may not be informed. The Russians may be a day's distance. They may be ten. Our boys may be holding them on the border…there may be a break through. Rumour has it they have thousands of tanks. What chance did we ever have?'

'Are you sure?'

'No. I am sure of nothing. I see no reason for this order. But I don't know. I see troops heading east and the roads from Viipuri thick with refugees. Like you I hear the Soviet planes overhead, see them sometimes when the cloud shifts. Who am I to know such things.'

The mother's throat dried. She swallowed the coffee, scalding her throat. Tuija began to sob and cry tearlessly. Merja sensing something was amiss curled into a ball on the rug and stared at the wall.

'How much time do we have?'

'This evening. There is a train at seven with places reserved. You have been prepared for some time I see,' he said looking at the packages by the door.

'We are ready but we hoped it would never come to this.'

'So did we all.'

There was a short silence. Tuija made huge efforts to pull herself together and stroked Merja's hair.

'I can help load the cart, and push it too.'

'My advice is to cook what fresh food you have, a warm meal will sustain you for the journey. Take what you need but no more. Leave the cart at the station.'

'But what of this place,' said mother casting her eyes around the cabin. 'What are we to do with it?'

'Secure the windows and doors, that's all you can do. There are no orders to burn everything. That at least means that district are not certain. This all may be a false alarm, a precaution. Who knows? God willing we will be here still for Christmas.'

'These are poisonous times master.'

'That's true…but it makes my task no easier. I am the black ram and all bolt their doors at my coming.'

'We will pray for you.'

'My thanks… but pray for we all. Pray that we should not be castaways. That I can undertake my duties and persuade everyone to leave.'

'Do some stay?'

'Not many, all are reluctant, that is understandable. This is home, I know as well as any. But they will leave though it unbuttons the heart to do so. Old man Hannu is creating. Many curses I've shot at him this day. First says he, it is too cold, then he stuffs a year's supply of tobacco in his pipe, smokes like a volcano till the whole cabin stinks with weed and you can't see his face for fumes. A blessing that is. Then decides that he will stay and fight. He's out there now building a barricade across the road east, laying man traps, eating all he can, smoking himself into the grave with that evil stuff of his. Says he's going to knock the first Ruski he meets on the head with his club. What am I to do?'

'He will either come round, or freeze to death.'

'There is that hope, yes,' said the master sarcastically. 'Well Mistress I must be going.'

'God Bless.'

'God Bless.'

The door closed. Snowflakes on the mat melted. The coffee cup still steamed though the coffee was gone. Tuija put her arms around her mother-in-law and neither of them spoke for a long time.'

'What shall we do?'

'Help me with the meal, we have hams, and potatoes and raisins. We'll have a feast. Who knows when the opportunity will arise again.'

So the kitchen became a hive of activity, not only in cooking but cleaning too. Every shelf was dusted, every floor swept. The table was laid with best tablecloth and crockery. Even Merja became more animated with the excitement. Once the meal was over, dishes were washed and carefully stacked, crumbs picked up. The cabin was immaculate. As time passed the activity helped conceal those uncertainties slumbering there. A few more articles were added to the pile by the door and then Tuija dressed and went outside to stow them on the cart. It did not take long.

When the time came to leave it was a moment of poignancy and irritation. Merja had dozed after the meal and woke in a state of disorientation, struggling with the coats and shawls and gloves that had to be forced upon her. Only the presence of a doll stopped her tears. Mother carefully bolted the windows, checked that nothing was left behind and filled the lantern on the window sill with oil.

In the lantern light she glanced around the cabin, trying to remember every nook and shadow. It was so unreal. But the lamp would burn through the night and comfort others as they trudged past.

Hannu will find us, she thought. He is a good lad, he will know where to look should he return with the village deserted. When the living had gone ghosts would return. The ancestors would see that all was well. With a silent prayer she turned the key, and put it in her pocket. At first she thought spectres had returned already but the silent movements of neighbours, the black and white shufflings, the glistening of snow, the whispers and the closing of doors one by one signalled a gradual evacuation of the village. Tuija pushed the cart while she held Merja's hand, the little one walked on in mute bewilderment, clutching her doll, wide-eyed at this bizarre adventure in the dark.

For a mile they walked to the little country railway station where sombre crowds were already gathering.

Only the mad old man remained watching as the sad lines of village folk trudged away. He turned his face to the east.

*

Walking on ice, the ice of the night is akin to walking across razor blades. Ruts and channels slice through leather and contort the feet no matter how well protected, it is a slow, painful process and the world is in negative. There is no colour, black and white and grey and silver from the moon, that's all.

Sound is amplified. The sickening shell and skull crushing crackle as boots fall and wheels turn. All frequencies and wavelengths combine to assault the ear drum with the patterings of hell. Soon cold numbs all feeling and what in summer is a journey of minutes in this deep world is spun into hours.

Then truth strikes like a hammer, ripping the body apart and exposing all flesh. It is as if some unjust punishment descends vandalising all that was once familiar. All sins splatter the soul, real and imagined, all regrets and sorrows, all apologies and atonements, all barbed words and consummations gush into the holes bored by anxiety. This slows you. This causes the brain to solidify and muscle to curl. All you can do is keep moving because there is no choice. There is nothing else that can be done and the sooner this fact is understood the easier life becomes. No backward glances. No wondering at divine punishment. Eyes on the road, concentration, no falls or slips, this is neither the time or place for broken bones.

So it has come to this, thought the mother.

The station wore a muffled light, wary of air raids for the sky was a rich sapphire blue and the consequent cold bitter. Stars shone and planets completed their orbits. Everyone was there, a whole tribe from villages and farmsteads busily unloading baggage. Knots of humanity in states of excitement, anxiety, despair.

Tuija rolled the cart up to the platform and unloaded. Merja sat on the resulting pile and watched all, missed nothing. Who knows what she made of the scene but her wariness scribbled its name on the walls. We have orders to wait, to wait with patience, taking care to be hidden, so ran the dictatorship of thoughts and all Karelians who massed in that place wondered what would happen if the trains did not arrive. Wondered at their destination. Could not believe that the Russians were really so close...there had been no signs of battle.

Not one farmer or fisherman or forester or blacksmith or gravedigger doubted that soon they would return. This was one of many temporary displacements for the people of this land. If the train did not arrive at seven then it would arrive sooner or later. There was a determination to be stoical about it. Yet what if? What if the train did not arrive? Would there still be time to escape? Was this waiting wise? And if it did not come there was still home. Hope enough.

My mother Mrs Juutilainen could not rest. Leaving Merja in her daughter-in-law's care she left the platform, climbed down steps laced in ice and walked to the goods yard alongside the tracks. Coal lay heaped, timber that could not be moved and what could have been oil drums with a coverlet of snow upon them. It was all virus and tentacles. An organism of movement yet to be swallowed.

How ordinary it all looked. She crossed the yard, opening the door to the main warehouse. It was empty, almost empty, a few chains, rope for haulage. When the door creaked shut behind her she jumped but did not leave. In the corner, where the moon's reflective glow bounced through the window she saw a line of four white coffins. Names scrawled in pencil on the lids, Private, corporal...

'You shouldn't be in here mistress,' said the stationmaster's voice. This is not a place for a woman.'

She ignored him.

'Who are they?'

'Lads from the front going home. Came in from Viipurri this morning. I've been here all day, when duties allowed. What a day it has been too.'

'Where are they going?'

'Not sure. Thought there might be some documentation with it, there usually is. Been a lot of coffins like this passing through recently. Maybe it's too rough at the front now to deal with formalities. When they first came in I thought my lad might be amongst them. Lost him yesterday you know.'

'I'm sorry to hear that sir.'

'When his mother knows it'll break her. I haven't the heart to tell her yet. Kept it to myself.' As he spoke the demons danced around him, pulling at his fob and tilting the peak of his railway cap.

Shrieking they were, revelling in his pain. He did not notice but the mother did, little red devils with claws like pincers. She shooed them away with a prayer and called upon the angels.

'She has a right to know.'

'Yes. So she has...but not yet. I haven't the courage.' So broken was the look of him her soul poured and her own tears had to be restrained. 'Such a waste mistress, such shocking waste. How we sow our seeds and the Lord in his mercy harvests the fruit. Such a good lad, our only child and his mother dreaming of grandchildren as women do. It will break her heart.'

'I can stay for awhile if you would like.'

'No mistress the train will be here shortly. As far as I know it is on time. When it pulls into the platform stay near the rear. Try and stay by the door, that way you can get out quickly if you need to. Chances are the planes will attack at some point...if they do, wait for the train to stop, don't try to jump while it moves and then rush for the trees, you will be quite safe there. Keep your eyes open, try to be ready.'

'I will, thank you.'

She turned for the exit, running her hands over the coffins, uttering a silent goodbye prayer.

'I hope you find your boy.'

'So do I mistress.'

'God Bless.'

With that she climbed back onto the platform and saw the steam rising and the crowd shuffling forward. Clutching Merja tight in one hand and a suitcase tight in the other she forced her way into a carriage. Tuija followed and stowed the remaining luggage onto the racks. It was a tight fit. There were hundreds of women and children aboard, old men too. From the window she saw the station for the last time. A small and frightened group of Russian prisoners under guard shuffled away and the cattle truck they had vacated was filled by more people and yet more bundles hopelessly tied with string.

The stationmaster emerged, his face blank, tranced in expression but he waved his flag and blew on his whistle and the train strained along the track puffing and bellowing. Yet no one cried. The warehouse faded. The trees settled. The winter solstice wrenched forward.

No one wept.

'Did you manage to find out where we are going?' asked Tuija.

'No I didn't. I forgot to ask.'

She tucked Merja's hair back into her woollen hat. It was always escaping.

'Don't take off you boots, either of you. Make sure you are not entangled. I have the handle of the door. If we need to, we can get out in seconds. If we need to, wait for the train to stop and run for the trees. Don't look back. Throw yourself down.'

Westwards ran the train, following an artery to the heart. The carriage lights were dimmed. Phosphorous and sulphur particled the occupants. Merja coughed as did others. Some fidgeted, some shuffled but no one cried.

So ends this verse and chapter.

Chapter 7

The key that springs the lock, the turf dam imprisoning flood, the portcullis and chemical membranes swelling blood behind their barriers, the clasp that holds the soul was the Isthmus. The Karelian Isthmus sweeping from the Gulf of Finland to Lake Ladoga. Myriad waterways bowed its granite. Forests thinned into plains across its width. This was the door on which invaders of countless ages hammered. All knew this. It was no secret.

So it was here that Mannerheim concentrated our forces, meagre as they were. Defences stretched in trench and bunker, ditches, anti-tank obstacles, mine fields, waves of barbed wire. We men, arms open to receive our Russian visitors, numbered amongst us the 11th, 5th and 4th Divisions and to the east in the Suvanto sector the 10th and 8th. The 6th Division was our reserve and no one but Mannerheim himself could call upon their assistance. All outsiders thought this defensive line impregnable, except we who knew better. More imagined than real, too few soldiers, too few cannon – the world and his wife thought this line demonic – but it was not – we knew – but we did not tell! So devious we Finns.

This was where the breech would be made if only the enemy came in full strength across our tender open fields, no force could prevent their passing. But they did not. Not at first.

Puzzlement was our initial reaction. A situation which we could not understand. Why did they not charge across? It was a war played out from nine to five. Let me explain.

We occupied advanced positions, about two miles in front of the main defensive line. These were no more than foxholes, surface blips with a dozen or so riflemen, no more.

Then reader, tuck away incredulity and mark my words. At 9 o'clock, on the dot, trucks would roll up before us and their soldiers jump out. They ran at us, supported by tanks and sporadic mortar fire. We withdrew from our forward positions. We gave them up. What value were they to us? None.

At 5 o'clock on the dot these Russians upped and left for their own lines for the night. So we moved back and re-occupied our original positions. This went on day by day. An office war with regular time keeping! As this strange charade continued we were able to train and learn, mark out the parameters of our fear. Our shortcomings could be overcome in this kindergarten, and while there was action, and some were lost, and many an unpleasant incident occurred (some already related) when the main attacks came we were in some sense battle hardened, we had grown in confidence. We had been given time to steel ourselves.

So here sat Harri, Simo and me. Three gentlemen clad in grey and camouflage white, grasping weaponry of many hues, sucking in our cold breath and sweating out our exertions. We had beaten them back and their dead lay spangled in the snow, and the souls of the fallen wandering the streets of a Soviet heaven. We at Taipale, simple men, country folk with limited horizons knew little of the machinations of higher command. Strategic thinking was not a task suited to our skills. We approached this war of the earth from foxhole to foxhole, meal to meal, stand to-stand down and thankful we were that such grand responsibilities did not fall on our shoulders.

*

If you can imagine the Russian approach to this war as a medusa with tentacles slashing hard in all directions west. Across the Isthmus and the northern shores of Lake Ladoga these tentacles slithered across bogs, frozen waterways, forests. Our axes had to slice wherever they appeared or we would be crushed, asphyxiated. If they could stretch around the Ladoga we would be trapped within their coils. In the far north from Murmansk they crept, across arctic wastes where few men dwelt, on the Kollaa river and splicing Finland at the waist. From the dangling air and pristine seas. What amputations they considered.

And into this jug of worms our commanders dived, into the organic, the multi-celled slime. But never enough of anything, men, materials, equipment, aid, to safeguard borders of a thousand miles. What hope did we ever have?

Well some.

We were stubborn. Stubborn as rock, as the crust. Immovable objects each. Our wives had always said it was thus! True, a mixed blessing but God be praised we knew this land and crossed it as water boatmen or pond skaters using the surface tension molecule by molecule. We did not blunder. General Winter led us and we were on friendly terms with him. As for our enemies they had their plans and executions but on the ground everything froze, froze solid, fuel, rifles, blood, air, hands, feet, hearts. It took a pick axe to complete even the smallest task and even then the body is sapped of energy if not treated with respect. The slightest wound turned black and gangrenous in hours, a needle prick, a mouth ulcer. Toes became stumps, brains soup, bodies a carcass hanging from the abattoir hook. Even in death was indignity, exhibition, contortions animated by frost. When we glanced across the fields of the fallen we noted how their blood sprayed and separated into crystals, heard the twang of bodies on the wire as the wind resolved to lullaby them.

Poor souls.

Some even smiled in their deaths as if this was all an enormous joke.

When as one we perceived this scene, as a battle from Old Testament times where ice was substituted for sand, it was impossible to determine our thoughts. Shock, sadness, exhilaration, relief, numbness. When Corporal Murto walked out alone we were all still transfixed. Mesmerised.

We could not understand what he was doing. Why he took a revolver from its holster, why he released the safety catch and fired. Then it dawned. A man slumped deeper on the wire and swayed. Another bullet to the body of a man already still, and a third we could not see. Transfixed we were. What was he doing?

When a final shot cracked we all jumped for it was unexpected. Did it come from our own lines? Was that possible? I looked around but could not make it out. Harri swore under his breath. Something clicked.

'Damn,' he said.

'What's the matter?' I asked but he did not reply.

We all saw Corporal Murto fall. We all saw his hair parted. Felt the vibrations of his landing.

'Damn,' said Harri. 'Where's Simo?'

'I don't know,' I answered. 'He must have left the line.'

Harri was always quicker than me. He made the connection immediately. He was worldly wise. It took awhile for me to comprehend this new genesis.

Scrambling from the rear a sergeant raced down.

'Who fired that shot?' he shrieked. 'Who fired?'

Blank looks.

Silence.

'What shot was that?' asked Harri.

The sergeant was in no mood for impertinence. 'You know damn well what shot. The whole company heard it. The whole company saw his head blown apart. Don't play the fool with me.'

He rushed away spitting teeth.

'What was all that about?' I asked.

'Wake up Hannu,' said Harri disgruntled. 'That shot came from our own lines. Look about you. Who's missing?'

'Simo?'

'Precisely.'

'Did he do it?'

'Keep your voice down.'

'But why?'

'Why do you think?'

'He's in trouble. Big trouble.'

'We are in trouble…mark my…'

He wasn't wrong.

A wiring party was organised that night and the sergeant took some pleasure in telling us we had been volunteered.

'You three,' snapped the sergeant. 'Are the wiring party. When you get back report to the Lieutenant. He wants a word with you.'

'What about?' shot back Harri, eyes glancing in my direction.

'What do you think? A right hornets' nest you stirred up.'

At that he left and we waited for darkness to envelop us. We sat with hands muffled, drinking coffee, trying to warm our insides.

Looking back, no one had rushed to retrieve Corporal Murto's body from the snow. It lay for a long time being quietly buried under new flakes until it became difficult to distinguish from the others, or a log, or a mollusc on a white beach. It was difficult to see him there. Any moment I expected him to rise snarling and barking orders. A true psychopath but still some mother's son. Somewhere there was weeping.

No, there was no rush, hours later a group of unfortunates plodded out, bent double for the enemy were likely to be watching. He was frozen by then, stiff as a pine bed and heavy he must have been for the four of them struggled to carry and drag the mortal remains. Snipers covered their retreat and a maxim gun poked out towards the horizon for any signs of trouble. There was none. The Russians were licking their wounds

There was more commotion from our lines. NCO's running around wild, like headless chickens trying to discover where the fatal shot had come from. Was it really so obvious? I suppose it was…the timing was great theatre, a statement. Now Harri and Simo and me were to go out and fix the wire, surely no coincidence.

The squid ink black descended on our world. A half-moon wobbled like plasma on the line opposite, craters on the surface oscillated as we breathed. It was bitter. I saw a shooting star and the triple hued solar system burst and fragmented. Stars were pearls and the elements radiating from their distances enamelled my eyes. Opalescent. Mother of pearl. The outside of a sea shanty. Into this world, into the clam we walked, loaded with wire and mallets and cutters like the magi following the star of Bethlehem.

The order for silence travelled down the line. We knew that we were covered by a hundred rifles but it provided no comfort.

It was like walking on gravel. Ice crystals exploded under our boots. We were walking on glass and half the civilised world could hear our progress. So much for silence. Simo too was muttering, cursing, moaning.

'For God's sake shut up,' spat Harri.

'I'm not happy.'

'Really,' replied Harri sarcastically.

We thundered. Wildebeest on the plains of Africa made less noise than we did. Every footfall amplified, we could have been in a concert hall.

'Don't make so much noise,' repeated Harri frantically.

'I'm trying, I'm trying,' I answered.

Simo plodded on, bent miserably.

Eventually we reached the ragged wire entanglements, zinging in the breeze. A metallic blister, a sizzling added accompaniment to footsteps as we dropped to our stomachs and crawled into the white; trying to be as one with the snow with only eyes and noses poking through clothing. Harri and Simo unravelled new wire from a spool, crouched, supplicating, fingers numb. Twice we had to unclasp the frozen bodies of Russians from the barbs. They fell with a thud which made us dive deep. With time eternal the gaps were filled and snags re-wired. It was heavy work; sweat dripped down the inside of my shirt and then froze into icicles, digging into the spine. We were porcupines scurrying in a lunar frost, that distant land of silver. It was a thankless task. Wire once cut would whip back and catch into camouflage capes as if caught by the fingers of the devil. At other times it slashed the face with only an arm to protect flesh, which was unhooked as a fish is taken from a line. And every second grew more dangerous, more obvious to the Russians opposite that a working party was on the ice. New fallen snow covered our tracks but still a grey calligraphy of movement could be discerned by the watchers and with every tick I expected the snap of a sniper's bullet to ripple. So exposed were we I uttered prayers to the almighty while Harri cursed and Simo moaned. If we did not hold the wire correctly it would zip along the whole line with the volume of a siren. Still ice needled our skin, we porcupines.

Hours later we finished. An inspection from our lowly vantage point indicated no breaks, repairs completed. A good job, the work of craftsmen. If I was not so tired and cold I would have felt a real sense of satisfaction. My face wore a luminous glow for the air was a mirror reflecting many images and the atmosphere metallic, sharp, slicing.

'That's it,' said Harri with relief attaching the wire cutters to his belt. 'Let's get out of here.'

We edged backwards, eyes front, reversing. Harri took a pistol out of a holster, our only weapon. But we had not gone far when a cry rang out, a heart wrenching cry. It was Simo.

'What is it Simo?'

'Keep your voice down,' urged Harri again, scanning the horizon with his pistol. We were truly exposed.

Then the flare exploded. A yellow flare, a star burst slowly descending, illuminating the scene for miles around.

'Freeze.'

So we buried ourselves and breathed not.

A burst of machine guns from the Russian side of the peninsula spat out. But not aimed at us, randomly searching. A response of rapid fire from rifle and maxim from Finnish lines shot over our heads, and then more response opposite, a few mortars, another flare, hay gold, crimson, beautiful, mesmerising, stupefying. Suddenly in the midst of a new battle, a real whirlpool we could do nothing but lie still, make ourselves invisible.

'We have to get out of here,' repeated Harri. 'Follow me,' and he started to crawl low and fast. Bullets from both armies inched above our heads. The noise was now so intense that silence was no longer needed. We shouted and released some fear in that way. But Simo floundered around in circles, burrowing into the snow with his arms.

'What's the matter? Are you hit?' I looked for red stains on the white, cherry dribbles spreading as I had seen them before but there were none.

'What is it?' I cried, now stationary. Simo was not following. I could hear Harri urging us back, swearing as an ancient, and all the time bullets and shrapnel skidding the air around us. Harri crawled back to me.

'Is he hit?'

'No…I don't think so.'

We watched as he prodded the snow frantically with his hands. I could tell Harri's temper was beginning to smoulder, still we edged nearer to him.

'Come on Simo!' Harri screamed. 'Do you want to get us all killed?'

'I can't.'

'Why?'

'I've lost my teeth,' answered Simo.

'You old fool,' Harri spat saliva out of his mouth. 'What do you mean? Come on!'

'My teeth…I can't find my dentures, they fell out round here somewhere.'

'You stupid old bark eater, leave them.'

'I can't. I need them to eat. I'll find them. They are white. They are here somewhere.'

'Everything is white,' I countered.

Despite the noise and patter-patter of machine guns, despite the flares floating down the unreality of it all and the horrified expression on Simo's face, his crazed slapping of the snow, caused me to laugh out loud. This only succeeded in enraging Harri even more.

'You're both mad, raving mad,' yelled Harri, but he did not retreat, instead with obvious reluctance, he started patting his hands too. 'If I get shot I'll kill you,' he threatened.

What the boys made of it I did not know. Secretly I hoped they could not see this weird moon-lit performance.

'I've found them. I've found them,' shrieked Simo and I saw him put his mittens to his mouth.

'Thank God for that,' said Harri.

I chuckled inside and crawled, rolled, slithered back towards our lines. There were no more flares and with time the firing died down, only the occasional rifle crack broke the silence.

We dropped, seriously frightened, into the trench and caught our breath.

'If you ever do anything like that again old man, I will shoot you myself.'

I said nothing, merely captured oxygen in my mouth and satisfied my lungs.

'You took your time lads,' said some soldier.

'Shut it,' replied Harri furiously.

We all three gasped and stretched our muscles, stamping to let blood flow into our toes again.

'What was all that nonsense out there?' asked Harri, but not in those words, in phrases coarse and blasphemous.

'I need my teeth. Without them I cannot eat. No one asked you to wait for me. It was stupid. You should have gone back.' He hooked the camouflage cape back over his head like a cowl. For a while, in a dimmed candlelight he took on the look of a monk from ages past, grizzled, two days' growth of beard on his chin and hair like a tonsure. Like rock, like time itself could not batter down his lean frame, tough as basalt. We were veterans now and this war business, well the mechanics of it were becoming natural and instinctive. This worried me some. It caused me concern that we should not become Abrahams, ready to sacrifice our own sons. This should not become a way of life. I was a carpenter accustomed to the turn and plane of wood, to grain and resin, joints and hinges. I laboured with chisels and awls as did Joseph of Nazareth. Always I longed to return to my workshop, the key to which I still held in my pocket as a talisman. As long as I could recall my past existence, that other life I knew, there was a seed of humanity within me. Simo was a hunter and fisherman, this was more game to him, more in tune with his daily life where cunning and guile and sharp shooting served him well. Though the quarry was different the rites and incantations he mumbled were the same.

Once warmed by coffee which in hands thawed would burn and scald we walked to the lieutenant's dugout, banging a support post with a rifle butt.

He grunted and we entered his lair. I was worried. I suppose we all were. The lieutenant was a good man, who in his own way and with the means at his disposal did his duty, however distasteful that might have been. But he had his duty. So beyond that brow, the brow of tiredness we all saw the eyes of ravenous anger.

'Who told you to sit down?' he snapped.

We stood up.

'At the end of the last engagement, when Corporal Murto was out there on the ice, he was shot, a single shot through the back of the head. I want to know who fired.'

We said nothing. I hoped Simo would keep his mouth shut and not utter some ridiculous remark. Harri was the man for this situation. He had talked his way out of many a tight corner.

'We only saw him fall Lieutenant. We heard the crack and saw him roll as did many others,' said Harri.

'So did I,' said the lieutenant. 'You two,' pointing at Harri and me, 'were in the trench to my right, and no disrespect to your pathetic soldiering skills, but you could not have been responsible.' He spat out the words with real venom. Never had we seen this mild mannered gentleman so enraged. 'But you,' and here he pointed his finger at Simo.

'You old man, so I'm told, can split a hair at a thousand metres.'

'So some say.'

'Where were you when Corporal Murto fell? Not in the line with others at that time. You did not maintain your position. Where were you?'

'I was beyond the trench, cleaning smoke from my eyes.'

'Were there any witnesses?'

'I don't know, I had smoke in my eyes.'

'Let me educate you Simo Seppalla, let me impart a little knowledge…it is a crime to murder a superior, even a corporal, in times of war the penalty for which is death. The firing squad, bang against a wall with the rest of the company to watch as a deterrent.' He paused for breath and the pistol in his hand dipped a little.

'It is well known that Corporal Murto bore you some ill will. He was a soldier, a regular and disliked slovenly ways. We are fighting for our lives here.'

'I did not kill Corporal Murto sir. It was not I.'

'We'll see,' said the lieutenant. 'The battalion medical officer is taking the bullet out of his skull as we speak. If it proves to be Finnish, from a sniper rifle. You are in big trouble.'

'It will not be so sir,' said Simo with confidence.

This confidence I did not share. I was weary. Harri was uneasy and I could tell he was a weighing up the wisdom of intervening. He did not. We stood there like statues, nervous and curiously embarrassed.

When the medical officer appeared and confirmed that it was indeed a Russian bullet lodged in his skull I almost fainted with relief. Simo did not move and the lieutenant's eyes never swerved from Simo's face.

'You can go,' he snapped, but his mood did not improve at Simo's disgraceful attempt at a salute or when his teeth looped into his lap when he turned for the exit.

'Sorry sir,' said Simo.

'Get out!' screamed the lieutenant who must have wondered at that time if the war was lost.

*

The roads to the past are always closed, bricked up, doorways block the path, locked, bolted and the walls encircling time do not crumble except in memory.

The lieutenant was angry, so enraged and Simo was so stupid looking, as if he didn't know what was going on. What was done, was done. There was no going back. We were in trouble, rather he was, and we by association. My thoughts I secreted away. It was a Russian bullet that did for Corporal Murto, scowling, twisted individual that he was. But then Russian guns and ammunition were easily come by. We gathered them all the time to add to our own meagre resources. Some also collected souvenirs, cap badges, insignia from uniforms and so on. But this practice was abhorrent to me, a desecration and I am sure that others felt the same way too. We had standing orders against the taking of trophies but could you blame some of the boys who were hardly out of school and find themselves in this situation. As for myself, I tried to keep myself clean, brush my hair, polish my boots for what it was worth. But the routine lay easy with me, one action followed another…because it did. Harri says I have changed in the last few weeks. This war had kneaded me like dough, out of the oven pops a new Hannu, more sociable, more forgiving. He is way off course. I have an office worker's mentality and like things to be just so. In the army it is just so, slick, spick and span. Do this because it needs to be done, be here because this is where you need to be. No questions, no analysis, straight. So when the storm breaks and we fight I sing my psalms and pull two sides of the seashell around my head, listen to the waves, do my duty, for I am a strong believer in duty. Pray that this tide does not engulf me, that I am not brutalised or drained of compassion even when I pull the trigger of my lahti and blast some poor soul into eternity. I do not aim but slip my mind back to those villages scorched with fire and the refugees with fingers frozen to jelly and ankles swollen to burst to motivate me, as a reminder. At the risk of repeating myself I pull the trigger but do not aim. Hate does not come easily, though at times I have known it parasite my feelings. That was my compromise, do not aim, do not deliberately kill. Morally questionable.

No, Harri was wrong. At heart I am still a worker with the metabolism of regular hours. Harri never really thought about anything but beer and girls and dances. He was so different to me. I liked him. He adopted me as a mascot. He laughed at my seriousness and adherence to rules. 'Why stand up when you can sit down?' he used to say. 'Why sit down when you can lie down?'

Harri was my shield, my protector from others who I could not like or hope to understand. Few people made connections, Harri was one, Merja, Maarit, my name's sake old man Hannu and Simo now. Though I cared for some, the numberless unknowns still earned my pity and I am definite, very definite about right and wrong, black and white, no grey. I claim closeness to very few. Let me tell you about Harri and that time we were in the school room in Imatra where we were sent to gain some manners and book learning. We had a young male teacher who was full of himself, superior, talked down to us and this lad, a much younger boy than myself wore callipers on both his legs. If I recall he was crippled by polio. Anyways when this master said move, you moved, you moved fast or a cane slashed your fingers and you yelled in pain. One day this boy did not move fast enough and the master swiped him hard across the back. A gasp went up from us as the boy fell to the ground. He tried to get up but did not have the mobility or strength. The more he struggled, the more the master swiped him, smash, smash, smash, lips pink pursed, red in the face, hair entangled across his brow which actually sweated with the exertion of it all. Even though it was the cruellest, blackest thing I had ever witnessed, no one moved to help, no one protested. We were so frightened. Eventually he hauled himself up by the arms, clutching the edge of the table, but only succeeded in toppling a fish tank on top of himself, water and all. The glass smashed, the fish jumped across the school room floor. And all I heard were the sobs of this little boy. Harri was a witness. He was next to me and tried to pull me back when I rose to pull him back onto his feet. He sat on a chair dripping and wailing and brushing shards of glass from his clothes. There were three goldfish on the floor and when I cupped my hands, in they jumped and I slid them into a pitcher of water we used to wash our hands. The master watched me and when I glared back at him his nose began to bleed and blood too oozed out of his ears but he was speechless. The master bled, the boy wept, the three goldfish circled the pitcher. I left. I'd had enough of schooling from that day on. Home I walked, which was a good distance, and Harri chased after me.

'How did you do it?' he gasped, trying to keep up with my long strides. 'How did you do that to the master. How could you order those fish into your hands…how did you do it?'

'Leave me alone,' I said. But he did not. We became friends eventually. Other things, unexplained, have happened since then. Things which cannot be deciphered or interpreted in any but the old ways. Harri is convinced I am a shaman. Maybe he is right about that.

But if I may shuttle this thread back across the loom I will reiterate that the roads to the past are closed, bricked up. We were moving, we three, transferred, no doubt as troublemakers from our comrades in the Taipale sector, to a new place of which we knew nothing. Our past constructed a barricade behind us, we were to move on.

That final night in the trench we spent huddled in sleep, exhausted by the day's events, weary, we rested as animals, unthinking. A cyclone would not carry us back to wakefulness.

There was no day break. In December the sun perches on the lid only to fall back, any warmth fragmentary and the dog, dark days of bleak winter moulds itself around the body.

At the appointed time we bestirred and trudged through lines of trenches to the rear, nodding to acquaintances as we disturbed their slumbers with our tread or momentarily deflecting the eyes of guards or lookouts.

'Good luck boys,' called Harri half-heartedly. 'See you in Leningrad.'

As for myself, I said nothing, concentrating as I did on keeping my feet in this dark metropolis of mud and ice and razor, which had been home. Occasional campfires glowed as the only colour in that monochrome scene. Inviting they were too, but we marched past impoverished, our breath vaporising on the flames.

We zig-zagged around the alignments of defences to open ground where a truck stood, engine running. The driver shouted to get in the back.

'I've orders to take you to Joensu, same place as this lot.' He pointed to crates and bags of materials. 'From there you can make your own way to Suomusssalmi.'

'What's it like up there?' asked Harri.

'Just a logging camp as far as I know, pretty rugged terrain, not as open as the Isthmus. General's rushing everything he can spare in that direction. Word is, he wants snipers. Looks like you've been specially selected.'

'We're not snipers,' said Harri. He looked across at Simo. 'Except one of us, and he has difficulty choosing the right target.'

'Lost me there, brother,' said the driver. 'But chances are you'll see more action soon.'

The lorry sped away, only brown exhaust fumes marking its presence.

*

The Russian commander looked at his map and saw that it was true. Strike from Suomussalmi, cleave Finland in half, cut the rail line to Oulu and the link with Sweden. So the war is won.

Chapter 8

The road northwards rumbled to the bickering of an engine, worn and tired. Needless to say it was a path frozen and from our vantage point amidst a jumble of stores and equipment we saw the serpentine ribbon of road exiting behind us, banks of snow on either side and no other traffic. Headlights were out for fear of air attack and it was as if we were within the human body itself, travelling down veins and arteries in sealed tubes and the engine was the heart pumping and spluttering, the pines and birches at the side were sinews and tendons dripping snow-blood onto the canvas roof.

I slept in part, hallucinating I'm sure and in my mind I was riding a bicycle on the village road where it ran parallel to the Saimaa canal. On the bridge above it I paused, resting on the handlebars. The waterway was still as silver but every time I breathed it rippled whispering thoughts back to me in dialects I could not understand – somewhere a dog barked the homeward journey, a freighter glided through the geometric shadow. And if you have ever wandered alone at day's end you will know what I mean, when dusk descends atom by atom and the ancestors murmur, murmur, murmur. A time between worlds. Except this stillness did not last, fear and foreboding overcame me and I cycled on down lanes where lizards crawled, hundreds, blue and curious. They did not move or try to escape but threw themselves at the spokes. Some I avoided, some I could not and were crushed under the wheels leaving a trail of mutilated and writhing bodies in my wake. I meant no harm and my accidental butchery caused great shame. But I did not dismount. I kept riding.

Only when Simo nudged me in my ribs did I stir and blink and let whatever phosphorescent light was available flood beneath my eyelids.

'Are you alright son?' he said jolting along.

'Yes...fine.'

'You were muttering something in your sleep.'

'Merely a dream.'

'How you can sleep in a rattle wagon like this, I know not,' responded Simo. 'Feels as if my bones will crack if it goes on any longer.'

Harri surfaced from beneath a flood of ropes and canvas.

'What did you dream Hannu?' he asked.

'Nothing.' I didn't want to share a dream. I was reluctant to describe what was private and indecipherable.

'Was it a premonition?' asked Harri expectantly.

'No...nothing of that sort.'

'Hannu can see things.'

''Tis a true gift,' interrupted Simo. 'Harri said you were a shaman. That you can read dreams.'

'Not that I know.' I didn't like the direction of the conversation and attempted to end it by yawning and feigning tiredness.

We stretched and uncurled but it was tortuously slow progress, sliding through black.

Finally Harri broke the silence.

'What is this place we are going to and why us?'

'Obviously we are an embarrassment after that business with Corporal Murto. We are out of the way, someone else's responsibility. Maybe they can't trust us to shoot the right person.'

'Don't look at me,' answered Simo, 'my aim is always true. As to where we are going, well, it is a lonely place, densely forested. Once in my youth I journeyed there with my father, following bear and wolf which are numerous in that region. It is taiga, teeming with pine marten, wolverine even and eagles.' He paused, as was his way and sucked in breath.

'Roads are sparse, but the rivers and lakes run with fish, a real paradise. There is some logging and charcoal burning but as to anything else, I am not aware it has value.'

'Then why are we going?'

'A holiday.' Simo laughed, ivory teeth chattering with the vibration of the lorry.

But I was aware. A voice collided with my brain, sucking in its ravenous word play. I was uneasy. While the ossified forests paled their pigmentations; while grasses fingered with icing, glazed by wind and frost I recorded the landscape into my memory. It took on the appearance of coral, satin, veiled, no human voice penetrated the confines of the transport from without. But eyes watched, eyes syringed my skull mixing with the babble accumulating there, transcribing a pattern. I was aware. I understood that this place was once carved by prehistoric glaciers, and I was once here, many eons of generations ago in genetic memory, in that part of me passed on and down and across. Where now the elk trod once pawed tigers and mammoths gouging trails and men scratched their axes for minerals from moraines heavy with illusion. When men's tongues still fused and uttered grunts, when speckled cowie shells rolled down slopes of red-grey granite I was there, so through this time I spoke back, my own image cast upon the tarpaulin, but this older me, more sunbronzed, wizened, tangled could see that Suomussalmi was the worm dragging us into its mouth, baring teeth red with blood. This was the nucleus and we the microscopic particles to be whirlpooled away.

Harri tethered my face with his gaze, riveted upon me.

'You have a bad feeling Hannu,' he said disturbed.

'Yes.'

'How bad?'

'I don't know.'

Simo sucked in his breath and watched us both.

Suddenly the lorry stopped. We were in a clearing where the road ended.

'Out you get boys,' shouted the driver. 'Don't leave any kit, you'll never get it back.'

'Where do we go?' asked Harri.

'I know,' I said, hoisting my pack, 'this place was once familiar to me.'

On we walked and as we walked through the trees other individuals and knots of men joined the snaking, threading stream ever growing to be bolstered by many more, young and old, in field grey or camouflage capes, in the uniform of border guards and military police and engineers and even in civilian dress, just men, until we were a mighty river of hundreds. No one spoke. Some paused for breath. Some shot their eyes about and still we rolled forward, a tribe in progress. They followed for I knew the way and after many hours of travelling we entered the village of Suomussalmi. Our personal Mount of Olives. Yet when I turned to cover our tracks, there were none. Just virgin snow.

We greeted the defenders of that place with handshakes and back slaps. Harri wondered what on earth was going on. Simo sought his sons in memory. I knew. I felt the hand of heaven on my shoulder and pushed my cap to the back of my head to take in my surroundings.

Smoke spiralled into the air and caught in the throat. Through the gaps the yellow sun snow dazed, barriers of pine grew everywhere. The village had been torched by the home guard who then withdrew to the outskirts. In we poured, a treacle of men mustering on the edges from where we were to be deployed. Only two roads led to this place, both poor. One from Juntusanta and one from Raate bounded by forests thicker than I had ever seen with snow banks higher than a man, higher than a house in some places. Who could get through this, an army in single file? There was a sense of determination seeping through this motley collection of Finns.

Colonel Siilasvuo climbed on a table and spoke to us. He growled and his eyes skipped to our faces one by one, drawing us into his sphere of influence.

'Glad you could spare the time to make it here,' he said.

We laughed.

'Let me tell you straight,' he began, 'there are two Russian divisions heading towards this place. The 163rd advancing from Juntusranta will be in the village by nightfall. The 44th heading from the south-east hope to join them. They must not. The two divisions must be kept apart and destroyed separately. If they combine we will be driven onto the ice of Haukipera and Niskanselka and annihilated. Speaking personally I am not ready for that.'

We cheered.

'The two divisions amount to 48,000 men, with armour and artillery. Our ski patrols and radio operators have made some interesting discoveries. Their progress is slow, a good many have succumbed to frost bite. Aside from their other accomplishments I am told they have a band to lead their victory parade into Oulu, printing presses, truck loads of propaganda, goodwill gifts for us Finnish workers.'

More cheers.

'Our task is quite simple. We have to stop the 163rd from reaching Suomussalmi. The 44th is moving slowly on the Raate road. We must destroy them before they join the 163rd. This will be the Wild West boys.'

We gave him a huge round of applause and whistled and clapped and dispersed to whatever shelter we could find.

Huddled in a makeshift tent with an oil burner to keep the ice from our hearts and many layers on our hands and feet we thawed bread so we might bite into it and gain nourishment. In this climate you had to eat. Warm soup we had from billycans and hot coffee. The body's core temperature had to maintained. This was vital. Biscuits and hard tack was insufficient. Field kitchens were more important than cannon. This much we had grown up with on our farms and crofts. These meals boosted our spirits and loosened our tongues and unleashed our memories. The cold would not claim us. The serene composure, that harbinger of death, that fatal final warmth as you slipped through a life that is like glass and easily shattered was kept at bay by raisins and potatoes and coffee beans. Such domestic incendiaries as these were a salvation.

When I looked into the horizon I saw only the ceramic squadrons of pine and fir, puff balls of light bouncing across them where the sun grazed the branches. This would be living in caves compared to the broad sweep of the Isthmus. Fate brought me here. I was led to this place as surely as the reindeer are led to summer pasture or the salmon to its spawning ground. It wrapped an intimacy around my back, a cloak, as if all that had gone before was mere confused preparation, a child's game. While men gathered hour by hour this battle would test our resolve and it would be a time for hunters, for stalk and strike. Orders could not be relayed through a landscape with the density of metal. Already engineers were at work constructing ice roads and what little artillery we possessed was wheeled into place. Skis were issued, equipment cleaned, ammunition checked, powerful flashlights distributed to every team.

Simo smoked his pipe. Harri combed his hair. I grasped my hunting knife slicing the bark from a piece of birch wood into fingers. We were at peace.

When the call to move spread through this shamble of shelters it was like a call to school. No urgency, matter of fact, quiet, understated. I thought, Lord Help Us and my heart beat. Harri glowed pale, a spectre in the corridors while Simo was no different to his usual self, putting on his skis as if they were extensions to his limbs, pipe still in his mouth. There were three hundred of us, divided into smaller teams and we were to cut the Raate road to prevent the two divisions joining up. This would be the first of many surgeries, a bringing down of the curtain.

Skiing to our assembly point, far beyond the reach of enemy patrols we scimitared the snow, slicing through the flesh of it like workers in an abattoir. Trying to conserve strength although our arms and legs ached and the ever present inhalation of frozen air scorched the lining of our lungs. Within an hour we approached the final jumping-off point secured by reconnaissance teams. Here in deathly silence we unpacked our heavy equipment, secured camouflage capes, burdened ourselves with machine guns, bullets, grenades, satchel charges, pistols. I heard a violin stringing through the woods and bird song, and the gentle chiming of a bell, and Leminkeinen's voice urging me forward, and the face of the pastor appeared upon my gloved hands. Fate brought me here.

So we were within sight and sound of the road. A scout led the way, we followed after him and I felt alone because we were all alike, we were polar bears on ice floes, disguised as mortals, gasping, snow blind. I could not tell which of the herd was Harri or Simo. Mere nameless mortals, primitive, without age and outside time.

I thought I could make out trucks, and conversation.

'Stay still. Move not,' whispered the scout as he spilled some incantation into his radio.

Seconds later mortar fire crashed into the road and the stutter of maxim fire caused pressure waves to flutter my eyelids. Snow avalanched from branches.

'Go!' he screamed 'Go!'

Down we swept, ski poles pressing into the ice and sharp shooters covering our backs, with instructions to shoot the officers first, no prisoners, no pity.

Life lapsed.

A slow animation in sepia or black and white played out against a cinematic back cloth.

I raked everything I could see with gun fire, spitting and cursing and screaming and bellowing as projectiles thudded into armour and tracks and the sides of transports, where blood shot into my face and the clang, clang of steel played counterpoint to the thudding of rounds into tissue. When my rifle failed I drew a pistol and thrust it through the cab of a lorry hysterical, salivating, red-eyed, unthinking. Some threw grenades into tank hatches, others hurled explosive charges. As I ran along the line I was felled by a mighty weight clinging and tearing at my back, grunting, a rifle butt swung and glanced my helmet as we rolled in surreal gymnastics across the road, a bizarre folk dance. My strength was failing but I drew a hunting knife slashing with fury. Swearing and cursing and crying tears of rage. A single rifle shot blew a hole in this man's head and his eye sockets burst, popped, viscous fluid dribbling onto my tunic. I pushed him away, this khaki-clad figure whom I did not know or hate. A corpse now. And I felt shame overwhelm me.

Taking shelter beside a tank track I saw the smoke from Simo's sniper rifle butterfly flutter and I knew that he had saved me. Reinforcements poured from the forest, a hundred, two hundred men yelling and firing their own bursts of gun fire until responses dwindled and only the occasional pistol shot put the wounded out of their misery. Then engineers skied down rushing barricades of logs and earth at both ends of the road. Trunks were driven into the breeches and overturned. Burning armour secured the gaps and the column was split in two. A fortress was carved, sculptured and strengthened at all its sides to be impregnable. We took up our positions but the road was cut and the Russians could neither advance or retreat. We were like so many ants upon a nest. We recovered, regrouped and waited for a counter attack but such was the confusion that no attack came. They had only a slither of roads down which to attack and this was within sight of our mortars. It would take an army of thousands to bulldoze through these barricades which were strengthened every minute. Nor could they skirt around it, so thick was the forest. We had bought some time and while our casualties were light theirs were heavy, for we counted them in hundreds and picked their pockets. Simo skied down towards me.

'You got him Simo.'

'Aye! Thought I would keep an eye on you. Are you hurt?'

'No…no this blood is not mine. It was the devil of a fight.' I felt suddenly nauseous, whether through shock or disgust I could not tell.

'Where's Harri?'

'I've not seen him. You stay there and clean yourself up. I'll find him.'

We had stung the scorpion and would hold this place for several days before picking up our packs and joining the rest of the battalion. The advance of the 44th Division had stalled for the time being. In the distance we could hear small arms fire and the harrying of the column further down the line. It was a matter of time but fate led me here.

When Simo returned with Harri they found me shivering, trembling with my tunic barely cleaned and fingers gripping the edge of the tank track.

'Wrap this blanket around you,' said Simo. 'You must have caught a chill, this will steady you.'

I took a swig of Simo's vodka but I merely vomited again.

'Do you want me to get the medical officer?'

'No, let me just wrap these around me and I'll be fine. The medical officer has better things to do.' When I glanced up at Harri I could see a touch of concern in his expression.

'Looks like you've been in a battle.'

'Where have you been?' I asked feeling comforted now we three were together again. 'We couldn't find you.'

'I went back for our packs before this new fall covered them. There's a storm coming. Better make ourselves at home. I think we'll be here for awhile.'

Simo handed out slabs of chocolate though how he acquired them, who knows?

'Job done,' said Simo. 'Still think I'm surrounded by the ugly battalion, same as Taipale.'

'At least I've still got my own teeth,' answered Harri.

'Temporarily. If either of you live long enough to lose them.'

'What do you mean?' I interrupted, feeling brighter.

'You need a man of my experience to keep you safe. One of you gets involved in a wrestling match with some Russian from the Steppes, nearly gets his skull cracked open. Another runs after tanks lobbing grenades, wailing like a siren and diving for cover when then bounce back at him. Who do you think you are, some kind of officer?'

'Fat chance.'

We settled, watching for any signs of movement. Snowflakes fell gently, covering the wreckage and bodies and paraphernalia and creating mounds and hills where they lay. As I scanned the horizon I saw scampering hordes of lizards criss-crossing the road, tails swishing and tongues tasting the air.

*

The flight from home for my mother and Merja and Tuija was not the exodus of later years. It was organised and ran to a timetable. Many considered it unnecessary for the front line was some distance away and apart from enemy aircraft flying overhead no other signs of enemy activity. Nevertheless the whole region was displaced with few remaining.

For the first time in her life my mother crossed the borders of Karelia. First to Imatra and then skirting Lake Saimaa pushed westwards. It was a tortuous journey. Many times the train stopped, steam was released and the wheels ground to a halt. No reasons were given but the claustrophobia of those packed and tangled compartments increased with time. A constant feature of that war, cold and darkness clamped the train as it did the soldiers in forest or trench and was never really alleviated. Each break in the journey intensified the feeling of being sealed underground, disconnected with the outside world. Nothing but ink could be seen through the windows. It might well have been the depths of the ocean, such was the sense of isolation.

'Why have we stopped,' uttered Tuija, rubbing her eyes and pushing hair behind her ears.

'I'm not sure. I heard that a woman was ill and had to be taken off. Others say the line is blocked.'

Mother felt trapped. Merja lay across her lap, cutting off the blood supply to her feet which had no sense of feeling in them. Thirst too caused great discomfort. It was difficult to speak and she tried to think of other things to take her mind away from a parched throat. There was water in the baggage somewhere but no opportunity of reaching it so closely knitted were the passengers with their life accumulations, boxes, suitcases, bags, textiles.

From outside the black screen of the windows flashed with white light and mother strained to make it out.

'What can you see?' asked Tuija.

'Some men with lanterns I think, examining the track.'

'You don't think the train has broken down?'

'I don't know,' she answered, a spark of irritation in her voice. Am I really responsible for everything, she thought.

The lanterns flashed outlining the figures of workmen. Glow worms were the trails of illumination they displayed, and in the absence of any colour she focused attention on the swinging, waving patterns they created. After a few minutes the workmen stomped away and the window was a black wall again.

Steam seeped from the engine and with a judder strained to re-start the journey. Sighs of relief issued from the slumberers for movement was good, a symptom of hope. Mother settled back and dozed into the regular percussion of the train as it ploughed steadily onwards. Merja slept on, hot and clammy, but there was nothing anyone could do.

In the early morning the train braked suddenly with such a screech and crack that at first people thought there had been an explosion. Many were thrown from their seats; others crashed against the wall or were enveloped by the contents of the luggage racks, struggling with fear and suffocation to their feet. Somewhere a leg was broken. High-pitched shrieks echoed down the tube.

'Get out...get out!' yelled mother, her hand already on the handle, pushing the door open.

'What's happening?'

'Get out.'

She grabbed Merja and with limbs stiff with cold and inaction jumped from the train, rolling into the snow. She pulled Merja to her feet and ran. Tuija followed breathless. Other figures could be seen racing for the trees, some holding hands, some carried, some as laboured individuals stumbling, falling, rising. Once in the forest she buried her face into the bark and covered Merja's sobbing frame with her body.

'I want to go home,' groaned the child.

Nothing could be said.

Two planes swooped, as if from outer space, as if from an alien planet where machines governed and men and women and children were termites, inconsequential. They flicked the tree tops with their wings and dropped two bombs which exploded yellow and orange and gold, shattering the windows and spraying shrapnel like confetti. It fizzed as it sank into the trackside snow, tiny plumes of vapour rising and for all the world it seemed that these planes were playing, creating mini volcanoes for the amusement of the watching passengers. After the first run, they arched and banked, the whooshing of propeller blades shaking the branches. On the second they flew lower and the features of the pilots could be seen fixed in concentration. This time there were no bombs but the whipping tingle of machine gun bullets peppering the track and spraying ever closer to the refugees, who sank deeper and cried louder. When they passed for a third time there were no bombs or bullets, just a cold assessment of damage inflicted.

Only when winter's meagre sun broke the tree tops did anyone move. The railway employees were first to inspect the train, others wandering down the track with a wary eye to the sky. There were bullet holes in some carriages and most of the windows had shattered but there was no serious damage. The track too was intact. From then on a series of frantic calls and waving beckoned everyone back onto the train. By some miracle there was only one casualty, an elderly man whose leg had snapped in the stampede. He was treated as well as was possible in the confines of that place.

At least the attack had given greater impetus to the driver; his cautious approach was overtaken by a desire to put as great a distance as possible between himself and the border.

While the bitter wind slabbed into the carriages now and the snow melted by body heat trickled as rivulets across the skin, greater speeds reassured the passengers. Only Merja caused concern, she had a temperature and her breathing rasped.

The train sidled through the industrial city of Lahti, deep in blackout, slowly, scythingly before picking up speed again. By mid-morning, with daylight pouring through the glassless windows, they finally pulled into Hämeenlinna. Pressure from the engine eased and stopped. On the platform Lotta Svard members were waiting, some banged on the sides of the carriage, others opened the doors and the passengers stumbled dazed and blinking onto the platform. The whole village was here, transplanted. The elderly man with a broken leg was rushed away on a stretcher. Boxes and cases were piled onto carts and a weary procession wound its way out of the station. Comments were made about the state of the train which was quickly shunted to sidings to be repaired.

So began a sojourn in the hinterland. For some there was no consoling. Truth struck like a hammer. All was left behind and perhaps there would be no return. Each step took them further from Karelia into unfamiliar lands. There were no leaders here. Tiredness made them pliable, willing to be directed by volunteers with crisp voices and shiny cheeks. Grateful that the journey was over, hungry, parched with thirst, desperate for sleep.

It was a clear day with some warmth within it. Blue sky, clouds, wisps. Along a dirt track, solid, marbleised, overhung with skeletal branches. Sunlight and shadow dappled the way ahead, shifting in a mosaic. This short walk to the bridge across the lake was a freeze frame series of steps with heads bowed and some of the characteristics of a dream. Too tired to take in much, mentally noting the red-brown castle in the distance and boats breeched on the ice, they shuffled to the creak of wheels and subdued conversation.

Tuija carried little Merja in her arms. She blazed with heat and being barely conscious sagged limp and inert. Mother wheeled their belongings in the file. When they entered the town square heads turned and watched. What a motley crew of renegades they must have resembled, hunched and disorientated. But at least they were together.

One more right turn and they were in the churchyard. From there they unloaded carts and entered the church. A white church still as a grave.

Quiet.

Bottles of water were distributed, and coffee and soup and bread, all gratefully received. Some had blankets draped around their shoulders. Officials worked through the crowds taking names and details. A police officer watched. There was talk in whispers. Tuija saw the painting above the altar, sucking in the colours. Merja was laid on a pew.

'Is there a doctor or nurse here?' asked my mother to one of the Lotta Svard. 'My child is not well, she is burning up.' A man in a suit and overcoat came across and with great seriousness placed a hand across Merja's brow. He looked in her eyes, pulled her head forward, pinched the skin between his fingers. Merja did not respond, which worried him. He pushed his spectacles back onto his head.

'We have to get her to the hospital. It's not far from here. There is no transport though. Can you carry her?'

' Yes…what is it doctor?'

'A fever of some kind. There needs to be more investigation.'

Mother choked.

'Is it serious?'

He smiled nervously.

'I can't say, not yet. Maybe with some rest and nourishment. We will know soon enough. Let me show you the way.'

Mother and Tuija embraced.

'You stay here, look after our things, try to find out where we are to go. As soon as I know anything I will send a message.'

'Take care.'

'I will.'

Out into the mid-morning air. People scurrying across the cobble stones of the market square. In the corner an anti-aircraft battery sandbagged and expectant. Wooden houses framing them on all four sides, faces at the windows. Another policeman pounding a beat.

The overcoated doctor strode purposefully down the side streets, mother struggling to keep up.

'This way,' he said leading through thick wooden doors of what appeared to be a workhouse. The floors were scrupulously clean and echoed with their footsteps. The doctor muttered something to a receptionist, turned and said, 'This way please.'

Chapter 9

In the beginning so says the Kalevala the water maiden left the realm of the sky for she was intensely lonely, into the stormy ocean she fell, tossed by the foaming, billowing sea, driven here and there by the wind. Yet still she remained alone. Yet still childless and tortured by anguish, praying in desperation to the ruler of heaven for relief from this isolation, entreating, pleading. And pity he had upon her decreeing that a swan of great beauty should find a dwelling place in the mighty ocean. But there was no landing place, no haven of rest until the water maiden raised her knee above the swirling waters, above the whirlpools and there the beauteous swan built her nest. Seven eggs she laid, six of gold and one of iron.

Over the eggs the swan sat brooding. Many, many years of care she lavished upon the nest, but so much heat was generated the water maiden's knee began to burn and melt. In pain she jerked her knee and the eggs rolled into the sea shattering and splintering into fragments. So then a true marvel occurred for the fragments fermented and changed. The lower parts became the earth and the upper became the arch of heaven. The yolk became the sun lustrous and the white the silvery moon. Whatever was mottled within the egg became the stars and whatever was black became cloudlets floating.

Then passed time.

Ten years in all beneath the shimmering sun and beaming moon until the water maiden raised her head from the sea and she commanded the world to order. Wherever her finger pointed was formed land, headlands and islands. Where her feet she rested formed the caves for fishes and water serpents. The ocean depths were formed with her diving beneath the water. So striding towards the land her fingers touched with the lightness of gossamer creating places for the siting of salmon nets, curving bays, rocks and reefs, pillars for the sky, mountains engraved with mysterious figures, fissures and cracks until commanding the stormy seas to be placid.

And so it was.

So we are told, so we understood, the water maiden made her landfall in the wildest region of Karelia and continued her creativity for many, many ages bequeathing this land to our ancestors. Myself, within moments of quiet, of stillness where the wind no longer roared and the sky refrained from ballistics I drew these images from my soul and wondered about them, turned them over and found it comforting.

Could it be the moon reflecting from my brow in particles of quicksilver is the same that shields the yellow hair of Maarit, the same moon creating shadows for the warriors and maidens of the Kalevala?

There had been no communication, no letters or notes passed along the line but this was no surprise, such was the turmoil we were experiencing.

I did not then know she wore the blue 'hakaristi' pin across her shirt or that her days of preparation for the front was coming to the end. Though the rules were relaxed at that time, discipline was still harsh and women would be sent home and made to resign should they drink or smoke or exhibit immoral behaviour. Should such discipline be applied to us soldiers our lines would be empty! Even their skirts had to extend to twenty-five centimetres from the ground. Such a dreadful waste of materials. No, it was only in the interlude between wars that I discovered the adventures she undertook and truly astonishing it was.

When I carve this tale, from a branch of aspen, from incidents of recall there are knots and diversions of grain for in the re-telling there are other voices, the mould of memory still shakes the sand from casting, and hesitations, modesty and unwillingness to remember detail all play a part in blurring. But it is the spirit of the story that drives and in this there are no inaccuracies.

To the Kollaa river she was sent to cook and mend and nurse as appropriate but no others with her. This was judged to be a place of obscurity, a region of thin soil and granite and rivers and rapids, thinly populated, looping north around the shore of Lake Ladoga, that mighty sea the southern shore of which we had so stubbornly defended at Taipale.

Few soldiers were there. A highway, the remains of three burned out Russian tanks, a few hundred men in hastily constructed dugouts, a sundered place wide of space, curling with time, de-populated. Ice roads were constructed, snow flattened, logs placed across and then sufficient water for a freeze to occur, allowing supplies to be brought up.

Maarit found herself in the remains of an old hunting lodge. Her sleeves were rolled up and she cooked by the light of a hurricane lamp. The stove blazed, two or three soldiers lounged on benches joking and laughing. Outside she could hear the zither of wood being sawed. It was almost impossible to see the lodge so deep was it buried in the forest. Tall black pine trees masked the light from inside; they creaked as the wind soothed them. Foxes scurried and scavenged.

Not everyone was pleased to see her. Some felt the front line was no place for a woman, others felt she was an ill omen, unlucky. No good would come of it, they said, and ignored her in their anxiety. Others asked shyly if she could find her way to fixing a button or sewing new insignia or stripes on their tunics. A young officer offered a pistol, to defend herself, he said. Maarit remonstrated that she had never fired a gun, and in any case could never kill a man. No, said the officer, you didn't need to kill a man, only make him think. Still she refused.

It was apparent to everyone that soon the Russians would come, drive through and then sweep around Ladoga to hit the Mannerheim line from behind. Then it would be all over for the Isthmus, for Karelia, for Finland. There might be a chance to escape, if you could ski well and slip like an eel through the trees. No one complained. This is how it was ordained.

Condensation in clouds raised the temperature of the room to an uncomfortable level. It gave Maarit a headache but still she stirred the soup and poured it into billycans to be distributed to the troops in scattered fox holes along the banks of the Kollaa. This ceaseless, mundane task was a life saver, and the men so grateful to clasp their hands around this steaming liquid, a transfusion, a drip, drip, drip of nourishment raising the spirits and thawing needles of ice in the veins and stomach.

Unnoticed the two soldiers left the lodge, clipped into their skis and vanished. Maarit was alone now and took the chance to sit and rest. She tied back her hair for the hundredth time that day and saw reflected in the window a face pale in pallor and mute in voice. She was losing weight, her eyes looked bruised, yellow and brown and weary. Perhaps her eyelids closed momentarily, she could not tell but she sat up with a start. Something startled her. What was it? The hurricane lamp shuddered, dust fell from the roof...water in a pan radiated waves. What was it? She got to her feet pulling the sleeve of her dress down her arms. There it was again. A rumbling, like a train. Then the whole room shook, a ladle fell from a hook and the floor vibrated. What was it? At first she thought it was the long awaited attack; but it was no bombardment more a steady drum, a rippling, an earthquake. She looked around and realised she was alone, realised that she was frightened. Throwing a coat over her shoulders she rushed outside but could find no one to ask, the site was deserted, lifeless. Had everyone gone? Had something happened while she slept and no one told her? Had there been a sudden retreat? Still the incessant rumbling continued. It grew in intensity and the rhythm lapped around her feet without ending, louder and louder. She tried to calm herself, breathed slow and deep. Still she could see no one; unnerved she ran through the trees to where a clearing, white and banked gave a greater field of vision. Plumes of snow shot into the air and the low beating of mahogany, of teak, of rose wood drums catapulted her senses and when the crescendo of noise slinged

142

into her face she understood that this was not the work of man but of nature. Thousands and thousands and thousands of reindeer stampeding through the forest where gaps allowed or trails funnelled them. Yet it was not many but one, a mutation of galactic proportions, many miles long, one body thundering through a fog of vapour and ice, a hydra-headed monster clashing antlers like swords and kicking spume in wings and taking flight. So thunderous was the noise, a sarcoma on bone, an amputation, a dragon conveyoring the senses, that Maarit felt her jaw drop and almost break as she pressed her body into the crevices of a tree trunk while swinging, swaying animals raced past.

Then, then as suddenly as the percussion began it filtered away, trickling beyond a low horizon. And the ground was churned into mud by the friction of a million hooves, steam rising from the baked earth. Only one animal remained, a young male struggling to rise, legs broken and blood dribbling through the nostrils. For a second his black eyes looked at Maarit until she turned her head.

Soldiers skied down and slit its throat and the blood on snow was still warm as the butchery commenced. One of the men escorted a still shaking Maarit back into the lodge and placed her on the bench. Another kicked open the door throwing hunks of meat onto the rafters where blood dripped to the floor.

'Meat today Maarit,' he exclaimed in triumph.

She nodded.

*

When the first attack came Maarit was still asleep, wrapped in blankets. There was a sudden commotion, men in far flung defensive positions rushed to their skis. Maarit saw some of them go as they swept through the trees grabbing whatever ammunition they could. Stoking the fire, boiling water, clearing spaces on the floor, she busied herself and thought of Hannu, of where he was, how he was feeling. It was a matter of waiting.

Down the only proper highway in the district ranged a column of Russian tanks firing as they advanced, barrels swinging from side to side and then a roar of ignition. In the distance, running to keep up, were mobs of infantry. Onto the sights of the Finnish guns they crawled. The first lumbering machine was quickly disabled, burst into flames, brewed up. The second flailed as the tracks were blown off, the third and fourth likewise exploded and the road was blocked. The spattering of small arms' fires sent the infantry racing back to their own lines and within minutes the site was one of cremation.

Yet the defenders knew, their comprehension was clear. This was only a probe, a sleight of hand to pinpoint strengths and positions, bought with lives that were expendable. Prisoners were taken, humble and polite and dazed and fearful of these white-caped men who would mount their heads on ski poles if they were ever taken. When they were rushed and hauled by the hair from their turrets and kicked and prodded to the rear it soon became apparent that this landscape, the sub-arctic conditions and the fear of God and political commissars that drove them forward filled them with despair, and the defenders with hope, sparse and under-equipped as they were.

Some of the captured did not even know the name of the country they had invaded, some believed they were on the outskirts of Helsinki, others stared in bewilderment at their predicament. One man with a hole the size of a pineapple in his leg, who later died of shock, related how he was picked up in the streets of a northern town and given a great coat. There was no training, no explanations, just a greatcoat and a rifle and three rounds. Soon the cleaning grease froze, and the biscuits broke his teeth and the snow he swallowed through parched lips caused stomach cramps which caused him to double up in pain. As he explained before he slid into that Soviet heaven he had only gone to town to buy his wife a headscarf for her birthday. The police caught him by the collar, bundled him into a lorry and here he was. Even his wife didn't know his whereabouts. The soldier who had neither washed or shaved for days took the scarf out of his pocket to prove the truth of his story.

With more bluster and confidence the Finn men waited for the second attack. Reinforcements were called for but in their hearts they knew none would come. There were none. When the artillery barrage blasted the road the tanks bounced and trees splintered. Shell holes opened the permafrost and men dug their bodies into rock. A single scream broke the mute and the injured man was pulled towards the rear on a sled leaving his legs on the snow. Aeroplanes circled, dropping their bombs haphazardly for there was no target. Pairs or individuals with skis propped upright. But no formations, no artillery, no supply columns. Just single men with binoculars glued to their eyes. Blasted was that forest, no longer green but weeping.

Again tanks rolled along the road and men scrambled in their tracks. This time the infantry left the roads, struggling through snow banks as the Finnish guns opened. But unused to such conditions made slow progress and with their khaki uniforms spotting the snow, teams of snipers picked them off, first in the legs, then the head, bang, bang, bang. While more tanks burned, their soldiers had bullets drilled into them mercilessly. From a crouched or sitting position they were lanced and left to solidify and statue amongst the trees. Yet how long could this last? With every advance more armour, more shells, wider arcs of infantry attempting to outflank the defenders whose numbers gradually thinned.

At the end of that first day the road lay shredded, the Russians retreating, but learning, gathering information, making ready.

Maarit heard the shells and drone of aeroplanes, she heard the pitter-patter of machine gun fire and the lazy crack of rifles, intermittent but deliberate. Twice she threw herself to the floor and in her heart wished someone was with her. When her name was called it was with some relief that she ran down to the clearing to help haul a man to the warmth of the lodge. Once inside she saw his face streaked with the sweat of pain and the wound to his shoulder. She quickly staunched the flow of blood, picking out shreds and fibres of clothing and dressing the wound as well as she could. His shivering pulled at her nerves and for some reason her teeth grated, but in the warmth, with an extra cape thrown across his back, he recovered, mouthed a thank you and settled back.

'He'll be fine,' she said to the stretcher-bearer as he helped himself to a mug of coffee. 'Why is he in civilian clothes?'

'A reservist…only arrived a couple of days ago. An old chap too by the look of him.'

There were streaks of grey in his beard and an uneasy composure about him as he lay by the bench.

'Should he close his eyes? Should he sleep?' she asked, watching him carefully.

'It will be alright. He's warm enough now and calm. Knocked him backwards that shot, but it's a clean wound and the cold helped stem the flow of blood. He's safe now, as long as we get him some more treatment before gangrene sets in. There's a sled coming soon, should be safe as houses then.'

'Thanks.'

'What's your name?' said the stretcher-bearer.

'Maarit.'

'Well Maarit, what brought you to a place like this?'

'I wanted to help. I wanted to do something.'

He sucked in his breath and took another sup of coffee. 'If I were you,' he considered, 'I would leave at the first opportunity. We held them today, maybe we will tomorrow, but after that… If I was your father I would want you home.'

'I don't know if I have a home.'

'You have a Karelian accent.'

'I live in a village to the north of Lappeenranta and the east of Imatra.'

'Perhaps they have been evacuated, as a precaution, but there has been no break through yet.' He stared at the wall. 'Myself I live in Helsinki, but no matter what, if I had daughter I would want you with me. This is no place for a women.' He looked at Maarit's face. 'I mean no disrespect. But you should go. Today this old boy was a casualty, there are more in other places. You should go, go quickly.'

Maarit tried to change the subject, busying herself with cleaning blood from the floor.

'I can't leave anymore than you,' she smiled. 'Though I feel halfway to my grave.'

'I've said my piece.'

After a few moments of silence there was a shout from outside. A sled arrived to take the old man away. She waved to the stretcher-bearer as he led the pony away, deep in conversation with his friend. She did not see him again.

During the rest of the day small groups of men came and went, drew rations, filled billycans, warmed their hands on the stove and then melted back into the forest. So many faces, so little talk, just bumping into each other as you would in a street or a library. So strange a way of doing things.

When Corporal Hayla made an appearance she noticed him more than the others due to his small stature, barely five foot tall, achingly bashful, nervous smiles, not a word, just spooned some soup into his mouth, cleaned his old-fashioned Swedish rifle, blushed when he said goodbye and disappeared. Later, as the battle of the Kollaa river ground remorselessly on she remembered him and the legend that grew around his exploits. A master marksman, five hundred kills, maybe more. Every morning skiing through the forests alone to hunt Russians then returning. He shot from a sitting position and once within his sights men were doomed. What went through his mind as he aimed? Revenge perhaps, for the farm he was to lose, or simply, as with others, that this is as it was. So great a threat, so renowned his fame, there was eventually a price on his head. Only a bullet through the jaw put an end to his marksmanship. A grim reaper, barely five foot tall, and so, so, so shy.

In the days and weeks that past beyond a Christmas barely noticed more attacks of similar savagery, each day repelled but at great cost, draining the defenders like a tap dripping. Every day more gaps and no replacements, more forces ranged upon the hills and ridges, the skies dense with the wings of iron mosquitoes biting and ripping at earth and flesh. Corporal Hayla they chased as a fox, tracking his ski tracks and strafing thousands upon thousands of bullets in his wake, but the wily animal outwitted them time after time until exhaustion felled him, and a bullet ripped into him.

Then one day, a day of clear skies, cumulus clouds variegating blue there was a pause. Everyone breathed. Men washed and shaved and changed their clothes for the first time in many weeks. Defences were repaired and sentries skimmed the horizon for signs of movement, for flurries of snow, or curling smoke.

A pause.

The enemy, gathering strength, feeding their muscles with steel wheeled in artillery without number, planes beyond measure and men, men countless. Waiting for a signal they were poised as athletes. This time there would be no repulse, no set back. Teeth were bared and the shield wall this time would be smashed by spear and arrow and sling shot. No quarter this day, no pity, no prisoners, these stubborn defenders would pay a price in blood. This day the army would cross the frozen Kollaa river, plant the flag in gravel beds, drive bayonets into the belly of these Finns and then march on. This day so spoke the commander's revenge, would pacify past pains and the Finnish fox would yelp, the hare turn on his heels. So cheered his soldiers, spinning helmets on their rifle barrels, yelling, slaughtering the air with their cries. Go now he said, go now and race as a thunderclap, as a torrent wash away these enemies of the revolution.

The cannon and howitzers checked their ranges, in a deathly synchronisation, stabbing upwards, row after row, battery after battery. Bombers circled, formations formed, the infantry crouched ready for departure. When the signal was given the sky sundered, atoms imploded and rippled, photons span, a cataract of rockets and projectiles thundered into the ground and all life there flew to cover. Seconds later men ran and dug into the earth and behind the barrage crept multitudes of the olive cloaked, stubble-faced, white-eyed.

Pulverised into satellite was the Kollaa river valley, as the moon. Shell holes scraped into granite, blisters of earth shimmered and the abyss of hell opened, fiery, sulphurous hell.

The hunting lodge disintegrated, what was once inside was outside, what was human became demonic. Maarit stood shocked, face puckered by pressure waves and lungs emptied of air. Figures in grey fled past her and a hand pulled at her arm.

'Run!' he shouted. 'For the love of God run!'

She joined them in their flight as the trees shredded of foliage became bamboo and the land surrendered. Then down a bank and through a door, a steel door slammed shut behind them, gasping in a concrete bunker devoid of light, not a pin-prick to illuminate their prison. Once more the door opened and a man bellowing in a voice like acid shrieked at the occupants.

'Do not worry, do not worry, my wife is coming and she is bringing more machine guns.' Out he went and was vaporised.

How that barrage bounced, how tremors travelled from wall to arm to brain. A solid sheet of noise, endless percussion, but now within the skull and Maarit could feel her brain simmer and nose bleed.

She screamed in the dark where no one could hear, and streaked her cheeks with nails where no one could see.

'I want to go home, let me go home!' she screamed. 'I want my Hannu, my Hannu, my Hannu let me go, take me home, take me home, take me home,' she continued until the chant became hypnotic. Blood trickled warm to her lips and tears of rage and humiliation soaked her dress. The bunker was inhabited by ghosts, by spectres who brushed against her but remained invisible.

When the bombs and shells stopped the walls still shook like a tuning fork. An officer found a torch and scanned the faces, eyes wide, staring, he drew a pistol and pointed it at the exit. Others sat against the walls with rifles raised, one man drew a hunting knife and when the final waves of bombardment died, they steadied themselves.

'Take me home,' whispered Maarit, 'take me home.'

She curled in a corner and waited for the grenade to fly through the door.

It did not come.

Nothing happened.

Nervously the officer pushed the steel aside and glanced about him. What he saw defied imagination, a flood of milk and shards of metal, stumps and canes, and elements of skin, shrapnel embedded in the concrete wall. What once was closed was now open; space existed where before there was none. A view, a vantage point where previously the forest grew. As he gazed he saw swarms of Russian infantry milling in the ridge below, unhurried, some resting.

'What's happening?' asked a soldier who followed him.

'I don't know.'

The soldier looked, puzzled. 'Why don't they come?'

Thinking to take advantage of this lull he ordered everybody out. What a sorry sight they must have looked.

'Move,' he said still brandishing a pistol. 'Let's get out of here while we still have a chance.'

Treading carefully through the debris, still hot, they skirted what cover remained, in a single file, seven, eight, nine individuals' ears still ringing and eyes bleary, in a daze they stumbled for a kilometre, maybe two or three and fell into the divisional headquarters. In amazement she saw troops heading back towards the river, the line still held and every man available be he sniper, or cook or clerk or engineer headed back to plug the gaps. The men dispersed and she was left alone, standing, at a loss but unable to move until a medic took her by the elbow and propelled her into a field kitchen.

'Get yourself cleaned up Miss and then report to me at the first aid post.'

In the cook house there was no one else. All had gone towards the river, a stove burbled, tin plates lay stacked on a table. Filling a bowl with water icy cold, she rubbed the blood from her hands, soaked dirt from beneath fingernails, wrung grime from her fingers and then pushed a tide of water as far as the elbows. Hardly daring to study her reflection in a shaving mirror she found on a shelf, she screwed up her face and smeared off the blood and soot. Red vertical welts where nails had scratched in panic now throbbed and a complexion once as

150

porcelain now had a rawness to it. It stung and freckles beneath her eyes winced, and her blood shot eyes were abnormally wide and her yellow hay hair streaked with brown and matted. She threw the water out and filled the bowl again. This time she soaked her hair, plunging it into the bowl, wringing, plunging, wringing, tying it back but more awake now, more human. As to her dress, well, she could do nothing about that, grease layered in fold after fold, it was stiff with dirt.

She sought out the medic and she saw his look of distaste.

'Are there wounded?'

'No sister. They have been evacuated, though more will come no doubt. I want you to see to the boys over there.'

He pointed to a large tent near the perimeter.

What she found in there caused grief to overwhelm her. She dropped to her knees beside the bodies of the four young men she found lying on the ground. Four young men who had hours before been living, breathing sons of God, made in his own image but now they lay still. Gentle Maarit closed their eyes, took off their boots. She emptied pockets and placed identity discs in a bag. Their tunics she buttoned up, hair she brushed, faces she cleaned with a towel. So sorrowful it was she could barely continue. We Finns, she thought, smile without smiling and cry without tears and grieve without comfort. Lips she touched. With deep love she wrapped the bodies in blankets as a mother or sister. With love she cared for them, masked their wounds, wiped their brows, placed their hands across their chests. As the stretcher-bearers placed the coffins outside and the chaplain struggled through the mire she embraced them as a mother or sister would, loved them as a mother or sister. So she wept. So her tears did flow and fall upon the blanket's hem.

'Fear not,' she said, 'on Good Friday when the earth trembles and the rocks split then your graves will open.'

'Sleep well my brothers,' she said, 'for the sun will dance once more upon your face on Easter morning.'

She tore herself away and reported back to the medic.

'What should I do now?'

'Get what rest you can,' he said matter of factly. 'The Colonel says you are to leave, to go home.' He paused for a moment. 'Follow the track south and west. There will be others, you will not be alone. Try to walk within the shelter of the trees, put on a camouflage cape and you should be safe enough. Don't allow yourself to be distracted. You must look after yourself now and…you will make it I'm sure.'

With that he turned away.

Maarit glanced once more over her shoulder to the tent, swept the hair from her face and decided there and then to set off for home. She did not bother with a cape, merely wrapped her coat tightly around her back, stuffed rags into her boots and began the long trek. In the week she travelled she hardly ate or slept. In a coma, almost stupefied, she walked step by step, sometimes for awhile in a truck, sometimes in the back of a cart or sled she inched towards home, to the village quartered by roads, to the station and timber mill, to the swinging hill and the Saimaa canal silvered by ice.

The journey with its many adventures is another tale and the arrival another tale too.

Chapter 10

The cottage hospital in Hämeenlinna had always been a source of pride for the inhabitants. It was compact and neat. Sparse, but a model of cleanliness. Only two wards with a few beds in each. One for men and one for women. It was not a place of luxury but in its way it exuded an air of quiet efficiency.

Merja was in the second of these wards, in a steel bed far too big for her tiny frame. She looked like a doll. The doctor was examining her. Looking into her eyes, lifting her head, checking her heart beat with a stethoscope. Merja's response alternated between a feeble passivity and defiance. It was obvious this was serious.

When he spoke with her mother it was in a gentle way, softly, almost weary. He combed his grey hair across his face and never took his gaze away from the girl in the bed.

'We have to get her temperature down. This we must do first.' A small electric fan already operated on the bedside table. A wet cloth lay across her brow. A saline drip snaked into her arm. From time to time a nurse came round and bathed her with a towel soaked in ice water but Merja found this distressing, she twisted and turned, and shrieked like a mouse almost before falling back exhausted in a restless sleep. Her skin was red and mottled, hair matted with perspiration.

You can imagine how her mother felt sitting by the bed, whispering encouragement.

'Do you know what it is?'

'I have my suspicions. She has a high temperature, she is in some discomfort when she moves.' Rubbing his chin he touched Merja's arm with his finger. 'When did this begin? When did she start to complain about feeling unwell?'

'Merja never complains doctor. She doesn't talk much...sometimes it's difficult to get through to her.'

'Has this always been the case?'

'Since she was a baby. She has always been withdrawn. Hannu can talk to her, she responds to him.'

'Hannu is you son?'

'Yes. He is at the front. I don't know where and of course we have been evacuated since then. He is unaware of all this. I don't want to trouble him, he has enough to deal with...this is serious isn't it.'

'I'm afraid so. There's no denying it.'

She sobbed quietly inside, sank into the chair and looked in despair at her daughter.

'It is serious...but not hopeless, not yet. You must give me some more information Mrs Juutalainen. When did this start, when did you notice something was wrong.'

She searched her memory.

'A week ago,' she said. 'We were at home in the village. She was even quieter than usual, and irritable. Usually she is no trouble, you hardly notice her but nothing was pleasing and she couldn't settle. I put it down to the upheaval of Hannu going away and packing things up. I couldn't explain what was happening; she saw all this disruption and sensed the anxiety, saw people upset. We left two days ago, in the morning with virtually nothing. We were packed on a train in the cold, hardly room to move and once came under attack and ran into the forest. It was frightening for a girl of Merja's age and disposition.'

'When did the symptoms begin,' he said patiently.

'There were signs, in the cabin before we left, looking back there were signs, but I missed them, in the tumult with so much worry I placed her to the back of my mind and I missed them.

She had a temperature, a cough, she was drowsy and slept a lot. I had to carry her to the station, part of the way at least.'

'Did she complain of a headache?'

'No...as I said Merja never complains. If something is wrong you have to pick it up in other ways. But in the train I could tell she was not well, as time progressed she became worse and I prayed for the journey to end.'

'When did the sickness begin?'

'Here. In the hospital for the first time.'

A nurse walked across the ward, turned in their direction and gave a shy smile.

'Are you going to tell me what it is doctor?'

He paused.

'I can tell you what I think it is. You must understand there is a combination of symptoms. The temperature and restlessness could be the result of almost anything – a virus, a bacterial infection – especially if Merja's immune system is low. In winter confined indoors, with no fresh air, with a lack of food, crammed together with others, the disruption. None of this helps. You can expect a reaction.'

'But there is more to it, isn't there?'

'Well yes. If it was merely as I've described a good rest would put things right. But as you say there is more to it. She has a high temperature, her eyes turn away from the light, I've checked and this is always so.' He looked at Merja again. 'You may have seen me lifting her head. Her neck is stiff, it resists the pressure of my arm...and she is sinking into delirium. She is not aware. I'm afraid I've seen this before.'

'It's meningitis isn't it?'

'I believe so. I don't think it can be anything else. I'm so sorry.'

A tidal wave ground through her body, and close to collapse she wrapped Merja's hand within her own. It burned, burned with a ferocity that frightened the mother.

The nurse came and wiped her down again.

'But how can it be so?'

'It is an infection, sometimes carried in droplets of water vapour. We breathe out, we cough, we sneeze. Some research indicates that we carry the seeds of it within us, in some it develops, in some it does not. Children are particularly susceptible to it. There is really nothing you could have done to prevent it. There is no blame.'

'But if I had taken more notice.'

'What would you have done? What could you have done?'

She began to struggle for breath.

'What now?'

'We will try to stabilise her. We must get her temperature down. This is possible, we have good staff here and we will do our best. We can make her comfortable, ease the pain a little and then it is a matter of waiting. Do you have anyone with you? Your husband perhaps?'

'Don't talk to me of husbands,' she said bitterly. 'Tuija, my daughter-in-law came with us. I left her at the church. I don't even know where we are.'

'Mrs Juutalainen,' said the doctor kindly, 'there is nothing you can do here. Merja is sleeping. We will continue to care for her. Go and rest, speak with your daughter-in-law. Prepare a place for her.'

Reluctantly, with a final look at Merja in the bed, she left the hospital and re-traced her steps through the market square, to the church.

The path had been cleared of snow and piled to the sides. A few carts lay propped against the walls. An elderly police volunteer opened the door for her and once inside it was obvious that most people had already been moved. There were members of the Lotta Svard milling around but no sign of Tuija. She explained who she was looking for and was directed to a desk near the vestry.

'I came with my daughter-in-law two days ago, but there is no sign of her.'

The strain on her face must have been obvious, for the man behind the desk looked though a sheaf of papers immediately.

She gave as many details as possible and he quietly, patiently, explained.

'Don't worry, madam. The majority of people have been moved to a series of holding stations. The church was felt to be too vulnerable to air attack, being in the centre of town.'

'Is it far? My child is in hospital, she is very ill.'

'I'm sorry to hear that...but it is not far, a plywood factory, about a mile west of here. Would you like me to escort you?'

'No, no thank you sir. The fresh air will do me good, and I have thoughts to carry.'

'God Bless,' he said gently

'God Bless,' she replied.

The road churned through a typical winter landscape. Negative, black, white, grey, sepia. How the heart yearned for colour in these bleak days, when the body is confined and there is nothing to stimulate the eyes. Reds, or yellows or summer greens, turquoise, the blue of a dragonfly's wings, the spectrum-sided trout, the amber of bonfires. How the heart yearned for respite. You are never burdened with more than you can carry, so the pastor always said. How did he know? Where was he, he and his bell, nowhere when you needed him.

The plywood factory was crowded, hardly a space remaining. Many of the faces she recognised and some came to console for they had heard of her misfortunes. More were weeping in the solitude of their hearts. News from the front had arrived and some of the boys had fallen, Tilda had lost her two boys, both of them, dear God how much more, she wept and rocked and sank into the floor. Rapidly she aged and fell into the arms of Jesus some years later. But there were others, and some stood with the anxiety of unknowing.

She caught sight of Tuija in the corner and they embraced.

'Come rest mother. I have reserved a space for us here in the corner. It is not much but it is better to rest on plywood than concrete. We are out of the wind here and the general commotion.' She continued to talk, almost as if she dared not pause and ask for news. 'Our things are stashed safely and the people say we are to be billeted on farms in this district. We will be able to make a home of sorts.' Then she asked.

'How is Merja?'

Mother shook her head and was crisp in response. She didn't want to falter or let the flood gates open. This room swam and heaved with sadness. Anxiety flicked the tongue and no matter how many neighbours gathered together such was the depth of displacement that solace could not be found. People were coming and going all the time, and when the door opened the cold wind blasted through. It was bitter. This place would live long in the memory.

'It is not so good,' she replied at last. 'When I left she seemed more settled. She is in the hands of God as are we all. I will go back soon but first I need to wash and change. It is humiliating to wear the same clothes for so long.'

Tuija strung blankets from the rafters to create a screen while mother washed and changed and tied back her hair. She ate bread and soup and coffee provided by the municipality. She sat on the leather chest and sank into the haziness, the unreality of their situation.

She picked up Merja's doll and put it in her pocket. If Merja wakes, she will want this, and the 'if' caught in her throat and travelled to the tear ducts. She held herself, not wishing to add to the secret sobs of the room. She had pride and her grief would be managed in the dark, where no one could see.

'Is there any news of Hannu?'

'Some,' responded Tuija, 'some rumours that he and others had been moved north, no one knows why. They were on the Isthmus, near the Savanto waterway and holding fast. We are holding them mother, there is still hope. Help will come soon.'

'How long can we hold? What help will come? But there is no other news?'

'None,' explained Tuija. 'I know Harri is still with him and well…good news is no news. Have you heard about some of our neighbours' boys?'

'Some,' she replied but did not say more.

In her thoughts she wished that Hannu was here. He would be a grand support. If anyone could talk Merja round it was him. But determined she was that he should not hear of this, not yet. His duty was to himself. To make sure that he came back home safe and well.

'I will return to the hospital this evening,' she said decidedly.

'I will come with you.'

'No...no stay here daughter. Look after our things, we will need them. Make sure the place we are to go to is clean and decent, and not too far. Do this for us.'

*

Inside Merja's head there was a battle raging. The skull pressed in on all sides and the optic nerves shot bolts from the eyes to the brain which was squeezed and pinched. It was so hot, molten. Why was it so hot and what was that liquid dripping, drip, drip, drip, from the back of her head down her spine? It tingled and glistened, even though her eyes were closed and she could not see she knew it was so. It was the darkness which truly frightened her. This is when she squirmed and called out. It descended like fog, as if in water spreading and circulating in wisps until what once was white was black. A tunnel or cavern closing around her. No matter how fast she ran the walls moved faster and never an opening. The ceiling dropped lower and lower until at first she bent double, them crouched, then lay flat until it enveloped her whole and the taste of it in her mouth made her sick, again and again without end until weakness, an inability to move or breathe encountered her soul with a bump. She did not know where she was. Surely her mother would come soon and take her away from this place. But she was nowhere to be seen. When the coiled red serpent caught the retina she was truly terrified. Crimson red, a worm unsaddled with black dagger teeth and rasping breath wheeling towards her and the jaws opened and bit into her head and the air stale as phosphorus filled her lungs until she vomited and drowned for still she could not move.

*

Even in the soft light of the ward, the nurse on duty could tell that something was wrong. She rang the bell for assistance and together they threw the blankets off her body and saw the little girl saturated, soaked to the skin and red raw. She writhed and screamed without sound, gasped for air, hair tangled and brow beaded. With real urgency they squeezed ice cold water on to her from towels, and wiped away the moisture and fanned her and opened the window and shuddered as freezing air entered the ward. With soothing words and quiet appeals they whispered to the little evacuee so small for her age, so thin, so lost. They pleaded with her, begged, threatened, cajoled.

When the gentle doctor came, he gazed and parted his grey hair with his fingers.

'Shall we send for her mother?' the younger nurse asked.

He waited and watched.

'No, not yet.'

'What more can we do?'

'Nothing more.'

'Is there any hope?'

'Not much,' he replied before turning and walking away.

When mother returned a few hours later the window was closed and a new sheet placed upon the bed. She sat on a chair and tucked Merja's doll beneath her arm. Not a muscle did she move nor complaint utter. Motionless she was in her guardianship.

The doctor called her immediately into his room and explained in that tired voice of his, that in her absence there had been a crisis, that they thought they had lost her. The two nurses on duty had now gone home, upset naturally, but she was welcome to stay the night if she so wished. Mother thanked the doctor and took up her station on the hard wood chair in the soft light and silence of the ward.

*

We were camped inside the road block in the forests of Suomussalmi. Hannu sensed something was wrong. A voice spoke to him but a storm was raging and the words were difficult to decipher. A female tone, a young girl's, a woman's voice splintered in the wind which tore through the encampment with stunning ferocity. There was no visibility, a whiteout, and pounding in the ears like a drum beating. They all sank low inside and covered themselves with whatever they could find. For hours it raged and for hours Hannu struggled with anxiety and felt the sickness return. Ice spears rattled across the surface and pinged into the burned-out tanks that formed the barricade, tumbling, blasting holes. Anything light or fragile, anything not riveted to the earth, was dentrified by the force of it. An angry tirade of nature turning blood to lanolin. When it burned out the defenders emerged from the avalanche brushing snow from hood and cape and weapon, stunned, anaesthetised, blinking at a scene transformed. Banks of snow twenty feet high, slopes, ridges and a chequerboard sky, white, black, grey rested on the canopies of trees with all vegetation stripped away. Stark branches sunk in snow and a crown of magenta and lime. It appeared that the sky was leaving, magnetised by the storm and sweeping upwards. An atmosphere sparse and clean, rigid as pancake ice with the fingers of earth and sky clasped together. Only then did I remember that Christmas had gone and mentally tried to work out the date. There was a roll call and some discussion amongst the officers about whether we should leave or stay.

Such was the pounding we had received I found it difficult to remember where we were, or why. Were we in another country? What was this place with its mysterious transformations and statues and sculpture? Was this the holy land? Were these towers and minarets and cupolas the skyline of Bethlehem? How did we come to be here? Such puzzling lasted some time and I could tell the others were equally amazed. There was a meandering amongst us. Fires were lit, some men began to shovel away the snow and think about how we might get back to our lines if we had to.

Then with his sharp eyes Simo noticed some movement on the edge of his vision. I strained my eyes but could see nothing. Others stopped working…and there it was, a disturbance. Activity of some sort, soundwaves carried through the echo chamber. Then up went the cry.

'Stand to…stand to.'

There was scrambling for machine guns and ammunition, fumbling with frozen hands for grenades, calculating ranges and lines of fire. On they came in a charge with screams and battle cries, onwards. And then I saw the blue of their coats, scales shimmering, claws fanned out and that curious lop-sided run of lizards, thousands, thousands in lines without end, tongues flicking, prehistoric, primeval faster and faster they came. I opened fire and saw the blood spurt out of their bodies, tails ripping, but nothing seemed to hold them back. Grenades I threw, ammunition clips swapped and more bursts, sporadic, targeted, personal and when I saw the giant leap, the king of lizards squealing mouth opened, exposed, my reflexes took over and I smashed his skull with my rifle butt again and again punching and gouging at the flesh until the blue scales covered my hands and glistened. By the time we had beaten them back my lahti had fallen to the ground, red hot. It sizzled in the snow. I was breathless. Fingers clenched, eyes wide.

So we repelled them again. This Moorish scene, Levantine almost for their bodies had the look of the Middle East about them. A touch of surprise. So little chance to even reach our barricades in drifts so deep without snow shoes or skis. So brave and pointless, wading through snow to the waist. What chance. Why?

There was nothing more we could do. The road was well and truly blocked for the time being and the column halted. The white-shawled maiden wrapped her arms around us and led us back wearily for rest.

*

Merja lay calmly all night. Mother slept intermittently. The hands of the clock traversed the face and all manner of dreams occupied the minds of the patients in the ward, though Merja was the only child. There were rumours that wounded would soon arrive from the front, more beds were made ready but no one came.

Tuija arrived and stayed for a time. They now had a place to live, a nice place, comfortable. When she left the hospital in the early morning she gave way to a terrible outburst of grief, crying, exclaiming, brandishing words to the almighty. When the air raid siren went off it only added tortures to her frayed nerves and it was a lonely walk back to the room they would call home, for a time at least.

Meanwhile in the routine of the ward nurses came and took temperatures, checked the pulse, towelled her down. Through it all Merja submitted weakly, unaware. Was there reason to hope? Any at all? Yes the pulse is strong, the temperature had not risen, it had stabilised at least and the little girl did not seem to be so much discomforted.

'How would I ever get on without you,' whispered the mother. 'So much travail in this world. Hannu gone for a soldier and Tuija to care for. Whatever next? Alone we are born and alone we die, so help me God.'

By the end of the third day the mother was dead beat. Her hair was lank and appearance neglectful. She considered meeting with Tuija to inspect the new room but found it difficult to leave the bedside. Somehow she knew that as long as she was there, Merja would be safe, that no harm would come to her, but the minute she left…well that was another matter. But she needed fresh air and stepped out of the hospital in the quiet of the evening. Everything was so unfamiliar. This was the furthest away from home she had ever been. To Viipuri once or twice but never beyond the borders of Karelia. What need was there? A few figures muffled against cold walked the pavements, trying to grip the icy surface as they walked. Across the market square again, all vision monochrome and the blackout rigorously enforced. To the church from where she had carried her child so fearfully. It was deserted now. The heavy oak door locked and bolted. She could make out the cream-coloured walls, the portico, the leaded dome but all became shadow as clouds drifted across the moon. She remembered the picture beyond the altar, but what it depicted she could not tell. There was the scent of candle smoke and beeswax and then the damp aroma of unwashed, displaced bodies, a kind of purification and all who mustered there were glad to leave. How long ago it all seemed.

A call roused her. Mrs Juutalainen, Mrs Juutalainen! Come quickly. And now it was confirmed that she should never have left that bedside, why ever was she dawdling in this town, in a trance, how ridiculous. She ran across the square, slipped and fell, ran, slipped and fell again grazing her knee and scraping her elbow on the frozen ground. It was an effort and she raced up the stairs never caring who she disturbed or woke.

She was directed to the doctor's office but could see a group of nurses round Merja's bed. A screen was pulled around. The doctor asked her to wait, he would be back soon. There would be nothing she could do as yet. Too tired and frightened to protest she slumped into a chair, knocking the back of her head against the wall. If she had only known that this scene had come to Hannu in his nightmares where the hag, aged and withered had crossed his path. This was the final battle she thought, the ending, in this ward for no-hopers and incurables, in this antiseptic corridor where mothers waited with complexions of marzipan, unable to save or comfort. Where hope is fearless and corrosive as battery acid. So this is where it had to be.

A few minutes later she was summoned. She drew what reserves of courage remained and sank onto the bottom of the bed. The nurses left her. Only the doctor stayed, seated in the chair she once considered her personal property.

'We called you back because there has been a new development.'

'What is it?'

'You have to remember that Merja's condition is complex. What I am about to say I say hesitantly. Perhaps I should not say it at all.' He paused and looked at his watch. 'Half an hour ago, when we took her temperature, we noticed that it had fallen a good deal. It is not normal but it is on the way. One of the nurses thinks that Merja has opened her eyes, fleetingly, and then closed them again. Now I have been watching since then, it is clear to me there are signs that perhaps the infection is easing. I have not seen her eyes open. But against my better judgement, and my experience, there is a slither of hope.'

The mother pushed her hands to her face and wept silently.

'You must watch. Talk to her. If she does awaken do not disturb her, display no emotion, stay your hand. At best she will be confused, at worst she may not know you at all. She is weak, so weak and that is a concern to me, there has been no nourishment for a long time. She may have dysfunction of the heart or liver or kidneys, such things are common. There is more you have to understand, Mrs Juutalalainen, and I truly wish that you could have someone here to share your burden but I would not be fulfilling my duty if I did not inform you.'

'What are you trying to say?'

'There will inevitably be complications. This illness causes swelling of the brain. It is a serious condition, with a high mortality rate. For those lucky enough to survive there is very often brain damage, visual problems, deafness, some sort of emotional instability is not unusual.'

'All I ask is that she lives doctor, that's all I ask,' she said stroking Merja's hair.

The doctor smiled. 'As you say. At these times small mercies.'

The vigil continued without pause, without change. Tuija made another appearance but her fussing began to irritate so she sent her away on an errand.

The nurses glided through rooms and the men's ward was emptied of patients ready to receive wounded from the Kollaa river. Already they were on their way.

For the first time she made plans, plans for the future. She designed meals and bedrooms, made clothes and considered a belated Christmas present, some little treats. All the while she sat in her chair, it soothed her mind. The stories she would read and the songs she would sing and the games she would play, and the lessons she would give...and one day, with a sob, one day they might be able to go home, and Hannu would walk through the door and all would be well. Such thoughts as these are precious commodities.

The first thing Merja noticed was a rectangular window high on the wall of her cell. Shafts of light penetrated the darkness, exposing a tiny yellow flower which must have grown somehow in the gloom. She touched it, pollen coated her fingers and the scent it produced filled her nostrils. Too tired to stir she gorged her eyes on sunlight surrendering to the warm rays on her arms. Every muscle was stiff, as if her body had been pinned down with ropes and manacles, but she began to forget about the horrifying black, the paralysis, the serpent red, the despair penetrating every sinew of her young soul. Puffs of cloud floated across the blue sky and more and more light flooded into the room. A doll flopped into her lap and a glass of water appeared on a table by her side. Strange she had not noticed it before. Thirstily she drank and it revived her. She devoured the eruption of another day...and through the grating flew a feather, a common dove's feather, pristine white. She cradled it in her arms.

Clambering to her feet she opened the door but curiously, though old, it did not squeak, nor did her foot falls echo on the stone steps. She skipped to the bed in a room bedimmed by memory and snuggled beneath clean sheets. When she looked up this time there was no cell, no grating, but the face of her mother, older now, in some pain, and she saw her wipe away some tears and smile and shake her arm and utter words she could not hear, and the man beside her moved his lips but no words came.

Chapter 11

The new year we spent encamped at Suuomussalmi. If anything the temperatures fell even lower, twenty or thirty degrees below freezing. Blizzards every other day, drifts of snow taller than a man.

Desperate conditions.

We coped as best we could, in tents heated by lamps, with hot soup, a sauna even. We were attuned to these conditions, it was our natural environment, but for the Russians stranded in a twenty mile snake of vehicles on the road it was a different matter. They were paralysed, chained together bumper to bumper; trapped. No advance and no retreat. No escape through the clawing forest surrounding them. The 44th Division was well and truly ensnared. Frostbite, fear and hunger and homesickness enfeebled their troops but any pity from our hearts had for the most part evaporated.

In desperation there was an attack across frozen lakes from the 163rd in an attempt to relieve their comrades on the road but they were mowed down in their thousands and we watched, as if in a huge, open-air cinema, the struggle through snow which glued their progress and hardly a shot could they fire in defence. All hope utterly lost they threw away their weapons and ran. For weeks we found them wandering, disorientated, more beast than man in forests that must have seemed endless to them, a hellish maze shifting constantly and drawing them ever nearer to a ravenous mouth. Like forget-me-nots they were, diadems on a glassy sea without thought or direction, leaderless and stumbling until they fell and froze. When we walked amongst them, salvaging equipment, it was as if we walked through some grotesque sculpture park for they froze in twisted dimensions like wax works, fingers clawing the air, arms raised, grins fixed, hair solid to the skull and all played out beneath a sinister amber light layering the horizon. Like primitive plants, cycads, they grew across the ice, and in spring when the thaw came they would slip into the water and be gone. How could this be? How could we farmboys wander between them in silence exchanging no word?

Alas our work was not complete. Any risk of breakout had to be eliminated. It was a simple matter of survival. We were few in number so attacks consisted of a series of local encircling movements. At a gap in the column an attack group would explode with charges and grenades and bursts of automatic fire, panicking defenders into flight. Those who fled into the forests were dispatched by knife or bayonet. They ran into us blind, almost knocked us over in their haste, thudding into our chests with their elbows. Those who remained were crushed by their own tanks, bones crunched and then trapped by barriers of logs and barbed wire in a circle without breech. Such was the confusion we knew them only by their green-peaked hats. If cannon was available they were obliterated into sores, if not, ski patrols watched until they froze to death within the barricades. Once trapped there was no hope, no relief, no food, no warmth, no light. The ravens circled and the light went out of their eyes. In this way the snake was chopped into pieces from head to tail. What a monstrous image we conjured and it stays with me still. That journey back to camp, shoulder to shoulder, skis ripping the cloth haunts my waking, we were becoming mute by then, almost sub-human and immune to suffering.

In the second week of January we were summoned to a briefing and informed that the column on the Raate road had to be destroyed completely, too many men were tied down carving it piecemeal. There had to be a decisive strike. Clearly some thought had already gone into this. We were informed that a great 'motti' would be created. In the language of foresters this is a stack of timber left by the axeman to be collected at a later time. In the new language, it meant the creation of an enemy enclave with no hope of escape or redemption. A knot of soldiers surrounded. This we had done many times in smaller fashion but now we understood that vast numbers of Russian men and equipment were trapped in a gigantic road block. Unable to move they had dug in, reinforced their defences and turned the barrels of their tanks and artillery outwards in a giant circle. Stores of ammunition were guarded in the centre but no food, no shelter, no petrol. This was a carbuncle they said and we were to root it out of the earth. A carcinogenic compound spreading disease.

We mustered in the great forests. In ones and twos, in groups and companies, and from a distance, the watchers watched and the imprisoned felt our presence. Soon many hundreds crouched in snow banks and saw through the lenses of binoculars the insect-like encroachments of the enemy, huddles of calcium crossing and re-crossing the circle with little purpose. In darkness their campfires glowed and the black outlines of their bodies silhouetted murderously against that background. How they whispered with their fingers in the flames and backs raw. How many numberless individuals slumped into the embers when a sniper's bullet tore open the back of their head. And how hurriedly were the fires extinguished adding to the misery of that place.

For a day and night we watched, noting layouts and strong points and routines. As a composition the motti reminded me of a sunflower, but colourless, opaque. At the centre were the seeds, an assortment of vehicles and baggage and empty ammunition cases. Horses were tethered, coated in ice crystals, vapour rising from their flanks and ribs exposed. No fodder and no respite. The gun barrels were the petals, periodically spouting fire, and stems, trails of barbed wire. A flower grimacing against a grievous wind and whitening as the day passed. Aeroplanes circled like bees and dropped their packages of pollen into the trees. Why did they remain? That was the puzzle. Why was more not done to rescue them? From our vantage point we saw everything and made our preparations, while remaining ourselves invisible. When I glanced to my left I saw Harri and Simo resting on their ski poles, frost on their eyes. It was a tense time, this waiting. But what was it like in the motti?

It is the end of our confinement, surely this cannot go on, how much more can men endure? God himself weeps for us, his tears fall as flakes upon my head. So many races here huddled in great coats that wither into the skin. We cannot control our shivering or the twitching of fingers ossified by cold, numbed to uselessness. Yet we wait for relief that does not come. Our aeroplanes swan above but deliver nothing, they bomb and strafe the forest to no effect for the enemy are ethereal, silken threads never snapping. For all my time in this god forsaken territory I have never seen a Finn man, not one, not even a shadow. In my dreams I disbelieve in their existence, it is an official plot to drive us out of our minds. These are tricks, mind games, ploys of the party to weaken our resolve and prove our insignificance. Well in that at least they have succeeded.

We do not see but hear them calling. 'Go home!' they shout 'go home!' If only we could. Home – what is that place of endearment? Another trick to play on men weak with deprivation. Best not to think about it. No we do not hear the Finn men but in their calls, as a crow caws or an eagle shrieks. The crack of a rifle bullet, the single mortar on the field kitchen, the targeting of campfires. Anything to bleed us of warmth and food and sleep. Well, they too have succeeded. In this corral there is no food or warmth and a sleep where men do not awake is the only blessing. Only the frantic spluttering of the radio operators breaks this silence, only the whistle of the wind and the turning of the rumour mill. At first we were told we could not retreat. Not a step backwards for the red army – nor forwards. This capacity for suffering, this docility in the jaws of monstrous injustice, is so tightly woven within our psyche that a pickaxe cannot crack it open. No, no retreat. No decisions made without the approval of the commissars, who will not approve for fear of the consequences. Then we hear the order for a strategic withdrawal has been given, whatever that means. First, so it goes, the horses will be driven onto the eastern ice to explode the mines scattered there, to create a path through which we will charge bayonets fixed and war cry in our throats. I hope not. In civilian life I am a waggoner and love my horses, care for them tenderly, they are children to me and it sparks my anger to see them ill-treated. Yet so much ill-intentioned cruelty have I witnessed in this war towards them. Such mute bewilderment in their eyes. 'Why do you do this?' I hear them say. 'Have I not served you well? There is no fodder, so like us they starve, except we slice them up alive and push their sticky flesh into our mouths and crawl into their bellies red for any glimmer of warmth. Like cavemen are we. We have regressed a million years. So now we are to drive these poor, suffering creatures across the mine field and step across the mutilations to save our own worthless skins.

So here I sit in what will be known as the great motti. The geometric prison. Every article of clothing I possess is wrapped around me yet still my back is a slab of ice. My stomach groans in emptiness. A square of hard tack yesterday was all I consumed, and that broke what remained of my teeth and caused my intestines to squirm. Even if supplies arrived my gums are sand and drain into my throat. I could eat nothing. I thirst for water but there is none. I yearn sleep but dare not. How feeble are a man's needs and how little satisfied. Crouched on my barrel (empty of course) in the shadow of an anti-aircraft gun I sometimes hear the cow bells of my native village and it soothes me much. I see vast heathlands stretching ahead, luxuriant tangles of vegetation traversed by black ants and the wriggle of earth worms disturbed by the wheels of my cart. But it is better not to think of home, we will never see it again, it will only deflate our spirits. So here I remain in the motti, in the location of my choosing beneath the anti-aircraft gun, on my barrel, lonely.

But let me tell you about my feet! Never did I consider I would speak those words. Old men talk about their feet, it is the conversation of the decrepit conversing with grasshoppers. But mine have a curious obsession for me. Ever since the feeling left them, ever since they ceased to respond to my brain's pleading I have watched them puff and turn to black, yes black as the ace of spades, and now the pain is devilish and many times in my musings I have considered amputation. I even held a butcher's cleaver in my hand but had not the courage to do the deed. Now pain sears my legs and I cannot move, for they are frozen to the ground, lumps of dead meat. So as I hear the whinnying of horses on the eastern edge I chuckle to myself. When the order comes, if the order comes, to break out, I cannot move, no matter how coarse or violent the incentives and I will be left behind.

But then what loss am I? A wastrel too fond of barley wine and shy of work. A grain of sand, a single example of times countless multitudes gone to dust. Unnoticed without leaving a mark.

An ill feeling I had that day. In the sky against the black outlines of fir trees 'sun dogs' hung like candles, false suns, mockeries of sunlight refracted by clouds of ice crystals and then halos, delicate circlets of light crowning the ridge. It sent shivers through me and caused all manner of whisperings through the forest as men made their final preparations for the attack. A bad omen, no doubt about it, a flesh tingling manifestation that went deep within me. I liken it to a piano playing inside my head, an obscure sonata, tunelessly hooking into my brain until its removal becomes impossible. A sibilant hissing, a whistle through reeds. So many times has this happened and much misfortune foretold. Merja I saw and the piano played on and the ivory keys tinkled and the sun dogs burst.

Something stirred in the motti. Unusual activity soon identified by our watchers. So subtle had been our approach that we still remained invisible to the Russians but something was stinging them into action. We strained ears for their orders and saw a sudden movement of men to the eastern side, then whoops and hollering and a stream of horses jumping the barricades into the mine field. First one blew into red pulp and its head skimmed across the surface detached, then another and another, thud, splash, panic-stricken horses slithering and slipping, rising, rearing, running on, bursting with a red thud. You would think that men with our experience of life's brutalities would be immune to such sights, but most of us were country folk and this act, the baseness of it and the jeering from the barricades tugged our heart strings. Simo in particular was disturbed. He spat his tobacco on to the snow and shuffled uneasily. Whatever we were doing we stopped, transfixed by this new drama.

As the Russians massed, a single mortar crashed into them, and those that remained dispersed into the motti again. Each to their own spot. What mentality was this? We were constantly bemused by these events, well beyond the understanding of us simple folk.

One horse lay on the ice.

Undead.

Grievously wounded but still living and thrashing about, moaning and screaming into the still air until all our nerves were shattered and many begged to be allowed to put it out of its misery, but the officers were clear, we must remain hidden until nightfall. We must put up with it. But after so many hours of this – well what can I say. I saw Simo pull his coat tight about him and march towards the ice.

'Where are you going?' I called. 'Come back.'

But he did not answer, he walked straight through the trees and onto the ice in full view of our officers who steamed with rage, and the Russians, who surely could see him so close to the guns of their defences. Any moment I expected a shot. I expected to see him fall to the ground. But none came. One step then another. I saw him stand above the horse's head, saw him utter some word of comfort and then put a bullet into him. Calmly he turned and walked away with his back exposed to the Russians daring them to shoot. It was almost a provocation and the tension was unbearable.

Harri whispered. 'The old fool, this will be the end of him,' and then he tugged my sleeve and pointed to the motti to the western edge where teams of twos and threes were slipping inside while the world and his wife watched the drama of the ice.

'Go!' yelled one of the officers 'Go now!'

Down the slopes we poured and into the motti. Already muffled explosions echoed along the machinery and equipment. The first teams in were busy with bayonet and Mauser, we followed, and those Russians at the Eastern extreme still watching the ice turned and screamed as if that was sufficient to frighten us away. Some ran towards us, where we felled them with bursts of machine gun fire and axes and hunting knives, our pistols swung right and left and they fell as corn. As they fell we kicked and trampled them under foot. There was no pity in our attack, no quarter.

'No prisoners!' yelled the officers, hoarse with rage and battle fury. 'No prisoners…leave no one alive.'

From the centre, batteries of flak opened, bullet and shell and tracer illuminating the sky but to no purpose, a dragon of noise with tongue of fire rumbling the ground and through it all we charged oblivious, the arm of God himself could not have held us back as we targeted radio sets, command posts, gun pits, ammunition stores, field kitchens, anything of value and then anything with a breath of life within it. So appalling was the furnace, so like the fires of hell, I fancied sulphur crept into my nostrils and the demon dead were cloven hooved and it was a duty to do this terrible, terrible, thing which overwhelmed us one and all. Into a dug out ran I, lahti in one hand and bayonet in the other and there an officer sat beside a vat of sausages and with the bayonet I stuck him, deep within the stomach, with a mighty thrust I carved him, in the fiery glow my talon ripped, until the firing ended and the noise subsided until he rolled into the corner, there beside his comrades dead already, some with sausages between their lips a'mocking.

Then the pistol shots rang out in isolation, one, one, one. Some escaped into the forest, some were unaccounted. One I noticed seated on a barrel with his feet frozen to the floor and throat dripping blood. Then it was I sank unto the ground and held my heart a-pounding in my chest and wiped my brow and gasped for air. From the distance I heard a cheer and saw the men of our army wandering stupefied though the camp, some in camouflage whites, some Finnish greys in helmets or fur caps.

Then it was that Simo saw me, then it was he beckoned and I followed where he leaned against a tank track.

'Seen anything like this before boy?'

'No,' I answered.

'Pray you never see its like again.'

*

Once the action was over we counted 5,000 bodies, such was the ferocity of our assault. Even then our superiors were not satisfied; some had escaped. But without skis and disorientated, blind, and surrounded, what chance did they have? The next day orders were issued to hunt then down. In teams of three we set about scouring the forests, following tracks as best we could and hunting them down. One man held a powerful flashlight and shone it directly into the eyes of our fugitives, who like rabbits froze and were mown down by bursts of machine gun fire. As time passed the mood softened and prisoners were gradually brought in bedraggled and bewildered. Some terrified, some stubborn, but all in poor physical shape. There were reports that some were punched and kicked, others taunted, but the officers put an end to such distasteful occurrences and generally they were fed, clothed, sent to holding camps. On interrogation it was clear they were ill-trained and ill-equipped and it was difficult not to feel sorry for them. But more disturbing still were indications that more men, more divisions, were crossing the border, an endless stream of troops, artillery, equipment, aeroplanes, tanks. There was no end, and we of the Finnish army grew increasingly weary, short of every conceivable article, desperate for rest and reinforcements, but there were none. Rumours too circulated that as winter grew on, as February dawned, events in other sectors were going badly, strong points were pressured and overrun, everywhere defences were leaking.

We expected new orders every day, a fresh deployment, but still we patrolled and watched the rib, repelling counter attacks, half-hearted as they were, but too weak, too few in number to advance ourselves. Such was the situation at that time.

Now the tale twists and turns and I will play the tune of it, the melody of my, of Hannu's story. Whether through exhaustion or disgust or the unrelenting dark and cold I know not but my sense of unease increased daily. A sense of foreboding, omens and portents abounded and I became careless. There had been no news of home or Maarit and this contributed to a lowering of my spirits. We boys of Suomussalmi talked much less and grumbled like the old men we were becoming. I grew careless on patrol, losing myself in thought, becoming isolated and at times lost in the wilderness. Not matter how much Simo and Harri rebuked me for this irresponsibility I could not focus, and drifted until inevitably a patrol went wrong and I found myself in trouble, deep and serious.

So hearken listener, turn your head in this direction and let me piece together this shattered tale, present it to you as a tableaux frozen.

It came about that Harri, Simo and me were in the wild, many miles from camp in a place of great physical severity and isolation. Our skis described long arcs across the snow. Darkness was receding, days sprinkling lighter as February unfolded though still iron with cold. Harri carried a powerful flashlight and we two automatic weapons…hunting down deserters and stragglers. There were reports of enemy patrols, new troops from Siberia used to conditions such as these, but we had seen no sign, a myth perhaps, propaganda.

In the crisp, with the hypnotic gliding of skis on ice and irregular patterning of pine trees striping my vision I fell into a trance, unthinking, unaware. So it came as a surprise to realise that in fact I was quite alone. That Harri and Simo were nowhere to be seen and while a glimmer of sun poked through cloud, the land was still an amalgam of shadows with that hint of the surreal that winter sometimes pressed upon the mind. I dared not call, nor could I distinguish any tracks but my own. Waiting, gazing through a gloom soaked air, I considered the best course of action. Finally determined to return to camp I took out my compass and attempted to plot a route, wary all the time for only my eyes were seeking signs of danger.

It was then the shot rang out. I felt a punch on my chest but thought nothing of it until the velocity of the punch caused my legs to crumble and I fell onto the snow. There was the merest trace of movement at the edge of my vision, a tainted green flash, a Russian cape retreating and then a dark tunnel down which I slid tumbling onto ground solid and unyielding. A sheet of steel at my back and head of clay. But where was I?

Beneath a birch tree heavy with frost, knobs of bark growing into my legs, lichen curled at my feet, fingers like willow leaves. Grievous was my position. I felt the sticky ooze of blood soak the inside of my tunic and then freeze. I felt the liquid pumping of the veins and the throb of my heart tightening and my hair grasped in a fury and the skin of my skull pulled back so my eyes burned like coals. Then it was I must have lapsed into unconsciousness. Sleepways sinking, fighting for quiet and that solitude of heart that only extremes of cold can unclasp. It is no smooth journey, twisting, casting, shuddering, an unholy trek full of pain, distantly eyeing worlds like a paradise seeker, immersed and alone, a fortress unbattered by events without, immune, slumbering, numbing, disowned.

How the snow glistened. How the stars fell like pearls from a sky rich in blue and the cranes flew across the face of the moon in quiet formations, and the wingless flurry of air prickled my skin and my eyes glazed in lens's misty. How horizons sucked land to sky and melted one into the other. Yet I was not alone. Conscious I was of someone coming, and I thought I recognised her soft tread. Straining on my elbows, lifted on arms like cherry rods I watched the slow advance of light, a single candle flame yellow and orange with the texture of citrus gliding through the forest, pine and fir and birch trees bowing and the magpies chattering silenced. She knelt beside me warm and cherished, hair of gold and topaz. In arms she cradled me and tears anointed, murmuring dialects unheard for ages so she said.

'Hannu. Poor Hannu the carpenter it has come to this.'

'I recognise your voice.'

'You have heard me many times Hannu, in the stillness of the workshop, in the splash of water when the oars are working, in passages, in waterfalls, in the swallow's wing freely yearning, in the boughs of the apple tree shading Adam from the sun. In your dreams you have heard my lullabies for I have always been with you and you have always known without seeking.'

'What is it I must do?'

'Follow…follow for your movements slow and laboured are sufficient for this journey of a thousand paces only, through the snow banks I will lead you, past the lairs of many demons, to our final destination.'

So it was I followed in her tread of liquid copper, in the whisper of her shadow. Beside a mighty river roaring, salmon leaping, beavers gnawing, turning whiskers at our passing. Lions and bison, elk and marten joined us on our journey weaving silky to the roaring, breathing vapour, meek, subdued but never slacking. Onwards where a bridge of hazel switches wove the river frenzied. But when I peered across, the other bank was fluid, white and glimmering.

'Now,' she said. 'This is our destination.'

'Should I cross the bridge?'

'That is for you to decide.'

'But what lies on the other bank?'

'You will see when you get there.'

'My task Hannu was to lead you to this place. If you decide to cross the bridge I will go with you…but you can never return.'

'But will I survive my wound. What will become of me, here or on the other bank?'

'I cannot say, it is not yet within my power or authority.'

'But still I bleed.'

She smiled and calmed me. Stroked my hair as if I was a child.

'If you decide to cross I will go with you, but there is no return. I can carry for you a memory, but only one, which will it be?'

My head swam and my thoughts tossed images of the village, of Merja, and Maarit, of the village splendidly unfashioned, of mother scolding, of haymaking and bonfires and wood turning and mist floating down the sides of curly birch hill, and the freighter plying the Saimaa Canal, of fish traps, and Harri and Simo with his teeth missing and the soup stirring.

'I cannot decide,' I said.

'In that case Hannu you are not ready. It is not your time. I can reveal that your wound will heal, but that many difficulties lie ahead, times of great sorrows and burdens which only your shoulders can carry. But remember that I am always with you, unheard and unseen by others...but on occasion you will feel my presence for the old blood runs through your veins. One day we will return to this spot where the bridge spans the mighty river and we will cross with your memory, when your time has come.'

She smiled again and lay me down with my back against a tree.

'How can I thank you?'

'There is no need for thanks or gratitude. You have been released into a life of suffering and at times you will curse the path you have chosen. But you are not alone and in dark hours that should be of comfort. Now Hannu let me depart with a song. Sing loud and sweetly as did Vainamoinen. Sing as the barley grows and the meadow flowers and the spring sunshine banishes winter's slab, and listen I will until the words dart no more. Do this for me.'

So I sang with such care and meaning that I felt my own heart burst with joy. I did not waver nor did I rest, nor did the melody fall and rise with any less skill, from morning till night, from sunset to sunrise, the words echoed through the forest and all who heard it raised their heads and turned their ears in the direction of the song. How long I sang, to this day I do not know.

*

Harri and Simo found me close to death. Frozen and pale through loss of blood they tied me to a sledge and hauled me back to a clearing station beyond Suomusssalmi. They did not have hopes for my recovery and they told me later that their hearts were sore with anguish and anger. From there I was taken by truck and train to the city of Tampere where I lay in bed, unconscious for the most part for many weeks. When I awoke the war was over, but bitterness there was and tears shed but I was too twisted in my mind to unravel the significance of it all. All I knew was warmth and quiet and solitude. So ends this chapter, this canto from a story mighty.

Chapter 12

When Maarit stumbled into her home village she was anxious about what she might find and equally the impression she would make. Days on the road in clothes worn for a month, without facilities to wash played on her mind more perhaps than it should have done.

A partial thaw had set in and roads became slush, a brief interlude before freezing again but uncomfortable all the same. Her clothes were damp and try as she might, she could not keep her hair from her eyes. Under her breath she mumbled in counterpoint to squelching on shoes encrusted with salt. She did know what to expect. The whole journey, arduous as it was, consisted of a powerful blocking out of recent experiences on the Kollaa river and the arrival home, long cherished but tormented by thoughts of what remained, if anything.

At long last she stepped across the solidified stream marking the parish boundary and skirted the hill. In the eastern sky the sun sparkled and a miserly warmth was generated. She saw the timber mill on the outskirts and the church and cabins dotted like toadstools randomly. A black cat she did not recognise stared and bristled, half-feral, making a claim to territory. It was quickly apparent that most of the place had been evacuated. There was no smoke, no sign of activity. The church doors were locked and bolted, cabin windows shuttered. Nothing stirred, no cattle in the stalls, no hens or horses, no human voices. In her heart she knew it was a possibility that the village was completely empty but hoped against hope…

So when old man Hannu challenged her with a raised club she nearly jumped out of her skin.

'Put that thing down, you idiot!' she screamed.

'Identify yourself,' replied the old man glowering like a maniac and swinging the club.

'It is Maarit Harmala, Jakko the farmer's daughter, friend of Hannu, resident of this village since birth and unimpressed by a welcome such as this.'

He studied her face, squinting his eyes, every feature, mentally calculating her height and posture.

'So it is,' he said at last, 'so it is.'

'Come,' he said more sympathetically. 'Come and rest. I have some soup on the stove and coffee.'

She allowed herself to be led away, sitting on the bench in Hannu's kitchen. The warm stove instilled feelings once more within her limbs. Old man Hannu didn't say much. He strayed regularly from lucidity to confusion. But this was not his first conflict. In his youth he had seen revolution and then a civil war of great brutality, and now in declining years sat talking quietly to Maarit as she spooned potato soup and luxuriated in a few moments of peace. Most people had departed, he explained, one night on a train, amongst them the Harmala family and the kin of Hannu the carpenter. Since then he had heard nothing but that they were somewhere in Haem province, transplanted together as it were. How they were faring…well who could say. As for the village she could see for herself that it was near deserted. Only one family remained, the Kuismas, and here his head hung low and he fell into a sleep. Unused to company her arrival seemed to be too much and he slipped away within himself.

Maarit took the opportunity to return to the old cabin. The doors were locked but the window shutters opened easily, so she climbed in, lighting the candle to survey rooms already gathering dust. It was bitterly cold inside but the yard pump still worked and she forced herself to undress and wash and change her clothes, which still lay folded in the drawer. Her Lotta uniform she threw into the laundry basket by habit and collected what remained in the storeroom. This was not much, some salt, sugar, wheatgerm, a few biscuits. Throwing a blanket over her shoulders she climbed out of the window again. She did not feel comfortable in this place; there were too many associations. Then it was she heard the old man calling her name frantically.

'Maarit...Maarit where are you?'

She raced back and saw the obvious relief on the old man's face when she returned to the stove side.

'I'm sorry, Hannu. I did not intend to frighten you.'

'You must take care child,' he uttered, 'this district is no longer safe.'

'I have seen worse than this believe me,' she answered, and as she said it she returned to the scene in the tent with the four dead boys laid out within it and she brushed her hair across her face and moved her hands closer to the stove. She did not wish to relay her story, for Hannu's part he made no enquiries. Fearing a pause in conversation she asked about family and friends. All the old man knew was that most except the Kuismas had gone. They did not leave because one of the children was ill and by the time she had recovered it was too late. Mrs Kuisma spent all day on the road looking for her husband, waiting for his return, but there had been no news since the Taipale battles where he had been listed as missing. Now she fretted about getting the girls away but had not the means or courage to do it. How cold and anxiety and loneliness saps the strength.

As the evening wore on old man Hannu lurched between complaints about the shortage of tobacco and snippets of information about the war. Planes flew over regularly and this seemed to concern him, mightily. He didn't like them, didn't understand what they were doing. Of her friend Hannu, he had heard nothing. There had been fighting on the shores of Lake Ladoga, that much he knew, and from time to time soldiers marched through on the way to the front, the wounded returned on the backs of wagons. He patrolled the village with club and lantern, he felt it was his duty as the only man left. There were packs of dogs scavenging through the lanes and fields mad with hunger, where they had come from he did not know but what a nuisance they were, and dangerous too if they should fall on one of the Kusima children. Then darkly, furtively, he talked of deserters and bandits in the forests. He had seen them once or twice and scared them away, but they returned at night stealing what they could and generally causing unease. This was the reason for not venturing outside alone, especially after dark. When he asked her what she intended to do Maarit could genuinely not explain. She had not thought about it. Hers had been the task to get home by any means, and now she was here? It might be possible to return to Helsinki, to Mrs Rajala, or make enquiries after her family. They would be worried and unable to comprehend her actions and certainly the lack of communication. But guilt did not consume her. She had witnessed too much for guilt.

By the end of the day old man Hannu furled himself in blankets and lay down beside the stove as had been his custom for many years. Maarit lay against the cabin wall on a straw mattress and fell into a deep sleep.

So refreshing was that rest, so touching a need that she woke late when the sun was almost above the horizon. Old man Hannu was gone, patrolling club in hand, a self-appointed watcher. Hurriedly putting on her shoes she ran outside. A blue sky, bird song, snow tumbling from branches, but the temperature had fallen again and the earth hardened beneath her feet. Much was achingly familiar, the geography of the settlement, boundary fences, orchards still dormant, outhouses, barns, small remembrances branded on the heart when young and ever with you. She took to wandering, for it was a day without purpose. She relished this respite from toil and decision-making. Still, gentle stirrings, a creak of wood from time to time, no more. Resisting the temptation to return to the family home she walked to the Kuisma cabin, knocking confidently on the door. She was greeted with squeals and embraces by the girls and their mother, grey-haired already and thin as a willow. She went inside and was made much of.

'So how are things Mrs Kuisma?' asked Maarit, aware that this conversation would be difficult.

'Not so good.'

'I'm sorry to hear about your husband.'

'Yes…it is a burden. Missing they say, but I have almost lost hope now. He is gone as are so many others. How we must have offended God to be tormented so…but I forget my manners Maarit. Why have you returned?'

'I was in the Lotta and posted north.' She raced the words, tumbling them out, unwilling to elaborate or answer questions. 'But I was ordered home and so I came.' She paused for a moment, tapping her foot on the floor.

'Only to discover that the village is deserted.'

'We three remain, myself and the two girls. Hannu, of course, but he frightens me. His wits leave him, all day backwards and forwards, up and down, swinging that club of his like a metronome.' She let out a sob, a tearless sob that shook the cabin. The two girls curled around her and she kissed them and held them and Maarit thought her heart would break once more as it had at Kollaa.

'You must leave Mrs Kuisma.'

'I know…but I cannot bring myself to do it. I know we must, there is little food left and besides, being alone, well I'm frightened. Too scared to stay and lacking the courage to move. What kind of a mother am I?'

'I can help. There is nothing for me here.'

'But if we go, if we break the chains that bind us here, what then? Generations of my family lie buried in the churchyard. I know of nothing else and then what would my husband say, if he were here, what would he advise?'

'I'm sure he would want you to take the children to safety.'

The window frames rattled and a mouse ran unnoticed to the corner.

'Yes…I'm sure you are right but it is so difficult. Every night I light a candle for him and leave it on the window sill, as did many others when they left for the railway station. Your own mother too God Bless her, thankful that she has not boys to lose in this war. She must be worried though, not hearing from you.'

'Do you know where she is, and father and the others?'

'Hämeenlinna…safe enough but struggling as are we all. You must go to them.'

'I will, and you must come with me. Four is better than three, and an extra pair of hands.'

'But if we leave, will we ever return?'

Maarit's silence betrayed her thoughts.

'One day we will come home,' she answered firmly. 'One day we will return to plough these fields and open the church again. This is our land, our ancestors tamed it from the wild and our boys fight and die for it. One day Mrs Kuisma.'

The mother with greying hair and children clinging to her dress poured coffee, spread chunks of black bread with butter retreating inwards as she spoke from far, far away.

'Have you any news of the others? Anything you can tell me? It's so long since we had any communication. Are they well? Is there any news of Hannu?'

She came back from that far away place, collecting her thoughts on the journey.

'No news of Hannu I'm afraid. Some of the others were stationed on the southern shore of Lake Ladoga but none spoke of him. I have heard that little Merja has been quite ill, in hospital I'm told but what ailed her I cannot say.'

'At least they are together.'

'Yes…there is some comfort in that. Well Maarit I'm sorry I could not be of more help, but you will stay here tonight, won't you? It is more comfortable than old Hannu's and more seemly. It heartens me to share conversation with another woman. These four walls crush my soul. Maybe there is light somewhere. I must be strong for the children.'

'And for yourself Mrs Kuisma.'

'As you say.'

'So you will prepare to leave?'

'We must do something, that much is clear before this place reverts to wilderness, carrying us all with it. Did Hannu warn you about the dogs?'

'Yes…where do they come from?'

'Who knows. The devil unleashing his pack to drive us closer to madness. Abandoned by farmers and now starving and out of control. There but for the grace of God go us, we poor Kareilans.'

Maarit smiled and gazed out of the window framed with light. Soon spring would come and what then? How the rhythm of life is torn apart. Where now is the seed to be found for planting and who will undertake the task? Sowers in trenches or dugouts or scouring the forests for fugitives while the land weeps with neglect. Where the harvest come autumn? Where the haymaking and fodder when the song and dances fade. How like the tribes of Israel we have become, living in the lands of strangers.

'You will prepare to leave then?' asked Maarit after this contemplation. She raised her eyes and sensed a slight flushing of the cheeks. The conversation entangled everything.

'We must. I suppose we have no choice. But there are no trains now, no transports. What horses were left have long since been requisitioned and the cold still bitter.'

'If we dress well and keep moving we shall be warm enough. There is a handcart still in the yard of my father's cabin, we can use it, and as for transport, once we meet the main roads we will be taken up, no fear. These last few days I have travelled from regions more wild and sparse than this. Folk will help, especially with the children. Now Mrs Kuisma let me gather wood for the stove and let you consider what is to be done. This evening by the firelight let us explain to the children what is happening, let us be brave and put it to them as an adventure, that way it may not be so frightening.'

'Yes Maarit, we will do these things.'

As she closed the door she heard the gentle, hopeless sobbing of the mother and felt both pity and exasperation. The village was too vulnerable for such innocents now. There was no protection and precious little food. The Russians may come. They may not but surely common sense dictated that Mrs Kuisma should find shelter for herself and the children.

She did not wander far between the cabins. There were log piles still untouched from autumn and as she surveyed the village with new unfamiliar emotions she wondered at the fabric of the buildings still fresh and this impressed her. The quietness lent a soothing hand to her brow and the cleanliness of her body and clothes gave fresh confidence. She was emerging from the deep to the sunlight. She saw the outline of Hannu's precious workshop with the padlock still in place. She touched it and felt him close and knew that he was still alive and something tingled within, so she smiled without smiling, gathering wood.

Then it was she heard the whistling, a man's whistle. At first she thought it might be old man Hannu but it was of a younger complexion so she paused and strained her ears. When the dog snarled she stopped dead still, wood heavy in her arms and blood cold. How many times had she been warned? She dropped the wood and ran panic stricken as the dog growled again and snapped. Half-blinded by light reflecting from snow she ran into the solid figure of a man, a big man, arms like tree trunks. He caught her wrist and twisted her so she cowered and felt the humiliation of her position and some anger too for she was not without spirit.

'No need to rush so, Miss', said a voice. 'Let me see what prey has been snared.'

'Let me go or I will scream,' yelled Maarit struggling.

'Scream if you wish, no one will hear but old men. It will put the fear of God into that stupid woman and her children. Scream if you wish.'

Maarit calmed but kept her wits about her, trying to discover the identity of her assailant. Something about the tone of his voice, his gestures, and the outline of his body was familiar, but she could not place it.

'All I want to do is talk, a firebrand I do not need.'

'Identify yourself then,' spat Maarit, no longer daunted, but angry and her mind racing, if only the sun was not so much in her eyes but white light burned and she could not decipher a miasma of impressions swirling through the day, assaulting the senses.

'You know me.'

Then it caught, the familiarity hooked into her senses and the truth struck.

'Paavo...Hannu's brother. What do you mean by this?'

'Half-brother – as he was always keen to point out.'

'As you say, now let me go.'

Paavo released his grip and stood before her. He was a big man, powerful in body and determined as ever. He had not shaved for several days, looking unkempt and rather forlorn.

'Why have you returned to this place?'

'It is my home, or have you forgotten?' she countered, smoothing her clothes and pulling away from him. 'I might ask the same of you. Why do you skulk in a village of women and old men? What business have you in this place? A deserter no doubt, you good for nothing.'

Maarit took the opportunity to scan the village for signs of life but there was none. The dog growled and saliva dribbled from its mouth and steam rose from its flanks where the ribs poked through as a cage. Paavo quietened it with a kick before tying the beast to a fence post. Always he looked round, his eyes constantly sweeping windows and trees with a nervousness she had not seen in him at other times.

'Deserter...no,' he scowled. 'I never joined my unit, what sense is there in dying with those fools. What value in losing life or limb when the outcome of this war was determined before it even started.'

'Spoken like a true hero,' she replied sarcastically.

Paavo grabbed her wrist again and twisted.

'Mind you don't go too far.'

'Let me go – you scum of the earth.'

He pushed her to the ground and glared but she did not turn away, instead returning with her own eyes the malice in his, and facing him down.

'How could they ever hope to win, to what purpose, an army of thousands matched against the millions of the Soviet Union?'

'We are not beaten yet.'

'It is a matter of time, even as I speak more divisions roll towards the Isthmus, the lines will soon break, the flood is too great, it is time to save yourself.'

'How do you know this? How can you have this information?'

'Many months ago I steered my course. It does not take a professor from your Institute to understand the outcome of this war. The Russians will be in Helsinki before the end of the month. I have seen the men and materials mustered at the border; unimaginable quantities of mortars, and cannon and tanks and aeroplanes to blacken the sky and bombs enough to pit this country like the moon. At Terijoki I saw it and nailed my colours to their mast. When they come, and they will, seeking vengeance for their losses only me and my kind will have the power and authority to stay their hand. So when the homesteads are re-distributed and the land parcelled out I will be first in line and the others the fools in their foxholes and trenches will take the long march to Siberia, if they are lucky. You have not heard from Hannu?'

Maarit remained silent.

'As I thought. Who knows what state he is in, alive or dead. Though he was a strange one, with his ramblings and arrogance. I would not wish to see him suffer uselessly. When this is over I can find him. I can bring him home if he lives.'

Maarit exploded into fury and flew at her tormenter, kicking and scratching, until he slapped her down, and took the dog once more into his control. The animal strained at the leash in excitement.

'He lives,' screamed Maarit, and when he hears of your deeds here he will seek you out and stick a bayonet in your stomach and the whole of Karelia will watch and kick your body into a ditch. So it will be! You scum, you monster without hope.'

'I think not Maarit once so pretty and now so coarse. I think you will be enslaved with the others. It is all they deserve for their stupidity.'

'And your wife too Paarvo. What did she ever do to deserve this fate?'

'She too was weak, full of poetry and false expectations. She must take her chances with the rest. If your paths ever cross, though I doubt they will, send her this message, that I release her from her vows, it is as if we were never married. Tell her to seek what comfort she can, with who so ever will take her. My task here is completed. I shall make my report and garner my reward as a true citizen of the world. Be thankful that I did not set the dog upon you. Goodbye and good riddance.' He turned and disappeared into the forest leaving no trace behind.

Maarit did not move, stupefied on the ground and unwilling to return to Mrs Kuisma until her tears had dried. She must not hear of this, she thought, it would only multiply her anxieties.

*

So pale February advanced. The threads of winter's coverlet loosened its grip reluctantly on rockpools icy and the moon's glow froze the land glimmering the thoughts of folk scanning their orbits. Reflections ruled the heavens, clouds bobbed in their sails above cabins in loops of spray garnered by the wind. Nails worked free of weatherboards and fishing nets strangled the fields in hemp lanyards. Spring would soon unclasp the tides and the whales of the north would head ever closer to Greenland's shore, followed no doubt by pirates, and the currents of warm air would sprout the earth in green and buds would burst and the cattle in the farmyard bellow. All would multiply.

While I slept and chased my dreams about the ward, events on the eastern borders of our land unfolded as we knew in our hearts they must. Men in their mortality can endure so much, suffer greatly, but in the end must give way to desolation, exhausted by bombardment, shaken to the core in concrete bunkers and concussed by projectiles never ceasing. Exhaustion crept upon our armies, exposure, sleeplessness, deafened by noise and lost in the disintegration of all that was familiar and human. One by one strong points were overrun. Despite tenacious and suicidal defence, sheer numbers of attackers could not be held as a plague of locusts descended on the Isthmus. This place was always the key. Our reservoirs of courage, of stubbornness of the bloody-minded ran dry beneath the unrelenting waves of infantry and armour. Our officers slapped the men in their stupor but were greeted only by the stares of men stumbling through nightmare. The skies filled ever darker with formations of bombers releasing cargo upon us, until there was no shelter, no hole deep enough to cover our bodies with soil. Yet still the pressure intensified, still they came. By night the headlights of their tanks were shot out by snipers, grenades and Molotov cocktails flung at slits and hatches until the darkness was illuminated by participants in some bizarre fireworks party. By day, we saw them stumbling through mine fields, but the wheels turned and the gears ground on. And notice reader that I talk as if I was there! In my mind I was with my brothers on the Isthmus, on the Kollaa, on the shores of Lake Ladoga in the far north of Lapland where still we fought and I in my hospital bed feeling all this activity through white sheets while the clock ticked and the doctors did their rounds. Alas, one by one by one, holes were punched in the dam and the waters flooded through in bursts of green. No matter how many walls we built, the Soviet juggernaut demolished them, and our armies retreated in single steps still facing the enemy and firing and in instances throwing stones and rocks at their soldiers but to no avail. So in the end, while other regions held fast until the end, this portion of our homeland crumbled atom by atom, this Karelia, this holy soil, succumbed. Russian troops flooded across until the order spread throughout the lines to hold, to bar the doors and keep these barbarians from our homes. We had to pray for a miracle and play for time.

Rumours of negotiations circulated, wild rumours, unbelievable tracts and propaganda leaflets dropped from the sky. We had too much common sense to be taken in but it was apparent that behind the scenes the politicians talked and wheedled and threatened and did as politicians did. The diplomats ferried themselves to Leningrad and Moscow negotiating concessions from a position that must have seemed hopeless. So many years later when I read about their endeavours, how I pitied them, how they must have placed their pride inside their pockets for the sake of our small country. But finally a cease fire was agreed. Peace was purchased with land, such a high price we paid, but we had the comfort of knowing an occupation was averted. They understood we Finns would not tolerate the terrors that other peoples endured, that we would make their lives hell if they advanced any further. Besides their heads were turned in other directions, to greater enemies.

*

I woke one morning in March after a hibernation of many weeks. At first I could not remember a thing! I thought I was in my own bed in the cabin or in the workshop and then in the trenches of Taipale. Such was my confusion that even my name had an unfamiliar ring to it. By the end of March some strength had returned and I was able to sit up in bed. I wore blue pyjamas, which were rather fetching, but I had a hole in my chest and breathing, well it was difficult, especially when I lay on my back to sleep. The nurses constructed a nest of pillows to make me more comfortable, and everyone I met was kindness itself.

Then one morning I had a visitor. My mother walked down the ward and could barely contain her emotions. Later she said I looked like a corpse, like an old man pale as death and wheezing. All I recall is being proud of my pyjamas and troubled when she had no news of Maarit and when she relayed the tribulations suffered by Tuija and Merja.

I said that I wanted to go home, and she replied sadly that it was not possible, not yet, that I was to rest and re-gain my strength. Then if I behaved myself I could move to the cottage in Hämeenlinna. It was a grand place, she said, very homely. In all she stayed for three days and never took her eyes from me. I asked after Harri, but she said nothing, so I didn't know what to make of it.

When the first rains of spring rattled the window pane she ventured to ask me what had happened. So I told her the truth, about the patrol and the fact that Harri and Simo carried me back to the first aid post. She liked the sound of Simo, thought he sounded like a real gentleman! If only she knew. I explained that it was only a flesh wound but she argued that a bullet had entered my chest, passed through my lung and exited my back. This was no flesh wound. Then I saw her frown and understood that she was happy to see me even in this state. Part of me expected to see her polishing the washstand but later I discovered that she had changed in subtle ways and grown older in the months since I had seen her last.

At the end of the third day she said goodbye and walked along the corridors to the outside, to the streets of Tampere, which at that time I had not seen. So began my recovery. I obeyed all medical instructions, ate food that had the texture of cardboard and allowed myself to be prodded by strangers in white coats who talked about me as if I wasn't there. All this time I tried not to complain and gained something of the reputation as a model patient. Some of the other boys were in a bad way, burns, frostbite cases, amputations, and when they slipped away it was always in the early hours of the morning, as if they wanted to cause as little inconvenience as possible. I prayed for them of course and sobbed inside and hid it all behind a mask of my own making.

What a day it was emerging in the sunlight, with a nurse at my elbow and an ambulance waiting to take me to Hämeenlinna.

Chapter 13

If in short steps you walk from the centre of Hämeenlinna in a north-easterly direction you cross the bridge spanning lake Vanaja and follow the road known as Viipurintie. It is here the town ebbs and the fields begin, rich farmland, pasture, oats, barley, prosperous farmhouses, now covered in snow, but in summer, rich and verdant. If on this road you were to meet inhabitants of this province you would find them reserved, polite but distant, quite a serious people without the exuberance and outward show of Karelians. Well meaning though, stoical and hardworking, such is their reputation, and I can vouch that it is so. A strange land to my mother, though a common language. None of the villagers displaced here had travelled so far. So you can imagine what a difficult time it was, full of unfamiliar sights and no anchor to cling to. Everyone's thoughts were attuned to the war. Everyday there was more sad news, another son, brother, husband, father lost to the enemy, until this place gained the appearance of a colony for widows and the tears flowed, how they flowed. It is said that no one slept and the mornings brought an ever greater emptiness which clearer skies only mocked. Items carried from the village were venerated, unhealthily so in some instances, and the talk was always of going home, the ancestral lands bequeathed to our people in ages before time. So listener if you follow my mother's tread along that track snaking ever thinner, basket in hand, you would see the vapour rising from warm lips, and a claret headscarf and thick boots. Across a stream, walking alongside a smaller lake, thawing in late winter, sunshine shaped with the head of a pony. It is here the land rises in a series of gentle ridges and a farmhouse stands. This is where she turned to follow an even smaller path, a tongue passing through stands of timber, a plank lies across a ditch which once traversed opens to a log cabin. A substantial building for its type, heavy and dark. A porch to the front and pipe chimney billowing smoke. Once inside you would notice the frost on the walls despite the stove burning. A large room with chairs and a rug and two beds equally substantial, but rustic, built to last rather than beautiful. Each bed had a mattress and blankets and pillows. In the corner there was another door leading to a store house, mostly empty. There were three windows, one to the side, two to the front. This was home, and in the circumstances, well it was sufficient. In the evening in the candle's glow there was an atmosphere of honey and mother knew they were fortunate to be allocated this place. She also suspected that the hospital doctor had exerted some influence on their behalf. God be thanked, she thought. Tuija had worked so hard cleaning and sweeping to make it habitable for their return. When she stamped slush from her boots and hung her coat on a hook the aroma of freshly ground coffee caught her attention. It was inviting, but they had to be careful – imagine such things as coffee and sugar being luxuries!

Merja sat on the bed playing with beads. When the door slammed she sensed the vibrations and looked up, giving her mother a shy smile. She exuded a contentment that surprised everybody. The loss of hearing had somehow released her from the need to communicate, that troublesome burden, and she retreated into privacy. Mother veered from anxiety to relief and back again at the vision of her daughter more active yet more alone than before. Tuija sat on a chair sewing, making new shirts for sale at the Wednesday market. Every little helped and food was really scarce. A constant stabbing hunger pain had to be endured. They would not starve, but neither would they thrive. It was so quiet. Old neighbours were scattered about the town and none lived close by. The cabin while homely was situated at the

196

end of a farm track and had once been some kind of lodge. It was all but invisible, surrounded as it was by trees which gave it the appearance of a peach stone in the middle of flesh. Conversation was limited. Mother longed to talk about home but dared not, she longed for news about myself but realised that no news was good news and in the candlelight, in the lonely, grey, outside light of early March knew something awful was about to happen. She had always been prone to premonitions like myself, and once, in the endless too'ing and fro'ing along the track, glanced across to a clump of birch trees where a spirit sat making dolls and figures out of twigs, tying them together with strips of reed. The spirit did not look up and my mother crept past unnoticed but this apparition disturbed her soul sowing uncertainty as to its meaning. Such sights, she believed, were limited to our eastern lands where the ancient magic still prospered in the wildernesses, not here, not in places where the new industries grew and machines growled. Witches and hags and miracle workers spoke in the dialects of Karelia, water spirits danced to our steps and demon dogs growled in intonations found only in the words of the Kalevala. Some people here did not even believe in such things! Some, bustling about in the market, even spoke with Swedish accents. All of these events only added to the widespread estrangement felt by the people of the village. Yes they were treated with kindness and consideration; homes had been opened to them. But it was foreign, another country. Some folk took to gathering in the church garden where they had first arrived, exchanging news and rumours. Each day the situation worsened and more boys whose faces only months ago had glistened with sweat in the barley fields or flamed the axe with effort were now listed as missing or killed or grievously hurt. All joy had flown and with each conversation the sense of separation and loss increased.

Then it was at midday she saw him, the telegraph boy wheeling his bicycle along the narrow track through the slush. His brow peeped out below a peaked cap and my mother's heart missed a beat. He was a most unwelcome visitor. When he knocked it crossed her mind to hide so he might think she was out.

'Who is it?' asked Tuija from the corner.

When my mother answered all she could do was utter a cry of 'Lord Preserve Us' and stand beside her.

'Hello to the one who brings the greeting and another to the one who sent it.'

He did not respond.

'Are you Mrs Juutilainen? They said at the farmhouse I could find you here. There is a telegram for you. Would you be so kind as to sign here.' He pointed to a space in a document book and registered with mild surprise that she was able to sign her name. As soon as the signature had been acquired he turned his bicycle and sped away.

Tuija watched as the envelope was opened and my mother, so she later said, sank into a chair when she realised that I was still on this earth but wounded in a hospital in Tampere. That was when she visited and plans to re-locate me to the new cabin were put into operation. In March, an ambulance transported me to the farmhouse and from there along the track on a stretcher swathed in blankets. My mother refurbished the storeroom with bed and chair and so on. For many hours I looked out of the tiny window and heard the erratic swishing of branches against the glass. Merja often came to wile away the time. She said nothing but smiled more than I remembered and within herself seemed to be content. I must say it was a shock to see her respond in such a way, to exhibit a liveliness and curiosity so much out of character. She would sit there plaiting grasses or looking with real concentration at the pictures in a book. Most days she would disappear into the forest only to emerge soaking wet with handfuls of pine cones or twigs or ferns. The news of her illness was relayed to me in episodes (everyone tiptoed around me) but all I could think was that someone was looking over her. Still, we all knew there would be difficulties ahead, she had so little education and…what would happen next?

The hole in my chest healed fairly well, all things considered. It looked a mess and hurt like fury when I moved but there was no infection and gradually I regained my strength. Tuija popped her head around the door from time to time although we never really talked. It was only later that I heard the details of her situation and it sent me mad with anger. I suppose people were careful not to overexcite me, not that there was any chance of that. I lived a kind of monastic existence with meals and entertainment provided. It was at night, in a darkness so deep, that my thoughts wandered to recent events. I prayed for news of Maarit, but there was none, and I worried constantly about my friends at the front, devouring greedily any information provided. Things did not look so good. Then, as always, I had these dreams.

One I recall vividly. If you can imagine me sitting on a gate, idling in the sunshine and looking up to see a sky full of clouds, billowing in all shapes and patterns, gliding, hardly moving at all. After awhile these shapes took a more solid form and became ships, huge ships with wooden sides and masts and sails and rigging. From the sides drop-anchors and the chains straddle the sky and earth. As I watch I see lines of men walk across the field and climb the chains hand over hand until they disappear. On closer inspection I see they are clad in field grey or camouflage white and they are mostly young men. Not one remarks upon my presence although they must have seen me. It is a never ending line. There are faces I recognise but cannot put names to them. Pekka walks up and shakes my hand and asks if I am coming with him. I say, no, not yet, so up he climbs like a sailor born. I get to wondering how he travelled from that shell hole on the Isthmus and why the countless multitudes are following.

'Who are you?' I ask, and a thousand eyes dart in my direction accusingly, as if it was a ridiculous question, as if I should know.

'We are the dead,' they say.

'We are the dead who will not awake when the earths quaking ceases and the final homeward waves have rolled ashore in fits and pieces.'

A chorus sang.

'We are the corpse, brother, the stench you covered with soil, the lips she kissed, the body you buried.'

And with the ferocity of injustice the chant continued.

'We rest, the dead who will not learn to turn away when the spade has ceased its swallowing our lips in clay.'

Still more did the voice of these once men render the sky.

'We are the sacks, the meat you carried away on a cart, the skull you shovelled, the hair you combed, the village boys.'

How sobs racked my body, how the earth quivered and my lungs burst, so many, so many, and I saw their children never born climb up after them calling and crying and appealing for their fathers never to be, to wait for them and comfort them. Such harrowing sights I would not wish upon my enemies. When the wind blew and the sails fluffed out, the anchors clanked ever upwards. I could not tear myself away and screamed and screamed, for then it was I saw Harri and Simo clinging to the anchor itself as it rose. Grim-faced and weary with exhaustion, gaunt, grey, solemn.

When I woke it was pitch black. I was covered in sweat, my eyes stung with salt, and it was many minutes before I stopped my screaming. Only when my mother rushed in with a lantern and lay me down did I realise it was a dream, merely a dream. I could not sleep again but waited for the first glimmers of daylight to break the fast. On the window sills were travellers robed in silk struggling through shifting sands and dunes and from that day I dreaded sleep and would do anything to hold its cruel malignancy at bay.

In the morning I was helped to a chair and remained there mostly. Tuija was silent. Merja wore a puzzled expression but made no attempt to communicate. My mother, overburdened as she was, never asked me what I witnessed in my dreams. I could not have explained, nor did I wish to repeat the experience but more furrows ploughed across her brow and more hair turned to grey. Still the cabin swam in the glow of honey and as March progressed a gentle rain fell and winter's slab receded.

The war ended. On what terms we knew not. The line did not break, not in one place were we overwhelmed, but exhaustion took us, our ammunition dwindled to nothing, and we could not raise our heavy arms to fire another shot. So it was. So it had to be.

*

The military police entered the village.

'Had we not heard?' they said.

'Heard what?' answered Maarit and Mrs Kuisma.

'The war is over. A peace treaty was signed days ago. Have you no radio?'

'We have nothing,' answered Mrs Kuisma bitterly.

'How many remain?'

'We four and Hannu the old man.'

'You must go now the Russians are hours away, they will be here before the embers in your stove have died.'

Mrs Kuisma began to sob loudly and the girls clung to her skirts. She did nothing, fear riveting her shoes to the snow.

'Go now!' yelled the policemen. 'We cannot help you further, this district should have been evacuated days ago.'

Maarit jostled Mrs Kuisma into the cabin, threw clothes upon them and blankets over their shoulders. Awake now, alert to the danger they were in, senses heightened to the drone of aeroplanes above, they fled towards the main road west. In their footsteps came the vanguard of a Russian column, a captain edging nervously across the Parish boundary, wary of booby traps, saw the smoke from the chimney and threw a grenade. All was obliterated. The thud carried to the fugitives and they quickened their steps.

The captain did not see old man Hannu lurking in the shadows. He did not expect to see him. Nor did he anticipate the vicious connection of the club on his head, a skull-splitting crash that killed him long before he hit the ground. Hannu looked down and saw the blood rivering the snow. He sucked on his pipe, shouldered his club and marched across the fields with a basket over his arm and small pack on his back. Not a single glance did he give, not one, no final look but the heavy, fatalistic tread of a peasant born and bred. He would not give in to those barbarians. They would not have the pleasure of his company. No sir. Where he walked and where he lay his head no one knew. That was the last that anyone ever heard of him. His boots scuffed the snow in clouds and his footsteps left a trail across fields he himself had ploughed for many decades. Cattle newly released from winter stalls raced past mad with freedom. Knots of refugees who had clung to their small holdings to the very end trudged across the ice bays. Finnish soldiers, terse and angry, along with a few individuals joined the throng. This was the picture painted that day.

Maarit and Mrs Kuisma and the children walked on for perhaps a kilometre, constantly looking over their shoulder.

'We should have moved long ago,' cried Mrs Kuisma helplessly. 'Everyone said so.'

Then God be praised a truck drove past and screeched to a halt. Two soldiers were in the cab heavy with fear and exertion.

'Get in the back!' they screamed. 'The enemy are minutes behind, we have to get to the new border.'

What did he mean, new border, wondered Maarit who was ignorant of the peace terms thrashed out in Moscow. But in they climbed grateful and relieved. There was a real jumble of materials on the floor, shoes, fabric, rolls of cloth the contents of a country store emptied to spite the Russians. It was all so unreal, a whirlwind of activity suddenly casting them from side to side on a road now crammed with refugees, carts, bicycles, soldiers, women and children, cows bellowing, horses straining at the bit, a tidal wave of humanity all desperate to reach safe ground, all eyes turned west. The road grew worse as the traffic increased, rutted and cratered. Straw and reeds tangled the wheels and progress slowed. An old man walked past with a stick and potted geranium under his arm. The green leaves shook as he tottered along. He carried nothing else, nothing.

'Whatever shall we do Maarit?'

'Let us worry about today Mrs Kuisma, tomorrow will take care of itself.'

Almost crawling now in an avenue congested with every form of transport. Broken packages, jam jars spilling soft red fruit into the mud, a grandfather clock standing vertically like a tombstone. In the rush to escape, people gathered whatever came to hand, without thought or logic. The results now littered this sad highway, lives discarded on the wayside, bit by bit and then trampled. But more disturbing still was the constant bellowing of cattle forced from their sheds into this chaos, hundreds of cows racing in circles, unbound by fences but lost and fearful, communicating an animal misery to all who could hear. It was a constant roar and these poor creatures did not rest but circled and herded together for comfort. Many a farmer witnessing this scene wished dearly they had put a bullet in their heads before this terrible exodus. It was too late now, too late for everything. When darkness fell the snow followed, light as a feather, a dove's feather from the ark, and the raven watched from the branches of a fir tree with an eye beady.

A long cold night they had of it. The sky was diamond, stars in sodium bulbs stretching light so faint across the column now parked along the road. It was too dark to move. Even Russians had to sleep, and were they really worth the chase? Somewhere a voice sang, a soft soprano voice breaking the air. Nestled in a bed of cotton and silk Maarit and Mrs Kuisma and the children slept fitfully and shivered. The old man with the stick and geranium died on the road side. The grandfather clock fell over with a crash. The cows bellowed, crazed with longing for the stalls.

When the sun rose on that final morning its warmth helped stir the multi-celled organism now stretching the cord of Karelia along this road.

The truck sparked into life, the wheels rolled, eyes squinted.

Where the burst of gun fire came from Maarit could never know. It just came...ripping through the canvas sides of the truck with a venom few experienced. Mrs Kuisma was the first to be hit, a gentle groan and she passed into eternity, almost as an aside, no drama, no fuss. Seconds later the two little girls followed before they were really awake. It was over so quickly that Maarit and the two soldiers were stunned. Before they could blink the day was quiet and calm, the sun shone, the frost thawed, the heron took to the wing and the cattle began their dance of madness. How strange this snuffing out of breath. How matter of fact.

She helped to lay their bodies on the road side. She planted a cross on their foreheads with her finger, pressed their hands together and left. What more was there to do?

The truck rattled onwards without clarity or thought to an unknown destination with Maarit in the back surrounded by the belongings of the now departed Kuisma family. How a line can so easily be wiped away, swatted as insects are, with no one left to remember them. Though she had physical strength there was a lameness to her spirit and the turbulence within her clattered along with the motion of the truck. She had not the energy to look out, to notice the ever increasing lines of refugees battling the cold, carrying whatever they could but determined, determined that while their homes, and farms and factories, and mills might soon become as one with the Soviet Union, they would not, not until hell freezes over. Fate picked Maarit up in her arms and she was willing to be carried wherever that universal river entered the sea.

*

All was quiet in Suomussalmi. It was a scene of inaction. A gentle thaw settled on the trees, droplets of water trickled down the branches when the sun was at its warmest, before freezing again as the sun settled low. Each drop reflected windows of turquoise and aquamarine, there was a sense of time passing. Crows cawed and scratched the hard earth, feathers dishevelled by the wind and the ice on rivers and lakes snapped with the acoustics of a rifle shot. No one spoke, no one shared their thoughts. In places wood smoke drifted into the air, a fire crackled. The final stretcher traversed the path to the clearing station.

Simo sat on a pile of logs smoking. His own thoughts he kept securely locked. Harri lent on his ski poles, face turned towards the Russian lines. Tears were streaming down his cheeks. He cried silently like a child and his eyes stung and his skull bled with bitterness on the inside. He did not care for anyone to see, and when he heard the lieutenant's tread in the snow behind him, he rubbed his face with the sleeve of his coat.

'Stay awake lads,' he said, 'the company will form up at the bottom of the ridge. We have orders to fall back, to the new border. I don't want anyone to get trapped behind their lines.'

'Do you know anything Lieutenant?' asked Simo.

'No more than yourselves…there is a new border, Viipuri is lost, as to anything else, well no one has informed me.'

'But we have beaten them sir!' cried Harri barely disguising the despair in his voice.

'So we have son,' replied the lieutenant, 'but we have lost the war. We never had much chance, not without help. Come on, follow me. There is no point waiting here.'

At the bottom of the ridge there was a road, heavily compacted by the passing of many armies. A sled waited there with a pony in the traces, a brown pony steaming in the cold. They piled their skis onto the back and formed two lines, one on either side of the road.

The lieutenant called them to attention, ordered the stragglers to tidy up their uniforms and in a voice full of seriousness and authority ordered the company to quick march. So they left that killing field marching like proper parade ground soldiers. Even Simo managed to keep in step. At first they were alone but after a time they were joined by others, also marching with the stamping of their boots on the road defiant and their numbers swelling. By midday they crossed the new border still in two long grey and white files. The civilians resting there applauded and clapped and slapped them on the back, and someone in the rear started to sing and the chorus was taken up along the whole length and the more they sang the more the crowds applauded and the men of Finland knew then that their spirit was not broken. They understood that this indeed was not the end. They did not hand in their weapons but cleaned and stored them. What ammunition remained they stockpiled and their skis they stroked and greased in readiness. The sobbing of their hearts they kept in check and their wounds they licked and the scaring of their minds they covered over. No this was not the end. So it was this mighty river withdrawing in good order, blooded but undefeated. From every crevice of the eastern lands the survivors poured, leaving their dead behind them. From the shores of Lake Ladoga, from the Kollaa and Kuhmo, from the northern outposts, from the rocky crags of the Arctic Ocean and the islands of the gulf, and finally…finally the Isthmus emptied. How God must have wept for them, but these men pushed out their jaws and sang a road to the new country.

*

So as the first part of this tale draws to a conclusion, I drill my memory for events clouded in fog and realise how much has changed within me since those days. If there are discrepancies and shifts in person or even tense please excuse it as the ramblings of a man not quite at his best and circumstances where many of the characters who flit in and out of this narrative are now gone, or like myself are utterly changed.

I was sitting in a chair with a rug over my legs. My mother entered the cabin and I could tell she was upset. She did not cry, a hard life wrings the tears out of you, it dries you out as if you were the inhabitant of a smoking shed. In a stern voice she stated clearly, without emotion, 'Well Hannu my son, and Tuija my daughter, it is over.'

She had just returned from the farm house where there was a radio. Many people had gathered that mid-March morning to hear the news and all departed in silence. 'We have lost our home. They have snatched it away from us and stolen all that we ever had. Viipuri is gone, Petsamo, Hanko, Ladoga, the whole of the Isthmus, there is hardly a thread of Karelia remaining. What a price we have paid in land and blood for our stubbornness and hostility. What was it all for? They have exactly what they wanted, what they had demanded. We should have handed it over to them before this war ever started.'

She sank into a chair shaking with emotion. Tuija simply cried uncontrollably and Merja followed her example even though the cause of this distress was incomprehensible to her.

For a few moments I sat rigid in the chair rubbing the wound in my chest. I almost…almost wished for the squeal of an air raid siren to break the silence and confirm that no, it was not over. But I had not the energy to fight on, even within myself. I was so fatigued. My fingers were heavy and lips blistered. 'We had to resist,' I said. 'We had no choice, had we surrendered they would have demanded more and more. That is the way of things. We had to show them what free men can do.'

Mother shook her head and rocked in the chair more disturbed than I had ever seen her.

'They have enough ground to bury their dead, no more,' I continued. 'What else was said?'

'Well the President gave a fine speech, as such people do and there is no arguing with the tone of it. We have responsibilities, he said, to the widows. God there are so many of them, we must aid the sick and the wounded and the homeless and the destitute. We must give what we have and show the same stubbornness in peace time as we did in war. Not one person chose to stay he said, and as his words tumbled out even in the farmhouse kitchen, even between we few, there was a spark of hatred and anger towards those monsters. He went on to list our losses, 40,000 farms, 400,000 Finns displaced, mostly our own people, Karelians…what will become of us?' On she talked as if her words would hold back the tide of sorrows welling behind her eyes. As for myself I took the workshop key from my pyjama pocket and caressed it. I turned it over in my fingers, polished the brass on my sleeve and saw a pale reflection of myself in the metal. And out of the window a single Finnish sun exploded, razored at the edges and slicing through the forest, trim like a burst of arrows turning all it met into a wall of blood.

PART TWO

Chapter 14

So dark is this green forest, so like charcoal are the atoms tumbling through the branches and colliding with my eyes. The track I follow, seldom trod has the look of the viper about it as it curls around roots and logs long since embarked upon a journey of decay. Sweat streams from my forehead and my tongue flicks out to taste the saltiness of the liquid. The steady pendulum of my boots raises clouds of dust, yellow as sand, emitting grunts with each step so progress is marked by the thundering of battalions, so much so that with each veering to the left or right swarms of chaffinches are flushed out and entertain my thoughts with their mockeries and histrionics. Still the heat steams, a haze rises and the journey becomes uncomfortable, my shirt is soaked and the pain in my chest simmers, a soreness designed to antagonise more than anything else. The cracking of twigs underfoot adds to the protest so the overwhelming impression is that of a world splintered or shrivelled due to summer's long assault.

But I know this place, its many tangled corridors hold no fears or strangeness for I have walked them inch by inch through all the seasons of this year, ever since my body found itself delivered to this province like a parcel. Even before the string was untied, before official issue brown paper was ripped from my skin I discovered these hidden pathways and gave myself over to exploration. It was the solitude that first attracted me to this spot. Not the silence. For anyone who seeks a silent refuge in a forest is devoid of hearing or perception. A forest is a single living organism teeming, one animal, a creature multi-celled with every membrane squeezed into utterance. Every step disturbs or kills, turns a stone, brushes a spore, dents the armour of an ammonite. If you pause, as I often do to drink air rustling with vibrations, you are aware that to our feeble ears these frequencies are blunt instruments, there are sounds too high and low for brains encased in bone to disassemble, the tapping of a woodpecker is all we can discern, but not the purring of a hornet's wing, the slither of an earthworm through litter, the drop of oil upon a beetle's back dripping to the floor. These are major orchestrations to creatures more sophisticated than we can ever hope to be, even with our crude technologies. We hear the timpani but not the harp. So I train myself to listen, to conceive, to funnel and filter all that flows in my direction. I discipline myself, straining all the senses so now I hear the forest as a colour, as cochineal, the colour of autumn, of life and death and replenishment. So now as summer's breath exhales I hear the red and green blasting a path through vegetation in a constant state of flux, falling as quicksand or fusing with the sky, harnessing sunlight with the force of a nuclear explosion. Blink once and it is all gone. All change, the scene has shifted.

But hark my destination lies before me. A clearing carved by hands where the sunlight is uncaptured by chlorophyll and a crown of yellow marks the ground. Grasses grow, dragonflies skim across the surface and the sap of the birch tree oozes forth and the ants scurrying across its bark are engulfed. It is the appointed time. I sit and wait and lose myself.

I stretch out my arms as does a lizard garnering warmth, with a smile upon my face, unseen, unobserved by the well meaning, curving mentally as I imagine an armadillo curls, though not in response to any threat, more in a sense of well-being, in this spot, where words are not hurled towards me and there was no need to field questions or explain those things that cannot be explained only experienced. You had to be there I would say, when I could bring myself to say anything. If only people knew how inclined to interrogation they were.

The scent of ramson drifted on the breeze and my eyes caught sight of a huge ant hill at the edge of the clearing. A cone dropped from the sky and now feverishly constructed and demolished, subsuming countless pine needles and twigs. Centipedes burrowed there, and a caterpillar lumpy as a pillow strayed too close and was attacked. In a fury of formic acid I saw it dissolve and with my ears fine-tuned fancied I heard it sizzling. This was no place for the squeamish. In the distance near and far were more nests, more cones and they reminded me of a photograph I had seen in a magazine of temples in the hills of Burma, now overrun no doubt by other armies. I recall their peculiar shape and the chocolate brown of the surface and the peculiar way they seem to have been dumped there, in a range of soft, rounded hills in the heat of the tropics where they melted...or so I thought. Now in this forest, in central Finland, far from home, ants squeak their antennae towards the merest hint of movement, assessing dangers and possibilities. Thousands of them trample the undergrowth foraging and submerge. A few walk across my boots gathering a yellow dust. One dies, another emerges from pupae. A butterfly rests its wings on my hand sucking mineral salts from the skin.

When Harri appeared I did not rise to greet him but left him alone to find his own way to my side. Likewise, he said nothing for awhile. I noticed his shock of white hair uncut and a vodka bottle in his back pocket.

'You look stronger Hannu,' he said.

'I feel good...my strength returns, I have some shortness of breath but it will improve. The doctor says I should get some gentle exercise everyday.'

'Bet he didn't mean find a spot like this.'

'There are worse places.'

'Tell me about it,' said Harri aggrieved, swatting midges from his face with a hand. 'If I stay in that house any longer I'll murder someone, probably my mother. The place is too small, three families sharing a space no bigger than a cowshed. So much noise and squabbling and all my mother can think about is the pots and pans she left behind. Why the hell did she bury

213

them in the garden? I wouldn't mind but she was the first to leave. She could have packed them no trouble. I tell you Hannu if ever I get back there, first thing I'm going to do is dig them up and obliterate them with a satchel charge.'

I paused and watched the butterfly spread its wings in the sun.

'Do you think we will go back?'

This time it was Harri's turn to consider.

'I don't know,' he said, 'we are rearming. I expect to be called up any day now. People say we are going to throw our lot in with the Germans; I don't like the sound of that, pact with the devil if you ask me. Still you should be safe enough with that wound of yours, for a time at least. Personally I can't wait to get back, out of this madness. I only have to walk down the street to be stopped, someone after something. Did you see Keke or Esko? No, I say, I was transferred from Taipale, I have no news, I saw nothing, I know only that the Russians didn't take many prisoners. My son is missing, could he be safe or lost or like you transferred to another unit? He could be I say, lying through my teeth, who knows, but I did not see him, there is no need to show me his photograph, leave it at home, there is no point waiting at the railway station, scanning every face on the platform. How can I say he will not come, I have enough to worry about. But this spot, it is well chosen, no one can disturb us here.'

The ferns swayed and the heat haze shimmed across the ground. The forest seemed to shake like a mirage, yet still the plants grew upwards and the squirrels watched and the breeze imparted new scents, of nectarine, of tobacco from Harri's cigarette and the resin of pine trees. Neither of us felt inclined to move.

'How is Merja?' added Harri, eager to keep the conversation going.

'She seems happy enough. Mother is worried, you know about her reading and so on. She has no friends, but then she doesn't feel the need for any.'

'Does she hear anything at all?'

'No, it will not return. Mother and Tuija find it frustrating and I'm sure she plays on it, to get her way. We will need patience, I can make her understand. Maybe she can actually hear something of what I say or maybe she lip reads, but I can communicate most of the time.'

'You have the gift Hannu, you predicted this war when we were still children, in your dreams you saw it, and can you remember that time you called the artillery down at Taipale?'

'It was a coincidence, no more.'

'As you say.'

Harri shuffled uneasily, he was growing restless again. Always he fidgeted, crossed from one place to another, then back again. Ever since he returned from the front and was reunited with the remains of the village folk in Hämeenlinna he displayed this sense of always wanting to be somewhere else. Some of that devil-may-care evaporated. The peace terms haunted him; he could not understand the loss of so much territory, so many lives. I had real fears for him. But now he said his goodbyes and walked back through the forest. We would meet here again when we wanted to talk, a verdant atoll free from prying eyes.

I did not leave for a long time, not until the swarms of mosquitoes cast their sirens into the air did I even begin to stir, not until the foxgloves bent a heavy head or the fronds of the hart's tongue fern incised the dusk did I amble along the track, casting my thoughts back, cutting out memories as a peat cutter works the land, one slab at a time. If truth be told I felt a little tired. The heat and humidity choked my lungs so the journey to the cabin was a difficult one. As I walked I pictured Simo searching for his son among the bogs and fells of Lapland where last he was seen and as the weary hours dragged and I entered the barley fields I knew I would have a difficult night. In the light of midsummer which dimmed but never set I saw the amber moon suspended and switched the bulrushes of the lakeside with a stick. Rose-bay-willow herb swayed at my passing until, many hours later, I pushed the cabin door open and crept inside.

Tuija and Merja were asleep. My mother, dozing in a chair, started at my entrance.

'Hannu,' she said, 'it's you.' As if it could be anybody else. 'Where have you been?'

'Walking…I met up with Harri, and well, time passed.'

'I have news for you.'

'O yes?'

'Farmer Jarvinen has some tools for you. They are old he says but they can be repaired. There may be some work, nothing too strenuous obviously, bench work mainly.'

'That's good,' I said genuinely pleased. I missed my work and ached to start, even in a small way. 'When can I collect them?'

'Tomorrow he said, but that is not all. Someone wants to meet you, has something for you.'

'Who?'

'I am sworn to secrecy but you must go to the church at Hattula tomorrow morning.'

I nodded when she mentioned the church. I was so tired by now that I didn't think anything of it, just assumed that the pastor had some use of me, something to do with his precious bell. I took off my shirt and slumped into bed.

That night the weather broke. Rain fell, torrential rain hammering the roof and swamping the windows. A thumping, violent, personal attack on the cabin and surrounding trees. Branches snapped and the wind roared angry deprecations into every corner of the room. What once was land now became ocean and the draining humidity of the last few days was replaced by spray. Summers heat dissipated in a hail of pins, stabbing and pulling swathes of grey clouds across the sky with bill hooks. How many slants the cabin rode and how many fixtures unhooked with the ferocity of it all I could not tell. The blankets covered my head for the thunder brought with it the time shaken memories of other bombardments and the blankets covering yielded fresh remembrances of my body prematurely covered with earth. And the great pike swam towards me once

216

more with a gaping mouth and gills sliced along the whole. Lightning cut the monster's throat lunging into all that was perpendicular until with a crash it found a mark. Fire burst from its long tongue which in its turn was quenched by water. In tangled veins drops pattered to the floor and I cupped my hand to capture liquid, drinking of it as a last supper. So the apples in the corner boxes released their scents and the atmosphere of this rustic storeroom permeated the bedding.

When at last I slept it was the sleep of stone, the slumbers of a man upon a funeral pyre.

Then morning.

Then the hayrick sun slipped through the window and I rubbed my face with it. Everyone slept, only the faintest mumbling of breath disturbed the outer room. My leaving went unnoticed.

I remember that morning vividly. There were marsh vapours rising from the ground, seeking me out and swirling wherever I walked. Like a benign stranger it followed my footsteps, splashing and sucking an earth now sodden and snared with traps cast down by the storm. How still was the sky but so refreshing and it cleansed my heart to be out so early. In all honesty I looked forward to my meeting with the pastor. I liked him and had the patience to bear his sermons. In his mannerisms I saw the loneliness and frustrations he dutifully suffered, and I suppose I felt a little sorry for the battles he lost. I was alike to him in some ways too. Things had to be just so, I appreciated that, it made sense to me that all human artefacts and possessions had a place within the scheme of things. We villagers were a disappointment to him, never quite reaching the standard. Too much drinking, carousing, cynicism. But then we too had our place...and it was not here.

The stillness of the air gave an eerie quality to the journey. The grey visibility made me stop and check my whereabouts. This district still bore much of the unfamiliar and, with the mist still cloaking my head, I stumbled into the village of Hattula almost before I realised I was there.

There was the church, a simple, red-bricked building with a tiled roof, with a dry stone wall around it. In this spot it had stood since the builders laid their trowels and peasants delved into the soil to lay foundations which had held firm for seven hundred years. Since first my eyes had garnered the heavy set interior I knew this place was dripping with prayer. A lingering fog of incense captured my senses. Ghosts walked the nave and chancel. I saw them in their furs and rough and ready clothing, grime-layered skin and hair wild. Some looked at me and others passed me by. Some spoke in languages I could hardly understand and the lips of others mumbled and their fingers clasped rosaries and the light diffusing from windows arched in stone illuminated their many comings and goings, sores and tumours and deformities and all. I saw the ghosts and they returned my interest with stares of inquisitiveness. They did not frighten me, their kind I had seen so many times. Yet I was curious as to why the pastor wished to meet with me. Perhaps some work, some restoration, but the church at Hattula was far from his roots and I could not believe he would approve of the images painted in browns and yellows and pale blues. All the saints walked the walls, climbed the pillars, some I recognised and some...well they were a mystery. There were swirls and ribbons and stunted trees and flowers and representations of Christ in all his agonies challenging the congregation. But then he was not here, only the slab-stoned floor caused the light to rebound into my face, no dust stirred, no vibrations, no hesitant steps. After a time I began to think perhaps I had made some mistake, misunderstood the time, the wrong church even for as I said this place was a most peculiar meeting place for a man so Lutheran!

I paced the walls examining icons, allowing the ghosts of peasants long since dead to pass through my body and the chill of them made my chest sting. To pass the time I ran my fingers over the pulpit carvings gouged to primitive life by craftsmen I could only envy. Saints and bishops in robes where every seam and line of fabric shimmered, grasping in their hands orbs and crucifixes. Above them skulls scowled and skeletons mocked them in their finery and knew one day their mortality would crumble.

When the door creaked open the spectres flew and I turned to greet the new arrival with some minor irritation for I had been kept waiting. I did not call out, my sense of decorum forbade it. In the gloom of the porch I saw the figure with a scarf and long dress. At first I took it to be some inhabitant of these ancient cloisters grown bold. But when she removed her scarf and shook her hair I knew it could not be so.

It was Maarit out of the blue, from a candle flame stepping down the nave towards me. I could not move, nor could I open my lips.

'A fine welcome I must say. All this time and all you can do is open your mouth like a goldfish. Don't you have anything to say to me?'

Eventually I summoned my senses but could only mumble, 'I thought you were the pastor.'

'Wonderful…I admit to some slight changes in appearance but the pastor?'

'Or a ghost.'

'Well I can assure you that I am neither.'

She stood by the door and the light encircled her. I must have stared for a few seconds but in the stillness of the church it seemed an age. Maarit was thinner, no that is not the correct word, slender, more grown up and her hair, while still the colour of barley, was shorter, cascading down her face to the shoulders. Her eyes still blue and freckles enhancing the prettiness of a face that had captured me from the first. Suddenly I felt weak and my muscles contracted with a real indiscipline. I though I might faint.

Then it was she shouted. She had a temper Maarit. Her voice shook the walls echoing and rebounding. 'Are you going to stand there all day you idiot.'

I stood.

'Well?' she said arching her eyebrows and placing her hands on her hips. 'Never mind…I'll do it.'

She raced towards me, and flung her arms around me and well…the tears flowed and I responded as I covered her in kisses and held on to her.

'You didn't write,' she said.

'Nor did you,' I responded.

'I was busy.'

'So was I.'

'At least that's settled.'

We stood as robeless spirits for awhile until Maarit, wiping her face on the sleeve of her shirt and rearranging her hair, pulled me outside. This place gave her the creeps, she said. I did not reply but let myself be pulled into the shadow of a lime tree in the churchyard. We sat down and I think I must have been still in a state of shock for whatever words I uttered came out as gibberish and all she could do was laugh and pull my fingers.

'My how you have changed,' she said.

'Do you think so?'

'You look like a skeleton and your eyes have grown tired.'

'I'd almost forgotten,' I said, looking at her lips, but I could not elaborate. I left it at that. Eventually with a real effort of will I managed to ask her where she had been, why it had taken so long to reach Hämeenlinna, why she had not contacted me. But enough of that.

'Enough,' she said, 'I'll explain about that later. I want to know what you've been doing to yourself. You promised me you would keep your head down, come back to me in one piece.'

I did not remember promising but took it as a compliment, so with time, under the lime tree we refreshed our memories and found our way back a year, to another time.

Time brought some recollections in with the tide and my shyness and uncertainty was exacerbated by the pain in my chest. My feelings, like lanterns in reeds, glowed and dimmed and I prayed that I would find the words to express myself. She gazed at me constantly and some times she interrupted but always she smiled and I discovered afresh the liveliness that was within her. Sometimes she caught my arm or gently pushed me away. I was aware of a mosaic of shadow and light as the breeze ruffled the branches of the lime tree. It was as if she didn't want to stop talking, that any interruption to the flow would break the spell and our conversation was a curious mix of intensity and silences, on my part, as I thought about the winter past and attempted to re-live it for her sake. I talked about Simo and his teeth and cooking pot, and when she laughed I dived deeper in the whirlpool, even my arms tingled and my head struggled to cope with new impressions flying. Some things I glossed over. I did not explain our reasons for leaving Taipale nor did I go into the detail concerning my wound. I was daydreaming, I said, and she stated gravely how lucky I had been. When I mentioned Harri's name she grew reticent so I guessed she knew about him and his wild ways and his drinking and the trouble he had caused in the town. He was gaining a reputation and while we knew the root of it, there was no excuse, we all bore a burden of bitterness. We were all homesick. I longed to see the village again and go back a year ago when the mid-summer bonfires threatened the forest and Old Man Hannu walked the fields. Neither of us dared to consider the havoc unleashed upon it now, the familiar being desecrated. No we could not bare it. So it came as yet another shock that she was there when it was finally overcome. She too kept her secrets and I did not enquire. As for her adventures in the Lotta Svard in Helsinki and the Kollaa river, words failed me, and I must admit to some sharpness in my voice when she recounted the details. I said that my Maarit should not put herself in such peril.

'So I am your Maarit,' she said, teasing.

I could not answer.

'It is a decency for my Hannu to get himself killed in the wilderness but not for his Maarit.'

'So am I your Hannu?' I asked before my shyness could prevent me.

'Maybe…it depends.'

And my reticence washed over though my heart burst and she looked beneath the lime tree like an angel and spoke and teased me gentle, with good humour drawing me towards her as she had done so many times before. My voice evaporated, it

221

would not operate, such is the curse of shyness, even to the one enfolded with you. My eyes were aqua lensed and I saw Maarit as a vision through water harmonising sky and glide, ripple and dew, flooding my hiding places.

She looked solemnly at my face and then burst out laughing once again. 'Oh my Hannu,' she cried.

'So I am yours.'

'Yes, you have always been though it drives me mad to say it. I'm sure some evil spirit smote me when I saw you scowling through the village all those years ago, annoying all and sundry.'

I started.

'Do I annoy you also?'

'Constantly,' she replied rather too quickly.

'Oh,' I said hurt.

'Come my wounded soldier, let me walk you home, you are paler than a birch tree and I fear I am too much for you.'

True it was I felt a little weak. The road to Hattula was many miles, and as yet I had but half my strength. For the first time I saw the edge of concern on her face as she linked her arm with mine and guided me home along the road. How I must have seemed to her, so broken in breath and leaning on her for support. But within my soul I grew strong. I realised on that road where the rose bay trickled into sand and the gorse thickets spiked my clothing that with time my body would heal. One day soon it would emerge from hibernation to surprise my family and friends, and that when war came once more, as I knew it would, I would rejoin my comrades and return home. My real home, the dwelled in place.

Of all my memories that journey to the cabin carved the deepest, to the bone. It was then I understood that when my time elapsed I would fold this one remembrance and pass it to the angel, saying take this for me. Take this, carry for me the time I walked with her arm in arm, and it felt as if I stepped upon the branches of an orchid tree, on the banks of a many saddled river looped down vales. Where the scents of pine unfolding slipped within and three not one earths merged. When her song glistened like silver and breezes haunted the many headed stranger I had seen so many times before. When the children gold combed the autumn rustle and she danced. She danced upon the steps of Hattula and spun the churchyard cat into a frenzy. Carry for me the moment when she laced the web with many layered reflections, do this for me.

By the time we reached the sanctuary of the cabin I was exhausted and had to sit on the chair before my breath recovered. It gave time for Maarit and my mother to catch up on events, they had always communicated freely. No mention was made of the village, it was a painful subject. There was talk of the storm and the damage it had caused...but then the gaping wound it had torn in the sky softened the air. Maarit seemed confident, at her ease, but I could not prevent myself from slipping into sleep such was my weariness. I noticed the concern they both exhibited, yet I felt despite the tiredness as if I was re-born, purposeful. Since those first attacks in the Taipale sector my life I had suspended, thinking merely of the day but now a future unfolded. It was my perception that an understanding now existed between us, and it was driven by Maarit for she had the energy and will, enough for us both. She was fearless in her pursuit of happiness and I was happy for her to be so.

Many were the experiences she re-counted, many more she censored or adapted, diminished or embroidered to an audience gasping. Even little Merja focused on expression and seemed to gain an inkling of the conversation. Weak coffee was distributed and oat cakes, and in the intimacy of that room time flowed in rivers and the light dimmed only marginally. Many things were agreed that day. Maarit would visit again from her room in the town when her duties as a nurse and cleaner at the hospital allowed. She would borrow a bicycle from the farm to return, for it was close to midnight and the walk would be too arduous at this hour...and yes she would pass on good wishes to her parents who could be found at a relative's house on the Baltic coast. When she stood to leave I said I would walk with her down the path but she would not hear of it and kissed me on the forehead and told me to do as I was told. We all noticed that kiss, a simple act that hastened my recovery more than any treatments or medications. She dripped good will onto the floor, draped her personality onto walls and furniture so we of the Juutalainen family felt at last as if the darkest hour had passed. We counted our blessings.

She waved across the lemon light skipping almost into the forest. Ions scattered through her hair, sparks flew from her so it seemed, fizzing sparks of yellow and blue. In the twilight where bats curved their orbits through the trees and chattered in frequencies unknown she slipped her body armour. I saw her lone diminishing figure casting spells upon the milk hamlets with her fingers, crisp the wayside berries and with kind words greet all who tilled the meadows salty. Her summer eyes poured magic on the lily pond. She was gone.

Yet.

Throughout this day fermenting I did not disclose the call I heard when deep within the bunker she cried my name. The thrust she parried to my ribs from that black interior, the lunge that tore me into pieces as the shrapnel rained. She must not know for horror would engulf her surely.

Chapter 15

At home I was never one of those people given over to thinking about the future. Few of us were. In that sense I would describe my approach to life as deciduous, in summer, water and nourishment, and winter losing leaves and battening down, living off the stores, riding the storm. We were educated to a basic level. We were expected to work the fields, care tenderly for cattle or horses, grasp the opportunities afforded by the forest. Some laboured in timber yard or mill, a few worked for the railways. Others like myself became apprentices as farriers or wheelwrights. Increasingly some boys took to the new fangled motor vehicles. You could tell them by their oil-smeared hands and a vocabulary littered with words like gasket and filter and cylinder head. Uncouth if you ask me. I never had much time for all that nonsense. If truth be told there were few decisions to be made. Work – it was one thing or the other, whatsoever your father decided, whatever you happened to drop into without thought or inclination, so there you stayed. Marriage – it happened somehow. One day you were a married man and children came along and with time you lost your hair and teeth and became dust, so it was without complaint or introspection. The seasons governed, spring sowing, harvest, cattle to the stalls, cattle to the meadow, fishing, gathering wood, hunting. For myself I participated in all these activities but supplemented my income by carving the handles of the hunting knife no man would be without. I repaired the wheels of carts, constructed frames for cabins, hung doors, fixed shelves, built tables of a primitive design, fixed roofs. I was pretty good at it, took a great pride in the work and took a fancy to being known as a craftsman.

Then there was the church to comb the irregularities out of you. The bell summoned good and bad. The services attended in best Sunday clothes without compunction. The pastor droning on and on and we listening politely. Christmas entombed in the warmth of the cabins with heat from the stove biting winter's darkness back, candles flickering and the cattle bellowing their satisfaction. Easter when in solemn tone we would all chant, 'At the last Eucharist Jesus sat down at the table to eat our Easter lamb.' All these events had significance and in our naïvety believed them carved in stone. True we had to join the Civic Guard but we did not consider the drills and parading a serious affair. We were famous for our incompetences in saluting, for the bedraggled way we wore our uniforms, for our difficulties in left and right turns. But our marksmanship we worked upon with religious fervour, we could ski well, we were tough and stubborn and enduring. This was a land we picked with the autumn mushroom and the glaze of ice on ponds and the mid-summer mosquito, we were as one with it. Its bite touched us not, the weal of discomfort we bore without noticing.

Yet our village was not a picture of isolation, not as others tended to be. Two roads quartered, one from north to south and the other east to west. There was a tiny station with a warehouse. The steam trains from Viipuri whistled down the track and we could hear them when the wind blew in the right direction. The Saimaa canal too cut through our district from the great lake systems of the west to Viipui itself and many times I stood upon the bridge at Malkia and watched the freighters glide the journey home. We were something of a hub with spokes radiating outwards. New opportunities unfolded, especially for young girls who carried school certificates in their pocket. Girls like Maarit who fancied a spell in Helsinki or Tampere or Turku before the pull of Karelia lured them home, as it always did.

226

Yet for all these subtle changes we still nailed ourselves to the old ways, to practises and superstitions long evolved. Many a battle we waged with pastors over our beliefs in demons and witches and hags and spells. We saw no contradiction in our following the church and adherence to this magic. Shamans were widely respected. Some lived amongst us, others travelled through the wildest, densest forests to emerge without eyes, with hair of tree moss and lichen-coated boots. We dared not antagonise them. When they offered recitations we listened, when herbal remedies in bottles green were pulled from pockets we poured them down the throats of our cattle as a defence against fever. We shared our dreams and premonitions with them, hanging on every word of response. Once when our current pastor was new he caught wind that a shaman of ancient years was holding court by the stream, he raced down and the shaman, on his approach, stood up. Keeping quite still he ceased his breathing and held out his arms in simulation of a tree so the pastor when he arrived red-faced and agitated, could nether see nor hear nor feel his presence. When he turned back to the church the shaman returned and our laughter wrenched the pine cones down.

This mingling of beliefs caused the tradition of placing crosses of wood in the forest. At every sighting of a ghost a cross was plunged into the ground as a warning. In the months before the war began there was a profusion of sightings and the crosses grew with the summer sun. All took this to be a sign of evil times to come. When there was a death, trees of the parish boundary were scratched with crosses to guide the spirits of the departed home. But they could not pass beyond the markers. They could look in upon the village but not enter. This we took to be a very good thing!

As for myself I saw the souls of our departed with greater clarity than others. From my childhood I saw ancient warriors rise from the ground and pass me by with the glint of battle upon them, many thousands of men with swords gripped tightly, of bow men, and heroes with battle axes and shields painted with the symbol of the raven or eagle. Many a time an arrow passed through me to embed itself in a tree. Once I saw a man sink in the mire that covers much of this land. Some peasant long forgotten with a staff that followed his terrified screams into the bog that leads to hell, where all believe he still burns. That frightened me, that experience. His shrieks followed me home and for many years I could not bring myself to return to that spot. Even now I am circumspect when traversing the marsh lands.

Yet gentler are the images of home brought to me when in the solitude of my room, or when traversing alone knee high in bracken in the forest, I cast my mind back. The youngsters gathered on the swinging hill, laughing and joking, fooling around…and quietly when adult eyes were otherwise preoccupied sipping cider borrowed from the storehouse and rolling down the slopes like logs to make the world giddy. Every youngster did it and every adult forgot that they had, too, once, while shaking heads in disapproval. Every cabin had a garden with an apple tree and lilac and patches of potatoes nowhere surpassed for succulence.

So what you may ask is the point of this ramble? Well, before I lose myself to memory I intend to convey the strangeness of the idea of forward planning, of constructing a future in your mind, committing it to paper even, and then working towards its fulfilment. This notion was quite foreign to me.

Events took an unexpected turn towards the end of that summer. The summer of 1940. My chest was healing faster than anyone could have expected. A medical assessment in August of that year indicated that I might eventually get back to full fitness as long as I didn't do anything stupid. There were bouts of shortness of breath, an occasional fever; that was all. Of more concern was my inability to sleep. When the lanterns dimmed and the cabin settled then it was my mind raced and in my dreams all manner of grotesques emerged from passages and assaulted my being verbally. There was little sense to it…yet it was real. I was buffeted and by morning exhausted. These dreams I did not mention to anyone but somehow I caught snippets of conversation between my mother and Tuija. Sometimes I shouted and woke them and the thoughts about what I might have called embarrassed me. My mother ministered as she always had but I think she too slept fitfully and seemed to age rapidly, always giving the appearance of tiredness. With hindsight she was torn between a desire to see me well again and a fear that if I did attain some level of fitness I might be liable to military service. They were hard times and when I look back I wonder that we ever got through them. Yet we did, and later endured even more.

Everyday I walked, it lifted my spirits. The sunshine browned my skin and lightened my hair. I liked to wander alone, and if you have ever wandered alone at day's end you will know what I mean. Hattula was a favourite haunt. The ghosts inhabiting this church were quite accustomed to my presence. I saw them haggling and quarrelling and kneeling on the rush floor in prayer. Women brought their children to be blessed and traders bore bundles of fur, beaver, marten and wolverine tied with cord and propped up and sniffed by prospective buyers. They looked at me, sometimes rolled out a few phrases I could not understand, but did not smile; such is the way of ghosts. Curiously if another person entered through the porch they disappeared, in a flash the church emptied and then it was I made my way back to the cabin. In other small ways our life of displacement began to take shape. I repaired the tools found for me and undertook small repairs for the locals. I fixed shelves in the cabin, strengthened the beds, constructed a stool and some play things for Merja. Tuija found work in a munitions factory though what she did and what she made was a mystery, even to her. It quickly became apparent that we were re-arming rapidly. There was a permanent guard at the railway station but the endless trucks laden with artillery and tanks and girders of steel could not be masked. Much of this new equipment came from Germany and we began to catch sight of German soldiers from time to time, not many it is true, but a number.

My solitary hikes were interrupted only by meetings with Harri. His moods swung unpredictably from despair to euphoria and back again. The military build up warmed his heart and the merest mention of a rifle or mortar caused the old grin to widen on his face. For awhile his drinking eased, he took up with a girl from Pori with impressive breasts and an unsavoury reputation. I suppose there were worse things. He was always expecting to be called up but for some reason he never was, not for awhile at least. I for one was glad. His company was a tonic for me. As I say we feathered our nest, if guiltily, for the sake of Merja mostly who would in the evenings walk with me through the forest with a canvas bag. She had a mania for collecting pine cones, taking them back to the cabin and tipping them into the corner. When she slept my mother would take them out and cast them away. Merja never seemed to notice.

One memory I have of that summer, was from the end of August, a day of balm and sultriness when the air was laden with a descending heat. I met with Maarit on the jetty jutting in to the lake known as Katuma. It was a small lake, not far from the cabin. It gave the impression of being scooped from granites when mighty glaciers melted but now it was a location of subtleness and gentility. Maarit was bare foot and she dangled her feet into the water. When she saw me coming she waved and pointed to the rowing boat tied at the end. She knew I was fond of rowing and with some cunning had arranged to borrow the boat more as an indulgence to me than anything else. With her legs still dripping she followed me onto the seat, untied the lanyard and pushed away. The day was the colour of her hair. The water was treacle, each stroke of the oar sucked up with a splash, and ripples bounced across the surface as we travelled ever so slowly out into the solitude. Reeds bordered the edges, amber reeds, cinnamon sticks rigid and scentful. Bulrushes too swayed and gossiped and murmured. Pine needles spun as we unsettled them, brown needles augmenting the texture of the lake with fresh patterns. I scrutinised the scene from above, as if we were two other people and it gave me intense joy to be both participant and observer. Maarit said very little, she trailed her hand from the bow and once remarked about the dragonflies and then the fish lumbering through syrup. We did not need words.

Hawks gazed upon us from adjacent pine trees; they did not stir, too lazy in that atmosphere. The sun encircled our shoulders, and the water was a sheet of gold disturbed only by the struggling of insects captured by the film.

Maarit looked at me and started to laugh. This was becoming quite a common occurrence. I don't know why. I have never been particularly humorous. I always considered myself a serious type.

'What are you thinking?' she asked, dipping her hand into the metal.

'I'm just rowing,' I answered puzzled.

This caused a fit of hysterics.

'Your brain is covered by a dust coat Hannu. I look at you and wonder what is going on in that mind of yours. Half the time I'm convinced there is nothing at all...it is an empty space. Sometimes it feels like...like when you enter a room two people leave. Then you utter some comment so out of synch with anything we've been discussing it takes me a week to catch up with you.'

'I'm sorry you feel that way.'

I started to row rapidly as if in some mad attempt at flight from a conversation that was well...confusing. It was all a little odd. Maarit noticed and shook with laughter so violently that the boat rocked and I had fears for our safety. She must have registered the alarmed expression on my face and calmed a little.

'Don't worry I'm not serious.'

The rest of the afternoon I spent rowing around the shore. Maarit dozed and I watched her. It was a time of true delight. We returned to the jetty late. The sky still folded in layers of lemon. The air still tanged with the scent of citrus. We walked home arm in arm and did not feel the need for conversation. The gentle pressure of our bodies close, touching, was sufficient. And I suppose from my imaginary vantage point high above I saw two young people leaning together, ambling along without consideration for time or direction, dwindling as the distance lengthened, becoming smaller and more silent as figures in a film set.

Sometimes a powerful sense of guilt broke upon me. This happiness we both experienced was...wrong. While we both longed for home and shared a sense of displacement with everyone else home mattered less and less. Karelia did not constantly occupy our thoughts as it did for others. Our time together mitigated that sense of loss. It enabled us to secure the moment from memories of pain and anguish. Within a few months my time as a soldier, of Taipale and Suomussalmi became an abstract, the experiences of a callow youth, a namesake but a different Hannu to the man idling around Hämeenlinna with a girl on his arm, eager to explore the lakes and forests of that province. We unearthed gems like the house of Emil Wikstrom, a mighty fine sculptor who worked in these parts, and sometimes we talked about his work and somehow I gained the impression that Maarit was trying to educate me, but I did not mind, I liked it.

Yet dark clouds remained. No human effort could push them away, like wheat bread they could not be unbaked but spat hot ashes at us from the oven. Harri got into even more trouble. He was arrested after a drunken binge in the town square and spent a couple of nights in the cells. His family came close to disowning him though it caused a rawness in them. They were hearth neighbours in the village and suffering more than most. Harri refused to stay at the house, it was too crowded. It wasn't home. He knew where his home was and it wasn't in this place. He was not a charity case and so it went on. We still met in the clearing but our conversations became stilted and short in exposure. Finally he was called back to his unit and it was a blessing. I waved him off from the station. Maarit gave him a bag of strawberries from the forest and he stuffed them into his mouth grinning from ear to ear. I gave him a hunting knife and he promised to stick a few Russians with it. When she heard him say it Maarit looked harshly in my direction and I had to explain in a fluster that it was no request of mine.

There was good news too. Simo found his son, unharmed in the marshlands of Lapland, wandering with some others, unable to believe that a peace treaty had been signed. He'd managed to persuade him to go back to the home village, which still lay in Finland. He wrote to tell me, it was very cheering. I was happy when all around were full of sadness and grieving. I showed Maarit the letter from my famous comrade but she could hardly decipher a thing. The letters were huge and rarely a one spelt correctly. He signed his name SIMO in letters which took up half the page.

Autumn came. The chill winds and amber death infected trees. Leaves bowed and stalks knelt. Most of the town rampaged through the forests searching for berries and mushrooms. Merja joined them and delighted in the task. I met with Maarit whenever I could but she was so busy now as were we all. The factories belched smoke and noise, every scrap of iron was collected. Young boys were drafted into work, armed with hammers they struck and moulded and riveted and turned their hands to lathes or grinding machines. The looms clattered ever louder and the walls of the mills ran with rivers of sweat. Tuija now worked in one – punishing, exhausting hours turning out tunics or shirts for the army. The saddlers and lorimers stitched or filed. Never had the harvest been gathered with such urgency, every man, woman and child advanced upon the fields with grim determination. They did not rest, they did not celebrate the harvest home, but moved on to the next task. Flour was sacked upon the sheaf!

I observed this. The minutiae of it all, and the expressions on faces, the clenching of teeth, the strangers nodding in the street then racing on, the dogs howling. The sycamore leaves floating on the Vanajavesi. I began to shiver inside.

There were bizarre anomalies. The alko factory poured thousands of litres of vodka down the drains which washed into the rivers and poisoned the fish. What was the meaning of this? Did they really fear an outbreak of alcoholism? Had Harri's antics of the last few months been so spectacular? For myself I was not concerned. I never drank the evil stuff, but for some old-timers it was an evil portent, a sign as deadly as the sudden appearance of a comet. They watched tearfully as the empty bottles were packed into crates and shipped away.

Then one morning, once the harvest was complete, I watched a herd of horses, all manner of beasts and nags and ponies beaten across the bridge to the railway station where they were whipped into cattle trucks...and off they went, dazed and confused to the east.

There was no civilian traffic, only army trucks, gasoline tankers, tractors all going in one direction. The goods yards were camouflaged afresh but tank transporters were easily discerned. We knew where they were going; it did not take a mastermind to calculate the meaning of it all. Aeroplanes flew across the town, practising manoeuvres, swooping and diving arrogantly. Everyday more German soldiers passed through. They shouted down to us, but we did not respond. Whatever were we getting ourselves into?

In November the first flakes of snow fell. It was poignant, a harbinger and recaller. The mobilisation began.

Sad bud.

The recruiting sergeant parried blows from a stick as he tried to take her youngest away. She cried and screamed and threatened and berated but he held his ground patiently and with forbearance. He talked quietly to her and suffered the blows until she slumped to the floor and he was able to summon assistance. A neighbour led her gently away.

'Already!' she screamed in parting, too distraught to utter words of any human semblance. 'I have lost my husband and my two eldest blown to pieces by the same shell. I have lost my home and my livelihood. I have only what you see me wearing and now you want to take my last remaining. May the devil rain curses down upon you.'

The sergeant took the boy away. He looked petrified. He was seventeen and looked twelve.

I walked away.

There was nothing I could do. There was no enthusiasm for this new call up. Few welcomed it and most were bitterly opposed, even we of the Isthmus who had most to gain from a new war shied away from it. It filled me with dread.

I walked away.

With my coat turned up and the snowflakes powdering my hair I crossed the bridge to the wood shop where I manufactured rifle stocks in ever increasing numbers. Hannu the carpenter turning plough shares into swords.

*

Harri along with many thousands like him spent the autumn and winter of 1940 working as a pioneer along the eastern borders. It was heavy labour digging new defensive positions into soil already solid, pouring concrete, and manipulating steel reinforcement cables. Deep bunkers were constructed with several levels one beneath the other for living accommodation, for signals, and for companies' headquarters. When this work was completed, which it never was, there were stores to be man-handled from the railhead. Ammunition dumps were gouged out of granite and heavily disguised. New roads proliferated, wide enough for tanks, and the hive reverberated with the thudding of pickaxes and the glow of acetylene torches, melting and pouring together, fabricating steel into armoured vehicles, mobile artillery batteries, bridging equipment. Even then it was not finished, for air strips were ripped out of the forests, hangars, observation posts. Firing ranges for new recruits and veterans alike who trained between bouts of feverish activity. It was the labour of slaves and not without its risks. There were landslides, trenches caved in, stores toppled over and men were crushed between the wheels of lorries for this construction was largely conducted in the dark, and in extreme cold. Many of the men were young and inexperienced, unused to the hazards, unaware of the dangers of such a widespread mechanisation and projects on a scale such as this. From time to time the generals came to inspect but they did not stay long. There were bigger fish to fry. Through Christmas and New Year this continued relentless. Too tired to question, the Israelites rolled closer to the frontier and their personal Moses watched with a monacled eye. They knew that liberation was near and some welcomed it, some bowed with apprehension, others hankered for their beds while most thought not but bent their backs because that was the way it was.

Overseeing it all were German officers. They did not dirty their hands nor condescend to speak to our own. You could touch the resentment, slice it with a knife and as more of their soldiers arrived the tension rose steadily. There was no outward hostility, it was much hidden, but present all the same. When they tried to make conversation our lads feigned not to understand, shook their heads, swung the axe or spade. Some like Harri mimicked their seriousness, the saluting and the clicking of heels. It was not our way. How fastidious they were...but with a hint of menace, an unnerving watchfulness. Yet the build up continued, in scale beyond imagination. A seismic shift in approach to the winter war which was purely defensive and unwelcome. These toneless characters, each the same as the next prickled the skin. It was truly an unholy alliance but without such men and equipment there would be no hope of recovering the lands lost. Once the dagger is unsheathed it has to be used, even if it makes you sick to plunge it forwards to the enemy. So it was until the end of spring, when work ceased and our armies placed new steel helmets on their heads, shouldered packs and tested the trigger. It was a matter of waiting.

*

Maarit was transferred at Easter. Ironically to the very hospital where I had lain a year before. She was to undergo more intensive training. She was to take qualifications, broaden the range of her skills so she said. But it meant nothing to me. I was no scholar nor did I possess a single certificate. I trusted her word that she should go and grieved at a second parting.

The interlude was over. Summer was long gone, as if it had never happened. The winter solstice passed and I spent many hours reading stories to Merja who understood much and gained new abilities of lip-reading. She thrived, unexpectedly, smiled more, became open of expression and I believe began to read.

She helped mother with the cooking and washing, grew taller. She was no more little Merja. Her hair she wore long and her manner became delicate, more aware. I even allowed myself to think that maybe, despite everything, she would find her niche, beguile the simple world she inhabited. Mother fretted, worried about the shortage of food and clothing, prayed that no one would fall sick. Tuija, we suspected, had taken up with a man at the mill. We did not know anything about him and were both of us unsure whether this was a good or a bad thing. Such moral dilemmas were a novelty. At home it was very much a case of black or white.

Still the mobilisation continued. I had another medical assessment and the doctor said I was not A1. Well, I could have told him that. Even so my muscles were stronger now and I was broad of back. He said I was fit enough to be conscripted again for light duties, whatever they were. I had no opinion on the matter.

So a few weeks later I found myself in field grey again but with a corporal's stripe because I was a veteran. I was to report to a training battalion in some place up north. I had no idea where it was but said my 'farewells' and departed. It was not exactly a difficult assignment. The barracks were comfortable. I spent my time teaching recruits field craft, how to shoot, how to drive bayonets into sandbags. That was it. A regular routine with hot meals, which suited me. I did not socialise. The recruits, most of them very young, were a mixture of innocents, keen to learn but no better than we at drill. I was not completely sure of the orders myself. Some asked about my experiences but I soon shut them up with a bark. Corporals could do that sort of thing. At least they looked smarter and were not a rag bag army as were we. Basic training passed without incident for most and they merged together and were replaced by others. To my disgrace I cannot recall the name of one, nor their features or fates. One batch in. one out, a military production line. Little distinguished one day from the next. During the course of my time at the barracks these snippets are all that are worthy of remembrance, small change in the pocket, a few coppers. There was talk of an armoured unit arriving, but it came to nothing. A signals specialist turned up for advanced training but he was in the wrong place. The commanding officer had a pet reindeer and gave it the rank of lieutenant until a rifleman with a grudge stuck a hunting knife into its neck and roasted it over a fire. And once, shortly before the war began, a grenade exploded prematurely and took the face and both hands of a private from Savonlinna. He did not die but what became of him...

I did not gossip or fraternise. I kept myself to myself. So when the barracks suddenly emptied and we who remained were ordered to pack and prepare to leave it took me by surprise. I was issued with new kit, a sub-machine gun and drums of ammunition. Everyone else seemed to know what was happening, they had kept abreast of the rumours and had an inkling as to our likely destination, which was somewhere to the south. Once more I found myself in a truck and paused to consider that I must now be A1.

Chapter 16

What became known as the 'Continuation War' started on 21 June, 1941 with the German invasion of the Soviet Union. Officially we were not allies mere co-belligerents but to many eyes it amounted to the same thing. What a pact with the devil it was and who could surmise the ending. But such was the hunger to reclaim lost lands our commanders would have descended into the fiery pit of hell itself.

Our armies tapped this malign serpent and waited on the roads to Karelia until the order to advance was spouted, gushed, cried. Long columns battle ready. Some primed for the Isthmus, some for the northern shore of Lake Ladoga. They nourished themselves on rumours, excitement mounted. Recruits new to this game of war could barely contain themselves. Veterans like Harri and Simo, together with the old unit, once more lazed upon the roadside meadows picking daisies and buttercups. The sky was full of birds, crows, finches, and herons all watching in anticipation and the growl of a half track scattering them in black clouds. Beetles scurried across the baked earth, the sun beat down, boredom bored into the bones, tempers prickled; the muse became a layer of dust coating the eyelids. Our soldiers swore and scratched and the Germans marched shouting orders and responses. Harri observed them with amusement. Simo saw it all as an irrelevance and wanted to get started, get the job done. He took care to cultivate the friendship of the field kitchen staff, ingratiating himself with the driver, gifts of tobacco, enquiries about family and friends…I'll give you a hand he said, and helped himself when the driver wasn't looking, filling his canteen.

The circus waited. The ringmaster hesitated under the burning sun while mosquitoes and midges gorged on the flesh of pale-skinned recruits suffering much from their attentions.

I was not there. I did not know of my location, nor did it trouble me. My transferences from barracks to barracks became a way of life and everywhere we landed the commanding officer looked at his paper work, furrowed his brow and said, 'No, we have no need of instructors, this is a vehicle workshop, a field hospital, a military prison…had we done anything wrong? No? Better get a move on then.' So we did.

But on the roads to the frontier, every lane and track and byway was bursting to capacity. Our men stood with cracked lips, coughing dust from their throats, trying to keep their rifles clean. Thirst was a company which cups of water could not satisfy. Disease threatened to break out. Patience wore thin as ribbon. Adders and grass snakes writhed around the ankles of the sleepers till they jumped or shuddered.

Through June and into July the false dawn suffocated. This serpent rumbled, bellowed, screeched, plucked fruit and lumbered. Played cards. Won money, lost money…

When the order to form up finally came it was with a sense of real relief. A carnival of animals scrolled out. First sloths, anteaters nuzzling the ground, tapirs, gazelles twitchy, giraffes, elephants, Assyrians in chariots, archers from Egypt, Goths, Etruscans, Saxons, Danes trampling the summer flowers under their feet. The trucks and tanks rolled forwards in dust clouds swarming with grasshoppers, horse-drawn wagons brought up the rear, combat engineers prodded and in files on either side the Infantry now stained yellow marched as their like had done for many centuries. The war of recovery had begun.

On the convoy roared, a cheer went up, someone unfurled a flag and the crocodile lumbered snarling. Saints and dragons rattled, flagons banged against the sides, the whinnying of horses aped those of chargers while men pocketed their feeling for later consideration. Poets searched for words. The Infantry tramped one behind the other. The anti-aircraft gunners scoured skies overhung with haze, picking specks from lenses smeared with sweat. A thousand hearts beat their drums.

Ten thousand.

A hundred thousand more briny complexions foreshortening horizons. Overhead flew allied fighters and bombers in arrow formations. Tongues loosened as they darted east toward Ladoga.

'We should have a band!' shouted Harri.

'That would be useful,' answered Simo coughing with sarcasm.

'At least it would drown the noise of your choking.'

'Well boy when your lungs are as old as mine they need a little accommodation.'

'When my lungs reach your age they will long be dead.'

'It's not wise to joke about death Harri, you know that.'

'Death is neither harsh or kind,' barked a voice behind them.

'Who said that?' shouted Harri tersely, coughing himself.

'Timo Visuri.'

'Simo and Timo, what a combination!'

'Well Timo Visuri, keep your thoughts to yourself.'

Onwards.

Through the corrugation of forests simmering in pans, grasses dried within stalks of baked clay, bogs stinking like cholera pits caused some to vomit for now the excitement had gone and the drudgery of this business imposed itself on their shoulders. One step at a time was the mantra of the rifleman. One step, one breath.

Halt.

They were closing on the enemy.

In groups they slipped between the trees. A capercaillie squawked, a squirrel circled the trunk as they fanned out in extended silent lines, brushing aside the bracken with their knees. Some fixed bayonets, others clipped new drums to their machine guns communicating one with the other by hand signals. Pollen smeared the grey of their uniforms. Ten paces forward, stop...scan, observe, move on, stop, kneel, watch and so unevenly through ground snared in vegetation the soldiers advanced and met nothing but waxwings. When night fell they were well beyond the armaments of the convoy. So they slept where they fell beneath the dizzying canopy. Few saw the spectres tracking them, some in chains, others running ever watchful.

At dawn the barrage opened, dropping a synthetic rain upon the strong points of the enemy. In parallel the armoured columns advanced with a new science, mechanical, automatic, synchronised – the first bunkers were overcome with flame and grapeshot. The monsters overrun them wiping out the runners with bulleted lassoes. A concentration of fire power unimagined in the winter war overwhelmed defences. So with these diversions the infantry pushed forward, avoiding trails and clearings, keeping to the cover of the spruce tree. Needles crunched under foot, bilberries and hair grass snatched at the ankles and the forest floor bounced as springs to the tread of their boots. So close the lichen brushed their shoulders, so blended forest and man in one relationship, advancing warily, eyes wide open.

With the morning sun barely wrestled above the horizon the company met their first objective. Before them the Hiittola railway line spliced through the belly of undergrowth. This was the neck to be broken. When snapped supplies and reinforcements could be strangled at the junctions. All along the line the Finn men crouched low into moss mats, fingering the podsol soil with fingers triggered for the off. A hundred officers trained their binoculars across the track, discerning movement or shadowy patrols. To break cover would wrench their nerves.

Harri and Simo lay side by side squinting through the architecture of thorns to the other side.

'Can you see anything?' asked Harri

'No...but that does not mean they are gone. Blow on the embers of a Russian and he will flame into life again.'

A breeze shifted the curtain. Midges swarmed, ants crawled over their bodies. Everyone was edgy. It was too quiet. There should be sentries. Surely this was too important an objective to be abandoned.

A captain detailed two men to cross the tracks.

Warily, stooping low, covering each other, they advanced. First across the gravel, then stepping the plates; almost there. When the second man triggered a mine there was a deep bass roar and his body slammed into the ground. The first was mown by machine gun fire, crumping down, writhing.

Though fettered they opened magazines into an enemy still in shadow. Bullets foamed sap from the birch bark and a sense of burning filled Harri's nostrils. He rose and threw a grenade into the direction of the fire. Others threw smoke and phosphorous bombs so when the order to charge was yelled all stumbled to their feet and raced forward mentally calculating their chances. Simo ran although his muscles ached now. I'm too old for all this nonsense, he thought to himself as he followed the others through clods of black clay. Amidst the firing and crashing of grenades he heard screams and curses. Men stumbled or smashed into each other, tripping over roots and branches honeycombing the forest. It was a deadly obstacle course. His eyes smarted and with the layering of light and dark could discern little but flashes.

'Keep moving...keep moving!' cried the captain until a bullet caught him in the throat and he gargled his life away.

An unholy bedlam ensued and some no doubt were cut down by their comrades. When the smoke cleared it was like the opening of a door. Vision and perception returned. Sounds died away, new appraisals made. Timo the boy with a clever way with words now lay on his back eyes open. Simo bent down to close them and muttered some prayer.

'You silly boy,' he said, 'tempt not death for it will claim you.' Red-stained his body. Already the flies gathered, blue bottles homing on the scent. 'I knew you once on the road to here, on the lonely trek, eyes front, rifle at the slope. One day, six words. Well son, death is harsh, it will follow us all, we cannot outrun it.'

A final glance and he was off.

The mustering of companies took place. Casualties were collected for their coffins. The railway line was theirs, cut in many places along its length. Engineers were busy clearing mines. Three platoons were detailed to secure the ground and the rest moved on, deeper into woods where taunts could be heard though Russian or Finnish he could not tell. Bats disturbed by noise and vibration bolted above them. The village long since abandoned waited for their rendezvous. They had crossed the border, the old border. They were home and when men realised the significance of this spot they cheered and placed helmets on rifle barrels, spinning them like plates.

'Happy now?' asked Simo to Harri.

The convoy joined them and this motley collection of soldiers reformed and continued east. Their work was not yet finished.

*

Maarit walked the wards of Tampere hospital under the supervision of a matron blunt both in figure and personality. Between lectures and classes she tramped many long hours across floors polished by her own hands. As yet there were no casualties from the front, only the victims of domestic or industrial accidents. Most of the beds were empty. Only the isolation ward was full; tuberculosis rampaged through a population weakened by diet. It was her task to wipe and scour, take out pans, manhandle laundry down the chute, fill water jugs. On occasion she was permitted to administer pills watched carefully by a superior buzzard. Once or twice she changed a bandage or took some poor soul's temperature but that was all.

When her shift was over she lay on the bed in a room shared with several other girls, all equally weary and bored. Most days she wrote to Hannu as promised though his responses were hardly works of great literature, consisting mostly of 'Got up, trained recruits, had tea, went to bed.' Scintillating it wasn't.

Still she composed as best she could informal, cheery, notes, full of insignificant details which Hannu intimated he appreciated. She knew the great war of recovery had started and while it filled her with hope, in common with many others she bore the taste of misgivings. This war was not so black and white, it wriggled with words unsaid and layers of deception.

It was a week now since Hannu had replied. One letter was returned without explanation so she guessed that he had departed the barracks, praying he was not enlisted at the front. He was not ready in body or mind for another pounding. He was not strong enough.

Waking hours occupied her thoughts of him, the shyness of expression, the coarse brown hair, untameable, the scowl that meant I am uncomfortable, please change the subject. In the ward last week a soldier lay in bed staring at the ceiling. A short man of pugilistic demeanour, all derision. An unpleasant individual who claimed to be acquainted with him at Taipale, stood with him in the trenches, with Harri too and the man called Simo whom Hannu talked about with affection. There was an incident he said involving the three of them where a corporal was shot. They were transferred to avoid an investigation but would not elaborate, merely grinning. How she could have slapped him but resolved that day to never mention the conversation. We all had our secrets she thought trawling up that encounter with Paavo in the village. Best to keep quiet. Instead she raked her consciousness for images that were not stained by others, personal memories to ease her into sleep.

Tomorrow she worked with the isolation cases, that ward for no-hopers and incurables, where even the atmosphere was corrosive. She shuddered and could not look the dying in the face as others did, could not smile or gift pleasantries unto them. This weakness shamed her and she dreaded the shift where men and women too far gone curled into the sheets and cried silently, dribbling blood onto counterpanes which sank into cloth and could never be removed, merely turning brown. A mud brown, the colour of indignity, and yet she could not force a smile to ease their suffering. How expectant they were when within those dustless corridors they heard the approach. How they gasped and pulled at their throats and chests to open up the body to oxygen. It was no use of course to drown their reason with the lungs. One by one the curtains drew around them and they were taken away. No, such images would not accompany her at this time when reserves of strength were needed and sleep without nightmares required. Instead she thought of summer where Hannu the carpenter, a singular person, swam with her beneath the granite overhang, where also swam shades and water bellies mirrored in that afternoon where only the husks of mayflies floated on the surface and the skimming of dragonflies plied a curved trajectory in aerial arithmetics. The sky mirrored us between this heaven and earth. The mother bird watched us tenderly and the curl of the lily became our lips unfastened by navigation. So come life or death we will not be parted, so she mused with her hands behind her head and blankets pulled up to the chin. So sleep summoned her with smiles and gentle carrying where the green land waited and thoughts of horror disturbed her not. Tomorrow was time enough for that.

I was now far beyond the old village. Our company of odds and ends skirted the perimeter for it had no significance for anyone but myself. I collected the familiar and stored them, gaining only tantalising glimpses of roof tops and telegraph poles. I asked permission to enter but it was not granted, so on we moved, jolting down roads busy with military activity of every kind. All manner of transport followed us and every roadside cavity burst with stores and equipment. It was an impressive scene, rich in confidence and expectation. I looked for my old comrades, for Harri and Simo, but knew there was little chance of re-joining them. Through the night we drove until, with a jolt, the convoy stopped and we were ordered to disembark. From there we marched in long files down lanes where there was no light. An atmosphere of eerie whispers caused some nervousness. No one seemed to know where we were, the heat was oppressive, our uniforms were soon drenched with sweat and by now many were beginning to struggle with the slog though this black, tripping over obstacles and each other. It was wearisome. So when the halt was called we fell out, took off our packs and slept wherever we could in heaps.

Dawn syringed us. Orders barked by dogs hurried our fumblings with equipment and we looked around astonished. The scent of salt air pervaded the nostrils and a marine breeze pimpled our cheeks. I could smell the grass unstewed by heat and the sun in arrows illuminating the stone walls of the jetty. The sea surrounded our encampment loosening our tongues with questions. Some men were brown as cloudberries, others lobster pink but all turned faces to the gently rippling Baltic towards which we marched. On the shore or tied to jetties were boats from many ages, water seeped through some of the planks, others were mere rafts tied with hemp. With no little trepidation we began to embark. Our vessels swayed and we shifted our positions front and aft to gain a measure of equilibrium. Once settled we dared not move. Casting about suddenly I realised we were on the Viipuri inlet and about to cross. I had the vaguest recollections of a visit to a place like this when as a child the scents of seaweed and shingle entered my experience. Was this the place? Rocky crags sculptured the coastline as if some giant had taken bites from the land. Boulders jutted above the waves. There were teeth marks in the granite and stands of spruce, bracken coiling onto the sand, and bones, ancient receptacles of humanity scattered…or what seemed like bones to minds drunk with disorientation.

Into the sea we drove in herringbone formation. Seagulls wheeled above and waves clouted, our craft paddled and oared across the inlet, slicing a veneer of water on a sun-soaked summer morning.

My stares drew the other shore towards us. It was an approach through reflections and starbursts framing brown-green islands, beautiful and picturesque and numberless in that early morning haze. Clouds of water vapour shrouded the inlet like veils of linen drifting, spiralling, ascending. Layers of pine surmounted every island and the remains of huts and fishing nets draped across them. All eyes peered through mist ever changing and a soft glide propelled us on but my own eyes saw what others could not see. The prows of many longboats side by side with our own. Warriors looped their shields onto the side and the raven-headed sails bellowed. Swords they brandished forged in the workshops of Sweden, fiery blades glinting and scabbards carved with runes running left and right and hilts of glinting gold. With every touch the steersman guided, answering our beckon. Swans settled on the bows and squalls rocked the bulwarks with a tingling music. Teal cooed upon the mastheads, seals swam along their sides and warriors with faces grim and battle fixed sharpened their features into flint. So when we butted hard into the shingle they faded with the mist and we stumbled ashore, into the forest cover, and made our way inland towards the city of Viipuri now our destination clear.

Forwards, always forwards, to the east we magi stumbled, through forest and stream, down tracks like deserts and villages where cabins still smoked and the charcoal of their rafters crumbled to our breath. More men joined us, and we them until we reckoned our part a tiny fraction of the whole. No shots rang out. No barricades hindered progress. The enemy had departed; our approach they shunned with backward glances and offered no response to our steady tread. The way ahead was open. No violence threatened our good fortune. A sun rose higher lifting the skyline as if it was on threads or laces and we were the audience entering a theatre open to the sky. Some among us chattered with anticipation. This was their home city. This was a homecoming. How that must have felt. How many prayers were answered on that day, how many cures successfully applied after the painful evacuation.

By late afternoon we were entering the portals of that city, mouths gaping in disbelief. Our boots rattled the cobblestones following tramlines into the centre. Buildings of stone, many stories high towered above us, windows banged, glass crunched. Doors swung open. Everywhere was debris and our entrance noted the many acts of vandalism executed by the previous inhabitants. There was a dead horse, a burned out car, statues pulled down, churches hacked into rubble and tombstones levelled and broken. It was difficult to comprehend it all and I must confess my feelings to be a swirl. This was the first city that Hannu the carpenter, Hannu the simple man, the seer, friend of ghosts had ever entered. It was deserted, not a soul remained. All fled before the Russian onslaught and none returned.

Many buildings were destroyed. It was an abattoir of masonry, blackened and tilting, precariously angled walls displaying the intimacies of rooms abandoned by their owners. It was a city of bereavements, not one civilian remained, only the remnants of domesticated animals, spitting cats or packs of dogs gone to the wild. It was a painful introduction and I felt a little overwhelmed by it all as I surveyed the scenes around me. A hastily organised parade took place. Someone unfurled a flag, a drum pounded a mournful beat more like a hiccup than anything else. We marched, or rather walked, with some recourse to discipline through the market square, beyond the round tower and down into the harbour where ships and warehouses and lifting gear had suffered the same fate as the rest of Viipuri. It was obvious that anything of value had already been looted and everything else vandalised. It must have been heartbreaking for those amongst us who were citizens, those who called this place home. Once it was a jewel set in the Baltic like a diamond in a ring, clasped by rivers and islets, pure of air and vital. But now besmirched, dirty, ragged. Through we tramped, steadily falling into step unwatched. A singled souled photographer capturing the occasion for posterity.

So the parade ended and a flush of cloud drew a blanket around us. The heat and humidity rose. We were dismissed, some made into the city, some were detailed for patrols or for construction work on new defensive positions on the outskirts. As for myself I took to wandering alone as was my nature. No friends had I made in my new company. Hastily it had been conglomerated and we all suspected it would soon be broken into parts and redistributed. I had applied to join my old unit but its whereabouts were unknown to me. Hence I made acquaintances but no more, and now as I reclaim my experiences of Viipuri it strikes me as surreal, as if I was not really there, as if it was not I. Nor do I recall a single name or face among the companions who crossed the inlet with me.

So my boots scuffed the cobblestones and I drank thirstily from a canteen, chewed black bread and peered into cracks and crevices of buildings with a childlike curiosity. Strolling up Castle Street like a proper tourist and for the first time in my life I felt the need for a camera. The castle loomed in red stone, cylindrical towers, the white tower, the brown dome, the ramparts and from that elevation the Belfry tower, and the railway stations and the bridges and the blue Baltic shimmering and the parks now overgrown, capturing steps unwashed and the crumbling of mortar in grainy falls, funnelling into long deserted streets. Such were my impressions and my head was made giddy by it all.

I found a bench and rested, draining the last of the canteen and mentally noting the need to refill it at the first opportunity. A pigeon watched me from a window ledge, hopping nervously from foot to foot, bowing its eyes sideways, ensuring always that I was in the frame of vision.

I must have dozed, for when I woke the sun was directly overhead. Its rays burned my neck and the collar of my shirt was dripping. From apartment blocks opposite hung windowboxes, snared by hinges and ready to fall. Soil dripped steadily down walls. The scent of herbs sailed on currents of air. The wind whistled through deserted streets, paper tumbled. Senses heightened, refrains and whispers carried, manifesting themselves in a cold shiver down my back. Conversations ricocheted round the corners, a silo of words, jack-o'-lantern phrases pitted the walls and rebounded towards me. Disturbing it was and I fidgeted on the bench preparing to leave for I was quite alone, not a single stranger in my vision, emptiness unrigged by walkers or the playfulness of children, or the tavern owner's pavement stance or the shoe shines to flicker my pedestrian explorations. Where I stood instinctively I glanced behind, nothing but flashes of light and beams of shade. Still the atmosphere teased my senses as a swaying bell rope or a creaking gibbet unhinges logic and sucks fancy into a body. So did this occur. With some hurry I made my way back towards the harbour, keeping to the widest avenues where now and then a grey clad figure lolled or a sentry uttered some greeting. Through the rectangular frame of a side street I saw the sea, and in that direction I ran, towards the harbour and openness and company.

In the shadows, with slabs uneven, I skidded towards the blue and realised how much my breathing had improved. At the exit, I collided with a soldier with such force that it sent both of us sprawling.

There was a good deal of cursing and the man, dusting himself down angrily, squared up to me and for a moment I thought I was in trouble.

'Idiot,' he spat, 'can't you look where you're going?'

'Sorry brother…I didn't see you there.'

There was something familiar about him. When he faced me I saw it was Simo, such is the nature of things it had to be him.

'Well son a simple handshake would be sufficient,' he said, smiling from ear to ear.

'Simo…is it you Simo.'

'Who else!'

There were mighty celebrations I can tell you, shouting and embracing, hot-faced was I and Simo bellowed, spitting out enthusiasm to anyone within range.

Then Harri came running across.

'My God,' he exclaimed, 'look what's dropped from the devil's pocket!'

'I can't believe it,' I answered, screwing my eyes in the light, 'what brings you here?'

'The whole division has been transferred. We took Hiitola and moved here for rest and recreation. More to the point, what causes you to fly through here in such haste?'

'Ghosts mostly.'

'Well…it is good to see you though I'd hoped you would be safe in bed in Hämeenlinna.'

'No such luck. I crossed the Inlet yesterday. I didn't realise we were so close to Viipuri until daylight.'

'Wait till the captain sees you,' said Harri.

'Do you think I can join up Simo?'

'Sure the captain will sort it out no bother. Come on we've carved a cosy little hole down by the harbour wall. Room enough for one more.'

So I followed glad of heart but still pinching myself, disbelieving.

As frail evening light speckled the harbour, as spars and rigging laced air buzzing with mosquitoes, I watched the sun fill Viipuri Bay with orange. Soldiers still ferried across in groups of ten and twenty, landed on the jetty and tramped inland. Anti-aircraft batteries poked barrels to the sky and binoculars were trained cloudways. All was quiet, the bay crinkling with light of many colours, gulls bobbing on the waves.

There was a brazier crackling and coffee steamed. We sat like gargoyles in the smoke, recounting adventures and pulling the threads of our separation together.

At our backs the old customs house provided shelter. The northern star brushed patterns on the walls and we shared our dismay at the destruction of this city while flame gilted our hair and moths singed their wings on candles. We felt our living at the margins, a transient existence, a lattice of life. With time, when we were once more comfortable with ourselves, Simo lit his pipe and watched the smoke spiral before speaking.

'Well Hannu the carpenter I thought we had parted forever that day in the snow. You must be tougher than you look.'

'Likewise,' I countered.

'Still ugly.'

'Thank you.'

'My pleasure.'

'I'm glad you found your son.'

'So am I. I'm sorry to see you here Hannu. You don't deserve to be thrown in this lot again.'

'I've seen no action yet.'

'That's something I suppose.'

Harri had disappeared, restless even now. We sat closer to the fire, blowing smoke into the flight paths of insects, scratching, brushing hair with fingers coated in dust.

'So the magician contrives to stumble into his friends again, once a shaman always...'

'A coincidence Simo.'

'That you should crash through a door at just such a time as I walked across the threshold. Grasp tight your gifts Hannu, value them, though I must say it is both joy and pain to see you so engrossed in this new war.'

'We had no choice.'

'I know...I know. We have sowed the seed, we will reap the harvest that's for sure.'

'Let's not dwell on things Simo, this is a grand place and we have taken it back.'

'True,' he said, resigned and musing at the coral ledges of a sunset. 'When last I was here it was as a newly wed.'

'Really?'

'Yes, on a mission of love for my new wife.' Simo seemed to be lost in thought momentarily, shuffling his back more comfortably against the wall.

'Some romantic assignment?'

'Oh yes. The purchase of gifts for the love of my life, my soulmate.'

'What did you buy her?'

'A lump hammer.'

'Really?'

'Yes,' he smiled.

Chapter 17

Like sparrows scattering sound, pecking and tangling for seeds, ruffling feathers, arguing and fussing in front of the church porch, so simmered the villagers in Hämeenlinna market place, more vocal now with words seeping through muslin, and the dialect rich.

Through the summer news filtered back that the old lands had been re-taken, Viipuri liberated and the Russians pushed back from both shores of Ladoga into the Soviet Union itself. The Finnish army halted within a few kilometres of Leningrad, at the old border. It was hardly believable but the offensive as far as we were concerned was over. But how the Germans gnashed their teeth and threatened, muttering darkly of ingratitude and betrayal when we refused to budge further. More fool them! Our lands recovered set the jewels in gold and we cared not for their ambitions. Never had we liked the cut of their cloth or the heavy lilt of their vowels. No Mannerheim, God Bless Him, would have none of it, curse as they might the advances stopped dead at the old border, not one step further. The taking of Leningrad had never been an option. What did we want with it? Render unto Stalin that which was his.

But news caused great consternation. It was imprecise, contradictory even. Refugees heard one day that with time they could return, the next that the land was still insecure. What to believe? Some, on their own initiative, took the road back east. Others waited. Still many more mourned another twenty thousand men lost to the grave. And the wounded and mutilated passed through this place trailing blood on tracks. The eyeless and the limbless and the faceless multitudes bundled their pain, and locomotive whistles drowned out the screams they uttered and the shudders they wrought as the mirror caught them. It was not without cost this victory.

The inhabitants of our village transplanted stood in knots across the market place in late summer sunshine, with head scarves bright and baskets over their arms. Feelings were mixed, uncertainty was not a quality hanging well with them. Would they undertake the pilgrimage and what would they find? Swallows skimmed the roof tops, and old men in caps that leaped from their foreheads, grey hair peeping out beneath, watched the scene bewildered, unable to contemplate another move. Benumbed by events that once carried them here, now offered a chance of return. It was hope that most exasperated these old men on benches mute. Hope clouded the lens. Some adjusted spectacles as if that alone would ease the decision. So they thought as if passing beneath vaults, stooping, unclear.

Tilda stood in the shadow of a tree beginning to turn. She had no sons, not now, nor a husband, not now, alone he lay at Hiitola, alone beneath the bracken curling, hushed, asleep.

'What say you Mrs Juutalainen?'

'I say wait and see. Leave now and what will greet us, what manner of destruction. No doubt the village will be stripped or burned to ashes. Much as I long for home, I long less for a death from cold devoid of shelter. The fields unsown, the cattle stalls empty, only the apple trees and those most likely in a torment of neglect.'

'So you will stay.'

'Until spring, until some warmth and then perhaps, God willing.'

'As for myself,' said a woman of fiery complexion, arms bare and hair tied back, 'come autumn I'm off to claim my own. This place sits uncomfortably with me. The people are so sullen. There is no life just husks. I cannot abide it.'

'There may be nothing left,' said a third older woman.

'We can rebuild.'

'I don't know. My child Merja, she has not been well. Silence cloaks her. She is too fragile for another journey.'

There were murmurings of agreement and many exchanges but the young one continued in the same vein.

'There is no friendship here. The people are ice cold. I sometimes feel like a charity case.'

'I cannot agree,' another responded.

The younger woman swung her hips and continued the conversation in a loud voice, loud enough for others to hear.

'Stiff as boards, the make up of these people. They are all in bed by seven. For myself I like a good time. I like to stay up late, and sing and dance. Boisterous am I.' Her actions caused mutterings of amusement as she danced in a circle, wind tugging on her skirts. 'We Karelians love life too much for a town as sombre as this.'

Tilda the bereaved one walked across to her, white faced, and planted herself face to face.

'Many a poor soul has lost their life, do well to remember. Show some decency, show respect.'

All knew of Tilda's loss.

'I meant nothing by it mistress,' said the dancer, shame faced. 'I just want to go home, back to our own lands.'

'Land is nothing,' she answered still white as a sheet. 'Return my boys and my husband and a rock in the ocean will suffice, land costs too much. Let them have it all. What use is land or pride or any such nonsense.'

She turned and walked away. Conversations petered and the group dispersed with their own thoughts but now holding them tight, reeling them in.

'Poor soul. May God pour his blessings upon her,' whispered mother on the long walk out of town. In essence she agreed with Tilda and dared not contemplate her pain. Soil soaked in blood is not soil, it will neither sustain nor nurture. Fresh anxieties surfaced. There are always black clouds, so ran her thoughts, sweep one away and another will appear. I will not return, not while the track leads us home. Merja is happy, she is content. We have sufficient. I will build a home for us all and when Hannu returns he will help provide. Such is the bounty of our creator. Nothing will compel me to return though it bites my memory with violence. So ran her arguments, counter and otherwise. Such was the decision made.

*

As in we marched so we left, in a straggle with units re-formed and reinforcements flooding from the plains. Myself, Harri and Simo more wizened now trooped along still in summer tunics. Packs were slung on backs and rifles carried in an easterly direction through a land of water courses and bog, marsh, reed beds, stands of pine and roads now rutted, pin cushioned with red and amber leaves where the wind rolled them or the rain rivered them away.

The air cooled and we prepared for winter. Never had we laboured with such intensity as those next few months. There was to be a new defensive line stretching from the shore of Lake Ladoga to the Gulf of Finland. The Vammelsuu-Taipale line. A series of dark corridors and alignments dug deep through black soil, one behind the other with communication and support trenches linking front to rear. At intervals were gun emplacements, cook houses, and ammunition dumps. Duckboards lined the floor and all was strengthened with timber, barbed wire, mine fields, observation posts. Our efforts warmed us and being Finns we chiselled out our saunas and shelled the interiors with logs. So when the first snows fell we were as comfortable as ever we could be. Well provisioned, well armed, clean, struggling more with boredom than anything else. We slipped into patterns of the winter war, as at Taipale in those days when this soldiering was new and we green buds yet to burst. Darkness descended, the all-encompassing onslaught clothing body and soul with sponge. We watched, stood to, repaired and mined, delved and pickaxed. From time to time patrols were sent forward or a flare despatched but on the whole both sides of this conflict snuggled into hibernation. I lived for letters from Maarit, cheery notes about life on the wards or in

Tampere, full of details and gossip. Mother wrote letters like shopping lists, she knitted them for me, and posted socks and gloves and candles and soap. Merja enclosed drawings full of colour and imagination which I pinned to the walls of a dugout. They were much admired, a touch of home from home, something to break up the bleakness of an environment without hue. Still we kept our heads below the parapet, it would not do to be careless. So when I wrote back I described our situation as something like a church without a roof, with aisles and chapels, and chantries and an altar where we gathered for refreshment and prayers, knees deep within the trench through which we waded boot high.

Then one night at Christmastide I sat and watched the sky star gazey dome across my vision and witnessed in the silence always gathered on its shoulders auroral storms battling in ribbons through the magnetosphere. Sapphire blue, lime green, mercury bursts emitting light soundlessly. And I quite lost myself. So reader if you have experienced such things as this you will understand how saints may wrap their arms around you and the prophets dispense their wisdom to men, even to those such as me. Days I sat in fascination, or so it seemed, for at that time there were no days. Leaning against the trench wall, smiling as the snowflakes fell, catching them in my fingers and watching them melt. Neither sleeping nor eating but stamping my feet and rocking forwards-backwards, forwards-backwards, hovering above the trenches immune from bullet or shell. I saw my comrades crouched above machine guns, sentries bleary-eyed, my friends cupping mugs of coffee, laughing, thinking, reading letters from home. And I loved them all, my men, my brothers tall and short, my children walking in the briars with lineaments familiar. I saw their families watching over them, jealously guarding with love too in their eyes from many generations many longs ago. Men with scythes and binding line, waggoners snapping whips against their legs, the draper's apprentice, brass till tinkling and the measuring tape snaking across the counter. The miller white, the cow herd, the goose boy and the wood yard worker bleeding sap onto the ground. For many days at that time without light my tapping, tapping, tapping, harvesting frost, capturing breath in ornamental fountains, unsought by cold, burning outside. My happiness knew no bounds, my abilities suffered no boundaries. I could swim if so I wished into air flavoured with the scents of flowers. I did not wish, I could not leave my comrades, nor would I desert them. Tapping, tapping, tapping, their faces drawn benignly to me. I waved and climbed the ladder rickety and noticed how the branching veins across my hands spread with the quality of music, with horn or timpani and with some amusement. Up the ladder, one step at a time, rungs without space or time disappearing. To the Lapps' encampment where the cauldron bubbled, where the salmon smoked beside it and the river swollen whispered still beneath the branches of a birch tree. How the embers flickered and the berry glistened like the headdress bobbing on the reindeer herder. How blue the tunics of the northmen.

Lord how I cried without end and shook and burned with fever and curled my body into spasms. How I fell from sky to ground and how the ladder splintered. So while I did not want to leave, the stretcher-bearers carried my bleached skin and stark hair to an ambulance once more into Viipuri. My, how branded was the memory of Haari's hand upon my shoulder and the face of Simo swinging side to side with feeling. He knew I was not ready for this war, was not healed or strong enough, too swarming with infection, too damaged. Simo the elder with his pipe and cooking pot and stubble armouring his chin, angry that I should have got this far when obviously the wound still chained chest to heart. Had I known. Had I then comprehended that I would see neither Harri or Simo again I would have smashed the stretcher into pieces and clung to the trench walls with my fingernails. But I did not know. My mind journeyed then to many times and places. I could do nothing. We would not meet again.

*

Spring brought mother home, she followed a path gilded by the sun and entered the village with some of her neighbours early one morning. It had been a long and tortuous journey of the road and mind, but concluding that she might ever regret the decision should she not return it was subsequently with mixed feelings and a beating heart that she wheeled a handcart from the remains of the station. Sound not vision mesmerised her. Long hours had she spent in fortifying her mind to the sights she might encounter, as one prepares to view a corpse so she imagined and braced herself. But she had not prepared for the gentle creaking of wheels on a rutted road, or the trembling of birch leaves. The hiss of grasses grown long unnerved her and a melody of sorrow sought her like a stranger. Bird song – were there ever so many birds? Was ever a greeting so tender or piercing to the breast? So try as she might, hardened by all that had preceded this time, she could not repel a tear, a single dew drop, a thorn. Hazel trees bowed at her passing and her eyes she resolved to keep fixedly on the ground or the trundling wheels, for then she thought images would neither startle or scare.

Only when the shadow of the timber mill loomed did she raise her eyes and see the figure of the mill owner waiting with an outstretched hand.

'Greetings mistress.'

'Hello to the one who brings the greeting and another to the one who sent it.'

'What is this mistress?' he asked, concerned, but with a teasing lilt to his words. 'Tears, never did I consider such a thing.'

'Well master forgive the weakness of an old woman.'

'Neither weak nor old. Let me be the first to welcome you home.' He motioned her towards the open door of the mill office. 'Come…I have been here some time. I have coffee and bread and an office newly repaired.'

'It is true I am tired and sore in need of refreshment,' admitted my mother.

'So it is settled.'

For an hour they rested, exchanging news, gossip even.

'I confess,' said the owner, 'that the situation is not nearly so bad as I expected. There is work to be done, but things are salvageable. People have returned in knots. The railway is restored. There are moves to plant the fields if sufficient labour can be found. I'm told that now the front has quietened men may be released. Praise God that it is so. And yourself Mrs Juutalainen, what news do you have?'

'What you have heard I do not know, it is family affairs, no more. Hannu is out of hospital now. You heard of his wound?'

'Yes…yes a friend informed me but did he not succumb to fever.'

'Absolutely! I was not happy. He was detailed only for light duties, training recruits but somehow he found himself in Viipuri and then the trenches. Only the Lord knows how. But that is Hannu, carried by the wind no doubt. One day he will wake. I have hopes that Maarit will take him under her wing and protect him from the ways of this mysterious life.'

The mill owner laughed.

'Truly I do not wish to criticise master. He is a son beyond measure, every mark of his pay comes to the household, it is a godsend to we…but, after all he has seen he is no more worldly wise.'

'Ever will it be so.'

Mother sipped her coffee and smiled.

'We have many reasons to be grateful.' She paused before continuing. 'Merja thrives, it is beyond my understanding. Tuija cares for her now, while I am here. It is as if some burden has been lifted from her shoulders so now she reads silently and expresses interest in visitors, and plays with others after a fashion. She is happy.'

'And yourself mistress. How are you?'

'Weary to be honest and in many minds about the future. It feels good to be home, comfortable but will it be permanent? Is this a false dawn?'

'Like you I had my reservations. I have no family to consider and in some ways this makes things easier. On the way here I held a similar conversation with a man from Summa. But he told the story of the child born with antlers and my understanding came and then I knew what will be will be.'

Mother nodded at the recollection. There is a folk tale relayed through many generations of the child born with reindeer antlers. No matter how unsightly or demeaning the parents knew that if the antlers were cut off the child would die. Such is the dilemma. And so it is with Karelia, if its people are divorced from this land long bequeathed to us, something dies, the heart, the soul, the light of our eyes.'

She sat up to move and winced. The mill owner caught the expression of pain.

'You are in distress?'

' Old age,' she smiled still pale. 'It is as if a hat pin sticks into my side.'

'Well…do not tire yourself. Let me help you.'

Together they wheeled the cart through the village. Gardens were overgrown and the lilac trees unkempt. When the dwelled in place appeared she groaned inside. Roses struggled through tangled vegetation and the cabin door swung open, creaking on the hinges.

'It is not so bad,' he added comfortingly.

'No.'

With that he left and mother pushed the door aside.

The living room was dark and smelt of damp. Mould grew on the window ledges and it was possible to trace the journey of water stains on the floor. Everywhere was cluttered with debris, articles of clothing, a helmet, half-opened tin cans, smashed bottles and windows, the glass shattering under foot. She walked with fingers clasped tight together. Some of Merja's clothes had been thrown in the corner. Every handle and every latch was torn apart. As she advanced the smell caused her to feel nauseous and she had to hold a handkerchief over her mouth and nose. There were dents in the doors and the walls had mighty cracks as if hammered deliberately. Bullet holes pockmarked the ceiling. Animals, wild and domestic, had obviously been allowed to roam freely. There was a chicken coop in the bedroom and the storerooms pilfered, piled with mattresses stained with blood. That such people should desecrate the family home, this much caused her much anger and pain. But it had not been burned down. The cabin was intact, structurally sound, so she gathered the strength inherited through ages, rolled up her sleeves and began to clear the cabin of much pollution. The thought that the family might one day return motivated this clearance to continue. First she piled the refuse high in the outside yard, a mighty heap on which she poured paraffin from a lamp, throwing a match upon it. The pyre exploded into flame and for a good while she watched it dissolve into flame, the black smoke carrying stench, the spluttering and crackling and spitting of protest harmonising with the anger she felt inside that strangers should make themselves comfortable at her hearth, in the rooms in which her children had been born. Then she swept the floors until no grain remained, until her muscles ached and her back grew sore. With time, as one day passed into another, every surface was wiped, sterilised with vinegar and fragrances of lavender and lilac brought inside to freshen the air. She said prayers in every room, daubing crosses on the walls, casting out demons and spirits. So with help from neighbours, many now returning, she whitewashed and filled cracks and fixed hinges and shelves, and placed handles through doors and realigned the cupboards into a semblance of order. Finally to beautify with wild flowers in vases. While devoid of furniture the cabin became home and she sat on the porch with some satisfaction and called to her friend who in frantic exercises of mime waved back. How grievously did the pain in her side attach itself, as a toothsaw through wood. But she banished it, dispelled the discomfort of it with the pleasure. On the step she sat and listened to the whistle of the unknown bird, masked by branches in the pine tree. Three notes trilled towards her. Three joyful words, of hope and new beginnings. And the birds flittered from one to another, and their nests they wove deep in foliage and the pain racked her body while she rested with complexion grey.

So then it was with timing impeccable I sauntered into the village, from the swinging hill. Stronger now and right glad to be home. Some tipped their caps, some raised a hand but my mother on the step did not notice my approach. Her eyes were closed so when I spoke she started, disassembling dream from life until with mute surprise she beheld my presence. How she clasped me to her. Where had I been, she asked, and was my health now fully restored. Yes, I answered grinning with the look of an idiot. I was quite well.

'God be praised,' she said.

'Yes,' I said.

Then scolding repeated the conversation, asking where had I been, and why, when all the work was done, had I idled home like a ghost?

'I am sorry,' I said, 'but I did not know that she would be here, or anyone, or the village itself for that matter would still exist.'

After some pause, she asked me, 'What do you think?'

'A fine job,' I answered, 'but you look gaunt and tired. Tomorrow I will help with the garden, things will soon be back to what they were.' This I said with a voice as much imbued with encouragement as I could muster but to my eyes she looked ill beyond weariness.

That night we slept in a clean house on borrowed mattresses. At sunrise I entered the garden clearing weeds and trimming back those plants gone to seed. Potatoes were planted, turnips too and the raspberries tidied on the stem. Soon roses emerged and I found the rhubarb stalks still robust. Each day the garden was unwrapped and this work eased body and mind. Each day more arrived, and I was kept busy fixing roofs and barns and stables until, by mid-summer the village bore the appearance once again of a living heart rather than a relic devoid of occupation. We shared what food we had in meals cooked over fires smoking black. Harvesting too of barley and oats and wheat occurred on a minor scale, where the very first arrivals had sown seeds early.

That the church was in a pitiful state was beyond conjecture. A deliberate and systematic regime of vandalism enacted upon it. The walls daubed in slogans. The communion table smashed along with half the pews. A bonfire had been lit in the corner and upon it placed remnants of furniture and prayer books, hymn sheets, property deeds and records from many ages past which I thought particularly unwarranted. When we brushed it out particles of ash still spiralled into the air; so when completed and painted afresh inside and out it was a shell, no more than husk. The calcified remains of life washed upon a beach. We spoke in whispers and I recalled the many times I had sat in this place, in Sunday clothes, collar biting into the neck, at harvest and Easter or when the walls reverberated with the tolling bell for another soul crossing. Changing shoes at the great stone or marking the boundaries with crosses so the spirits of the departed would not wander lanes in loneliness or sorrow or throw their eyes in our direction. It was here, when snow in high drifts piled against the door that I listened to our pastor relay the news of the first shots of the winter war. He could hardly speak. Harri smirked as was his way. No bells chimed in this sepulchre now. The pastor hugged his bell in the central provinces. He would not return. Many thought he was happier there, some were disappointed, many gave it no consideration.

The final task was to clear the churchyard. It was mightily overgrown, a veritable jungle, so we slashed at it with sickles, and bees murmured between strokes visiting flowers placed upon the tombstones. Every stone lay horizontal, not one survived the ridicule of Russians, some were smashed into pieces, all were beyond repair. For many hours I was busy making new markers, and when the vegetation was cleared it became obvious that others had been interred within the grounds, in a haphazard way, facing north or south or angled south-west without thought or inclination to the day of judgement. So sorry for the souls corrupting beneath I gathered golden rod and dog rose as a tribute. Some who watched me thought it mad, irreverent even, but I cared not. I had a reputation to maintain!

Finally, in the stillest of days, when the sky was gold we planted a new cross many metres high and reclaimed the village for ourselves and Christ. It was re-consecrated by a minister from the neighbouring parish who had a deeper love for this place. When he spoke the cattle bellowed and the crane flies skipped across his boots. We chanted psalms and said prayers with our hearts dripping to the floor. We could hardly stop our throats from trembling and glimpsed paradise. At his suggestion we carried a boulder from the barley field, sliced it in half and carved the names of the fallen upon it. It was a task both sad and joyful. Once complete he blessed it with holy water and the sign of the cross.

We turned and walked away.

All night mother and I debated the merits of sending for Merja. Tuija we thought would stay in Hämeenlinna where she had work and was developing friendships. She would not want to return; she had expressed this view on many occasions. Perhaps a neighbour would bring her. Perhaps I could make the journey. By nightfall we had made no decision and mother slumped grey in a chair. How she had aged in these few months. How much weight she had lost, now skin and bone with hair almost white. It was a shock to see her thus in the candlelight. Yet she would not seek help, took only herbal remedies which had not the strength to remove this malady. She groaned as if a wolf devoured her from the inside, each bite snapping another nerve. She mumbled in a half-sleep. I heard her as I lay in bed, murmuring disconnected thoughts, and in the morning when I questioned her, she said she was raising her thoughts to heaven and collecting her memories. This dwelling on things was most unlike her. She spoke with a borrowed voice, a tone channelled from others. So another worry pressed upon my forehead, yet she would not seek help from a doctor. She was most insistent, aggressive even. I watched her wasting.

Is this an opportune moment to turn the discourse away from the confines of the dwelled-in place? While the scene will be forever etched in memory, to other matters I turned my attention. Many mischiefs had been done to the village, both of deliberate and neglectful natures. It was a time for thinking in runes, rather than calculation. Each day carved in a script which

266

later generations would not care to decipher. Yet each day was real enough, monumental in its way.

Nature furnished this world with many riches, some caught in the roots of alder or hazel or pine, some of the earth itself, like Adam constituted from the soil, like we Karelians desiring only that our bones lie softly alongside his. Some treasure glistened on the surface, garnet, copper ore, coins of bronze and silver. Items of sombre value, elements ungrown, but appreciated for a beauty, as a butterfly wing or the rainbow in a salmon's side bravely leaping. Some flew with wings towards the sun, some growled, others poked heads above the frost when spring raised them from sleep. My own treasure lay accumulated in my fingers, in the turning and chiselling of wood. As each day passed the need to return to work, to make recompense for foul deeds committed by these hands in the name of necessity grew stronger. With fortitude I crossed the lane to where my workshop once stood, no longer could I avoid this day, or construct any contrivance for delay. It was not there of course, how could it be? A pile of blackened timbers once smouldering marked the outline. Like a grave. There were no tools, no door to lock myself away, no bench or chest or scent of wood dust. But I had to see. As hope carries more pain than despair I kicked sticks of charcoal away and cursed silently.

Chapter 18

Daybreak.

Beyond our trenches.

In lands darkened by the enemy.

He raised his head, peering carefully through the early morning haze. Cobwebs brushed his hair. Delicate strands of silk in branches and parallels, with spheres of water balancing the rigging. Like the lanyards on a sailing ship or the floats of fishermen. Simo watched the many suns rise upon his final day; one beyond the other in an amber sky curving. Reflections mirrored these flames in stagnant water where may fly nymphs and whirligigs paddled on the surface tension. Flat, sinking into matting, sponge mosses sucked him down and the dampness simmered his old bones, and the binoculars clamped to his eyes gave the appearance of crustaceans awatching prey, ready to bolt or scurry away. Deep inside Russia. Way beyond aid this party of three on deep reconnaissance moulded themselves into contours, of hollow or hummock. Acid smoked the grey of their uniform, sizzling undetected. Skin turned brown to green to red and their bodies became as one with the many coloured carpet. Sundews smeared a glue upon their sleeves and the bog, the endless shivering mire that was this land began the long, slow process of digestion. They were being eaten alive.

'What do you see?' asked a comrade. A young man, barely out of school, terror burned into his face.

'As before.'

'Then we are lost.'

A sky lark shot into the air. Ravens circled and the young man's face, now close to madness, swollen with mosquito bites looked pitifully at Simo.

'There is no one here, there is no one to track, no horizon, no paths, nothing.'

'Then we are lost,' he repeated despairingly.

Simo did not answer at first but scanned their bleak environment one last time.

'We go west.'

'To what purpose?'

' None that I can tell.'

Two men rose. One did not stir. Already half-reclaimed by marsh his body succumbed to the long, slow descent. So soon had midges laid their eggs within his hair and worms enclosed his fingers. While still warm the frenzy started, and the chemicals that once were Private Alapuro synthesised. Blood drained out of him. Humanity took flight. He sank and bubbled and the two remaining soldiers struggled through water and mud up to their knees.

Daylight magnified them. Steam issued from them. Dense clouds of insects flew into their eyes and blinded them. Weed wrapped around their ankles. Thirst parched them. Disease turned their stomachs over and this life such as it was oozed from every pore. Still the ravens circled and a marsh harrier watched their progress with a natural curiosity.

The younger man stumbled. With a splash he caught his breath, calling out. 'Simo…Simo I can't go on.'

'You have no choice. Do you want to join your friend as carrion? Say and it will be so.'

'You will not leave me Simo?'

'If I must.'

He spat out his words, cruel utterances born of exhaustion. But relent he did and returned to the younger man. His face bore some resemblance to his own son. His anger subsided. Faith returned and compassion speaking softly urged the boy soldier to continue. 'All is not lost. Once we have stumbled from this hell, if we can avoid enemy patrols, we can regain our own lines.'

'Is it possible?'

' It is,' he answered, pulling the boy forward by the straps on his backpack. 'I've been in deeper water than this I can tell you.'

There was hope. Always hope. The marsh was not endless, it merged with forest, with dry land at some point hence...but how far? On they staggered, caring little now for the enemy. No human had they seen for many days, nor any sign of habitation. Spurts of gas shot upwards when the pressure of their boots pressed down.

Blue flames.

Mirages. Foulness. Mildew. Skin in sore halfway gone. Devils dogged them. Red-suited devils mocking. Tails flashing. Simo saw them.

In circles, where what passed for land haunted the memory and the shape of it, the outline was familiar. The waterways and rivulets without feature they crossed and re-crossed. Oxygen evaporated, the air itself was brackish.

The many suns beat down. Mud dried in slabs across their backs and the weight of it disfigured the walk. Mud jumped on them, earth dragged in great clumps and mosquitoes stabbed their fine syringes into every vein until blood too seeped from the pores and bluebottles feasted on it.

More feverish the soldiers battled on, splashing through reeds and then falling. Simo urged caution, explained that if they kept their heads and continued west, they would eventually escape. But he would have none of it; compelled, driven, the distance between the two men lengthened.

The scream awakened him. Simo struggled to the spot and saw the soldier waist high in mud and sinking deeper.

'Don't struggle...stay still.'

The eyes covered that earth bespeckled face, so wide in terror were they, white as dinner plates.

'Get me out…get me out. For the love of God!' he screeched a cry returning to childhood, higher pitched, a voice primeval.

Simo lay flat and stretched across the mire, holding his rifle as a branch. There was nothing else. But try as he might the soldier could not reach it, and worse, with every muscle spasm he sank deeper, demons pulled his legs and now his chest was encased in this muck.

'Damn it!' shouted Simo. 'Damn it!' He looked around for anything that might aid his rescue. 'Take off your pack, it is dragging you down! But it was like concrete and his fingers did not have the strength to unclasp the buckles. They merely served to drag him deeper.

'Simo!' he screamed and the mud flowed over his mouth and nose and the eyes poking above the surface grasped one final image of sky. Then it was that Simo saw the face of his own son once again, until it was gone and globes of air puckered the mud and the surface levelled again and the trapdoor closed.

Simo sank to his knees. At that moment he knew that all was lost. He would not sleep again; the closure of his eyelids drew the curtain back to many images of death. There was no hope. None.

He stood and threw his rifle away. His own pack he took from his shoulders and dumped that too, keeping only a water bottle mostly empty. Onwards and onwards he advanced. There was nothing else to do. Many strange encounters with witches and sprites and miasmas he had in that place. Too sore to repeat, too lacking in sleep to re-tell. Then at the edge of life, a breeze wafted cleaner air into his lungs. He saw the rising of new land and the dark green of conifers topping the horizon.

When the devil tapped him on the shoulder he was not surprised. Many a one had followed him, guided by ravens.

'Wait a moment. What is the hurry?'

Simo stared, but did not reply.

'What's new in your world old man?'

'How should I know?'

'Pause a while. Speak with me.' He hissed, flicking a long red tongue in and out of a black mouth.

'I have no time to waste on such as you.'

The devil smiled. 'Then let me entertain you.'

The devil clicked his fingers and a horse galloped through his frame of vision pursued by clouds of mosquitoes. When the horse stumbled, rearing its head and swishing his mane the mosquitoes fell upon it, devouring, tearing it apart, sucking up blood until…still writhing the horse was soon reduced to bone. Only the eyes remained and the skeleton, eyes frantic, galloped away. And the devil laughed and slapped Simo on the shoulder. A bolt cold as ice shot through his spine.

Simo had enough and turned to face the devil, angry as hell itself. A foul stench caught him, but Simo did not flinch.

'Be gone and take your pestilence with you.'

So he sank, waving and mocking into the mire and flicking a serpent tongue.

Simo strode purposefully forwards. When thankfully solid ground was reached he paused to drink what little water remained. So clogged were his eyes and ears that he could only stagger in a daze. He could neither see nor hear, only feel the air cooler to the skin and the ground firm.

So it was that Simo followed the track, unaware that at a road block Finnish troops at the very edge of the line had watched this curious brown and olive green figure emerge from the mire. They were nervous, jumpy and beyond contact with their officers.

'Halt!' shouted one.

'Halt or we fire,' was the second's response.

A warning shot rang out. Simo glanced into the tree canopy but could make nothing of it, so disorientated were his senses that he merely advanced, unaware of countless warnings shouted with increasing intensity.

The bullet that killed him entered his brain between the eyes. He keeled over onto his back and just had time to close his eyes until death claimed him. The two sentries ran across and stared down at this creature, part human, part vegetation. What was the meaning of this?

*

I was glad the forest ended. The alternation of shadow and blinding light became oppressive after awhile. My senses filled with aromas of mint, wild garlic, grass dried by the sun. It was difficult to think.

At one time the very act of seeking solitude was enough, sufficient to enable those processes of contemplation so valuable to me to be undertaken and the knots unravelled. But today it was all froth. This return from exile was not as I envisaged. The village was largely empty still, a struggle to crank up an agriculture too lacking in manpower and equipment. The heart had gone and those childhood associations mere wounds. I have to confess that there were times when I considered a return to Hämmenlinna but a natural impulse of loyalty to the dwelled-in place and the hope that things would improve, caused me to stay my hand. I was needed I suppose. So much work to do.

As reader, you know by now that I do not respond well to confusion. I feel most secure when everything is in its place. It is good to know that tomorrow such and such is built, and the next day repairs are to be completed, like so, just so. Uncertainty and anxieties sit uneasily with me and causes much agitation.

When I emerged from the trees the hum of bees accompanied me. I tasted sunlight on my tongue, the honey texture of it causing me to lick my lips. A woodpecker tapped, a kestrel hovered. Straw from the barn tumbled across the path and somewhere in the distance I could hear the whinny of a horse. I strode in no particular direction between the cabins unable to shake this melancholy despite the gentle gurgling of water, dulcimer sweet. No human voices did I crave, neither friend nor foe, indeed I positively avoided contact. Through meadows crowned with buttercups, warbling with birds I could not see, crows cawing alarms at my tread. Pollen brushed my trousers to the knees, with every step a butterfly rose. Tall nettles covered up the boundaries masking their stings. And in the midst of all this life, well hidden, I turned a circle with my arms outstretched and spun and spun and spun as once we had as youngsters on the swinging hill. Faster and faster until the blood rushed to my head and the ground became a trench and air a parapet. Then it was I sank beneath the meadow safe. Certainty came, like a catch of wire. Then I understood, in a moment, that out of us all, all who walk this earth, God chooses some to hear his words carried on the wind as through the crack in a wall. Like it or not, words seep into a consciousness as scents whisper or the burnet rose gathers raindrops.

One blow.

Light engulfed my mind, streaming to every corner. It was so quiet.

'All acts are irreversible,' said He. 'There can be no regrets, no sorrows, no punishments for misdemeanours, no apologies, no atonement, no unconsummation.'

It felt as if...as if I had been ripped apart and put back together again. There would be no return to soldiering for me; I was not fit for it. Maarit would soon write and the disturbance rippling my sleep would calm. We would find permanence, all of us, whether here or in some other place God would determine.

Only the scream broke this spell. An ear-splitting cry reaching even here, when all the laws of physics denoted that it should fade. I recognised the voice and raced back into the village where others had responded. Of course I knew it was my mother. There was no doubt.

By the time I reached the cabin she had been carried to a chair. A pool of blood swam across the floor. She was grey and beads of perspiration riveted her scalp. Her hair much whitened by sorrow hung limp and while still conscious she mumbled, making little sense, turning the same words over and over again. A doctor was sent for and all I could do was prepare a bed. Someone threw sand onto the floor to soak the blood. Neighbours carried her into the bedroom and a woman near in age to herself prepared her. Mopping and coaxing and whispering in domestic intricacies. Soon she was encased in blankets. A mother tipped a cup of water to her lips but she could not take it. The men disappeared, only the women remained.

'There is nothing you can do Hannu,' one of them said. I nodded. The silence of the cabin was punctuated only by screams, intermittent but biting, raw.

When the doctor arrived he hurried through carrying a black bag and slipping off his coat in one smooth movement. He did not need to spend much time in there. Through the door I heard him asking questions which received no answer. I imagine he examined her; every action met with groans and wicked, wicked, screams which could not be held. He emerged with his sleeves rolled up and washed his hands in a basin.

'It is not good,' I said.

'No,' he replied. 'There is a tumour, a large one in the colon. It has most likely spread to other organs. I'm afraid there is little anyone can do but make her comfortable. I have morphine to alleviate the pain. The next few days will be difficult. She will lapse in and out of consciousness but even now she is not aware, be thankful of that.'

I combed my hair with my fingers, tapping my foot on the floor.

'Is there no one else to help?'

'My sister-in-law will come if I summon her. I have a sister but she is still young.' I considered my next response. 'I can stay. I have a medical discharge from the army and there are neighbours who will assist.'

'No husband?'

'Somewhere.'

'If you need anything, send for me. The morphine is in an ampoule at the side of the bed. Take care with it, it is like gold.'

I thanked him and helped him on with his coat. An elderly man I had not seen before, barely able to catch his own breath. His hands were stained yellow by tobacco and his bag wore some imperial emblem.

Later that evening when the cabin was empty and the floor brushed I took a candle into my mother's room and steeled

275

myself for a long night. She looked comfortable now with her eyes closed and the counterpane rising gently as she breathed. The candle flame flickered and shadows danced on the walls. In this room she had given birth to three children, one lost, one without hearing, one damaged by war. Such are the injustices of this existence. No recollections snared her now in sleep uneasy. In this room she would die at the hour appointed when first she grasped this life laden with dew. At each ticking I raised my head. I slipped in and out of sleep myself. I was aware that I participated in a ceremony which many generations of my ancestors had fashioned from their fascinations and griefs. At dawn a tapping on glass roused me. A wagtail hopping on the ledge peered in and flew away.

She was gone. At the time anointed in a quiet way, without fuss. Out of one door and into another.

The village came to pay their respects, offering condolences, and the elderly, the ones with hair white as snow prepared her for the grave. Towards nightfall Tuija and Merja arrived. Many tears we shed and much lamenting, though restraining our upset for the sake of decency. My mother was not inclined to ritual or display. We said farewells as was the custom and awaited the interment stoically.

Our footprints sank a thousand tombs. As a crashing of mauve heather on the winding hill towards the church. The cortège halted by the great stone where many times we had paused to change our Sunday shoes. It made me smile, as if my mother had a hand in this small act. We said our prayers and sang our psalms before the coffin was carried to the graveside. To the little cemetery surrounded by birch trees.

Sad rose.

Soil covered her. She succumbed wearily one cell at a time. Ferns folded over the edge, a feather was carried by the wind. Aye, it is she who once walked yonder hills, whose kin dwelt once among the longhouses when this land was wild and untamed. Her cabin sucked this earth like a limpet. Wind screamed through the rafters but it would not budge her, nor

would the death she witnessed or the spitting of fire or pain
searing like hot pokers on cold temples move her spirit one
grain. So we grind summer grasses under foot, hovering in limp
blades over the hole, eyes descending. She who once walked
yonder hills now gathered crisp clear clouds like an orange bay
as soil sank blind her cancerous body.

*

To my mind Tampere was a metropolis. A great many mills
and factories churning out war materials at gargantuan rates. So I
am told, for I only saw the inside of a hospital ward, that it is a
place of motor cars and trams, where life is taken in your hands
when crossing the road. The air is yellow apparently and the
thud, thud, thud of power presses and spinning machines and
turning of lathes is the music of that place. It is rumoured the
city rotates with the activity of it all. The people are solid and
workman-like. So different to the quiet of the village but it takes
all sorts. It was here throughout the greater part of the
continuation war that Maarit lived. It was a dark period about
which I knew very little, and of which she did not speak to any
great extent. We kept in touch through letters, although the
frequency dwindled; we both had preoccupations and in all that
time we did not meet. I confess to some disappointment that her
letters were infrequent, sometimes bursting with energy,
sometimes a log of daily events or a formula. Not that my own
correspondence was a mighty tome. A few years later I had
occasion to read them and goodness! Dull as ditch water. They
read like orders of the day and when I glanced at the vocabulary
I realised with embarrassment how barren it all was. The word
'tea' and 'bed' and 'work' appearing with chronic regularity, a
few articles, the odd adjective and that was about it. When I
wrote about the loss of my mother she replied rather touchingly.
They had always got on well. It was some comfort and I longed
to meet but our plans came to nothing, events always overtook
us. And, well I always found it difficult to express myself in
words either in the flesh or on paper. I must have been hard
work.

But to pick up her story, it goes thus.

Maarit escaped the monotony of hospital life, more a cleaner than a nurse, by long walks, in all weathers, rain or shine, winter, summer or spring. There were many parks and as a creature of habit she followed a route from the railway station to one of these green spaces where an ornamental lake provided a focus for her thoughts. It had the air of solitude about it and some sad neglect. Flowerbeds provided a back drop and a fountain from another age stood severely in the centre. Wild fowl visited the water, mallard, teal, pochard, scrambling after vegetation or eyeing visitors expectantly for bread. Of course there was none. Bread was in short supply but their eyes were ever hopeful. High-buttoned humanity gravitated to this spot in twos and threes, as individuals seeking respite from the grey grind or anxieties of the war. Often air raid sirens punctuated the silence but this soon achieved the flavour of normality. There was a low rumble of traffic and the clattering of wagons on the railway track, soldiers sauntered along the paths, children raced across the grass. Maarit watched it all with detached amusement.

One elderly man caught her attention. He wore a black suit, dated, but clean and pressed with a sombre black tie and homburg. She waved and he came to sit beside her on the bench.

'A fine morning Maarit?'

'Indeed Mr Lehto. You are early. I didn't expect to see you here.'

He sat bolt upright and brushed imaginary dust from his jacket. A fob and chain hung from his waistcoat. He screwed up his eyes in the sunlight, tapping his foot on the floor.

'You know it's strange but the older you get the less sleep you need and the more time you have for doing nothing. What a peculiar turn of events that is.'

Maarit smiled.

'What a sad reflection.'

They both sat drawing in sunlight feeling little compunction to talk. It was Mr Lehto who opened the conversation again.

'That's true…tell me Maarit how are you coping with this irregular existence? Any news of a transfer?'

278

'None I'm afraid. I have to finish my training, which consists mostly of scrubbing floors or emptying bed pans! They think me too young for the front now, though I have more experience than the matrons. It is all regulations and procedure. To be honest I am becoming disillusioned.'

'One day at a time. When you get to my age you learn to appreciate the smaller things in life. A nice meal, a cigar, a walk in the park. Such a sorry state the young men sent away and suffering monstrous injustice and the old and useless passing their time in parks or libraries, shuffling newspapers. Sometimes I see a line outside a shop and stand in it. Just to pass a little time.'

'Really Mr Lehto, you wouldn't want me to feel sorry for you?' teased Maarit.

'No...no. You are right. I am quite capable of doing that myself.'

There was another pause. A cloud covered the sun and the air turned momentarily cooler. Mr Lehto continued.

'Have you considered my offer Maarit?'

'Yes, most carefully and I must say I have been tempted. The hospital bores me to tears, and the girls I live with, well I have no patience with them or their gossip. I'm sure they don't like me. Not that I care.'

'I'm disappointed … but not surprised.'

'It was most kind. In other circumstances I would have jumped at the chance, nurse and housekeeper in a fine house like yours. But I feel I must complete my training. While it drives me to distraction, it will provide a future. If things go badly in this war I will be needed. One way or another there will come a time to settle down.'

'Mrs Lehto will be disappointed too. She likes you Maarit, she likes to hear you talk of Karelia. She left the village of Inkila on her wedding day, and never returned, yet still she calls it home.'

'Home, I cannot imagine it, my mind mists over in clouds of carbolic soap and floor polish.'

This time it was Mr Lehto's turn to laugh. 'There are worse things you know.'

'I'm sure there are. I'm not totally serious. One day soon it will come together. I look at the faces in the hospital wards, the pain and anxiety, the boredom of it all and make my plans for a little house by a lake. A garden, a lilac tree, a front step polished like quartz. Then Hannu comes through the door in a state of permanent confusion, trying to remember if he's eaten his lunch or left it in the workshop and all I can do is laugh at him. Then he feels hurt and I laugh some more so he storms out...and he creeps back sheepishly, with his empty lunchbox and some clothes pegs as a peace offering. You must meet him Mr Lehto, he really is something. Now he is in the village and the cares fall heavily on his shoulders and his losses mount and all I can do is sit here in the park moaning.'

'You must go to him.'

'I will. When next we meet I will grab him by the hair and pull him to me and never let him go, come hell or high water we will not be parted again. It will drive me mad, to the edge of insanity. Within a year I will be a wreck or smothered in spindles and brackets and wood glue.'

Mr Lehto shook with laughter, his walking stick pattered the gravel path. He was young again.

'Will you miss me when I'm carried to the lunatic asylum?'

'Of course...but I will visit you, most certainly I will visit with gifts of chocolate cake and brandy.'

'I will need it. In his last letter he talked about getting a dog. Where that came from I know not. He has always been disparaging about them. What kind of dog I asked him. A dog with four legs says he, or three, a black one, maybe white with a bark, a good bark. What am I supposed to answer to that?'

'Suggest a cat. He will soon grow out of the idea.'

'Hannu doesn't grow out of ideas, he picks them up and puts them in his pocket. Some he loses, some drop back to the ground and others take hold like measles.'

'But you will meet again soon.'

'We will God willing. I must write to him.'

'Come Maarit I'll treat you to a coffee.'

It was almost two years since that meeting took place and much occurred in the intervening period. She continued with her work and qualified as a nurse. Mr Lehto cared for his wife with a saintly patience. Maarit often visited, she shared meals at Easter and Christmas, helped around the house and steadily outgrew the girls with whom she shared a room. From time to time there were air raids, but little damage resulted, random attacks, tokens of aggression. German troops embarked and disembarked at the station, more subdued, bitter, scowling on platforms as they waited for trains. Our people turned their faces away from them, the majority at least. News from the front filtered back, sometimes good, sometimes bad. Seasons flowed one into the other, snow blizzards rimed rooftops, darkness descended. Winter's dead drumbeat scorched eyes, cold numbed the fingers of Maarit and Mr Lehto and the many thousand inhabitants of Tampere caught their taunt breath casting glances down alleyways black as ink. Smiles became scars. Hearts pulled the sharp strings of winter's thin threads like music, like rivulets of ice, feet stamping at doors. Snow spilled from trees and the windows crystallised producing many imaged ghosts. Winds whipped into fury forcing all beyond doors bolted. Time elapsed.

In the village Merja sank beneath the blankets of her old bed. I shared the storm in candlelight. Winter's coverlet iced the watering places and a mooning glow reflected planets into a room where many spirits swirled. Slab winter covered the fields. Barren and cauterised in comfortless shrieks. Like meat stripped from bone the trees clung tight in the ice bay winds, garnering earth's loot. Breath vaporised to salt and the stones were clasped in frost's grip. Somewhere in the darkness Tuija made her way to Hämeenlinna. We spent a final winter in the country. Had I known it would be so I would have gathered every snowflake to my heart and sucked the life from it.

Chapter 19

Share in a cup of suffering as this tale long in the telling recalls its sting. In trenches stretching deep unto horizons as black scars. On lands now defended for a second time. Like an army of ants toiling through time and space many thousands of men clad in grey sank ever deeper in frantic activity.

Summer storms tumbled upon them, sun baked the surface into crusts and those whose eyes moved not from loam knew in their hearts that a final reckoning was near. In all regions men retreated. The Germans annihilated in Stalingrad now fell back from the Crimea to the Arctic. That gamble with the gods which Finland once had made now came back to haunt us. Already Finnish forces had been cleared from vast tracks of land to the east. With our erstwhile allies we exchanged hard stares and it was only a matter of time before one betrayed the other. Now the line was drawn and we dug in. Here the sledgehammer would fall. Harri knew it when he swung the pick, when his back drenched in sweat and sore was a dull reminder of humanity he remembered the agonies of winter war and counted the many years since this fightback had begun and Karelia re-gained. Now as the summer of 1944 tore a path through lives caught in its web the waiting would soon be over and one way or another all our fates decided.

There would be resolution and in the mean time work continued with the energy of desperation. Building fire steps and block houses, re-aligning communication networks, filling sandbags. Hard, cruel, unremitting work. At dawn stand-to. The sun rose above the trenches of the enemy. The sentries silhouetted in that golden glare for several minutes of the day, our snipers took a toll of them. Harri, with grim satisfaction carved notches on his rifle butt, and with every kill spat out his bile. As every morning ebbed the boys dipped their heads and prepared. When new drafts of the trigger-happy swelled the ranks, old hands, veterans of many years of war cursed them for their stupidity.

'Hold your fire,' they would say, 'save your ammunition. You will need it soon enough. If you fire with ill discipline they will mark you as jumpy and bring all hell upon us. Now stay quiet and keep your heads down.'

Some did and some knew better. Some lived, some were scalped by bullet. So the daily grind of trench warfare continued. Stand to at dawn, repair work, routine maintenance, inspect rifles, sentry duty, stand to at dusk, double the guard at night. In between snatch sleep, brew coffee in a billycan, de-louse, make sure food was not left around…it encouraged vermin.

Harri accepted this as his lot. He witnessed the power of bombardment and the shrapnel inscriptions etched into the walls, the wail of random mortars. He peered across the parapet from time to time, saw wisps of smoke, craters. Through the lens of a periscope he watched the gradual decay of a Russian soldier no one had bothered to remove. The observable became a fascination. At first he rested with his back against a tree stump, legs blown off. Now he was black and bloated, his face green. Shaven hair, spectacles dangling comically from a nose dribbling black blood. As the days progressed the ravens picked him piecemeal and the pink tails whipped his face. To one more philosophical it might represent the loot of Karelia, but to Harri it was soldier, a dead Russian, one of many he had seen, it meant nothing to him. On patrol, at night, in a silvery light, starkly beautiful his hands disturbed the bones of skeletons, rattling his imagination and memory. He watched two rats tussle over a severed hand and as he sheltered in those pits slugs crawled across his skin and frogs jumped into his mouth. He felt old, he felt he had had enough. In those silent hours the darkness moved and the ground shivered. Hallucinations confused the senses, bushes crawling, saps and listening posts advanced and retreated. This was a deadly time, casualties mounted steadily, pitter-pattering, in ones and twos remorseless.

In the dugouts, around the campfires, he did not mix, nor did he socialise or share his thoughts with others. Too many friends had passed this way and out of sight. He did not trust himself. Nor did he consider a future so uncertain in dimension. It was irrelevant. Only the past interested him; those images of village life gnawed him out. So while outwardly he gave the impression of being morose, volatile even, within himself he saw the steam of the engine approaching the station, cut barley with scythes like sabres, and slept in a bed without nightmares. None read him. No one disturbed his musings when he studied the stars and imagined them as dot to dots. Words did not come to his lips to either question or reply. A solitude cloaked his shoulders, isolation compounded his darkness seeping through every vein and artery and he was quite alone. He was comfortable with this.

A mere two hundred metres away, preparations for the final onslaught were being prepared, more confidently now, more professional, single-minded, ruthless. In the airfields of Leningrad squadrons swarmed, armour and artillery turned their wheels towards Karelia and men without number trudged west.

The Finns awaited them. In the giants jaw life kindled or sparked and quiet orations drifted in a multitude of dialects through a land which would soon despatch them. The mouth opened, the teeth snarled, the days darkened into shadow and all felt its cold crawl upon their backs. They wrote and drank and laughed and checked rifle bolts. Meanwhile, with a grin, the jaws clenched and the trap began to close, the pulse quickened and all the mutations of war straining at the leash seared the air with demonic howls.

*

We were having a hard time of it in the village. Everything was scarce, food, coffee, clothing. Many were half-starving, and while the harvests had been good, we had not the manpower to sow or gather in the crops and much of the land began a slow descent to wilderness. I did my best to repair buildings and cabins but timber, cut and treated, was in short supply. Many times I reflected that to build a home it was necessary to start with the smoke from the chimney.

I took to watching Russian prisoners working the fields. They had no love for the task, doing the bare minimum and it was a time of many frustrations. Some people returned, some left, but it was difficult to re-capture the essence of the dwelled-in place. So many once familiar voices departed. I'm afraid to confess that Merja ran wild in the forests, splashed in the stream and was neither clean nor well kept. But what was I to do? Almost three years we were there, until in that final summer we heard the drone of aeroplanes overhead and the vibrations of aerial bombardments in the nearby towns. The sun seared the ground into a solid ridge, harder than concrete and the footsteps of many malefactors drummed upon it. We were always on our guard. In the night we heard footsteps, escaping prisoners, spies, deserters, criminals taking advantage of the chaos to steal all that was not nailed down. In my belt I kept a service revolver and while I did not consider I would ever use it, its presence gave me confidence and would, if the need arose, at least serve as a deterrent.

I must have been accumulating visions as others accumulated wealth, knowing that the hill and the church and the very sky under which I stood might soon be lost. Others may have shared this sense of finality, if they did, they did not share their thoughts with me. On this particular day I stood gazing oblivious on a field of potatoes, and beyond to the churchyard where a grave was being prepared for a Russian airman come down not far from here. The bottom of my trousers were stained brown with dust. Weeds wrapped their talons around my legs and grass seeds speckled my boots. A sultriness caused my breathing to catch and spurt. It was a scene of shimmering stillness. A water tank creaked, a wheelbarrow lay up-ended in a ditch. Merja ran between my line of vision. She had been crying, tears stained her cheeks, but she would not tell me why she cried, or why she carried her shoes in her hands. I did not have the energy or inclination to follow her back to the cabin, but stood gazing covertly at the little things, pocketing them for posterity. Empty flower tubs, sweet briars twanging like bowstrings, the smell of zinc in the nostrils, a black bird calling alarms.

What made me turn I could not say, maybe a gentle tapping on the shoulder by some apparition but turn I did, and saw him standing there, arms folded across his chest and the buttons of his jacket fastened unevenly.

'Paavo.'

'You remember me then little brother,' he said, stretching out his hand. I would not take it.

'What is it you want?' I questioned him. I was determined to be on my guard.

'You look well. Stronger than the last time we met.'

'I wish I could say the same of you.' I answered, glancing disparagingly at his shabby appearance. 'Don't you want news of your kin?' I barked.

'No need to be like that Hannu. I know all that concerns me. I have ways of knowing. Tuija is happy enough. Merja, is there something wrong with the girl? I'm afraid I startled her by the stream and she ran away.'

I gritted my teeth.

'And yes I am aware of our deep loss. Mother lies in the churchyard. I have visited her grave several times after dark. Times must be hard.'

'We manage...but why have you returned? Why not stay with your friends the Russians in Terijoki, or wherever they now reside.'

He strode towards me and I took one pace back. This caused him to smirk and raise an eyebrow. Unkempt he might be but he was still strong, well-built, powerful in frame and temperament.

'God forgive that I should try to help my ungrateful brother.'

'Half-brother.'

At this he screwed up his face, and his cheek browned by the sun took on the appearance of an old broad bean, shrivelled and splitting. Rage surged into his heart, but he held it in check. I was unprepared for this encounter, taken completely by surprise so I was careful not to provoke him, at least until I had a plan.

'Are you really so ignorant?' he exclaimed. His adam's apple jolted and I discerned a new huskiness to his voice. 'The Red Army is poised across the border, not twenty miles from here. Have you not seen the fighters and bombers overhead, countless formations, do you suspect nothing? Any day now the signal will be given and the hounds of hell themselves will be unleashed.'

'Let them come, we have mauled them many times.'

'Not this time,' he said, softening his voice. 'This time they will not be held. This time their rage and cries for vengeance know no bounds. They will be in Helsinki within a week.'

'So why are you here?'

'I come to salvage what little remains. A month from now Finland will be absorbed into the Soviet Union. A great power, a mighty new order and no one will be come to your aid. This country is tarred with the same brush as the Germans, you reap as you sow. Come with me before it is too late, bring Merja with you and as many as will come. Hand over the village and there will be a home for you. Do this now before it is too late.'

'Go!' I growled trying to contain my anger. 'Leave this place before it is polluted by your presence.'

'Such fools,' he ranted and his shirt collar shot up to his chin. 'I'll waste no more time.' Shards of words were catapulted towards me but I turned my back on him and started to walk away.

'Idiot.'

I kept walking.

'Even Maarit had more sense to leave you here.'

My anger cracked and as I watched him striding back into the forest some turbulence, some years of pent up rage and anger and fire was instantly eroded. I calmly took the revolver from my belt, flicked off the safety catch and fired. The bullet smashed into the back of his head. He fell instantly into the undergrowth. The blackbird flew away. I did not glance around. I did not care if the shot was noticed or if a witness saw the act. It was all one to me. Later that night, when Merja was fast asleep I returned to that spot. I dragged the remains of my dead half-brother across the potato field and laid him flat in the grave of the Russian airman. I shovelled a few inches of soil into the hole and when satisfied that he was invisible returned to my bed.

In the morning the airman's coffin was placed on top of him. No one noticed. Why would they? I even helped to fill it in. That was a Friday if my memory serves me well. The beginning of the final week.

The village slept in a state of dormancy. The pebbles swirled in the riverbed. Kingfishers dived, trout sought the shade of overhanging trees. Apples glistened. Butterflies flickered in and out of the lilac tree. I packed my rucksack and bundled Merja's scanty belongings into a pillowcase. Most of the week I spent in a kaleidoscope, sitting on the porch. On Wednesday I dug up the rhubarb, roots and all and deposited it in a sack. One Thursday I walked down to the stream and filled a bottle with water, ramming the cork into the top. On Friday morning I made my way to the churchyard to place flowers on my mother's grave. A few hours later the guns opened up, and while they were a long way off the earth still trembled.

*

At dawn the Finnish line was prepared. There was an uneasy silence. Harri peered over the parapet into the awakening of a beautiful day. There were new dead on the wire. They swelled and burst in the heat. The colour of those young faces changed from white to yellow to red to green to black. The smell of their putrefaction drifted across the line and some men vomited.

Then the punch came. A giant fist pummelling the surface of the Isthmus, a vindictive arm tattooed with the grinning, smirking, face of Stalin punching the land, holes and craters, and all beneath it smashed to smithereens. How the belligerents cowered and laughed one to the other. This barrage more terrific than any gone before cracked the granite core itself and the air was sucked from lungs and all men could do beneath its deadly imprecations was pray to almighty God and breathe whatever oxygen was spared to them. Some were vaporised, some buried alive, some so shattered into pieces that even the raven's eye could not discern their composition. All day rained down metal and cordite with a blistering intensity. Air attacks compounded the ferocity and when the rumbling of armour crept through the smoke there was nothing to be done but to withdraw, in good order but well shaken, ears vibrating and eyes besmirched with smoke. A week of retreat and desperate delaying tactics saw Viipuri lost, that jewel fell into the sea with a ripple spreading through the Gulf of Finland. Many villages now reduced to rubble fell into enemy hands. There was one line more to stand, one defensive structure where the armies of Finland rallied. On the eastern banks of the Vuokski waterway men unpacked their weapons and vowed they would not move. At Tali-Ihantala Harri found himself with the remnants of many units disordered by retreat. In wonder, spying through the lenses of binoculars, he saw a flow of reinforcements flooding to the line. All that moved, on horses, on armoured vehicles, on foot shouldering rifles thousands poured across the Isthmus and dug into the earth. Some later said that women and children were among their number, but it was legend only. But all knew that it was here fate would decide their future. There was a grim determination to concede nothing, to leave no one. Among men bandaged round the head, shaking with shellshock, stuttering, unable to string plain sentences together there was an understanding that this was it. After a preliminary bombardment hordes of Russian Infantry charged screaming across the plain. The minefields scattered their numbers and the intimate crack of sniper fire ensured that none were rescued. There was a breathing space; further reinforcements and supplies rushed forward.

'When will they come again?' the soldier next to Harri said. He wore a corporal's stripe now and carried the authority of a veteran.

'Soon enough,' he answered. 'Make sure your ammunition pouches are full and scan the front for cover or shell holes; mark the territory with your eyes.'

The soldier did as he was told and only raised his head when the sound of singing blew across from the enemy lines. Louder it grew, marching songs sung by long extended lines of Russian soldiers carrying no weapons but with arms linked as if this was some kind of dance. Onwards they marched without wavering. At their backs, squads of machine gunners. At a distance they followed, unable to turn their attention aside.

'God help us,' called out Harri in dismay.

'What is it?'

'A punishment battalion. I have seen this once before. Hold your fire. Be prepared for the rush when this is over.'

'But what's happening?' cried out the soldier now alarmed. His eyes skipped across the horizon and fingers shook.

'Wait and see,' said Harri. 'This will be something to tell your grandchildren about.'

Onwards, in long, extended, lines, ripples of green marched with arms linked. The singing did not cease but took on a mournful, hypnotic quality. It tore the air like paper ripping, it tore at the hearts of the watchers.

'What are they doing?' screamed the soldier in disbelief.

'Can't you see…are you stupid, look.' Harri jerked the soldier's face towards the front; he slapped him over and over, pulling his hair, angry, bursting with rage.

One man turned his head and was instantly shot in the head. He fell, the line closed, the gap was filled, onwards they strode. Some wore grins, some closed their eyes, a small number, younger men, mere boys, studied the ground over which they marched with a terrible intensity. As creatures of the deep are washed ashore so these men of the punishment battalion advanced to desiccation. The first explosion tossed three into the air, limbs flew into the faces of the others, cries sundered the air some started to cry…threats moved them on, more lines blew until the writhings and moans and deprecations grew too terrible for the Finnish gunners and they sprayed the line with machine gun fire. The sultry scents of blood and cordite, the green sea of faith rolled shorewards, ever nearer, edges ragged now, unfurling onto the wire.

One man stood defiant, legs akimbo, arms folded, unarmed and daring until a bullet felled him and the unlamented one burrowed his head into the ground; where bodies stacked, gaps within the mine field opened. Infantry from the rear charged forward, lips quivering, and a desperate glare burning the mouth, white-eyed, stubble-faced, heads bobbing they came. Armour followed in their wake undaunted by the dead and dying pulverised between their growling tracks. These monsters too were stopped by artillery, by mortars, by bottles filled with kerosene and hurled at the advance. The smash of glass, the seep of liquid and the phut of ignition transformed those dwellers within into incineration. No vision eluded the smoke of battle nor balm from any herbs soothed the wounds. Yet still we stood with stubbornness defying logic. Not one step backwards, we could not yield.

Harri, half-blind, fired until the rifle's heat charred his hand and when grenades were spent and bullet casings spat empty to the face he flung rocks and stones and earth and screamed as a beserker and all along the line it was so. Projectiles sundered the air and those few who broke the tide line were dashed by rifle butts and skewered with bayonets and none writhing in the mud were shown mercy. Pity did not exist in those days. God wept, God cried from heaven, but the wiping of his forehead did not soften pounding hearts and the beating of his breast was merely amplified by shells. Aircraft dodged his tears and wiped away their impact from perspex cockpits.

When it was over.

At the end.

White pavilions rose in spirals and a morning star gleamed through mists, illuminating gaunt battalions of spectres abandoning this earth. Nothing stirred. Not one man stood untroubled by the hosts of dead shining; no smiles on the black soil of Karelia. Some wandered in circles. Some gathered thoughts and watched ranks of Russian soldiers furling banners and abandoning their posts.

We had fought them to a stand still and, their stomachs filled with bile, they had not the strength to charge again. Greater demons called them from the field. Other suns caused their shadows to leap from this place to the plains of Poland...to the crossing of many rivers and the blood-soaked roads of Prussia, we would not be moved, our boots were riveted to this land. Shouldering their pikes and sounding bugles we watched them leave, and one man waved in mock salute. I was there. I saw those scenes in premonitions rarefied by fear and tension.

The army turned away, collecting wounded and the dead on stretchers in never-ending trains. The Russians we left for wolves, they saw no clouds nor witnessed other dawns. Steel won that day.

That night, huddled in blankets, the campfires spluttered. Harri smoked and the soldier once beside him did not speak, not then or at any other time until the day he died. Words could not devour the visions revealed to him and conversations, sympathetic or otherwise, could not dispel the nightmare of those long, extended lines walking in a dance macabre through minefields.

'What now?' a comrade asked.

Harri, aged soldier, warrior now of many battles merely shook his head and did not answer. He chewed a crust of bread and his teeth bled sweet and his nostrils caught the stench of many hells and his eyes covered by a veil of smoke refused to judge. Rumours soon spread that the army would fall back to the last defensive line along the shores of Lake Saima. Exhaustion caused most to dismiss this news, not one more step forward or back could they make.

Yet with a new day it was apparent that the politicians had decided that this war could not be won.

The order to withdraw was given, so wearily, for a second time the Isthmus was cleared of Finnish soldiers and the trek, the final trek, took place within an atmosphere not short of despair.

What had been the point? At what cost had these latest battles been fought? How many grieved or hugged their stumps or took a final glance at corpses covered in blankets as once these men were warmed in beds.

So long to sleep now.

In Helsinki bells rang in slow, morbid, tones. Flags were lowered. Crowds gathered around radio sets and newspapers were snatched from the hands of vendors. In a daze all work stopped and conversations were muted. Some shook their heads, some whispered that it had to be so. Many questioned the sacrifice. The maimed and wounded struck their heads, grasping only at the idea that for a second time the greater part of Karelia would be ceded. The ancestral lands, half re-built, half re-populated would be passed to Soviet hands. There were some who sought solace in the end of war, for whom hope was the enemy and struggle too unrelenting to maintain. The worst had come and now it was over. To others it was a shock. A bolt from the blue, these men and women both, now without homes or attachments raged, raged against the dwindling of the summer light and slipped into darkness. They knew the terms of peace would once again be onerous, worse than before because we had allied ourselves to armies now loathed and themselves on the brink of catastrophic defeat. Many tears ran on to sun-soaked pavements, many doors slammed to privacy. We had fought the serpent and lost. Only the dead did not stir in agitation but set their faces to the east awaiting resurrection.

In Tampere Maarit heard the wails of patients in the wards and stood stony faced at a window where the mills, and factories and workshops basked. Too stunned, too sad at heart to contemplate any domestic thoughts. Strain was evident everywhere, etched in every face young and old. Muscles tightened, throats convulsed and mighty efforts were expended in the maintenance of dignity. Maarit watched the people far below milling aimlessly, wandering back and forth across the same slice of land, accosting total strangers to ask, 'is it true? Is it true? Has God so deserted us?' Even the flowers paled on the stem and birds sought shadows.

In Hämeenlinna Tuija placed the tools upon her workbench and walked home. To the cabin, where reminders of Karelia caught her breath. She slumped into a chair, covered her face with her hands and quietly wept. How much time would they have to escape? How much time to leave the land? And would their footsteps be dogged by aircraft strafing and bombing?

Tilda gave away her mind that day. She had lost her boys all three in foreign lands now. She strode around the market place in huge circles and could not be dissuaded from her ramblings. She mumbled but could not be understood, she slept in doorways and at the first glint of dawn continued with her pathetic circuit of the stalls until nightfall or exhaustion caused her to stop. Until the next day. No end of consternation did she instigate and sometimes she would call the names of her dead children and talk to them and scold them for never coming home. She was side stepped and ignored. Until one day she simply disappeared.

Haari marched across the Isthmus but would not glance to left or right, tying his eyes to a road of yellow dust where stands of pine offered some protection from the sun. It was as if the landscape melted at his tread. He acknowledged nothing. And perversely in his thoughts he felt betrayed, not only by the generals and politicians but by Karelia itself, which had not kept faith with him, had surrendered its magic to those who would not value or cherish or understand. In anger he slashed at trees with his rifle and kicked stones into the air. When the new border was crossed and the order to halt called out, he sat on a rock, put a cigarette to his lips and watched the fumes curl upwards. In the distance plumes of black smoke began to rise and the trundling of many thousand wheels shivered the soil beneath his feet. He did not care, not any more.

Chapter 20

Even waterfalls lunging from the highest mountains, even those supported by mighty rivers, by snow and the flow of glaciers cannot endure forever; drought or the movement of the earth may kill their roar in times without limit, in ages incomprehensible to human imagination. So our time in the village of the Isthmus was coming to an end. This time we had some warning and the Russians, while advancing, were still twenty miles away. For days refugees had passed through. Carts and wagons loaded high with mattresses and beds, stools, bicycles, farm implements, sacks of corn and potatoes. The wooden shafts creaked and the horses snorted and the wheels threw up clouds of dust. Long, long, lines of transport. Farmers led horses by the reins and whipped them and prodded them in frustration. Their hats and waistcoats were soaked with sweat. Cattle were pressed along with this mass and the noise and stink of the column became sometimes unbearable. Our own village was almost deserted. The majority had fled and abandoned their homesteads to the elements and enemy. I could not tear myself away. Merja and I did not have much to carry and the border was only a morning's walk to the west.

Instead we sat on the porch and watched an army of grim-faced Karelians stream away from their homeland. There were no smiles, occasional nods of acknowledgment but nothing else. Their thoughts were preoccupied. Some looked back, a final glance, a nervous search for soldiers. Children dangled their legs over the back, buckets and cauldrons swung on pegs clanking. When they halted Merja ran out with mugs of chicory coffee while I helped to water the horses. No one said very much. I watched them continue their journey, struggling up the gradient of the hill. Pressing hard and cursing.

As days passed the stream receded to a trickle and I began to consider a time for our own embarkation. That final morning I took to wandering the paths and alleyways, touching those once familiar landmarks with my fingers. I looked to the fields and recorded them growing one last time, checking my emotions. The mill was locked. The railway station empty of passengers. In the forests the leaves rustled and beetles crawled upon the bark. A cuckoo sang. In the sky the sun still glowed but it was no longer our sun and the heat it radiated was of inferior quality. Its rays still shot the spiralling hawk. I touched the scene with my fingers and gathered my memories. Would this really be the final time, the last few hours of my life here? Would we never return? I knew it would be so. Summer was twining to a close, daggers ripped the sinews apart like coarse hemp and in those hours I bled inside and the bloodless flow of me ebbed into the soil. My hair was tangled by breezes my bones gnawed by invisible parasites. I stepped from stone to stone and the spear tips dripped.

It was time to leave.

I turned towards the cabin. Spells I cast on the sleepy hamlet to ward off evil. I said farewell to the tillers of salt earth, to the carriers of crisp harvest, to the murmur of the lily pond. In my pocket, soil from mother's grave seeped to the ground. In my mind's eye I fancied she waved to me from the churchyard and the tears flowed down her cheeks.

Between us we piled wheelbarrow with bread and cheese, with the rhubarb plants and the bottle of water from the stream. Merja carried a flour sack of belongings. I pulled the rucksack onto my back. Already I had locked the doors and flung my revolver into the trees, and catching one final breath I scanned the village plot by plot, cabin by cabin. A lump rose in my throat and I saw Merja looking up at me. I smiled at her.

'We have to go now.'

She nodded, seemingly understanding the gravity of our situation. What she thought I could not tell but she struck me as very 'matter of fact'. She started to walk ahead. The road was empty. We were the last to leave.

Then...then the last ghosts I ever saw walked into view. Men from the battlefields rose up and walked towards me. Through the forests they walked: grim, pale-faced apparitions. Some were unblemished, some with hideous wounds, eyes burned out, gaps in the skull. Some were carried on the backs of comrades, others pulled themselves along with their arms, slithering like snakes without legs. Blood drained from them and all advanced in our direction away from the Russians, without haste they walked, passing through trees and bushes. We have not come to comfort, they seemed to say, we have come to judge. You who remain, what was it for? Why did we suffer death and mutilation? To what purpose? They passed through me and the chill of it froze my heart. I saw them stride along the road ahead, an army of the dead, and then fade into crystals of sunlight. No more came, I knew it was time to go.

I raced to catch up with Merja. The wheelbarrow soon stung my hands and the road was pitted with craters. It was hard work. We caught up with the stragglers from the column, twenty, thirty, maybe more from babies carried in arms to old men, all tramping forwards at a monotonous pace...we fell in with them. All you could see was the back of the person in front. My back began to ache from stooping over the barrow. We rested on the roadside, cutting huge slices of pork from a joint and slabbing it onto bread. I poured coffee from a flask and Merja dipped her finger into a pot of jam. Red strawberry scars smeared her upper lip. I laughed at her and she frowned. Once rested we took to our heels again, re-joining the column just as we crossed the new border. There was a muffled cheer as we crossed, shortly to slump to the floor with exhaustion. We carried on until nightfall.

That night we spent on the kitchen floor of a cottage. It was cold and uncomfortable but we were tired. The occupants said very little, we did not receive much of a welcome and in some ways were treated with suspicion. Nevertheless in the morning we bought fresh milk and continued in this way for many days. Walking, finding shelter as and when we could. Our road took us to the Gulf of Finland and open water. One night we slept on the beach watching flocks of birds scrambling through the dunes. Cranes flew overhead, screaming into a sky in silhouettes of turquoise and amber and aquamarine. Salt bit into my cheeks, Merja slept curled in a blanket.

Then.

One fine day we stepped onto the platform of Hämeenlinna railway station and paced Viipurirantie to the cottage in the clearing. Tuija greeted us there. It was not much changed. The same chair, the same beds, the same deficiency of light. I crept into the storeroom where a pile of letters from Maarit were stacked upon the shelf. I lay down, tore open the envelopes and devoured them with eyes wide open and mouth agape.

*

The echo of war, the reflections of it spread outwards. A necklace of hands linked the peoples of many lands while rain pelted their hair and fingers grasped tender ropes, while gates swung on their hinges, and buds burrowed back into the tree. It was not over this torment.

Not yet.

Birds dropped dead from the sky and the bodies of fish lapped the shore. While some stared in hope from windows, others embraced. While some tore their hair or banged their heads in grief against a wall the tramp of boots once more pounded roads military. In autumn the final reckoning approached. Daybreak at that time is of black milk. We drink it and dig it out whistling strange fugues with hearts made ashen by the pointlessness of it all.

So what is it I mean?

Simply this.

While the ceasefire held on the eastern frontier we could not lay our heads on pillows. We scrambled down scree and our armies close to collapse headed north, to the mythical lands, to

Pojohla. A place once moulded by lava and crushed into basalt where the rocks are of iron and the clefts within them steel. There was one more task to complete. Expel the armies of the arctic, destroy the Germans loitering there before escaping into Norway. Do this thing or our anger will know no bounds, so screamed our new masters, the one whose voice must be obeyed. The images of those poor souls sent north now seem to be grainy. An unpleasant and unnecessary episode completed under duress. A convoy of images, shaking on the film, hardly existing.

Harri swore he would never swap his uniform for civilian dress, not he. So he journeyed with them, many hundreds of miles into chasms of emptiness. Beneath the northern constellations he travelled, blinded by comets and the black milk sky. If death comes now I will hold it, so he thought. It will not fall from my arms. If it be in fighting German or Russian, I care not. I will dip my spear into their blood, stab deeper into the flesh than ever before. Already the ground has turned to yellow and red, plasma and blood.

Cloudberries oozed scarlet ink beneath the tread. All things wild fled at their approach. And events played out within that treeless wilderness took upon the tone of a symphonic poem, a soft drawing of a bow across the strings, the gentle rumble of a kettle drum, a harp from which a woman's voice called them softly from their beds.

At first we thought the Germans might depart of their own accord, despite our betrayal. A little sprinkling of ochre into the eyes would send then scurrying to the mountains but it would not be so. There had been a gentleman's agreement but how could this stand? We, we valiant Finns had to fight this little blood-soaked war for Stalin and we pictured him grinning ear to ear at the irony of it. Do this thing, his loudspeakers blasted, or we...we will occupy your land once and for all as we have in Poland, and Latvia, and Estonia and the Ukraine...

There was no choice. We had no magic left. It had evaporated with the loss of Karelia and all that remained was this alien technology and way of doing things.

Through fells and moors and bogs and sweeping horizons the infantry divisions moved warily. Delaying actions, snipers, booby traps, and minefields slowed our advance and picked off our men one by one. Rovaniemi was the goal. The only town of any consequence in the whole of Lapland. On the approach vast fields of butchery opened as a vista. Reindeer herds decimated, hacked to pieces, dead eyes staring, antlers clattering in the wind and fur ruffled by breezes. There was no need for this. Spite and vengeance held sway at that time. Such actions caused great bitterness. Harri beheld the town from a distance of a dozen miles. Clouds of black smoke billowed from its centre, ashes and embers flew into his eyes, burning his cheeks, and even from this spot the heat scorched heather and lichen and the trees glowed. On entry...well there was nothing left. A few bodies. The railway station and marshalling yards twisted piles of metal, every rod, every bridge blown apart and not a building left in tact. It was difficult to breathe. Harri put a scarf across his mouth and shielded his eyes with his hands. He caught his reflection in the only window left. It caused him great alarm for his hair had turned white as snow, as an old man, and the face and expression he wore were also that of the aged.

The Germans had escaped but left a bitter harvest of a thousand Finnish dead, and many more with wounds. Through Tornio and west into Norway's mountains, where other fates and battles awaited them. More mothers cursing, more ghosts.

Harri's unit camped outside the town, waiting for the heat to subside before venturing in to clean the mess as best they could. It was filthy, dangerous work, but there were rumours of a general demobilisation and most welcomed this news. They were war weary. They had earned this respite. Harri did not speak to them. He was a stranger this old man with his silences and scars. He did not rejoice but took to wandering in the outskirts with his rifle still slung over his shoulder. To be honest no one bothered with him. They didn't want their head bitten off.

One afternoon, in fading daylight, he watched a company of sappers loading their tools onto a lorry. Young chaps, earnest, keen. One of them noticed him and called across.

'Hey Corporal...watch your step. Stay between the tapes. We haven't cleared that area yet. There are still mines.'

'Thanks lads,' he shouted in response and watched the lorry disappear. He looked into the sky, and then behind him. Carefully, with great deliberation, he walked into the mine field. A few seconds later there was an explosion. The lorry stopped, turned around and raced back to the spot where Harri's body lay twisted in the mud.

*

The following spring. The first of peace for many years. Maarit and I were married. I was deliciously happy...and surprised. I had no recollection of proposing, though Maarit intimated that she thought I wouldn't mind and organised it all. The tide carried me, and well, there are worse places to be washed up! I was not complaining. Merja followed us out of the church with a bouquet of flowers and a new white dress. Tuija was there and some of the villagers remaining in the vicinity added their voices to the proceedings. They must have participated with mixed emotions and I have to admit there was a moment as we walked down the aisle towards the doors when I wished to God that Simo and Harri were there. They would never have believed it, and Harri would have put it down to a spell or potion. Maarit had her family around her and looked more beautiful than I had ever seen her. Our own pastor led the service. His thin speech brought back memories and the ringing of our own church bell now ensconced in a new church pealed for hope.

Soon after we left the cabin. We had been allocated a piece of land. Not much, and not very promising, but it would be ours and I determined to make the most of the opportunity. It was a long, long road through the forest. Sentinel pine, larch, spruce carved a corridor to the new homestead. Tiny ferns loped over the path, flowers of wintergreen dotted the forest floor. It was damp. Droplets of water rolled down stems and leaves, wild strawberries, ant nests, squirrels ovaling branches. This now was our world and the labour needed to transform it was a daunting prospect. My health was reasonable apart from a throat grown coarse; I was no tenor. Nor did I dream or see visions any more. Joseph my patron had ceased to visit. There were no more conversations with him and the heat of Palestine did not prickle my skin.

First I stripped the bark from our birch trees with the sap till running. I coiled it and carried it into town to sell. While Maarit worked her shifts at the hospital I spent the day on our plot of land. It had to be cleared, mounds of stone shifted to the boundary. Merja sometimes helped but she was so easily distracted I was more efficient on my own. Huge rocks and boulders had to be manhandled from the soil with pickaxe and crow bar. I split them as a mason would, manoeuvring and rolling them as a lining for our new house. A wall of rocks marked the kitchen and the living room, two bedrooms, store house. This labour was an organism, ever growing, and when I stopped to wipe my brow I wondered at the might of this earth, how it relinquished its treasures so reluctantly, always having to pull and claw. Many a time Maarit would visit and see no progress. She would purse her lips and I would return despondently to the rooms we shared by the market place.

When she saw the wooden frame she jumped delightedly, hopping and skipping and saying how clever I was! This was better and on that day we walked home arm in arm and she told me all the gruesome details of her stint in the operating theatre. I nodded approvingly but didn't understand a word. Sometimes I went quiet. She knew to leave me on my own at such moments, and she never asked or bothered me about it. Sometimes a loud noise would make me jump or dive to the ground, sometimes...I still saw lizards scurrying beneath my feet and would have to control my screams and check my actions.

Still I laboured with spade and axe; digging, felling trees. The walls rose, a shingle roof, window frames and a door. When the glass was fitted, we three moved in, even though there was no stove and we cooked on an open fire. I had not started with the smoke from the chimney but it curled rightly enough now. God be praised for His mercy and His glorious bounty. I built a cow shed now, a simple lean-to, and a hay store and before we knew it we had a cow for fresh milk and company. In the fields I planted barley and potatoes and sawed logs for fences. I stacked timber in mighty temples in the corner of the yard. Before very long we had a stove installed, flowers in a vase on the table, and a radio. In winter I earned an extra crust with maintenance work and repairs. I did not carve in wood, I had no time for such childish things. Instead I constructed drains and ditches, tempering the soil, improving it, preparing the ground. The crown of rhubarb I carried from the village grew well. It grows now and the fruit cannot be beaten for succulence when sprinkled with a little sugar.

Merja grew taller and took an interest in clothes and hair styles. She communicated through signs and after school worked in the houses of neighbours washing and cleaning, paid a few marks, which she quickly spent.

Potatoes thrived in this soil. Huge harvests every year. There was nothing better on a plate than potatoes, butter, herring and a bowl of milk. No better pastime in an evening that sitting on the porch with a clean red shirt and a candle spluttering.

Maarit and me, we had our ups and downs. I considered myself to be a difficult companion. I did not respond to change so well, my moods and silences grated I know. Maarit had to put up with a lot. She was always right. While the province wrapped its arms around us, our hearts would always lie in the east, to the Isthmus, now resting in another country. We constructed an uneasy peace with our mighty neighbour, careful never to provoke, maintaining a low profile, which seemed to suit everyone.

Our first born we christened Arja. We used the water from the stream back home for the baptism, it was blessed and smelled sweetly of water lily. When he made the sign of the cross with it on Arja's forehead she smiled as if she understood the significance. Three more children arrived. Two boys and a girl all of whom thankfully took after Maarit. They played and went to school and scraped knees causing no end of anxiety and joy. Merja helped to look after them until she took the position of a housekeeper in Helsinki, which suited her very well. Life was difficult at first. Reparations had to be paid to Russia and the country undertook a period of hibernation. We managed, although food was scarce and clothing patched. The small holding kept us from starvation. Our homestead grew, new rooms added as the children arrived. With time we bought curtains and carpets and furniture, we never acquired great wealth but we were comfortable and better off than most. Gradually we adapted to our new life. The villagers who first arrived at Hämeenlinna church in the winter of 1940 thinned by degrees, some met their maker prematurely, others moved away. The rest including ourselves became assimilated. We still wept for Karelia with shiny and metallic tears. Our birthplace stamped itself into our bones, flowing with the marrow. The skies were never so blue nor the grass so green. Magic rarely showed itself to us, my heart did not skip as once it did. At odd moments sitting on the step or pulling up potatoes I would pause to close my eyes and visualise the village, the mill and meadows or the whistle of the distant train. Old man Hannu was the last of his kind and talk of shamans met with puzzlement, as though we spoke a different language. Some of us dreamed that one day we would go home, some could not settle and became the wandering tribes of Israel. There were times I could not bear to open my eyes. But these moments passed and life continued in its ordinary ways. I took to making commissioned pieces, furniture of high quality which gained me something of a reputation as a craftsman, and with time I became less uncertain; more sociable. Maarit was a wonder, a real blessing to we, tireless and imperturbable. She raised a family and still worked at the hospital gaining many plaudits for her quiet efficiency. She cared for me, which was no easy task.

I still took to wandering in the forest, solitude bore its attractions and when I knew I was quite alone I would lean against a tree and think of the battles in Taipale and the storming of the motti and patrols through snow and ice. Glimmers of Viipuri entered my consciousness, that beautiful pearl, no longer ours. Such occasions caused my brain to shiver but I found they kept the worst of recollection at bay. Others suffered; I saw them dive to the floor when motor cars backfired and their embarrassment at rising to their feet. I saw their shaking frames and mumbling lips, these old soldiers walking with the students and the shoppers and musicians on the cobblestones, wiping their faces with sleeves.

*

So reader how did this tale begin all those many years ago? Yes I remember now. The quiet milk-white sky drifts to a merging of conifer green, as soft autumn lays the hay dry and a single Finnish sun splinters my hair. Corn licks the lakeside and a morning mist whispers its way across the water to those vague and distant hills. And from those hills pours melting black the universe from another night and the day rising across the pastel-layered horizon in its wake. It is the beginning...

Well now it is the end. There comes a time to cease from speaking, to bind my tongue, abandon my song. I sit now on a bench on the shores of lake Vanajevesi as it meanders though the centre of Hämeenlinna. The stone bridge is to my left. I am frail now but many times I have gathered my thoughts on this spot and watched the world go by. Maarit I lost several years ago to a cancer eating her away, such a sad death, the children long since fled the nest to lead their own lives. While I tire easily my shoes are still polished, my tie straight and a smart hat covers my grey hair.

It is midday. Light blinks from eyelids heavy with time. I strain to discern faces. A fountain arches upwards, rippling the waters into shades of grey. Neatly mown lawns skirt the bank, flowerbeds with yellow-red tulips poking through. In the distance the waters snake towards a mill with piles of fresh timber bleeding amber. The *Aulanko* boat bobs gently at the jetty. Colours diffuse and merge: white, lemon, grey, the colours of tobacco and ash. Snatches of conversation from the lakeside café drift in particles across the water and I hear the sucking in of air and words, old Norse, Russian, English, whispered laments among the sugar cubes. The trees are twisted and the buildings whiter than chalk.

I am not alone. Harri and Simo are beside me, clad in field grey as in the old days, chattering excitedly and nudging me in the ribs. In all this time they have not changed, not one iota, it was a miracle they recognised me. On my lap I hold a parcel, a plain brown paper parcel tied with string. It contains my memory. And as I wait with Simo and Harri, on the bench I see her walking on the lake shore, hair of gold, trailing copper. I see her smiling and she calls to me.

'Hannu the carpenter, it is time to go.'

Appendix

These works have been invaluable to the production of *Karelia*. I highly recommend them.

Armstrong, Karen (2004) *Remembering Karelia*, Berghahn Books
Eagle, Eloise and Paanen, Lauri (1991) *The Winter War,* Stockpole Books
Tillotson, H.M. (1993) *Finland at Peace and War,* Michael Pound
Trotter, William (1991) *A Frozen Hell,* Algonguin Books
Voipio, Tilda *The Road to Evacuation*